SANTA MARIA PUBLIC LIBRARY
P9-CKV-607

BY THE SAME AUTHOR

A Breed of Heroes
Short of Glory
The Noonday Devil

TANGO

ALAN JUDD

SUMMIT BOOKS

New York London Toronto Sydney
Tokyo Singapore

Summit Books
Simon & Schuster Building
Rockefeller Center
1230 Avenue of the Americas
New York, New York 10020

This book is a work of fiction. Names, characters, places and incidents are either the product of the author's imagination or are used fictitiously. Any resemblance to actual events or locales or persons, living or dead, is entirely coincidental.

Originally published in Great Britain by Hutchinson, a division of Century Hutchinson Ltd.
SUMMIT BOOKS and colophon are trademarks of Simon & Schuster Inc.

Designed by Caroline Cunningham
Manufactured in the United States of America

1 3 5 7 9 10 8 6 4 2

Library of Congress Cataloging in Publication Data

Judd, Alan
Tango / by Alan Judd.
p. cm.
I. Title.
PR6060.U32T3 1990
823′.914—dc20 89-26333
CIP

ISBN 0-671-70710-8

To
Nick Langman
and with thanks to
Anthony and Caroline Rowell

1

In appearance, at least, she was so dramatically, so extravagantly concupiscent that for his first six months in the city William ignored her. He believed himself susceptible only to subtlety and indirection, and therefore impervious to such shameless blazing beauty.

He only ever saw her from a distance. Once, in the old quarter of quiet squares and crumbling government buildings, the tall faded doors of the treasury opened for her, narrowly and inexplicably. Twice he saw her in the streets where the traders from the country had their stalls, once coming out of a bar near the cathedral. On a brisk afternoon in an avenue that led to the sea she was talking to some other girls when the wind flung her dark hair across her face and harried her skirt about her thighs. All the girls tottered and laughed, clutching at their clothes. She wore red gloves.

By then it was winter, his first in South America. Many of the women huddled in needless furs, the men in sheepskin jackets and berets, but for William it was like a cool summer's day in England. The sky was blue and white, the sun pleasantly warm and there were welcome sea breezes. During his evening walk home across the golf course he could view the sea on one side and the angled red roofs of the city on the other. It was a small city, tolerant of trees and green spaces, its wide unhurried avenues fed by winding cobbled streets and alleyways. Often in the early evening there would be black clouds over the sombre tranquil sea, their undersides reddened by the sun. He would linger by the stunted trees before taking the coast road home. He could easily have driven to and from work, but saving time wasn't the point; he was in no hurry either way.

That morning he left the office for lunch earlier than

usual; there was little point in remaining. For the third day running there was no post; the telephone was still out of order; there had been no customers in the shop below and no response from any of the potential clients he had contacted. Ricardo, the young man he had been obliged to employ as his assistant, had not returned since taking some parcel orders to the post office two hours before. He would be at home drinking coffee with his mother, or with one of his married sisters, or drinking brandy with his father, or with some girl.

There was an anticipatory bustle in the streets as the lunch interval approached. Cars pulled up and parked anywhere, people walked with a shade more purpose, waiters laid tables rather than taking trays of brandies and coffees to the civil servants in their offices. William ambled, clutching his latest week-old copy of the *Telegraph*. It was a good city in which to amble; in London you felt in the way, but here there were things that kept pace with you – horses and carts, street traders pushing their barrows, even some of the cars. These were mostly of 1930s and 40s vintage, the results of a few decades of prosperity and international competitiveness, but years of cannibalising meant that many were of an age and type indeterminate to any but the enthusiast. There was nothing like an MOT system and no one paid any road tax. It seemed a tolerant and sensible system. William strolled among the decrepit and dignified beasts, ignoring – as they appeared to – the intrusion of a few Mercedes and BMWs, and a rather larger number of Japanese cars.

Beneath plane trees in a small square fruit traders spread oranges, apples, bananas and lemons. The traders were short, wizened, cheerful people who at this time of the year huddled beneath scarves and sheepskins. Most of them were drinking maté, a green tea which was sipped through tubes stuck in gourds. The gourds were topped up with hot water from flasks clutched in mittened hands. There was a universal and – judging by the nasal evidence – wholly unfounded belief that maté prevented colds.

William had meant to try it but Sally, his wife, was very keen on hygiene.

It was not with any thought of seeing the girl that he went to the covered market that day. He thought no more about her than he thought about the sun; when it was there he felt it, when it wasn't he didn't think about it. Buried deep in his mind, though, there was perhaps a connection between her and the market. It was the city's great meeting place, particularly during the lunch interval which occupied the middle third of daylight hours. Ricardo said that everyone went there – lawyers, bankers, business-men, prostitutes, even the new president and his generals. Being Ricardo, he had of course implied that there was an intimate connection between presidents and prostitutes, and William knew him well enough now to know that the other three categories were simply the next in his list of most important persons. Nevertheless, like many of Ricardo's assertions and exaggerations, this had taken root.

It did so because buried even deeper in William's mind was the connection between beauty and prostitution. It was not that his experience suggested any correlation – indeed, casual observation in Shepherds Market and around Kings Cross station in London had suggested the reverse – but there was an unconscious assumption that beauty so startling could not be freely available. It was too marketable.

The covered market was actually a British Victorian railway station minus trains, platforms and rails. It was a small Liverpool Street with the same massive girders and towering pillars and in the middle a clock tower that looked like an iron Big Ben and always said ten past four. It had been built near the docks in 1901, having been destined for Paraguay or somewhere – Ricardo was always vague about places – but a revolution in Paraguay or somewhere meant that it never got there. The building was now given over to the national obsession: eating. Steaks fit for giants were barbecued on great wooden charcoal fires tended by loud happy fat men. They poured

red wine from old whisky bottles, splashed coffee into tiny cups, expertly slid huge sizzling steaks on to huge plates, threw salads, sheep intestines, tomatoes, thyroids, mushrooms, sausages and bull's penises on top, shouted, smoked cigars, drank and knew everybody. Each fire was surrounded by a wooden bar at which customers sat elbow to elbow on high stools. Between the barbecues were tobacconists' kiosks and tiny places selling just drinks or coffee. Frequent power cuts cast the building into a cavernous gloom, lit only by the fires. Smoke coiled around the clock face and among the high girders. In London, William reflected, it would have been condemned as a fire risk.

He eased himself on to a stool. The weight problem, already established in London, had increased alarmingly during the past six months. The abundance and cheapness of red meat and wine had caused a sudden shrinkage of clothes, chairs and even doors. The trouble was, he felt more comfortable like that; and Sally seemed to have given up complaining.

He sat watching the sweating, busy men. They were fatter than he and with less excuse since most of them looked younger. William was 35 which meant – if the days of the week were to be accorded with the seven ages of man – that he was at Thursday lunch-time. The weekend was not far ahead. By Thursday lunch-time a man had a right to a little expansion. Anyway, the *padrón* was considerably fatter than he was and looked as if he might only be on Thursday afternoon, evening at most. The only irritant was the two men seated on either side of him. They ate and drank hugely while talking to their neighbours in prolonged bursts; they were almost unforgivably thin. But this was a place in which to eat and drink, to meet and talk. That was what it meant to be alive in this city, unlike London where being alive meant working and hurrying. William forgave them.

His order was scribbled on a piece of paper which disappeared. Orders were always written, but later always paid for without any reference to paper. He had to shout above the noise. It had been good for his Spanish, all this competitive shouting in recent months, not because it increased his vocabulary but because shouting the language had given him confidence. He did not order wine this time, since red wine at lunch meant a heavy afternoon in which he could neither work nor sleep. Despite this, a glass was banged down before him and abruptly filled from an old Johnny Walker bottle. Perhaps they remembered his earlier visits? A different hand pushed bread across the counter; he broke it resignedly and dipped it in the wine.

It was in fact her friend he noticed first, a big girl with big white teeth and bushy red hair. She was laughing at him. Embarrassed, he looked up and down so quickly that he noticed nothing apart from that; he did not even see that she was not alone. A woman's voice shouted something and he glanced up again, this time seeing her companion. The big girl was shouting at the *padrón* but she – her – was looking at him. She was dark, watchful, poised. They were seated across the other side of the fire and she had moved her stool back, perhaps to keep out of the smoke. She looked away from him, smiling slightly, and spoke to the other girl who laughed and looked directly across, shouting something he still couldn't catch.

The *padrón* was before him, bald and grinning.

'They want to know, *señor*, are you a priest?'

'No, I am English.'

The *padrón* shouted the information and another question was shouted back.

'They want to know, is it English custom to take mass in the market?'

They all laughed and William smiled. He nearly essayed a reply on the some-men-live-by-bread-alone theme, but was not sure how it would translate.

'You wait for your food?' asked the *padrón*, his eyes glistening.

'Yes, but I am in no hurry.'

'It is ready.'

'Good.'

'There.' The *padrón* pointed to a place which had been cleared next to the two girls; a plate of steak filled it. Other steaks were put before the girls.

William took his wine and sat next to the big girl. Her smile enveloped him.

'You come from England to join us?'

'Especially for this.'

'You speak Spanish very well.'

'Not very well.'

'No, but for *un Inglés*.' She turned her hand, heavily beringed. 'I am Ines. This is Theresa.'

William introduced himself and they shook hands. Theresa's hand was firm but quickly withdrawn. He talked rapidly to Ines, who asked many questions. Yes, she knew the English Bookshop, now renamed Britbooks by the parent company in London. What did it mean, Britbooks, and why had they changed? If William did not like it, why had he agreed? Surely he could paint it out and put back the old name that everyone knew? And why did they not sell so many books now, why was there so much paper, so many envelopes? What did wholesale mean? Why did he leave London to come and be manager here when London was so much bigger a city? Was he married? Why had he no children?

They ate as fast as they talked, like everyone else. All around them chunks of meat were being pushed into mouths, great slabs sizzled on the fire, even greater slabs and sides, inches thick and feet across, hung waiting to be cooked. The air was thick with smoke and voices. Sally had never been to the covered market, though he had once tried to tell her about it. She had gone vegetarian about a year before.

William kept talking. Ines needed everything explained, which was useful at that moment but made him suspect that she was boring. He wanted to talk to Theresa, but she ate and said nothing. Perhaps she was boring, too, in a different way. Sometimes she looked round, but not as if for anyone in particular. Perhaps it was he that was boring. Once or twice, though, he felt her eyes upon him but when he looked up her eyelids were lowered and she too was pushing meat between her lips.

More wine came. He asked Ines what she did but didn't listen to the reply because he was thinking of how he had never been unfaithful to Sally. Maybe he was afraid or maybe he had never really wanted to. Whatever it was that Ines was explaining, it didn't sound like very much. She kept repeating the words for 'sometimes' – '*de vez en cuando*'. He had never seriously considered having an affair. He wasn't doing so now; he wasn't even talking to her.

The voices around them quietened. Ines whispered to Theresa and they both looked away. Others did the same. The source of the growing silence was something he couldn't see. Heads and shoulders turned and he got off his stool and stood. Both women had their backs to him.

It was a group of military men wearing olive greens and caps with long peaks. Three or four carried sub-machine guns with exaggerated nonchalance, the others puffed at fat cigars and wore beards like young Castros. They walked slowly, smiling and greeting people. At their head, young, handsome and hatless, was the new president, General Calvaros. He looked as if he had stepped out of his own newspaper photographs, slim and smiling, a sensitive, intelligent face marred by a loose undisciplined mouth. Educated in England and Sandhurst-trained, he and his junta of colonels had seized power about a year before from the corrupt but elected Liberal Democrats. The putsch was now called a revolution but it had never had popular support. Nor had it met with real opposition apart from certain sections of the press, at first.

The party disappeared behind Ines's bush of hair as she turned to William.

'The general, our new president,' she said, smiling hugely.

The group continued to move slowly, stopping to talk to people. They had at first promised elections within months once certain economic measures had been taken, necessary because of the widely acknowledged corruption and inadequacy of the previous administration. There was less talk of that now, though; rather, the talk was of the new political party, the People's Party, which had been formed by the junta. Elections would be held when arrangements were complete. The old Liberal Democrat leaders would be released when their financial positions had been fully investigated and accounted for.

William waited for the group to reappear from behind Ines's hair. Yes, there was no doubt. President Calvaros walked with his hands clasped behind his back and grinned with impersonal goodwill, like any British Army officer at any military open day. His cohorts kept reaching out to shake hands with and good-naturedly slap surprised onlookers. The guards were relaxed and pleased with themselves. Yet despite the good humour and jokes a silence surrounded the junta's advance. Talk ceased at their approach, people were fearful in their presence, subdued when they had passed.

Ines turned her head again and whispered: 'The president is walking with his colonels to meet the people.'

'I had heard that he does this.'

She looked pleased. 'He likes to meet people.'

Behind the president was a tall calm man whose smile showed teeth as large as but more regular than Ines's. Ines whispered to Theresa.

The president stopped by Theresa and spoke. William watched the back of her head as she replied.

'Also on Wednesdays?' the president asked.

'Yes.'

The president's smiling young eyes moved to Ines. 'You, too. I have seen you at the same place.'

'Yes, I am there also.'

'I will come again.'

His eyes moved to William. 'William Wooding.'

'Carlos.'

'What are you doing here?'

William explained. The whole party stopped and looked at him. He stumbled in his Spanish, partly because the sentences he tried to form were interspersed by memories of Carlos at school in Shropshire: Carlos pale and reluctant on the rugby field, crying in a maths lesson. He had long wondered if it could be the same man but the name was common and many of the officer class had been educated in Europe or America. There was no mistaking the vulnerable mobile mouth, though, nor the hazel eyes of his English mother. He remembered helping Carlos with his English prep in return for chocolate.

'I am pleased you are bringing business to our country,' Carlos said when William had finished.

William inclined his head. 'As you brought some to mine.'

'But your company must not bleed us. You must give as well as take.' Carlos spoke more loudly than before.

'At present we take nothing. We put money in.'

'Neither do we want your charity. Remember that.' Carlos looked about him. 'We ask no charity of anyone. Only honest dealing, non-interference and the chance to achieve social justice.'

His escorts nodded to the crowd. The tall man looked at Carlos who looked back at William, smiled and switched into English.

'Actually, I enjoyed my time in England. People were kind to me. I think I was popular, especially with women. You were not always so fat?'

'No, I wasn't. It's since coming here.'

'But you were always quite fat.'

'I suppose I was.'

'See you.'

He spoke the words as if they were chic or daring, and moved on.

The tall man stopped before William. 'I am sorry, *señor*, I did not hear your name.'

He spoke with courteous deliberation. When William had introduced himself the man shook hands, once, very firmly.

'I am pleased to have met you, *Señor* Wooding. My name is Manuel Herrera.'

The presidential party left. Cigars were re-lit, wine

poured, conversation began again. A number of people stared at William.

'You know the president?' asked Ines, wide-eyed.

'We were at school together in England.'

'And he remembers you?'

'So it seems.' He caught Theresa's eye. 'Who was the man, the tall one?' he asked her across Ines.

'Manuel Herrera.'

'Is he part of the junta – of the government?'

'Yes, he is one of the colonels. But he was trained in Cuba.'

She spoke slowly, perhaps for his benefit. He wanted to go on talking but quite suddenly they were leaving, their steaks unfinished.

'What do you do?' he asked hurriedly, addressing both. 'Where do you work?'

They hesitated.

'We are singers,' replied Ines. They both said '*chau*' and left.

William went back to his steak. His appetite returned with eating. When he paid, the bald *padrón* took his money.

'*Gracias, señor*. And the *señoras?*'

'Have they not paid?'

The *padrón* smiled with his head on one side. '*Señor*, you are far from England.' He held out his hand.

2

The office was above the shop and that afternoon William continued his task of cleaning the window-panes. Having sorted out the stock, the filing system, the records and the stores, this was all that was left for him to do when there was no Ricardo, no telephone and no customers. Every five minutes or so he picked up the telephone to see if it had come on again. Meanwhile, by turning his creaking wooden swivel chair – with arms, a definite improvement since in London he had had an uncomfortable modern contraption with no arms – he could reach each of the twelve small panes in the bow window by his desk. He cleaned them with an old shirt he had found in the 'complaints' file, scratching with his fingernail at every speck of ingrained grime. Ten panes were now spotless. In the cold sunlight of the street below was a solitary stall laden with hundreds of oranges; by it a huddled figure sipped the inevitable maté from a gourd. No one went and no one came. Farther up the street was the wreck of a 1930s Dodge saloon, rusty and lopsided with one headlight hanging loose like a disgorged eye. Unlike the orange-seller, it had not been there yesterday.

From downstairs came the sound of the two shopgirls giggling. They often giggled. At first he had thought it was at him, then that it was because Ricardo flirted with them. Now he had concluded that they simply giggled. There was little else to do. It was over fifty years since the London company had set up the English Bookshop with its small paper mill and packaging factory out of town. For most of that time the operation had run quietly into the ground, largely unnoticed by London. The Britons who had been sent to manage it had been either misfits or casualties of the greasy pole that led some to the Board. Several had been re-treads looking for a quiet life.

None had retired. All had died in harness, usually of heart attacks or strokes brought on, it was said, by too much eating and drinking. Stress was not thought to be a factor, although one had had his final moments in a bordello. Wicks, William's immediate predecessor, had actually reached retirement age alive but had then refused to retire, refusing also all summonses to return to London. Dixon of Personnel had been sent out to see him but something had gone wrong; Dixon had stayed three weeks instead of three days, had returned in order to resign and get divorced and was now said to be living with a dance-hall girl in La Paz. Wicks had died shortly afterwards in the usual way.

The Board's attention had thus been drawn to the operation. Because decline had been gradual, people had become accustomed to the idea of losses that were only now, suddenly, seen to be significant. This coincided with a fashion for restructuring, rationalising and retrenching, and a review of the company's operations worldwide. At the same time the military take-over had brought in laws forbidding the withdrawal of capital and compelling foreign-owned businesses to employ local people at managerial level. This was a popular move which meant that many younger sons of members of the People's Party were now possessed of more money and status without having to do anything for it. It was part of what the government called 'democratic socialism'. The result was that William had to employ managers at the mill and the factory and have Ricardo as his deputy.

He had been sent out with a simple brief: get a grip of the operation, turn it round and make it pay or it would be wound up, capital transfer difficulties notwithstanding. He had been selected, he was told, because he was a relatively young man still at the point of his career where he could make his name if he wanted; it was his big chance. Afterwards he had discovered from one of the clerks in Personnel that he was the fifth person to have been asked. The previous four had turned it down because it was seen as a dead end, perhaps not only metaphorically. Also, it was far from England and a foreign tongue had to be learned.

For William, though, there was the romantic appeal of running a book-shop, something he had always thought he would like even though it wasn't in Marlborough or Norwich or Harrogate and even though there was a mill and a factory attached. Further, it meant escape from daily humiliation by British Rail, a sentence otherwise destined to last – according to his way of measuring age – from now, Thursday lunch-time, until retirement at Sunday lunch-time, followed by death by Sunday evening. Sally, whose job was teaching English as a foreign language, had been keen on the idea at first but had become less enthusiastic as the time approached. Now that they were there he couldn't tell whether she was happy or not; she didn't say much.

There was a shout from below followed by thundering on the stairs. Ricardo entered with his usual rush, his young face bursting.

'You know the president?'

It was not often that William could impress or surprise Ricardo. 'Well, yes, though we haven't seen much of each other for some years.'

'But he speaks to you?'

'Yes.'

'Also Manuel Herrera. Already you are a famous man.'

Ricardo spent so little time at his desk that whenever he sat at it he did so with relish. He would pick up the papers, shuffle them, move them from one tray to another, sign a few, then tip his chair back on its hind legs, put up his feet and talk.

'How's business?' He always tried to make it sound like a technical question.

'So-so.'

'You were trying to telephone someone?'

'The factory. Still no dialling tone.'

'Give up. There's no one there anyway. They've all gone home.'

'Why?'

'They're all striking. Today is cold; they want to go home.'

William replaced the receiver. 'How did you know I had seen the president?'

'Everything in the market is public. That is why he goes there. He wishes his people to see him.'

William wanted to talk about Theresa and Ines, but asked instead about Manuel Herrera.

'He's from an old family, he has great influence with the president. The other colonels, they don't like him so much, but for the president he is a good friend because he knows the Cubans. The Cubans have strong military. Also he knows the Russians and they can give help for the economy. But no one knows what the president is really thinking.'

While he was speaking Ricardo threaded a biro between the fingers of his left hand, straightened his arm and abruptly clenched his fist, breaking the biro. He grinned.

'Also you were with two women?'

'I had lunch with them.'

'Two women are better than one.'

'I didn't know them before.' William paused. 'What do they do?'

Ricardo shrugged and pursed his lips, affecting a connoisseur's disinterest. 'They live as all women would live if they could. They dance and they sing. They are comfortable.'

'Dance and sing?'

'Of course, it's part of it. Ines's father makes clothes but he was put in prison by the old government. He killed a man with the scissors for the cloth. Ines was very bitter against the old government and now she likes the president, but her father is still in prison.'

William didn't like Ricardo knowing the girls. 'What's happened at the factory? Why are they on strike? It can't simply be the cold.'

'Nothing has happened. They are fed up. They want more money, less work – what all workers want.'

'What does Miguel say?' Miguel was the manager.

'Nothing. He is not there. Those two men from the ports have made the workers angry.'

The two men were union officials. The new government had taken a great interest in the unions and had strengthened them, particularly in the foreign-owned companies. Union members could not be sacked except by their unions.

Ricardo threw the broken pieces of his pen like darts into the wastepaper bin. 'We must sack those two men.'

'We can't.'

'Put things in their clothes and cars – stolen things or drugs.'

'No.'

This method was now the only way to get rid of anyone and was increasingly used, judging by the talk in the Foreign Traders' Association. William would not contemplate it, but he had no idea what he would do if troublemakers made the operation unworkable. He felt slightly guilty at not being more ruthless and consoled himself by saying that there was nothing he could do about it. Because of the new laws he had no authority over the factory or the mill, although as far as headquarters in London was concerned he was still responsible. They refused to understand.

'That's where you've been, is it – the factory?' he asked.

'Yes.' Ricardo stood, stretched and looked at his fingertips.

There was nothing to be gained by confronting him with his lie. He hardly ever went to the factory or the mill and had no doubt got his information from someone in the town; but demonstration of a falsehood only increased the fervour with which Ricardo asserted it. It was easier to get him to contradict himself later, provided the contradiction was not pointed out.

Ricardo lingered by the door. He obviously wanted to

go but was probably uncomfortable at having only just arrived, and so thought of something to say instead.

'There have been no customers in the shop today?'

'There were two this morning.'

'Did they buy any books?'

'One bought some paper.'

'There were more customers when *Señor* Wicks was here.'

William was sensitive about this. He had no adequate explanation.

'But then it was called the English Bookshop; everyone knew it. Britbooks is not the same.' He had not forgiven the company for forcing that upon him, nor for the envelopes, the coloured wrapping, the knick-knacks, the toys and 'gifts' that they called diversification.

'It was because of the pornography. *Señor* Wicks was famous for that. It was a very big secret; everyone knew and they all came to the shop.'

'Pornography? Here?'

'Of course.' Ricardo raised his slender eyebrows. 'He kept it in boxes behind your desk. It was free to anyone who bought a novel. There were many customers.'

William was sure they didn't know that in London. 'We're not selling pornography.'

Ricardo shrugged. He probably felt he could leave with honour now. 'I will go the factory again tomorrow and report.'

'You'll be in late, then?'

Ricardo looked injured. 'Not late.'

'Later, I mean.'

Ricardo grinned. 'Yes, later. *Chau*, William.'

William returned to the unfinished window-cleaning. The small figure with many oranges had not moved. William wondered if he was being prudish in ruling out pornography. Would London regard that as lack of initiative? Would they think pornography an acceptable diversification? But surely one should be able to sell books – novels – without that? Novels, were after all . . . well, they were important. If the time came when we needed pornography to help sell them, then the world had no place for novels any more. Oranges – even oranges – could still be sold on their merits, or so it appeared. Perhaps it would be better to sell oranges. He'd never actually seen the little man make a sale.

A loud clatter and a cloud of blue smoke announced that the lopsided Dodge up the street was not after all abandoned. It jerked away from the kerb, gear-box crunching, loose headlight banging against the mudguard. As it passed he saw a flash of eyes and a cloud of dark hair – not enough of her to recognise, strictly speaking, but he knew. No one else blazed like that. He felt a surge of confidence. Of course he could make the shop work, the factory and the mill were not a hopeless drain on the whole operation, novels would be sold, he would not be defeated; he would see her again. Things would happen.

3

A plate slipped in the kitchen and Sally swore. William asked if she wanted a hand. There was a muted negative.

He was out on the balcony with his binoculars and would have gone in but his presence in the kitchen annoyed her. The room's narrowness did not well accommodate his width and she became flustered if he hung around when it was her turn to cook. She had so often remarked that he was always in the way wherever he stood that now, metaphorically and literally, he tiptoed around her. It did not help that he was the better cook.

The rest of the flat was spacious and light. It was on the corner of the building and every window had a view of the sea. There were balconies on either side and from one William could look down into the trees bordering the golf course. Large green parrots lived in them. After six months he had still not tired of watching the birds. They were unnaturally vivid, almost surreal.

This evening he was using the binoculars to try to see a man he had christened *Señor* Finn, a tramp who lived a kind of Huckleberry Finn existence amidst clumps of very tall pampas grass just off the beach. He had a shack made of driftwood, a chair, a table, pots and pans hanging on sticks and an old upturned rowing-boat. When William walked home from work, coming off the golf course and along the coast, the elderly Huck would be sitting over his fire, bulky and red-faced, a grey kitten and a scruffy terrier at his feet. Their acquaintance had developed from nodding to waving to bidding good day or good night to – very recently – the exchange of a word or two about the weather. Even the terrier now barked only once and with a kind of gruff familiarity.

But this night *Señor* Finn had not been there. His fire was unlit and there was no sign of dog or cat. The boat was in its place. William was uneasy. He liked routine, drawing from it a sustaining strength, and felt obscurely threatened by the old man's disappearance. There was no need, he told himself, since the precariousness of *Señor* Finn's foothold on the beach was probably only apparent and his place in the world, being anywhere, was perhaps more secure than William's own. Nevertheless, William was sufficiently concerned to spend thirty minutes out on the balcony while Sally cooked. It was better to be out of the way, anyway.

The sea was brown that night, indicating rain inland. Mud brought down by the great river spread from the estuary for miles along either coast and as far out as could be seen. Corpses of cattle and horses were sometimes washed up on the beach. In the days of civil war they had apparently been outnumbered by the friendless bodies of unburied men. According to Ricardo, it had started happening again but only in ones and twos; and only according to Ricardo.

The sun slid down beneath the indigo clouds and its rim touched the horizon. The sea reddened as if heated by a furnace. *Señor* Finn's hut was now in deep shadow, but as the sun sank William saw something on the beach that might have been firelight. He watched for some minutes in case it was a maverick reflection; but, no, it was definitely firelight.

The banging of plates on the table indicated supper. Sally had said that morning that she'd do them both a salad, which was partly how he had justified lunching at the covered market, but when she got home she declared for spaghetti bolognese. He said he liked 'spag bog', but it had irritated her to hear it called that and she had altered course for mince, potatoes and brussels. Sally's brussels sprouts were William's least favourite food. Suspecting that she cooked them so often because they were easy and less likely to trouble her than something equally easy but less familiar, he had maintained through four and a half years of marriage a self-sacrificing silence. Sally, being now a vegetarian, had salad for herself.

'Lovely,' he said. He could see that the mince was half-cooked but kept silent because it probably represented a generous intention. There was no wine, though. She thought he drank too much, which he did because wine was good and cheap, but he had to have something with the food. He fetched a bottle and a couple of glasses.

'Would you like some?' She shook her head. The wine bubbled happily into his glass.

'You really do drink too much,' she said.

'Less than I did.'

'Still too much. You'll end up with cirrhosis of the liver, like the French.'

'How was work today?'

'I resigned.' She smiled at his surprise. 'That is, I told them I'd leave if I didn't get a move.'

'Where to?'

'One of the more advanced classes. It's boring, what I'm doing, boring and repetitive, and when I started they said I'd be doing more advanced work within weeks. It's been six months now.'

She worked at an American-owned school of English which had flourished in the gap left by the closure of the British Council school. She was well qualified and felt she was wasted.

'What did they say?' he asked.

'Nothing much. They're going to ask the executive vice-president.'

'Isn't he the one you don't like – the Hitler man?'

'Hueffer, Max Hueffer. I never said I didn't like him. I said I thought he didn't like me.'

'Will he now?'

'I don't know.' She pushed back a strand of hair that had escaped from the elastic binding her pony-tail.

William returned to the subject when they were washing up. 'Did you feel any better for having said it?'

She brightened. 'I did, actually, the more so for not having planned it. I just came out with it when old Riley asked how I was getting on. It quite shook him, I think. About time something did.'

'What happens now?'

'I'm going to see Max tomorrow.'

'Sounds as if they might want to keep you.'

'I don't know. I don't mind much either way. It's up to them.'

Later, as William sat down with a book, she put on a medley of local dance tunes. He could not read and listen, so took out his stamps instead.

'Why don't you get a home computer?' she asked.

'What for?'

'Something for you to do in the evenings.'

'Is that what they're for?'

'It's what people seem to do with them. It would make a change from reading and stamp-collecting.'

'I suppose it would.' So would dancing, he thought, listening to the tango. He used to do a lot but Sally was a stiff and awkward dancer, more so when with him. It was odd because her movements were normally graceful. Perhaps knowing that he danced well spoiled her confidence or perhaps she felt awkward because of his bulk although, like many men of his size, he had rhythm and poise on the dance floor. Anyway, they never danced now.

'Oh, someone from the embassy was after you,' she said.

'Which embassy?'

'Ours, of course. He was one of those two secretaries or whatever they are that everyone's always on about. I never know which is which.'

'Feather and Nightingale.'

'Yes, one of them. He wanted you to go and see him. He was trying to get you after lunch and eventually rang me. Wouldn't say why.'

'I must have been out.'

'Do you think they are?' she asked after a pause.

'Everyone says so.'

'I didn't think it was allowed in the diplomatic service.'

'Used to be traditional.'

'Really?'

William smiled. 'No, not really.' Her occasional literal-mindedness had always attracted him. It made him feel protective.

'I'm going to have a bath.' She turned up the music so that it would carry.

The British Embassy was an old white house built for bankers in more prosperous days. It stood out from similar houses in the street because it was festooned with cameras and anti-terrorist devices. In the entrance hall was a magnificent chandelier that was lit day and night.

'The inspectors tried to make us turn it off when they were out last year,' said Nightingale, the youngest and, because of his flamboyant bow-ties, best-known of the embassy staff. 'They also tried to make us move into some awful modern building with glass all over the place but Nigel made one of his great Feather fusses and they took fright, poor things.' He laughed. 'Of course, the ambassador having been on the panel of inspectors in his last post helped a bit. We actually got an increase in allowances. Only one in the world this year. I wonder where the beast is?'

'Who?' They were climbing a wide curving staircase and William, who had the outer lane, was finding it hard to keep up.

'Peter, the ambassador. Not that he'd be very keen to do it himself, but he'd probably like to squeeze hands.'

'Do what?'

Nightingale appeared not to hear. He touched his bow-tie which, that day, was blue with white spots and very floppy. They turned off along a corridor and into an office where a girl sat at a desk reading the horoscope in the *Daily Mail*.

'Angie, dear, is Peter in?'

The girl did not look up. 'Don't think so, no.'

'Oh, drat, he's such a nuisance. Do you think he'll mind not being introduced to William?'

She glanced at William. 'Shouldn't think so.'

'We can always say we tried.'

The stairs narrowed and wound more tightly upwards

and William was happy for Nightingale to go first. 'Peter's a bit of a stick-in-the-mud but he's not bad really,' Nightingale said. He had thin lips and an unrelenting smile. 'Came up the commercial side. Not very bright but terribly pleased to have got a bit of status. Rather touching. Nice enough so long as you make him feel he's been consulted, like all these commercial people.' He hesitated, then turned to William with sudden enthusiasm. 'Of course, you're in business yourself, aren't you? How very interesting that must be. It's a jolly good thing to make ambassadors out of commercial officers; they know what's important.'

The stairs gave on to a narrow corridor in the roof. 'Used to be the maids' quarters,' Nightingale continued. 'They were used for lumber and old files for years, but we thought they were so much nicer than the chancery rooms that we nagged Peter into letting us move. We're both much happier here, so much more private.' They entered a sitting room with a sofa and armchairs and matching curtains over dormer windows. 'The main problem was the admin. officer. He fought with native Celtic guile and an obstinacy all his own. In the end we won him over by letting him have the chancery rooms all to himself. Enormous increase in status. We're all so very corruptible, aren't we?' He laughed. 'Actually, Peter was the only loser because now he has to work within spitting distance of the said awful admin. officer. But then someone in life always loses. Nigel had to explain that to him. I expect you're wondering what all this is leading up to?'

'Yes.'

'Thought you were. Awfully restrained of you not to have asked before.' Nightingale put his finger to his thin lips and pointed at the door at the far end of the room. 'In there, in the office - the scriptorium, we call it – there's a little man called Box who's come all the way from London to see you. Nigel's making him happy.'

'What for?'

'Oh, just being friendly, you know. Don't want London to think we don't like their little people.'

'I mean, what does Box want to see me for?'

Nightingale held up his hands in mock horror. 'My dear, I can't possibly tell you that. All frightfully hush-hush. We had a *telegram*, one of those eat-before-reading ones. You know what they're like. Perhaps you don't. Come on, I'll wheel you in, then scuttle off with Nigel.'

Two more armchairs and another sofa, this time larger and leather, were grouped round a fireplace at the far end of the room. The sofa had its back to the door. By the window two desks faced each other, one very tidy, the other strewn with papers, mugs, bottles and glasses. Feather was a big man in a stained and crumpled white suit. His tie hung loosely round his unbuttoned collar, his hair was long and he was unshaven, giving the effect of an ageing Baudelaire. He sat in one of the armchairs with a Turkish cigarette and a glass of brandy, addressing the sofa.

'Nigel, what a sight for our visitors!' Nightingale exclaimed delightedly. 'I told you this morning this would probably be William's formative experience of the inner workings of diplomatic life. You'll leave a lasting impression.'

Feather turned towards William. 'Brandy?'

'No, thanks.'

'Coffee?'

'Yes, please.'

A percolator bubbled by the fireplace. Nightingale hurried to it and sniffed. 'Nigel, it's not Brazilian.'

Feather stared for a long time like a dying man trying to remember. 'Is it not?'

'No, it is not and I went to the market especially when I knew we'd have guests. I do wish you'd pay a little more attention sometimes.'

Feather's gaze traversed slowly back to the sofa. His eyes were the most melancholy that William had seen, dark holes in a handsome, dissolute face. It was impossible to tell whether he was contemplating the futility of all human endeavour or simply having trouble formulating a thought.

'Don't need us, do you?' he said to the sofa. He got up and shuffled past William to the door. 'Leave that now,' he told Nightingale.

'But it's not ready yet.'

'They can do it themselves.'

Nightingale followed him crossly out of the room.

William stared at the back of the sofa. There was a movement and then a very short man stood and faced him as if from behind a parapet. The man was the contrary of Feather in every particular: small and dapper with thining dark hair pressed ruthlessly down upon his skull, gold-rimmed glasses and a disciplined moustache. He wore a dark three-piece suit with a thin gold watch-chain across the waistcoat, a tight triangle of white handkerchief showing above the breast pocket and a half-inch of white cuff beneath the sleeves. His face had a London pallor.

He held out his hand. 'Arthur Box.' They had to negotiate the sofa before contact could be made. Box looked around the room. 'Is there anywhere we can go?'

'Go?'

'To talk.'

'Can't we talk here?'

'Walls.'

'Walls?'

'Have ears.'

Box went to the window. It was set high in the eaves and he had to go up on his toes in order to peer out. He turned and put his thumbs in his waistcoat pockets, standing very upright, then nodded at something behind William. 'That'll do.'

Behind the door was an old white sink, probably Victorian. Box strode over and tried to turn the tap. He had to use both hands and another handkerchief taken from his trouser pocket. After a couple of splutters, water gushed out.

'Better than nothing,' he said. He indicated to William to stand at the other side of the sink, then continued in a low voice. 'Apologies for the irregularity, but we need your help. You no doubt know where I'm from?'

'London?'

'What I represent, I should say.'

William thought. He had sometimes imagined being asked to work for the secret service but not like this. The suggestion should have been made on a yacht or a ski slope or, since he had never been on either, in an expensive bar, preferably by someone who looked like Theresa. 'The Secret Service?'

Box shook his head. 'Nearly but not exactly, at least not any more. There's been a recent change. We're now Special Information Services plc; we've been privatised. A very successful flotation. Surprisingly. Her Majesty's Government is still the major shareholder, of course, as well as our major customer. They buy most of our information. That's why I'm here.'

For William, spies began with Bulldog Drummond and ended with Bond. After that they were all victims. Nevertheless, it was a call to be answered. He would rather have been on Her Majesty's Secret Service but if Special Information Services plc was the nearest to it that Her Majesty would permit, so be it. He waited for Box to explain. They stared at each other across the gurgling tap.

'Why are you here?' William asked eventually.

'Cobalt.' There were raised voices in the next room and a door slammed. Box took no notice. 'You've read about cobalt?'

'Not recently.'

'You are in business?'

'Yes, but books and paper, that sort of thing.'

'Nothing to do with cobalt?'

'No.'

Box leaned across the sink. He lowered his voice further and rapidly explained that problems in Zaire had led to a world shortage of cobalt, that this was one of the very few countries with sufficient unexploited reserves to make up the shortage, that there were worrying signs that the Russians were moving in to corner the market and starve the West of a mineral essential for rocketry, certain kinds of jet engine and, as everyone knew, artificial hips. Indeed, the Russians seemed to be doing more than that: they had negotiated a fishing agreement highly favourable to themselves, had influenced the way this country voted in the UN, were secretly training elements of the armed forces and were believed to have the new president at least half-way into their pocket. Whether he was being pocketed willingly or under pressure or through mere foolishness no one knew – but being pocketed he was. Cubans were in evidence, East Germans were about, the Russian Embassy was being enlarged into a fortress, there were food shortages in rural areas caused by the diversion of grain to the Soviet Union – in short, all the symptoms of a further expansion of Russian imperialism, a generally fatal disease. It was not only bad for the country, it was bad for the free world as a whole and for Britain in particular.

'That's why I needed to talk to you,' he concluded. 'It's a very big contract, this one, a bonus job. If we can stop this place going down the drain, we'll keep the Firm going for the next few years while we build up the private sector commercial intelligence side.'

There were sounds of sobbing in the next room. Another contrast with Feather, William noticed, was Box's eyes: they had neither depth nor expression and, being an uncertain mixture of grey and white, seemed not quite to achieve a proper colour.

'That's if you wouldn't mind helping out Queen and country and whatever,' added Box. His neat white hands gripped the edge of the sink.

'Not at all.' William was embarrassed. 'Very happy.'

'Some people don't these days, you see. Don't seem to care any more.'

'I can imagine that.'

'Could be something in it for you, too, of course. Not that that's important, I know.'

'No.'

'But the Firm would see you all right.'

There was renewed altercation in the next room, cut short again by the slamming of a door. After a soft knock, Nightingale's thin face appeared. He looked upset and his bow-tie flopped more on one side than the other.

'Feather's impossible. I'm at my wits' end. I hope we haven't disturbed you.' His eyes sought the running water. 'Oh, it is you. I said it couldn't be. How embarrassing. Would you mind awfully if I asked you to turn if off? Don't want to be more of a bore than I am' – he smiled – 'but it's coming through the ceiling below. They think we do it deliberately. They get frightfully upset.'

Box put both hands to the tap. 'We'll go into the garden.'

There were two buckets catching water in the corridor below and a green plastic bowl on the desk of the girl who had been reading. Nightingale left them in order to placate her. As they descended the stairs they heard his plaintive tones and her irritated protests eclipsed by harsh croaking admonitions from Feather. Everyone was saying that they were going to tell Peter.

The garden was large and well kept. An almost English lawn sloped down to burgeoning banks of shrubbery. Box clasped his hands behind his back and sniffed the air.

'I think a stroll, don't you?' he said loudly. They paced the perimeter of the lawn as far as the first corner. Box turned to face the embassy. 'This should be okay. No one's watching. You stay where you are while I check.' He ducked into the bushes.

A green parrot flew across the lawn and perched in a tree. William had heard about this bird. It lived at the embassy and was famous for its imitations of staff being rude about each other and their guests. It stared at him and slowly raised one claw. William raised his hand.

'Someone coming?' Box's voice was urgent.

'It's all right, I was waving at the parrot.'

When Box spoke again his tone was gentler. 'Just pretend you're enjoying the garden. I'll stay in here so that we're not seen together. We can talk like this, but try not to move your lips too much. If anyone does see you, they'll think you're talking to yourself.'

William turned to the bushes. 'But we walked down here together. Anyone might have seen us.'

'Memories are short. Out of sight, out of mind. Find that very often in this business.'

William turned away. 'What is it you want me to do?'

'Try to look normal. Stay as you are.'

'I mean, help. You said you wanted help?'

'Wait. I'm thinking.'

The sky was blue with fluffy white clouds and there was now a nip in the breeze. William buttoned his jacket by the centre button, which reminded him again of his stomach, then of Theresa. The parrot cocked its head on one side.

'You had lunch with the president?' asked Box.

'I met him while I was having lunch.'

'You were with two women.'

'Well, not really, but in a sense, yes.'

'You bought them lunch.'

'Only after they'd gone.' William turned to the bushes again. 'How do you know all this?'

'Better not face me when you're talking.'

William turned away. 'How do you know?'

'The whole town knows if the president talks to anyone in public. That's what I mean about not being seen together. In this business you have to be careful in small towns.' There was some rustling as Box moved. 'The president knows you from university?'

'From school. I didn't go to university.'

'Never mind. Makes no difference after a year or two. Could you get to know him again, talk to him, find out what he's thinking?'

'This is the first time we've met since.'

'And then introduce me if he's amenable.'

'What for?'

'So that I could influence him.'

William tried to imagine Box influencing Carlos. 'I don't know. I don't know how he would take it.'

'Don't worry, you haven't been with the Firm five minutes. You need experience.' Box sounded as if he were encouraging a child. 'Look, you've been in the same place for a long time. Better move about a bit. Looks more natural. Walk slowly and I'll keep pace. Talk as we go.'

William turned to his right. 'The trouble is, I'm not very likely to run into him again. I don't think he goes very often to the market and neither do I. Well, not that often, anyway.'

Box's reply was inaudible. William stopped. 'Which way are you going?'

'I'll come to you.' There was more rustling and movement. 'Okay.'

William began walking again. 'I'm not sure how I can meet him – I mean, I can't exactly call on him.'

'Can't you?'

'Not with all those guards and generals and Cubans and whatever.'

'Cubans? Were there any with him?'

'No, but there was a chap who'd been trained in Cuba. I met him. His name is Mañuel Herrera.'

'Now we're on to something.'

William stopped. 'I'm at the corner now. Shall I go on or turn round?'

'Go on.'

William turned the corner. There was a crash in the bushes and a grunt. 'Are you all right?'

'Wire.'

'Shall I turn back?'

'I'll catch up.'

William went on. Presently he heard a movement beside him. 'All right now?'

'What?' The voice sounded strained.

'You're sure you're all right?'

The bushes parted and a stocky middle-aged man in shirt and tie stepped out. He looked red-faced and awkward, his grey hair was ruffled and there was a biro in his shirt pocket.

'I'm sorry,' said William. 'I thought you were someone else.'

'I thought *you* were.' They shook hands. The man introduced himself as Peter White. 'I'm the ambassador here.'

'I'm William Wooding.'

William almost shook hands again but stopped himself in time. 'I've just been in the embassy with . . . with some of your –'

'With them?'

Something in the ambassador's tone made William relax. 'Yes, with them, but it wasn't them I came to see. I came to see a Mr Box from London. He's in the bushes, too, but farther down.'

'Ah, the funny hush-hush business.' The ambassador had a plain, honest, troubled face. 'Not in there with him, are they?'

'No, they're in the embassy.'

'Ah.' The ambassador's features cleared. 'I was out for a stroll round the gardens. Popped in the bushes to make myself comfortable.'

'Very wise.'

'Helps to get out of the office now and again.'

'Yes.'

'Well, better get back. Pop in if you're visiting. Door's always open.'

They shook hands again and the ambassador walked briskly towards the embassy, adjusting his tie.

William went back along the bushes. 'Are you there?'

'Who was it?'

'The ambassador. I think he was relieving himself.'

'Where?'

'In the bushes.'

'Where?'

'Farther up. It's all right.'

There was a pause. 'We must meet to discuss modalities.'

'What?'

'Plans. Can I contact you at home?'

'Yes, or at work.'

'Who should I say I am?'

'Well – you're who you are, aren't you?'

'We use other names. I'll have to explain all that. I'll be Harry. We can say we met in a bar. Who will you be?'

'Myself, I suppose. Síince you're ringing me.'

'Fair enough.'

On his way out William paused by the tree in which the parrot was sitting. He raised his hand and waited while the parrot, shifting its weight, slowly raised its claw.

4

'Who is Harry?' Sally asked.

William paused in the ironing. 'Who?'

'Harry. That's twice he's rung. He won't leave a message.'

'He's rung again?'

'The phone was ringing when I got in from work. Who is he?'

'Chap I met in a bar.'

The telephone rang once more. She answered it and fortunately it was for her. He tried to think of some less obviously evasive explanation. When she came back into the kitchen she stretched from tip to toe, pointing as she used to do when she went to ballet classes.

'He's a chap who might be buying some books,' William said. 'South American studies, that sort of thing.' He couldn't remember having lied to her before. Though this should hardly have counted as one, it was a deceit and he felt it.

'What?' Sally looked blank. 'Oh, Harry, yes.' She put on the kettle. They usually had tea before going to bed. She looked at his shirts. 'You're miles better than Angelica or me, you really are.'

Angelica, the maid, was on holiday. 'She's improving under tuition.'

'She's being courted, I think. She wants to learn.'

He didn't ask who had telephoned because any display of curiosity might bounce back. 'Good news about the job, isn't it?'

'Mmm.' She warmed the pot.

'That chap – the American vice-president or whatever – wasn't as bad as you thought, then?'

'No, he was quite nice. He's no fool, though.'

'Clearly.' He smiled but she didn't notice. 'What's his name again – Heffner?'

'Hueffer, Max Hueffer. But I'm going to have to work hard with these advanced specialist groups. I shall be directly under him. He could be a mean master.'

'That's good, isn't it? You said you wanted to be stretched.'

When he had finished the ironing he took his tea into the sitting room and joined her on the sofa. They sipped in silence. He wanted to read but didn't in case this was one of the times she wanted to talk. His eye wandered surreptitiously to the closed book on the arm of the sofa, less than a foot from his lap.

'What did the embassy want?' she asked.

'They wanted me to talk about business here to some chap out from London.'

'Why you?'

'They seemed to think I know about it.'

'Funny.'

'That's what I thought.' He would talk to Box about this subterfuge. It was as awkward as it was unnecessary.

She reached across him and picked up the book, Jeffrey Archer's *First Among Equals*. 'Any good?'

'Makes you want to turn the pages.'

She tossed the book back on to the coffee table and got up. 'I'm going to bed. Good-night.'

Ricardo was unusually early the next morning. The seriousness of the situation at the factory had impressed him. 'They're all back today but not for long and they are doing nothing. We have to get rid of the two union men. They intimidate the others and Miguel is too frightened to manage. He does nothing except what they tell him.'

'Why is he so frightened?'

'Because the union will beat him up and the police will do nothing.'

William stared through the latest clean window-pane. The orange man still stood alongside his barrow, muffled and solitary. 'I'll go out to the factory myself.'

'What can you do? You can do nothing. You do not have authority.'

'I'll talk to Miguel. It might be possible to work out something. Then at least we can report to London.'

Ricardo gestured impatiently. 'London, what can London do? You must plant something on them and get rid of them, I told you. It is now the only way.'

Ricardo's face was intelligent and fine-featured. He smiled with treacherous charm. 'You are a reasonable man, William, very English, very nice. It is because of men like you that your country has always been popular here. Without you we would not have become a country. But because you are reasonable you are also blind. You cannot see that others are not reasonable. Because you have no nastiness you do not see it in others. But you must fight them with their own weapons or they will win.'

'We must also try to do what is right.'

'It does not work any more.' Ricardo had been half-sitting, half-lying on his desk. He slid gracefully off it. '*Chau*, William.'

'*Chau*.'

That was probably Ricardo's appearance for the day. He might come back in the afternoon if he ran out of people to see. More likely, he would find a girl. William looked once more at the quarterly returns, at the list of questions London had sent, at the incomprehensible local tax demand. This was the sort of thing that Ricardo was supposed to help with. Perhaps he had been too reasonable with Ricardo, reasonable to the point of weakness, but it was easier in the end to do things himself. At least they got done.

The factory was a worry, though. It produced paper products mainly for the wholesale trade but a small amount was retailed through the shop. Because trade was slack they had wholesale stocks for four to six weeks but if the trouble were prolonged they would be out of business. There was enough competition to see to that. Neither the mill nor the shop would survive without the factory; it was the engine that kept the operation afloat, in so far as anything did, yet in London they seemed to think that the shop was the main thing. Indeed, the job had been sold to William on that basis and he had been trying since his first weeks to correct London's view. But they would not accept it, any more than they accepted that although he was formally responsible for the factory he had authority neither in it nor over it. He had responsibility without power, the worst of all worlds.

The idea of planting things on trouble-makers stuck in his throat. It was not the sort of thing one should do, even if it were done. One might pay them off, perhaps – bribe them to go – but wrongful arrest was another matter. Catching them doing something illegal would be best of all. That was what he would talk to Miguel about. It was important to try to be reasonable even if no one else did. Perhaps particularly important then. After all, the world was fundamentally reasonable. No matter how badly people behaved they tried to justify themselves, to make themselves seem reasonable; and no matter how far and wide the aberrations, everyone in the end had to adjust. It was a condition of existence.

The orange-seller had a customer, a man as short as himself but wearing a flat hat rather than a beret. They were negotiating over an orange. It was a protracted business involving argument, shaking heads, gesticulations and a prolonged searching of pockets. The seller appeared to be insisting on the sale of more than one orange, indicating that he had no change, while the buyer appeared willing to spend the rest of the morning searching his pockets rather than pay for more than he needed. Eventually a coin fell from the buyer's pocket and rolled under the barrow. He followed it on his hands and knees and it was then that William recognised Box.

He tapped on the window and tried vainly to open it. He was very keen to talk. Apart from the calls to the flat there had been one to the office taken – a rare event – by Ricardo, who had then asked who 'Mr Harry' was. William had told the same lie he had told Sally. Repetition had not made it sound any more convincing.

The window came open as Box turned away clutching his orange. William was about to call to him but stopped. Box wouldn't like it. He closed the window and hurried down through the shop.

The orange man was rearranging his stack, though it was hard to see why, and Box was walking quickly towards the square at the top of the hill. William hurried after him, regretting yet again that morning the absence of the lopsided Dodge. Box had turned the corner into the square before William, breathless, caught up with him.

Box spoke without turning his face. 'Drop back a few paces. Don't want to be more obvious than we have to be.'

William dropped back. He supposed this sort of thing was one of the necessary irritations of spying.

'Hoped you'd spot me and come out, but didn't mean to make you hurry,' Box continued loudly. 'Important we weren't seen together by that spy.'

'Which spy?'

'Chap with the oranges.'

'Is he a spy?'

'Of course he is. He's spying on you. That's why he sets up there. No other earthly reason. No trade. No change. Has he been there long?'

'No – well – I'm not sure. A couple of weeks, I suppose.'

'There you are, then.'

There were more stalls and barrows in the square but business was desultory. They walked rapidly between customers, children and the battered lorries and shooting-brakes belonging to the traders. Old-fashioned upright bicycles – Raleighs, BSAs, Triumphs – leaned against the plane trees. Box spoke crisply without turning his head. Presumably he relied on the locals having no English or on sheer speed making it difficult to overhear. He was now in an hotel, he explained, which meant that they would be able to devise a satisfactory contact procedure – with fall-back, of course. He would brief William on the name he was using etc. in due course. Meanwhile, had William got anywhere with the president?

'No.'

'We'd better discuss how you can. Are you free for lunch?'

'Yes.'

'Good. That's something.'

William was further irritated. 'Are you sure you should risk being seen with me?' He didn't catch the reply and had to ask for a repeat. People were staring after them.

'You have to take some chances in this game,' Box repeated, more loudly than before. 'Which way for lunch?'

'Right at the next corner.'

When they left the square Box slowed up and indicated that they could walk side by side. William headed for the covered market. The thought put him in better humour.

'Tell me, why did you buy just one orange? It seemed to cause a lot of trouble.'

'I wanted to spend long enough with him so that I'd know him again. Also, I'm only allowed one on expenses.'

'One orange?'

'Two if you'd been there . . . or more. They're quite generous if you're entertaining professional contacts. It's only with us they're mean. This is all post-privatisation, of course. Where are we going?'

When William told him Box shook his head. 'Sorry, won't do. Too public, too crowded, you're too well-known there now. Wrong kind of risk. Unjustified.'

'But we might meet the president.'

'Worse still. He'll suspect a plot.'

'Does he know you, then?'

'Of course not. No one here knows me, that's why I was sent. But his cronies would do their damnedest to find out – be round the hotel in no time, checking everything.'

They headed instead for Gustav's, a German restaurant William had heard about but never used. The entrance was a small black door at the end of an alleyway. There was no sign outside.

Box stopped. 'What is this place?'

'Gustav's, known locally as the Nazi restaurant.'

'Nazis?'

'Not really. One or two, maybe. They must be pretty old now, mustn't they?'

'Runs in families.'

'But at least we won't bump into the president or any of his left-wing cronies. Opposite ends of the political spectrum.'

'The spectrum is circular. The two ends meet on the other side. Totalitarians always have more in common with each other than with the rest of us.' Behind his gold-rimmed glasses Box's eyes were unblinking and expressionless.

'Well, there's nowhere else I'm not known,' William lied.

They went in. The furnishings and decorations looked a mixture of *Bierkeller* and alpine hut. There were racks of German wines, bottles of German beer, German newspapers on the counter and, on the walls, German regimental insignia and pictures of German warships. The background music sounded like a German drinking-song. The few customers looked native.

The waiter spoke Spanish. '*Para dos, señor?*'

'*Gracias.*'

'No.' Box pointed to a table for four. 'That one.'

The waiter appealed to William. '*Pero para dos personas, señor?*'

'*Sí*, for two people.'

'No.' Box stood by the other table. 'Johnny's coming. That makes three. So we'll need a table for four.'

'Johnny?'

'Coming later.' Box explained to the waiter in halting Spanish that a friend was coming. The waiter glanced again at William, shrugged and showed them to a table for four.

The other customers watched.

William had not seen Box's smile before. It was a fleeting parting of the lips, slightly disconcerting. 'Better table separation,' Box explained. 'Makes it harder for observers to overhear. Useful chap, Johnny.'

'What happens when he doesn't turn up?'

'We go on saying he's late. Typical of him. Useful but unreliable, as the actress said.' He laughed, a sharp bark. The other customers looked up again. The waiter's head reappeared round the kitchen door.

They ordered wild boar and wine. Box repeated what he had previously said about the country subsiding beneath Soviet dominion. William presumed he didn't realise he was repeating himself and listened with the appearance of polite attention while his mind wandered. He wanted to know why he had been chosen. It was true that there weren't many other British businessmen in the city. What few British commercial operations remained after years of complacency were generally serviced by managers travelling down from Rio for a few days. They never seemed to be the same people for more than two visits. Predecessors had always just been sacked or sent for drying out or found to be transvestite or discovered with their fingers in the till. Rio seemed to have that effect on the British. William supposed that he, by comparison, was on the spot, stable, patriotic and as yet unsacked. Also, he knew Carlos. But how did they know that?

Box finished his peroration and looked suddenly self-conscious. 'I expect you think I'm seeing Reds under every bed.'

'Not necessarily. I don't know.'

'But you believe what I say?'

William hesitated. 'Yes.'

'And you're happy to help us?'

'Yes. But why me? There must be others you could have asked.'

'You know Carlos. No one else does.'

'But how did you know?'

Box's lips parted briefly. 'Trade secret, really, but I'll tell you since you're one of us now. We checked through all the records we could find of anyone who could have known him in England, and then checked them against the list of expatriates who'd registered with the embassy here. Yours was the only name that came up twice. Hope you don't mind?'

'Not at all. I was just curious.'

'You really are happy to help?'

'Yes.'

Box's pallor was tinged with a faint blush. 'My first recruitment since privatisation.'

'Recruitment?'

'Yes, I've recruited you. That's what it's called.'

'But I've only said I'd help you.'

'Yes, that's it. That's recruitment. I get a bonus, you see – so much for a Brit, more for a foreigner. You don't have the right to any other passport, I suppose?'

''Fraid not.'

'Never mind, can't be helped. Let's drink to our success.'

Afterwards Box wiped his lips with his handkerchief and leaned forward. 'What I always say is, supposing there really are Reds under the beds? Are we supposed to stay silent?'

'Of course not.'

'But if we do speak we're accused of saying there are Reds under the beds and no one takes any notice.'

'I suppose not.'

'It's jolly hard to know what's for the best.' Box put down his glass and, his elbows on the table, clasped his hands and clenched them until his knuckles showed white and his pale cheeks shook. Then he relaxed and sat back, his palms flat on the table. 'Always ease mental tension with the physical. Clears the arteries and the mind. Prolongs life. Keeps weight down, too.'

'Do you think I should try it?'

'You could try. But we must sort out how you're going to meet the president. Brandy with your coffee? All on expenses.'

'Can't someone from the embassy see him?'

'No good if it's official; you can't bribe a chap in front

of his pals. Actually, "subvert" is what we call it now. Bribery has got such a bad name.'

'How much?'

Box looked at his glass. 'A million or two. Plus favourable trade deals, that sort of thing. As I said, it's a big contract.'

The door opened and Theresa entered, behind her Ines and Manuel Herrera. She smiled quickly at William, who was facing them, and turned to a table in the corner. Ines smiled fulsomely, showing nearly all her teeth. Manuel raised his hand.

'What's happened?' Box had his back to them.

William told him. Theresa shook her head as she sat and pushed back her hair with both hands. Her fingers lingered a moment before running through it and leaving it spread over her shoulders.

'Keep your head still,' said Box. 'I'm trying to see their reflections in your glasses. 'What did you say they do, those women?'

'They're singers, I think. They dance and sing.' Ricardo had added something about that being part of it. 'I don't know where.'

'Herrera's up to no good.'

'How do you know?'

'Because he's Herrera. Half Cuban by birth and all Cuban by training. Also a communist. I checked. He can't be up to good.'

'Perhaps he just likes girls.'

'Of course he likes girls, he's half-Cuban. They spend their lives liking girls. But it won't be only that.'

Box stared into William's left eye. The waiter had gone to the table. Herrera was saying something serious, one hand on the waiter's arm.

'Every problem is an opportunity,' Box continued in an undertone. 'It's unfortunate that we're seen together and Herrera's probably as unhappy to see us as we are to see him. But no one's seen my face, so we're one up. And he's probably with the girls because the president took an interest in them, so this is your chance to get to know them better and use them to take you to the president.'

It had not occurred to William that he could legitimise getting to know Theresa. It was a thought both appealing and worrying. 'I'm not sure how I could.'

'Initiative.' Box spoke the word as if it were a code. 'Always have an aim, then you find a way of achieving it. Bit of a boy-scout approach but it serves me well. My aim is to leave here without my face being seen. Yours is not to leave without having had a conversation leading to a further meeting with at least one of the group. I'll go first. Contact me when you have something to report: Hotel Britannia, room 42, name of Welling.'

He stood, stepped sideways from the table so as not to show his profile and walked quickly through the nearest swing-door, which led to the kitchen. There were raised voices in a mixture of Spanish and German. Box backed out and, still without facing the restaurant, walked smartly down the corridor to the toilets. The waiter, who with his three new customers had been watching the spectacle, hurried into the kitchen. He came out with another man, went to the till and came across to William with the bill. He stood by while William paid.

William had to pass the group on his way to the door.

'You like German food?' Ines asked.

'But your friend does not?' Manuel held out his hand to be shaken. It was like his face – strong, smooth and confident.

'Client,' William said. 'A prospective client.'

'Not an obliging one. Is he all right? He seemed to be hurrying.'

Ines laughed. 'The food does not agree with him?'

'He said he was going. Perhaps there's a back way out.'

Manuel pursed his lips. 'Only the window. A very small window. He must be very determined, your client.'

'I don't know. I don't know him very well.' William felt he should be doing better. Theresa stared down at her spoon, edging it backwards and forwards with her little finger.

'I daresay it would be impolite to follow and find out. Unnecessary, perhaps.' Manuel smiled.

'I liked your car,' William said to Theresa. 'Your Dodge, the old one. It was parked near my shop yesterday. You drove off with a great noise.'

She looked up. 'It always makes a great noise. But not now. No more noise.'

'It doesn't go?'

'Kaput, they would say here.'

The waiter reappeared with plates. On his way back to the kitchen he hesitated, eyeing the toilet. He took a step towards it, hesitated again, then walked determinedly in.

Everyone laughed. William felt easier. Anything out of the ordinary was more acceptable now. 'Would you like me to have a look at it?' he asked.

'You know about engines?'

'A little.'

'It's a very big engine.'

'They're easier to work on.' One of the company drivers in London had told him that.

She looked down and touched her spoon again. 'If you like. It's very kind. You don't need to.'

'Where is it and when shall I come?'

'Plaza San Marco. I will meet you there at seven this evening.' Her tone was definite, as if to conclude the discussion.

The waiter came out of the toilet and walked thoughtfully into the kitchen. They laughed again.

'I hope you have better luck with cars than with clients, *Señor* Wooding,' said Manuel.

5

William knew nothing about repairing cars. He knew they had big-ends that went, gaskets that blew, clutches that slipped, brakes that seized, gaps that narrowed or widened, points that corroded; but he didn't know what to do about any of them. Also, it was his turn to cook and seven was an awkward time. He couldn't very well start, rush out, repair the car and rush back, nor did he want to ask Sally to swap nights at the last minute. Nor did he want to lie to her. He spent the afternoon in wretched and futile indecision.

He walked home as usual across the golf course and as he came off the hill towards the sea he saw that *Señor* Finn was there again, hunched over his fire in the clump of pampas grass. The fire flickered uncertainly and a brisk damp breeze worried the small trees and bushes. The clouds were spitting rain and the sea was leaden and surly.

Señor Finn, bulky in assorted clothes, sat with his elbows on his knees and poked at the fire. The terrier barked once and got half up before subsiding. The cat sat on the upturned boat. William raised his hand in greeting. *Señor* Finn did the same.

'Not so good this evening,' William called.

'Rain is coming.' The wind in the pampas grass and the waves beyond made the old man's voice indistinct.

'I didn't see you the other night.'

Señor Finn pointed north along the beach. 'Fish. Good fish.'

'I see. Good.' They grinned and nodded at each other. '*Buenas noches.*'

'*Buenas noches.*'

William felt happier during the latter part of his walk. He would tell Sally everything. It was better to be truthful, certainly easier, and lying probably wouldn't work anyway. He would tell Box afterwards.

Sally seemed neither surprised nor impressed. William was disappointed.

'Are you sure he's not having you on?' she asked. 'A privatised secret service seems a bit odd. He might be a gangster or the mafia or something.'

'I was introduced to him at the embassy by Nightingale and Feather.'

'That could mean anything. And who exactly are these people you know who know the president?'

'Well, there's Herrera – and me, of course – and those two women the president talked to in the market and who were in the restaurant today.'

'But you hardly count. You haven't seen Carlos since school and you weren't all that friendly then. Who are these women?'

'Singers, I think.'

'Where from?'

'I don't know.'

She laughed. 'You do get yourself into pickles sometimes. Only you would get mixed up with a privatised secret service, a president, a sinister colonel and a chorus. And now you've got to mend a car and you don't know one end from another.'

'It's just a way of getting closer to the president.'

'It might get you as far as his garage.'

She was amused in the way she used to be when they had first known each other. He was glad he had done nothing for which he need feel guilty. Nor would he now. He would enjoy Theresa's company, certainly, but that was all. Anyway, he wasn't doing it for that.

'Might it not be dangerous?' she asked as he was preparing to go.

'Oh no, nothing like that.' The notion of danger hadn't occured to him.

'Max Hueffer says that the Russians really are moving

in a big way economically and that the government is getting more extreme. People have started disappearing.'

'Which people?'

'I don't know. People who oppose the government.'

'I wonder if that really is true. The press is fairly free.'

'Is it?'

'Well, not much less free than it ever was. People still hold protest demonstrations. There was one at the weekend.'

'I thought that was a government rally.'

'Maybe, but anyway . . .' He was less confident now; he kept thinking of Manuel Herrera. 'How does Max know all this?'

'I don't know. He just seems to know things.'

He searched for the car keys. He would take the company Datsun in case he needed to pull or push the lame Dodge. 'Perhaps I should take some tools.'

'Are there any?'

'I don't know.'

She found a hammer in one of the kitchen cupboards, a solid piece with a heavy head and claw. He put it in his duffle-coat pocket. 'Might be better than nothing,' he said, to encourage himself.

He dithered over leaving. She seemed much better-humoured and he no longer wanted to go. The whole business was an uncomfortable mixture of the serious and the absurd. She kissed him, which she hadn't done for some time. 'I won't be long,' he said.

Plaza San Marco was in the old part of the city, not far from his shop, an area of cobbled streets and large faded buildings. The darkness spawned a fine invisible rain and the wind flapped William's duffle-coat against his legs as he walked from the car, except where the hammer weighed it down. Theresa was already beside her Dodge, holding an umbrella and shivering beneath a long dress and shawl.

'There is no need, really, we don't have to do this,' she said straight away. 'You can come in.'

'No, no, it's quite all right.'

'Are you an expert with cars?'

'It depends what's wrong.'

She smiled. 'I think you are not an expert.'

High heels made her as tall as him. She stood close while they talked, trying to shield them both with the small umbrella. Her bare arm was across her breast, clutching the shawl.

It was a while before he realised that the chrome handles on each side of the bonnet served instead of a bonnet catch. Propping one side open, he switched on the torch he had brought. The engine looked massive and intractable.

'I'll have a look at the other side.'

The second side didn't seem to open properly and he struggled for a time before realising he had to close the first. From the other side the engine seemed to be mainly metal pipes. 'Try to start it.'

It gave a groan and expired. 'Would you like to try?' she asked.

There was some pleasing awkwardness with the umbrella as she got out to make way for him. Her dress rustled and she wore an arousing perfume – whether cheap or expensive he had no idea, but it was obvious, which was how he liked it. He sat on the leather seats and contemplated the wooden dash-board. The ignition light was on but the key wouldn't turn.

'No, no, you press this.' Her bare arm, which had a few dark hairs on it, reached across him.

He pressed the button marked S but nothing happened. He pulled the button marked C, presumably for choke, and again pressed S, again without result. He remembered his father's countless old cars. 'Does it have a starting-handle?'

They found one in the boot. It was heavy and long. He had to get down on his knees in the wet road and struggle to slot it in. 'Make sure the car's out of gear.' He was impressed by how masterful he sounded. He tried to turn the handle. 'Are you sure it isn't in gear?'

'Yes, quite sure.'

He tried again. It felt as if he were trying to rotate the whole car.

'Shall I help you?' she called.

'No, no, it's all right.' He paused to regain control of his breathing and then put both hands on the handle, one on top of the other. He had learned from his father to grip with thumb and fingers together rather than opposed in case the handle kicked back on firing. He remembered stories of broken thumbs and wrists. Straining with both hands, he had moved it nearly half a turn when there was a violent cough. He was thrown sideways and left sitting in the road. The handle spun harmlessly in its socket. The car shook and spluttered, relapsed, then heaved itself into life with a great clattering roar as the handle fell out. The back of his right hand started to hurt.

'William, where are you?' Theresa called above the noise. 'Are you all right?'

'Yes.' He wanted to get up elegantly and quickly, but couldn't before she reached him. Water from her umbrella dripped on to his head.

'William, your hand. You can't be all right.'

There was a little blood. He got to his feet protesting that there was nothing wrong. He liked to hear her use his name.

She touched his arm. 'Come inside and clean it. You must be poisoned.'

'No. Okay.'

She led him to a house in the corner of the square. An unlit board outside announced that it was Maria's Tango Club. Inside it seemed a mixture of club, bar, dance hall and somebody's house. The worn furnishings had once been good and the rooms were large, each giving on to another. In one was a bar, in another a band, in another tables and food. There were drinkers of most ages, nearly all of whom greeted Theresa as she passed. William followed, feeling uncouth in his duffle-coat and holding his now aching hand as inconspicuously as possible. The glances which fell upon Theresa flipped back on to him like branches that had parted before her. In a hall they passed a huge sofa on which seven or eight colourfully dressed and made-up girls were sitting. They greeted Theresa in an uneven chorus.

She swept through, her shawl fluttering. They went down some stairs, past a noisome lavatory and into a dressing-room strewn with womens' clothes. Three or four women were in various stages of dressing. None paid him any attention except Ines who, bulging through black underwear and stockings, was bent over looking in her handbag. She waved and smiled and said something about his coat which he didn't understand. The others looked at him. One, a thin woman in a long skin-tight red dress, was putting on lipstick before a mirror encircled by bulbs. She paused with her mouth open and the stick at her lip, regarded him indifferently and carried on.

'Here, come here,' called Theresa. She was removing clothes from a pink wash-basin.

Trying to smile in a genial and unembarrassed manner, William picked his way between the garments on the floor. He knocked against a chair on which a tabby cat lay curled up on a skirt.

'Take off your coat,' Theresa said.

He did so slowly, hoping neither to make it bloody nor to let his eye be caught by the reflection of the other women in the mirror above the basin.

She took the coat. 'It's so heavy.'

'That's the hammer.'

'A hammer? To mend my car?' She laughed and shook her head. 'Oh, William.'

Some of the skin was torn and there was a slight swelling; it looked worse than it was. She wanted to bandage it but he said there was no need. When the water made it sting he pretended it didn't. Ines called loudly to know what had happened. One of the other women said Theresa was stupid to persist with such an absurd car now that she could afford a new one.

'Not yet,' said Theresa.

'After tonight, then?'

'It's not certain.'

There was a chorus of good-natured disbelief.

When the hand was clean she took Wiliam to the room where the four-piece band was playing a rumba. Three couples were dancing. More couples and a number of single women sat at tables at the side.

Theresa led him to a separate table. 'You can wait a while?'

'Yes.'

'They will bring you a drink. I cannot talk now. I will come and talk later.'

More people came in. Men asked some of the girls to dance and after a while he noticed that there seemed to be a high turnover in girls. Some were danced with once only, others for several dances, others disappeared with the men. More couples came and stayed together, then more men and girls who came and danced and went. William assumed they were prostitutes but couldn't be sure. It was true that some held the eye for a fraction longer than normal, but perhaps that was because he was doing the same. It was true, too, that some had a knowing look but then almost all women were entitled to that, so far as he was concerned. Being married had taught him little. He and Sally had gone out with each other in the usual way but after the initial excitement had worn off they had got engaged instead of finishing, at the very time they had become bored with each other. It had added excitement, progress, focus to the relationship.

He had been grateful to her for marrying him and afterwards had begun to love her. He didn't know whether she really loved him. She used to say she did, and there were times when he thought she must, but most of the time – and especially now – she seemed to accept his being there in the simple unreflecting way in which she might have accepted a brother. By being careful with each other, they got on well enough.

A waiter appeared with a tray and a tall glass. He gave a glacial smile and put the glass very precisely on William's table. The drink had ice and lemon in it and was very cold.

More people came. A cha-cha caused a crowded floor. The dancers smiled, talking and swinging their hips ostentatiously. William sipped his drink, resenting the grace of the slim-hipped men; they were disagreeably feline. The women, more generously hipped, danced with a rhythm which involved little movement, depending for its effectiveness on the time between movements. He realised he was staring rather fixedly only when he noticed the guitar-player doing the same. The man was sitting upright except for his head which projected forward to an unnatural degree. He had an expression of concentrated gloom. It was impossible to tell whether he was focusing on what he saw, or saw nothing. His long fingers wandered expertly across the strings. The dancers laughed and swung their hips. William permitted one foot to tap.

An infusion of yet more people on to the floor, a crowd who had come in together, raised the tempo and temperature. William was still staring at the staring guitarist when he felt a hand on his shoulder.

'You do not have to be a spectator. Here even *un Inglés* who is married can enjoy himself.' Ricardo smiled.

William stood quickly as if caught out. 'What are you doing here?'

Ricardo laughed. 'I should ask you that question. I have come to dance. But you?' He held up his hand. 'You have come for Ines and Theresa?'

'No, not just that, I was helping –'

'Do not worry, you are not the only man who comes for this reason.' He turned to a girl at his side. 'Maria, this is William. He is my very English partner.'

Maria was small, pretty and dark. They shook hands and William moved his duffle-coat from one of the free chairs. The hammer clonked against the table. 'Won't you sit down? There's plenty of room.'

'Yes, but first we will dance. We are with others but we will all join you and you can dance with Maria.' Ricardo smiled again. 'Then you need not feel guilty. You look very married tonight, William.'

William smiled back. 'I am.'

For Ricardo dancing was an exhibition, his partner a necessary prop. He curled and cavorted, swayed and swung, taking up more room than anyone else. It was a good exhibition, energetic and graceful, but vitiated by being a performance. He danced as if before a mirror and William soon wearied of watching. Instead he watched Maria, who at least was trying to dance with her partner, her movements modest but responsive. William's attention was again distracted by the guitarist, whose stare was fixed in its concentration or vacuity.

When the cha-cha finished another table was pulled alongside, more chairs gathered, drinks ordered. Ricardo's companions were boisterous with each other and elaborately polite and uninterested with William. Ricardo continued to call him his 'English partner', implying inferior status. Maria smiled and was quiet. William exchanged smiles with her but did not speak. The music and the clamour of rapid simultaneous conversations strained his Spanish.

Ricardo lit a cigarette and leaned back in his chair. 'Does your wife know you are here?'

'Of course, yes. I came to help Theresa start her car. I told her.'

'Of course, yes, to start her car.' Ricardo smiled. 'Does Theresa know you are married?'

'Oh yes. Well, no, I don't know. It doesn't matter, anyway; it's not like that.'

Ricardo put his hand on William's shoulder again. 'Maybe you forgot to mention it, yes? It has slipped your mind. But William, I have news for you: you have competition for that woman.'

'I'm not in competition for her.'

'Big competition. From the president himself. He is coming here tonight. If he likes her, he will take her as his mistress. It is her big chance.'

'Good for her.'

He tried to sound nonchalant. No doubt this was what Box would call an opportunity. It was important not to show too much interest. He looked around. 'Who owns this place?'

Ricardo pointed to the staring guitarist. 'He does. He is a very rich man who never spends anything unless it is to earn something. Your predecessor, *Señor* Wicks, used to make arrangements with him. The best girls are here.'

'Does he always play the guitar?'

'When he wishes. It is a hobby for him. And the girls here, they are examined medically and have to audition just to work. They cannot come in off the street. He is a very strict man. He is famous for his money and his principles.'

'Does he always stare like that?'

'Always. He is famous for it. He is known as *una lagarta* – in English, El Lizard.'

'How do you know the president is coming?'

'Ines told me.'

'You know Ines?' It seemed that everyone knew everyone in this city.

Ricardo grinned. 'Of course.'

There was a growing sense of expectancy. More people crowded in, the curtain was drawn back to reveal the further width of the stage, extra tables were set out. El Lizard gave his guitar to another man and went off with a uniformed man who wore white gloves. William recognised some of the girls he had seen in the dressing-room. They were taller than most women and wore long shimmering dresses with slits up the sides. They moved through the dancers with regal disdain, concerning themselves with preparations on stage or with each other or with the white-gloved supervisor. William could see neither Ines nor Theresa.

The music and dancing stopped abruptly, conversation with it. Everyone stood as the presidential party entered in silence. Carlos Calvaros was more colourfully uniformed than in the market and wore more decorations. He looked slimly and smilingly perfect but for the threatened indiscipline of his mouth. There was about half a dozen with him, all officers, among them Manuel Herrera and two portly men whose uniforms were more sober. It was a few moments before William recognised the Russian insignia; he had never seen Russians before.

El Lizard led the party to their tables, his expression unchanged and his head projected nearly a foot before his body. When the band struck up the national anthem the presidential party stood to attention and saluted in the Russian, or Nazi, style. The anthem lasted six minutes and there was palpable relief when it finished.

The president waved his non-saluting arm. 'Please – continue.'

Everyone sat, the band struck up again, conversation resumed, but no one danced. William faced the presidential party across the empty floor. Without wanting to, he caught Manuel's eye. Manuel inclined his head and said something to the president, who looked across with raised eyebrows and smiled. The two plump Russians stared.

'Now you can dance with Maria,' Ricardo whispered.

William shook his head. 'Not on an empty floor in front of them.' He turned back to Ricardo. 'Perhaps you should dance? You do it so well.'

'I know. It would give them great pleasure to see me dance. But it is not me they have come to see. They want samba.'

'Can't you samba?'

'Not in this way. Wait.'

There was a roll of drums and the lights were dimmed, except those on stage. The drums stopped, paused, and began again with a fast samba rhythm. It was throbbing insistent music, like a fast stream that swirled, tumbled, convoluted and turned back on itself while rushing onward, ever onward. It was the kind of music William usually resisted but now he could feel his stomach tighten.

The back-stage curtains parted and first one girl, then another, then another entered dancing. Soon there was a dozen of them spread across the stage and off it, flowing down the steps on either side on to the dance floor. They were the girls William had seen earlier, all now in their long tight dresses with slits up the sides and frilly tops.

Their samba, little more than a shuffle of the feet and a motion of the hips, was mesmeric. Holding their arms high, they shimmered over stage and floor. Led by Carlos, people started clapping rhythmically. Gradually the girls sorted themselves into two vibrating lines which led down the sides of the floor and focused on the stage. William could see neither Theresa nor Ines. He sat at the edge of the floor, his head very close to the pullulating hips of the nearest dancer. Ricardo was still talking.

There was a drum crescendo and then silence. One of the Russians shouted something. Carlos smiled politely at him and turned back to the stage. Manuel sat unsmiling but the other officers all acknowledged the Russian. The silence continued.

'Come on,' said Ricardo. His words carried and one or two of the presidential party looked across. The dancer next to William shifted on her feet and her tight dress rustled. Like all the others, she wore a carnation at the point where the slit in her skirt exposed her stocking top. Ricardo nudged William, indicating that he should stretch forward and take it.

The silence was tense and as becoming oppressive when the drummer began again, very slowly, very softly, a gentle suggestive momentum. The curtains parted and Theresa and Ines samba'd slowly on to the stage. Ines wore shimmering white and Theresa a tight-fitting black dress that flared out from her hips. Each danced down one line of girls, who themselves began gyrating again on the spot. Both were stunning and flamboyant but Theresa, to William's eye, gave the impression of something extra, something hidden, something kept back. Her eyes were veiled by black gauze, leaving only her lips visible. Her movements were hardly more than suggestions. The essence seemed to be not in the movements themselves but in something between and behind, a kind of latent prolonged explosion, imminent, hinted at, not quite occurring.

When they reached the end of the lines they began leading the other girls back and round, then across and through each other. The drum tempo increased and the rest of the band joined in. The girls seemed to be going anywhere and everywhere, to no pattern but to an irresistible rhythm. They coalesced, separated, circled, came together, all the time shuffling, advancing, hesitating, withdrawing in seamless liquid movement. William kept making himself look away from Theresa but each time his eyes came back to her. It was as when he had first noticed her – she was too blatantly attractive, she ought not to be real. As the pace of the dance increased she moved even less, her feet just inching forward, her lips slightly parted, her outstretched arms quite still, her hips in hypnotic coaxial rotation.

After another crescendo, the dance ceased. The girls stood as they were, all smiling, surrounded now by clapping, whistling and whooping. The president stood to clap and soon everyone was standing. Carlos and his party walked among the girls, talking and smiling. The band began a sedate cha-cha and dancing restarted. Carlos danced with Theresa, one of the Russians with Ines. The Russian was not as tall as Ines and stood indignantly upright. Herrera remained at the table. William looked to see whether Ricardo would dance, but he was saying something to Maria, possibly his apologies since he then, with a quick grin at William, got up and selected one of the dancers.

The president and Theresa were in the middle of the floor, a wide space around them. Carlos talked all the time. Theresa was attentive and smiling, her movements graciously confined to his. William did not want to look at them. Ines was firing salvoes of delight at her Russian, who was either more than usually clumsy or slightly the worse for drink. Several times he made as if to come closer and missed, like a ship in heavy seas. Ricardo performed around a slim mulatto, repeatedly spinning her or himself and then basking again in her wide admiring gaze. Manuel sat smoking a cigar. William again inadvertently caught his eye. Manuel smiled and let the smoke seep from his mouth.

William supposed he should go over and talk to him; that was what Box would want. Box would no doubt say that Willaim's aim for the evening should now be a conversation with Carlos, not – as at the begining – simply seeing Theresa. The aim would be best achieved by talking to Manuel, so as to be at the table when the president returned. Perhaps Theresa would be there, on her way to Carlos's bed, and he could strengthen his claim to her acquaintance with a view to making use of her later. Box would be well pleased with such an evening's work. The thought of it depressed William. He wanted to talk to Theresa but not to anyone else. It was time he got back to Sally.

'Wooding.'

The tone was instantly reminiscent of school. Carlos stood before him, holding Theresa's hand. He looked pleased with himself.

'I understand you are helpful with cars. Can you be helpful on the dance floor? It would not do for the president to be seen dancing all evening with the same lady, however much he might wish to' – his lips slackened into a smile – 'and so I wonder if you would take care of her for a while? I must talk to my boring guests. Please deliver her to me when you have finished. She knows how to dance, I can guarantee that.' He gave Theresa's hand to William, bowed slightly and walked back to his table.

William kept hold of Theresa's hand. He could see her eyes through the veil but not their expression.

'Do you really want to dance?' he asked.

'You must not think about what I want. I don't.'

'We don't have to dance.'

'We do.'

She led him on to the floor and began a gentle cha-cha. They danced with each other very carefully. William could remember the steps so long as he did not think about them.

'I'm sorry if you've been forced into this,' he said.

'Don't worry about me.' Her lips parted in a quick smile. 'I like to dance with you, William.'

'But also I mean – all the rest. I don't want to be in your way.'

'You are not in my way.'

'I suppose not.' He was seized by a spasm of resentment. 'It's your big chance, tonight, I know. To be the mistress of the president is . . .'

'Much money.'

They touched fingertip to fingertip as she turned under his arm. Her movements matched his. Not by the smallest flourish did she betray how much better she was, but to his fingertips she felt cold and detached.

'I'm sorry,' he said. 'I shouldn't have said that.'

'Please understand' – her lips were set firm and she paused while she turned away from him – 'it is not *my* big chance. It is not for me.'

Most of the president's party were now back at their table, smoking cigars and surveying the dancers with complacent propriety. The president said something and they all laughed. The Russian was still cavorting with Ines, who gave the appearance of enjoying herself hugely even when he staggered and she had to support him. The president pointed his cigar at them and said something else. His companions laughed again. Nearby, Ricardo was executing increasingly flamboyant manoeuvres around his smiling mulatto. At the end of each he would kick one leg in the air and spin on the other. William looked across for Maria, Ricardo's companion. She was talking to others at his table, her back to the dance floor.

The cha-cha stopped. William stood back so that Theresa could leave the floor. The band began a tango.

'You can tango?' she asked.

'I used to.'

They clasped each other, joined from knee to breastbone. A friendly dance, his instructor in London had called it. She pressed herself confidently against him but was so light in her movements that it was as if he had only his own to think about. They went through the smooth – staccato, slow – quick steps with an ease he did not think he had.

'Are you sure Carlos won't mind?' he asked.

She was looking back over his shoulder, her head turned away from the direction of dance. 'Perhaps it is good for him to mind a little. You dance well.'

'I think that's you.'

'No, you are better than most, even most here.'

'I love the tango.'

'So do I. Anyway, I don't mind if he minds.'

'Why are you doing it – you know, with him?'

'Not for myself.'

'Why do it, then, unless you are compelled? You could just refuse.' Box, he thought, would not have approved.

'I am not compelled. I am determined.' Her lips set firmly again.

The floor was less crowded than before but there were still too many for a proper tango. William kept having to hold back and at one point seemed unable to get away from Ricardo. Each way he turned the floor was blocked by Ricardo's exotic steps which came closer to gymnastics than to any normal dance. The mulatto girl looked either entranced or dazed. Twice they nearly collided with Ines and her Russian, who continued to lurch around the floor. Ines's face was creased into a wide, fixed smile. Out of context, it would have been impossible to tell whether she was laughing or screaming.

William did not see what started the fight but it seemed that Ricardo had cannoned into either the Russian or Ines. Ines was suddenly sitting on the floor with very nearly the same expression, her legs splayed and her dress off her shoulder. She looked like big ugly doll thrown down by a child. The Russian, a burly man with a crew-cut and a grizzled face, had pulled Ricardo down by the hair with one hand and with his other was slapping Ricardo's face. He shouted as he slapped, pushing and pulling Ricardo backwards and forwards across the floor. No sound came from Ricardo.

Theresa went to Ines. William started to follow but hesitated. He felt he should help Ricardo somehow. The floor was quickly filled with uniformed men and he was jostled to one side. A woman screamed. His glasses were dislodged and for a moment he couldn't see what was happening. He could still hear the shouting and slapping. Trying to get round the side, he was pushed back against the table and half fell amongst some chairs, including the one which had his duffle-coat. He picked up the coat with a vague intention of saving it and pushed on round the floor.

Soldiers had their backs to him. He tried to peer over but was pushed back. Then the soldiers parted and he saw Ricardo on his side on the floor, his head in his arms, his knees doubled up. There was blood on his hands and on the floor. The Russian was kicking him.

William shouted, 'Stop! Leave him!' in English. One or two of the soldiers looked round, but the Russian went on kicking. Small grunting and snuffling noises came from Ricardo. William couldn't get near enough. He shouted again, this time in Spanish, and looked for someone to help but the soldiers were all laughing. He swung his coat back and threw it, intending it to fall between the Russian and Ricardo like a towel in a boxing-ring. He swung it hard and only as he did so remembered the hammer in the pocket. The coat left his hand with surprising velocity and struck the Russian in the face, flopping over his shoulders. The Russian pushed it off him and stood, blinking. A trickle of blood came from his nose.

For a second or two no one moved. Through the soldiers on the other side of Ricardo William glimpsed Carlos still sitting at his table, pale and staring. He felt someone grab him by the arms. For a few moments he was pushed and pulled, then abruptly released. Manuel Herrera stood before him, cigar in one hand and William's hammer in the other.

'An unusual instrument to bring to a dance, *Señor* Wooding,' he said. 'I wonder what your wife would think.'

William didn't remember having told Manuel he was married. 'It was her suggestion. I had to repair something.'

Manuel did not smile. 'Of course. There is usually something to repair at dances.' He indicated Ricardo with his cigar. 'Bodies, for instance. But not with hammers. You have injured a senior representative of a friendly power. Perhaps you have caused an international incident. A serious matter.'

Ricardo was being helped to his feet. William did not regret what he had done but he was frightened of Manuel and the soldiers. 'I'm sorry. I didn't mean to.'

'Of course not. Please do not leave until we have spoken again.' Manuel turned to Ricardo's friends and told them sharply to take him away.

Ricardo hobbled out, his arms round the shoulders of those nearest him. He coughed and his face was still bleeding. There was a fragment of tooth in the blood on the floor. Maria walked behind him with her hand on his shoulder.

William was glad to be ignored. He made his way round the edge of the dance-floor. Some people were leaving but many were milling about. The band, which had stopped playing, were being told something by El Lizard. William wondered where his coat was but didn't like to go back and look; he didn't want to meet the Russian. Without having planned it, he found himself near the presidential table. Carlos was sitting there alone, his colonels and companions still engaged with the remnants of the fracas. His slim face looked thoughtful, even mournful.

'Wooding,' he said. 'Come and sit here. No one will bother you.'

William sat. Despite what had happened to Ricardo, he had an urge to apologise. 'I'm sorry, Carlos. I didn't mean to cause all this trouble.'

'It wasn't you, was it? I thought it was your clumsy friend.'

'No, I mean the officer. I threw my coat at the officer who was beating him. There was a hammer in the pocket.'

'A hammer?'

'For repairing Theresa's car.'

'Of course, yes, she told me.'

On the dance floor the Russian was holding his nose and arguing with everyone near him. Carlos toyed with the champagne cork on the table, pushing it backwards and forwards with his long middle finger. 'Well, that's Theresa for tonight, anyway. It wouldn't be the same now. I am no longer in the mood.'

William was more relieved than he would have thought possible. 'That's a pity.'

'It's like this with everything now. Either it gets out of control and goes wrong or I can have it whenever I want but I stop wanting it. It was better before.' He looked at William. 'Do you know what became of Charles Chatsworth?'

William thought. He remembered Chatsworth from school, a gangling youth who collected catapults. He was often in trouble. 'No, except that he joined the Army. He struck me as a bit mad.'

'He was a genius. He was below me at Sandhurst.'

'Was he?'

'Promotion in the British Army is slow. I don't imagine he became a general, like me. They would not recognise his genius.'

'Probably not.'

'He was in prison for a while in Bogata. Then he got out. I should like to know how he is doing.'

Presumably this was what Box would call an opportunity. 'Would you like me to find out and let you know?'

'No, it's not important. He wasn't a particular friend.'

William couldn't remember Carlos having had any particular friends. He had been an isolated figure at school who nevertheless did not appear lonely, as if he didn't realise he had no particular friends or perhaps didn't know what they were.

'You have done very well yourself,' said William.

'Yes, I have. Am I famous in England?'

'Oh yes.'

'That is what our embassy in London says.' Carlos gazed at his officers, who were all still arguing with each other. The Russian held his handkerchief to his nose and gesticulated with his other hand. El Lizard stood obediently to one side while Manuel nodded and spoke calmly. Theresa and Ines were not to be seen.

'I have noticed a strange thing, William,' Carlos continued. 'The more powerful I become, the less I can do. Power does not increase in proportion to one's advance and never can one do as much as one thinks. Of course, there are some things one can do – execute most of the people who were dancing, for instance, or have them imprisoned for injuring Russian officers–' he smiled '–but not much else. One can do that, but it is hard to do less, if you see what I mean. There is not much between that and leaving everything alone. In fact, there is much to be said for leaving things alone but one does not necessarily have the power to do even that.'

William tried vainly to think of the question Arthur Box would have him ask. It wasn't so much that what he was doing seemed unreal as that it was almost too ordinary to be significant. 'Why pursue power?' he asked, after a pause.

'One does not necessarily have much choice about that, either.' Carlos's eyes were on Manuel and the Russian, both now talking to El Lizard. When Carlos resumed he spoke rapidly. 'Power also means one loses all choice in one's personal affairs. Tonight is an example. When I was a captain I could have had Theresa, but now I am general and president it becomes a very complicated business involving many people and so it goes wrong. But you can help me.' Manuel and the Russian were approaching. Carlos turned to William. 'I don't want all these people involved any more. I want you to arrange it for me secretly. You know her, you can bring her to me without anyone knowing. It is better that way. I will contact you with instructions.'

William stood as the two reached them. Neither acknowledged him. Manuel turned to Carlos.

'Excellency, Colonel Scherbitsky wishes to speak to you about the woman he was dancing with.'

William backed away. The band struck up again.

He found his coat but not the hammer. At least now he would have something to report to Box: the president was unhappy and less in control than was thought. Also there was a good chance of further contact. Presumably this was the sort of thing that would please Box, though William was not so sure that it pleased him. Pimping was one thing – perhaps – but pimping for Theresa another. He already felt possessive about her. Anyway, there were limits, he told himself.

She was in the next room with a lot of other people. She turned when she saw him. 'I was worried about you but it's all right now.'

'It seems to be.'

'Ines is going with him.'

'With whom?'

'The Russian colonel. At first he wanted you beaten but now Ines is going with him and Manuel Herrera says it doesn't matter, you don't have to be beaten. He will forget about it for you.'

'Good. I'm glad about that.'

'Good for Ines, too.'

They stood back to allow some people to pass.

'What are you doing now?' he asked.

'I am going home. The president will not see me again tonight.'

'I'll come with you to your car, to see if it will start.'

'You are kind but it is not necessary.'

'No, but I shall.'

She became passive, as if suddenly hopeless. 'All right.'

'I'll meet you outside.'

'Yes.'

It was still raining. The old Dodge gleamed balefully in the light of the street-lamp. Theresa joined him wrapped in her shawl and he held the umbrella for her while she got in. When she pressed the starter it produced the same tired groan as before.

'I'll get the starting handle,' he said.

She put her hand on his arm. 'No, William, you must not do that.'

'Don't worry. It worked before.'

'No, you must not. You'll make your hand worse. You won't be able to do it.'

'All right, I'll give you a lift in mine.'

'No.'

'How will you get home?'

'I don't know.' Her passivity seemed to deepen, as if she were sinking away from him. 'Do you normally drive?' he asked. 'How far is it?'

'Normally, if I don't have my car, my father or my brothers collect me. But tonight I did not make arrangements for going home.'

'Can you telephone them?'

'I have no money.'

'I have plenty of change.'

'They have no telephone.'

The rain dripped from the umbrella on to the inside of the car's open door. She stared at the windscreen, one hand on the wheel and the other negligently in her lap.

'Let me take you home,' he said.

She shook her head.

'I have a message for you from the president.'

She looked at him.

'I'll tell you, anyway,' he added quickly, ashamed of himself. 'You don't have to come with me. I'll tell you now.'

She let go of the steering wheel, took out the ignition key and swung her legs towards him. 'Where is your car?'

The route lay through the centre of the city, past the docks and towards some steep hills farther up the estuary. He didn't know the area but knew of it as the shanties, a sprawling conglomeration of shanty towns that had grown up over the past twenty years. He had seen it both in daylight when it appeared a generally cloudy or misty region of wooden buildings on muddy hills, and at night when it was identifiable by its lights. These were fewer and yellower than the white lights of the city, the result, he had heard, of the fact that power was illegally siphoned from the mains. There were frequent fires and during wet weather landslips that washed away dozens of shacks and their occupants. Someone had told him that the shanties were now larger than the city itself, teeming carbuncles of the poor and dispossessed who had chosen urban rather than rural poverty.

She directed him monosyllabically. He wanted to say something but couldn't think what and anyway had to concentrate on the muddy pot-holed roads. His headlights picked out the wrecks of vehicles, ramshackle buildings heaped on top of each other like boxes, mangy furtive dogs and, as they went higher, shacks on rickety stilts built into seemingly impossible hillsides. All around there were people, a constant, swarming, variegated stream. It contrasted with the city, which had been near deserted in the rain. Every shack had a light of some sort and from most came the sounds of television or loud music. Scantily-clad children swarmed like insects, oblivious of the rain.

She seemed to relax and he felt her look at him. 'You are afraid you will be lost when you go back?' she asked, smiling.

'Only a little.'

'It's not so difficult. I live high up. So long as you keep going down in any direction you will come to a road that leads to the city.'

He turned hard left where the track narrowed and became much steeper, holding his breath as they lurched into another hole. He had his window open and the leaves of a bush brushed his face. Beside the bush was an open door in which a man stood smoking. Behind him was the usual dull yellow light and blaring music.

'I was ashamed for you to come here,' she said.

'You shouldn't be ashamed.'

'No. Anyway, my shame does not matter.'

'I spoke to Carlos again after the fight.'

'Does he still want me?'

'Yes.'

'Turn right and go slowly because it's very rough.'

'He wants me to take you to him next time without anyone knowing. He says he will send instructions.'

'Will you do it?'

'If that's what you want.'

She stared ahead. 'Yes, I want it. The rest does not matter. I told you.'

The buildings petered out in an haphazard conglomeration of wood and corrugated iron. The track continued up into the darkness.

'Here,' she said.

It was hard to see where her home began or ended. 'Are there many of you?' he asked.

'Eleven. That is the children. Then my parents, my grandmother and some others.'

He pointed up the track. 'What's up there?'

'Nothing.'

'Is there room to turn round?'

'Yes.'

He took his time in order to delay the moment of parting. 'What do they do, the people who live here?'

'Anything. Nothing. They work in the canning factories or the mines, some in the city.'

'Perhaps they work in my company's factory.'

'Perhaps.'

'What does your father do?'

'He worked for a builder but he hurt his back. Now he cannot work. He lies down nearly all the time. It is for me and my brothers and sisters to earn money.'

When he had completed his seven-point turn they were facing downhill towards the house. The headlights showed barrels beneath the broken guttering, a rusty water-tank on a ledge and two cats. No one came out to see whose the headlights were.

'Our water,' she said, indicating the barrels. 'The rain is good for us.'

'Is it you that supports your family?'

'I help. I told you, it was not *my* big chance.'

'Yes.' He kept the engine running, fearing that the silence after switching it off might prompt her to leave.

'Do you dislike me?' she asked.

'No – no, I don't at all.'

'You sound as if you do.'

'No – no, I like you very much. Really, I do.' He was so surprised and pleased that he felt he must sound unconvincing. 'I like you very much but I don't like . . . what you are having to do.'

She looked at him. 'You will not help me?'

'Oh yes, yes. I will help you.'

She opened the door and got out.

'How do I contact you?' he asked.

'At Maria's. I am there every day.'

'Every day?'

She nodded as she closed the door.

'You dance beautifully,' he called.

She had to come back to hear him repeat it, then thanked him and complimented him on his own efforts with a professional courtesy that had not been present before. He drove away feeling miserable and reckless, more unhappy at the distancing effect of his remark than at the fact of pimping for her. Eventually, though, it was the thought that perhaps she liked him, perhaps even found him attractive despite his shape – or at least was not obviously repelled – that reconciled him to the frequent wrong turnings and dead ends of his meandering route home.

6

Next morning the office was busier than usual. An unexpected resurgence in paper supply from the mill coincided with a surprise order from the newly-formed Ministry of Information which was responsible for propaganda and for overseeing the press. William visited the ministry, made arrangements via the now functioning telephone to visit the factory and the mill that afternoon, sent letters, calculated costs and composed his first optimistic report to London. Despite only a few hours' sleep, he felt fresh and vigorous. Ricardo rang, saying he would be in later and apologising for not being in already. It was as rare for Ricardo to apologise as to appear any earlier than later; to ring and say was a sign of special effort. For once he sounded respectful, as if William were a wealthy patron. He said his injuries were not too bad, there seemed to be nothing serious though his lip was cut and he ached a lot.

'I must thank you,' he concluded.

'No need.'

'You must permit me to thank you.'

William realised that honour was at stake. 'Of course. When you come in.'

'Later.'

'Yes, later.'

William hardly had time to think about the previous night. He would have liked to wallow, recalling each of his sensations, feeling its texture, then placing it somewhere airtight so that it would not decay. But he had no time and the events were already assuming the unreality and distance of dreams. Even Sally's reaction to his lateness now had something unreal about it, though at the time it had seemed merely muted.

It was gone four by the time he had returned home. He had undressed in the dark but had woken her when groping for the bed. He gave an outline description of the evening, slightly exaggerating the pain of his hand because he felt she might find it more acceptable if he had suffered a little. In fact, all she had asked was whether he would often have to go out like that.

'I shouldn't think so,' he said without thinking. 'Well, maybe once or twice. It depends on the president's demands.'

'What demands?'

'On Theresa.'

'She's the prostitute?'

'The dancer.'

'The one who's also a prostitute?'

'Well, yes, but only with the president.'

'Is that what she told you?'

'Not in so many words, no.'

In the morning Sally was cheerful and brisk. She was to have one of her more stimulating advanced classes that day as well as embarking on a new project with Max Hueffer, the American boss.

'One thing about your fun and games last night,' she said as she was doing her hair, 'is that your friend Box should be pleased.'

'He certainly should.'

She put a grip in her hair and pushed it back behind one ear, removed the grip, replaced it, removed it again and substituted for it a larger one. William had watched her, wondering why he didn't feel more guilty. It wasn't because he hadn't done anything – that wasn't really the point – so much as that everything to do with Theresa seemed separate and unreal, as if it didn't really count. And, in a way, the more exciting it was the less it seemed to have to do with real life. Exciting things, in William's experience, were frothy, not real and not serious. What was real was his marriage to Sally for whom, as he watched her, he felt a familial, reasoning, domestic affection. He didn't want to be unfaithful.

He picked up the telephone to ring Box and put it down again. Lunch the day before seemed at least a month away. Hotel Britannia, Box had said, but William couldn't remember the name he was using. He gazed through the window at the orange-seller. It has hard to believe that the man was really sent to spy on him. It seemed far too obvious. Also, the man's presence pre-dated William's meeting Box. Therefore, if he were being spied upon, he must have been under suspicion anyway. But it was harder still to believe that the man was really selling oranges. After all, his only customer in the past three weeks had been Box, another spy. Perhaps all over the world spies were keeping each other in business by spying on other spies and pretending not to. Perhaps spying made for greater universal happiness. William was happy to be doing his bit, Carlos seemed happy to want to confide, the orange-seller was presumably happy to be employed, while his employers – Manuel Herrera? the police? Carlos himself? – were presumably happy because William was being spied upon. Finally Box, the professional spy, was happy because he had identified an opposition spy and because his own spying plans were going ahead. So, too, presumably, would be Box's employers and shareholders when they knew about it. Perhaps all was well so long as everyone went on spying; anguish and anger would come about only if someone blew the whistle, or defected, or simply stopped.

He remembered the name – Welling. After he had asked for it he remembered that spies in books and films were wary of the telephone. No doubt he was making an elementary mistake for which Box would reprove him, but it was too late. However, after a pause the receptionist said that *Senõr* Welling was not available.

'Did he say when he would be back?'

'He is not out. He is here but he has asked not to be disturbed.'

'Could you please disturb him nonetheless? It is important.'

'He refuses.'

The hotel was on the outskirts of the city along the coast towards the airport and the unexpected business meant that William was pushed for time that day. On the other hand, Box ought to know the news. Also, William was pleased to have found it out and wanted to tell him. He left a message for Ricardo and went. Once out of sight of the orange-seller, he took a taxi. It felt almost daring.

The hotel was late Victorian Scottish gothic, a huge turreted pile that faced across the coast road to the sea. There was no other building in the city – possibly in the continent – like it. It was grey and massive, and years of non-repair and sea air had still not made it look more than comfortably ravaged. It had a reputation for spacious rooms, excellent service, inadequate heating and appalling food. It was said to have been bankrupt for years but had somehow survived. William had never known anyone except Box stay there, business visitors now going to the American Hilton near the airport. As he entered under a vast portico he had the impression that a mere count of guests was not something this hotel would bother about. The place seemed sufficient to itself.

The entrance hall was like a cathedral. He was directed to room 42 and had to pay a uniformed bell-boy not to show him the way. The hall was draped in faded tartans that matched the carpets. There was a polished marble floor and inside the capacious, jangling lift there was more polished wood and brass. The wide corridor was festooned with stags' heads and antlers which alternated with paintings of Scottish glens in the rain.

All the rooms had massive doors. William's first knock was too feeble. He knocked again, then again, and was already irritated when a voice behind him whispered, 'This way.' Turning, he saw Box's head protruding from the open door across the corridor.

'Sorry,' William said. 'I thought it was room 42.'

Box raised his finger to his lips and beckoned. William followed him in. The room was large and high with casement windows opening on to a small balcony. Beyond was the coast road and the sea. Still with his finger to his lips, Box walked over to the casement. He wore firmly pressed twill trousers and a blue guernsey, his shoes were brown with highly polished toe-caps, his moustache gleamed as if recently polished. When he had forced the window open he stepped out on to the balcony and stood with his hands clasped above his head, breathing deeply. William remained in the room, which was filled with cold air and the sounds of sea and traffic.

Box turned so that his back was to the sea. 'Better you stay in and not be seen,' he said. 'We can talk like this. The background noise will drown our speech. Have a seat.' He waited until William was seated. 'I should explain, in case we're interrupted, that I am not Welling in this room. I am Kronstadt, a German entrepreneur who hopes to buy into your company. We are meeting secretly to discuss it.' His smile switched on and off. 'Always better to hide a big secret with a little one.'

'Why?'

'People look no further.'

'No, why Kronstadt?'

'Double blind. You'll have to learn about this sort of thing. I booked in as Welling during the day and again in the evening as Kronstadt, when the night staff were on. That means anyone trying to keep tabs on me who gets as far as Welling thinks he's done it and pays no attention to Kronstadt. The trouble is, it also means that Welling can appear only during the day and Kronstadt only at night.'

'Why aren't you Welling now?'

'Well spotted. I am testing the EEC and I set it up in Welling's room since it's rather a lot to lug around. We'll pop across later and see how it's getting on. Emergency Equipment brackets Communications brackets off. You'll soon learn. Now, did you have any luck?'

'Some.' Box's feet-astride, addressing-the-troops posture made William uneasy. 'Won't you sit down?'

'No chairs out here.'

'You could have one of these.'

Box frowned. 'I suppose that would be all right. Yes, I'll get it. Don't show yourself.' He came into the room and took a curved armchair which he placed sideways to

William on the balcony. He came back and took a glass from the bedside table. 'Looks better if you have a glass in hand.'

'No chance of a coffee, is there?'

'Not really. It would mean them bringing it up and they might see you. Looks odd if the chap who calls for Welling ends up with Kronstadt.'

'Do you suspect the hotel staff, then?'

'Always, on principle. You'll find water in the bathroom if you're really thirsty. Hotels are nearly always in league with the police.'

William began his report tardily but as he talked his enthusiasm took over. Box's pleasure was expressed by interjections of 'Splendid', 'Well done', 'Excellent – very straight bat'. At the end he got up from his wicker chair and stood looking out across the sea, his hands on the balcony. When he turned back to William his pale face was near to shining with pleasure.

'Well done,' he repeated, stressing each word. 'A wonderful night's work. No professional could have done more. You not only achieve access to the president, you find reason for seeing him again and in clandestine circumstances. What's more, you get an insight into his state of mind and attitudes and discover that he's not happy and he's not his own man. Just what we need for the next stage. I congratulate you. London will be delighted.'

William was pleased. 'It was a bit of luck, really.'

'And you clonk a Russian into the bargain!' Box barked his laugh. 'We'll reimburse you for the hammer.'

'No need.'

'No, it's important.' Box pulled up his guernsey and took a notepad and biro from his shirt pocket. 'And the petrol, of course. Don't worry – I encode such notes as shopping lists. Your name doesn't appear. Make of car?'

'Datsun.'

'Engine size?'

'Eleven hundred.'

'How many miles?'

'To where?'

'That you travelled. Sounds quite a long way out to this whore's house.'

'Not that far,' said William, his mood changing.

'Now don't be modest.' Box wagged his pen and made another of his disconcerting smiles. It wasn't that they were inauthentic or forced so much as that they didn't suit him. His natural solemnity of expression, tight-lipped but not ill-natured, had no room for them. It was as if he had made an effort for each occasion. 'You get so much a mile, you know. Not as generous since privatisation – the old civil service rates were wonderful – but it more than compensates. How many do you think?'

'I don't want to claim.'

Box frowned again. 'Nothing worrying you, is there? Mustn't let the stress get to you. Say if it is.'

'No.'

'I'll put down fifty.'

'No.'

'Thirty, then.'

'I don't want to claim for taking her home.'

'Why not?'

'I don't want to take money for that.'

Box closed his notebook. 'It is rare nowdays to find someone willing to give his services and take nothing for them. I congratulate you.'

'No need – it's not really – really no need.'

'Service to one's country is its own reward.'

'It is.'

'Despite my personal – some say idiosyncratic – unease about privatisation, I still regard service to the company as service to one's country. It is that that gives meaning to our work.'

'Quite.'

'That and the pursuit of truth. So far from patriotism not being enough, it is – alas – too much for many, beyond their reach. Most are merely selfish.'

Box stood for a few moments more in thoughtful silence before stepping briskly into the room. 'Now – London. We must tell them.'

He explained that he would draft a signal which William could deliver to the embassy on his way back. Box did not want to go to the embassy too often whereas it would look natural for William to go because, as a resident British business man, he could be consulting the commercial section.

'I've never heard that they had one.'

'Doesn't mean they haven't. Anyway, you can pretend you're going to find out. Ask for one of those ornithological gentlemen and give the signal to them. They'll send it under secret cypher. I'm rather surprised not to have heard from London already. I told them you'd been recruited. You'd think they'd be pleased.'

He added that he would have to go back into Welling's room to draft the signal. William was to wait.

'I'm very busy today,' William said. 'I haven't got long.'

'Won't take long. Second thoughts.' Box looked thoughtful again. 'Strictly against the rules, of course, because I'm supposed to await authorisation from London but – well, since you are keen and already one of us, as it were, you can come and have a look at the EEC kit. Might be useful if anything happens to me and you have to operate it.'

'Is that likely?'

'No. Provided you can get to the embassy, they can always pass messages. So it's only if anything happens to me and you can't get to the embassy.'

Box opened the door and peered along the corridor. He signalled to William and they crossed to room 42. It looked across woods to the airport. On the lawn at the back of the hotel a man held a hosepipe with nothing coming out.

Box pointed at a large black suitcase on the bed. It was closed and made the bed sag. A wire ran from it to a power point on the wall and there was a low hum. 'Charging the batteries,' he explained. 'We're on standby for testing. In fact' – he looked at his watch – 'London should be open now. We don't have to send a signal. We can test by receiving: if it receives it can send.'

He opened the case to reveal dials, switches, wires and

boxes. The lid, which was similarly furnished, folded flat on to the bed. Box used both hands to move it. 'This is the control panel,' he whispered. 'I'll show you how to operate it. Looks complicated but it's easy and very robust. Bit dated now, of course, but you can always trust it, that's what I say. Since privatisation they've got all these new-fangled pocket-handkerchief-sized squirters linked up to satellites, but I'm still attached to the old mark five.' He patted it.

'Isn't it rather big and heavy?'

'Nothing's perfect.'

'How did you carry it?'

'It came out in the diplomatic bag to the embassy. I picked it up in a car at night.'

Box knelt on the bed and pored over his machine, adjusting, switching and connecting while consulting a set of tables. Red, green and white lights came on and off. Once there was a brief noise which he swiftly stopped. It was a labour of love and his features were taut with concentration.

'I can't stay long,' William said again. He badly wanted coffee. The man on the lawn dropped the hosepipe and walked slowly back towards the shed from which it came.

'No need,' Box said. 'Here's what you do. You can watch it while I do the signal.' He unplugged the suitcase and showed William how to switch on to battery/receive. 'The red light means you're capable of receiving, the green one that they're sending. There'll be a signal any time now. You won't hear anything, but you'll know it's coming through because the white light flashes. Press those when you see it. Don't bother with that lot – that's for when you're sending – and that there is the auto-encode stuff. I'll show you how to send a message later. Quite simple. You'll love it once you can do it.'

Outside, the hose sprouted water and the man walked slowly back to it.

When the machine indicated that it was receiving William flicked the switches. There was a whirring noise and Box came over and pressed a button. A series of letters showed up on a small screen.

'It's all right. Standard test format. For the operational signal you simply put in a different cypher cassette.' He looked more closely. 'Hang on. There's more. Perhaps a real message. Maybe congratulations'. He frowned. 'Share prices are up.'

'Share prices?'

'The company's. They congratulate us.'

'That's good, isn't it?'

'I suppose so.' Box looked thoughtful. 'I daresay you're used to this sort of thing, being in business yourself, but I must say it leaves me a bit cold.'

Out on the lawn the water from the hose pipe stopped again and the man shuffled back to the shed. William tried to go but Box insisted they rehearse a formula for arranging meetings over the telephone.

'We've got to do two more things,' he added as William was finally leaving. 'Establish RCMPs – Regular Confidential Meeting Places – and find a hiding-place for the mark five, somewhere we could both get to in an emergency. Leave that to me. We should both think about the RCMPs, though, especially you with your local knowledge. I'll be in touch tomorrow. Meanwhile, let's consider what you're going to say to the president when you see him.'

'We don't know when that will be.'

'Can't be helped. Be prepared.' Box held out his hand. 'Once more, well done and thank you.' His colourless eyes stared unflinchingly into William's.

The parrot at the embassy ignored William's wave. Nightingale met him under the huge chandelier.

'So sweet of you to drop in. I was just saying to Peter that we needed a nice surprise.'

William tapped his pocket. 'I've got a message.'

'A message? How exciting. Do tell.'

They went downstairs into a basement room with no windows. It had in it several machines like enormous typewriters. The floor was almost covered in a confusion of punched white tape. One of the machines was making a loud clattering noise and producing typescript at the same time as emitting tape from one side. An untidy middle-aged man sprawled in an armchair reading *Penthouse*.

'Is London still open?' asked Nightingale.

'Yep.'

'Could you ask them to stay open because we've got something else now?'

The man glanced at the two clocks on the wall, one set at local and one at London time. 'They won't like it.'

'Well, it's their job. It's what they're there for.'

'Is it urgent?'

'It might be.'

'They won't like it if it isn't.' The man resumed his reading of *Penthouse*.

William and Nightingale went back upstairs to the corridor leading to the ambassador's office. The same girl sat reading in the outer room. 'Are they both still there?' asked Nightingale.

'Think so. Door's closed. I've been in the loo.'

They entered without knocking. The ambassador's office overlooked the garden. William's first reaction was that the carpet was smouldering but then he saw that the smoke came from Feather's cigar. Feather lay full-length on a low sofa. On the floor beside him was a saucer surrounded by ash and cigar butts. The ambassador was sitting at his desk, writing. Feather, who had been speaking, broke off as they entered. His dark liquid eyes traversed the room, then returned to the ambassador.

'– and essentially the stability of the government rests upon the three solid props of the energetic young president's personal appeal,' Feather said slowly, while the ambassador wrote to his dictation, 'on the new economic measures with their emphasis on democratic worker-participation and on the increasing popularity of the new People's Party through which the president intends to submit himself for election in due course. The government neither needs nor seeks outside assistance beyond the normal framework of international aid. It is in hock to no one.'

'Is that last bit right?' asked the ambassador tentatively. He gave William a worried smile.

'It's what London wants to hear. That's what "right" is.' Feather's voice croaked lazily and he pulled on his cigar. 'They don't know whether it's right or not but they want to be able to say it is so that they can tell everybody there's nothing to worry about.'

'But what if it isn't and it gets out that it isn't?'

'Then the situation's changed and it either gets better by itself or it's too late to do anything about it. Our job – your job – is simply to get on with the powers that be.'

The ambassador put down his pen, his honest face creased. 'You're the brains here. I don't dispute that. I've no experience of diplomacy. But is that really my job?'

'Of course it's not really, no. Your job is to represent your country's interests. But no one realises that any more. They think you're here to get on with people.'

'I'd much rather get on with people.'

'Naturally.'

The ambassador glanced apologetically at William and Nightingale. 'London want an assessment.'

Nightingale nodded sympathetically. 'I know, Peter. Frightful.'

Feather flicked ash in the area of the saucer. 'They don't want an assessment, they want reassurance.'

'William's brought a signal from that funny little man,' said Nightingale.

The ambassador raised his eyebrows. 'Thank you, William. Very kind.'

'Very tedious,' said Feather. 'Show.'

Feather read Box's message rapidly and handed it to Nightingale without a word. Nightingale read it and then dropped it on the desk in front of the ambassador, who read it slowly.

'Oh dear,' he said. 'This contradicts what we're saying. It says the president is unhappy because he feels he has no power and may already be a virtual prisoner. And there are all these colonels including this chap trained in Cuba who won't let him out of his sight. It also says that there's widespread repression and that economic changes are not going to work and are being made only for political reasons. Bit strong, isn't it?' He smiled uncomfortably at William.

Feather stared at his smoke. 'Doesn't matter. It'll reach London long after our assessment and it'll be yet another example of the funnies being late and wrong.'

'What if it's right?' asked William. He was beginning to feel protective of Box.

'If it's right it'll be right later, by which time we too shall have reported in similar vein. Things will be different then. Context is all.'

The ambassador shifted in his chair. 'But what about this business of repression and the economy? Supposing the foreign press report the same? Then London will want to know why we don't.'

'Quite,' said William. He was also beginning to feel protective of the ambassador. Feather waved his cigar at the immaculate garden. 'Can you see any signs of repression and economic failure? There'll be no problem so long as the funny report gets there later.'

The ambassador shrugged. 'Oh, well. We'll send it later.'

'By which time the president will no doubt have caught something interesting from his whore,' said Nightingale. 'Nothing would do more to ensure his popularity than that.'

'Any message back?' William asked abruptly.

There was no message. 'Thank you so much for coming,' said Nightingale. 'Lovely to see you.'

Ricardo was waiting at the office and they set out at once for the factory. William went without lunch, which made him feel virtuous. Ricardo had also acquired virtue in his eyes by having suffered and by being – for the present at least – tirelessly anxious to please. Ricardo's lips and one eye were swollen and he complained of pains in his back which hurt when he turned. But his gratitude exceeded his complaints.

'You are the saviour of my life. I have told my father. He will meet you.'

'That's very nice of him but it's really not necessary. All I did was swing my duffle-coat.'

'Now you are my friend. At first I did not like you.'

'Oh – well, that's an improvement.'

'Then – I told my father – after the first I thought you were all right, you know – not bad, not hot, not cold, just English – but now I can see you are a man.'

They shook hands for the third time that day. Ricardo was driving his Toyota sports saloon with his usual skilful nonchalance. They were outside the city and heading inland towards the factory. Through the haze caused by the power station and the metal-processing plant William could see the shanties where Theresa lived. The rickety shacks crowded precariously on the hillside, each wooden and corrugated structure supported by the one below. They were festooned with washing. Even through the haze William could see that the hills swarmed with people. He cleaned his glasses, but the haze remained.

He forced himself to stop thinking of Theresa. 'Your father is in the army, isn't he?' he asked.

'Yes, he is already a colonel. But he does not know those people who were there last night. The Russians, the security police and the junta are separate from the rest of the army. They are always with the president and they are very political. They are not popular with the rest of the army. Especially, the Russians and Cubans are not popular.'

'What about the president?'

'No, the president is very popular. He is a patriot. But not the people with him.'

'Why not?'

'They are political.'

'Isn't the president?'

'No, I told you. He is a patriot.'

It was too subtle a distinction for William's knowledge of the country. 'Are there people in the army who are against the government?'

Ricardo nodded. 'Many, my father says, but they are frightened. People are disappearing.'

'Who is doing it?'

'No one knows. Probably the security police.'

There were farms in the hills and on the road an occasional straggle of huts marked a village. There were few trees but a great deal of long grass studded with boulders. Ricardo sped past ponies and carts and small flocks of sheep or goats. William wished he would slow down but knew it was no use asking. He felt listless now. The countryside, the smell of cigarette ash in the car, the prospect of difficulty at the factory and Ricardo's friendly but persistent conversation all combined to increase his tiredness. It was like being in the sway of a great wave. He let himself go, trusting that waves passed.

Ricardo lit another cigarette, flicking the car's lighter in and out between his two fingers. 'Also, I can help you in your work.'

'But you do anyway.' The mutual pretence had become so habitual that William barely noticed it.

'No, your real work.'

'My real work?'

Ricardo smiled. 'Of course, you have to be secret. I realise that. I mean your spying.'

William felt now as if the wave had dumped him on cold wet sand. 'My spying?'

'William, we are friends. You are an English spy. I know it, everyone knows it. But now I am prepared to help you.'

Box's briefings had not extended to this sort of thing. A straightforward accusation he could deny but offers of assistance were another matter; offers from Ricardo another again.

'I can tell you what is going on and maybe help you kill people,' continued Ricardo.

'I don't know what you mean.'

Ricardo took no notice. 'The people like the president but they do not like the government. They are frightened of it. We – you and me – should kill the Russians and Cubans and colonels and save the president.'

'I don't know what you're talking about.'

'I will not tell anybody.'

'No, you mustn't.'

'I promised my father: I will tell nobody, I said.'

'What did he say?'

'He was very pleased. He told my mother and my sisters and they all congratulated me.'

They overtook a battered lorry on a blind corner. Ricardo's pleasure in himself was so complete and unquestioning that he took no notice of silence in others.

'What exactly do people say about me?' William asked.

'Not very much, not yet, because they know you have not done anything. But we will change that.'

'Why do they think I am a spy?'

Ricardo frowned. 'You are, aren't you?'

William gave up. 'Well, of a sort, I suppose. Not a very important one.'

Ricardo put his hand on William's shoulder. 'William, so modest, so English. Everyone knows because of your company. It has been here so many years, it makes no money. Everyone knows it is really British Intelligence that keeps it going and that everyone who comes from London to run it is a British spy.'

'Why is it necessary to put the orange-seller on the pavement opposite to spy on me, if everyone knows already?'

Ricardo shrugged. 'I don't know that he is a spy. Maybe he is in love with one of the girls in the shop. Anyway, he cannot be important. They wouldn't ask *un campesino* – a peasant – like him to spy on you alone. That is why they asked me.'

'Who asked you?'

'The security police.'

'Did you agree?'

'Of course. They are the security police.'

'What have you told them?'

Ricardo smiled. 'I told them you are in love with Ines.'

'But that's not true. Nor is the bit about the company. It just makes a loss, that's all.' William paused. He would ask Box about his predecessors in the company. 'So far as I know.'

Ricardo held up his hand. 'William, please. We are friends, not children. Of course you are not in love with Ines. That is why I told them. You are in love with Theresa. Everyone knows that. But please do not pretend about the company. There is no other explanation. Who would go on with such a hopeless business, making such a loss? Not even the British. Someone must be paying for it.'

A flock of brown goats scattered inches ahead of their speeding bonnet. William, no longer alarmed, sat in thoughtful silence.

The factory and the mill were on the far side of the hills in a fertile plain not yet denuded of trees. They were about a mile apart, both on the bank of a river. The factory resembled a half-finished building site. The only buildings were open-sided sheds stacked with wood and long corrugated huts with no windows. Instead of gates there was a makeshift barrier of oil-drums and planks. An ancient Morris van was parked by it and a few yards away some soldiers stood warming themselves around a small fire. They had sub-machine guns slung across their backs and gazed indifferently as Ricardo spun the Toyota with gratuitous violence to pull up by the van. The ground was churned and holed. Everything looked scruffy, unfinished and uncared-for.

Miguel, the foreman, got out of the van. He was a round man with a balding head, a round face and a rounded shambling gait that made him appear to roll along the ground like a deflated rubber ball. His handshake and voice were soft, his lips rubbery and mobile. He greeted William with an almost oriental politeness, followed by a minute or two of reminiscence about where and when they had last met. He came from the interior and his accent was hard for William to follow.

'It is sad, *señor*' he said, indicating the deserted factory.

Lopsided coaches used for bringing the workers from the city stood empty. They looked as if they would never move again. The whole place looked as if it would never work again. 'How long do you think the strike will last?' William asked.

Miguel raised his arms. 'It is impossible to say, señor. A day, a week, a year.'

'Unless we give them more money,' said Ricardo.

'Maybe.'

'It's not only money, is it?' asked William.

'Not only.'

'What else?'

'Also the cold.' When Miguel smiled his eyes were nearly invisible between the folds of flesh. 'Yes, the cold. Even when it is not cold.'

'What else?' repeated William. 'Have they made no demands?'

'They do not want to work.'

'Is that what they say?'

'No, but – the union men, it is what they say.'

'Is that all?'

'They say they will present demands when they are ready.'

'Are the workers frightened of the union men?'

'*Sí, señor.*'

They had been walking slowly towards the barrier. Ricardo vaulted it, cigarette in mouth.

'We must get rid of the union men,' he said. 'I keep telling him. Eh, Miguel?'

Miguel grinned uneasily. His head shrank into his shoulders when he shrugged.

There was a shout from one of the soldiers standing by the fire. He waved to them to go back the way they had come.

'What do you want?' Ricardo shouted back.

The soldier shouted again.

Miguel shook his head. 'We must not go into the factory, *señor*, they do not let us.'

'What is it to do with the army?' asked William. He noticed a small encampment of olive-green vehicles and brown tents in a clearing behind the trees.

'They are not normal soldiers. They are troops of the security police.'

'And they stop you going into your own factory?' asked Ricardo.

'They say they are told to help the union. That is why there are no pickets. They say it is a national question, because we are a foreign firm.'

'I'll talk to them,' said Ricardo. He vaulted back over the barrier and strode towards the soldiers. William wanted to call after him to be tactful but his Spanish deserted him. Miguel touched his arm.

'It is not your fault, *señor*. Please tell London there is nothing you can do. It is a political matter, this strike.'

'Have you talked to the workers yourself?'

'Some of them, some, but in private. They want more money, of course, but they do not want to strike.'

'Why do they obey, then?'

Miguel turned his round head from side to side, smiling and looking down. 'They have families, *señor*.'

'But surely their families are hurt by their being on strike?'

'Not hurt. They suffer, that is all. It is better.'

William waited but Miguel did not look up again. 'You have family also, Miguel?'

Miguel nodded.

Ricardo was still with the soldiers. It seemed a good-humoured negotiation. There was laughter and he handed round cigarettes. When he came back he grinned resignedly.

'No good. They are friendly but it is not possible. They are acting on orders of the Party.'

'Party?'

'The People's Party. There is a political officer who visits the camp. He tells them what to do.'

Miguel, looking even more like a crumpled ball, walked back with them towards the car. 'I will let you know everything I hear, *señor*,' he said as they shook hands again. 'Please tell London it is not your fault. They must not blame you.'

Ricardo put his hand on Miguel's shoulder. 'Nor yours, Miguel. They will not blame you, either.'

'*Gracias, señor.*'

They took off for the mill at Ricardo's normal speed.

'I feel sorry for Miguel,' said William.

'No need. It was he who told the workers to strike.'

'Are you sure?'

Ricardo looked pleased with himself. 'The soldiers told me. It is a sad fact about my countrymen, William, that most of them will do anything for a cigarette.'

'Perhaps Miguel had no choice.'

'He could have refused.'

'He has family.'

'I have family, you have family, but it does not stop us fighting back, eh? Together we struggle, divided we relapse – you have the same in English?' Ricardo laughed. 'The security police will expect a report from me on our visit. They will get reports from Miguel and from the soldiers. But I will make a top secret one. I will say that you are afraid that because of the strike you will lose your job because London cannot understand. They will believe that.'

'They may be right.'

It was William's turn to cook, to make up for the previous night out. He grilled two trout – Sally's vegetarianism did not extend to fish – with mushrooms, potatoes and spinach. While he was cooking she continued a long letter to a girl-friend in London. She had started it three days previously and there were now, he noticed as he laid the table, eleven pages of her large circular handwriting. She seemed engrossed, so he said nothing until they sat down to eat.

'How's the job going?' he asked.

'All right.'

'Only all right?'

'No, really all right. Good. Harder work than before but more interesting.'

'And what about this chap, this American' – tiredness threatened to overwhelm him and he groped in vain for the name – 'your boss.'

'Max.'

'Yes, Max. How do you get on with him?'

'All right.' She ate with relish, which pleased him. During the last month or two she had seemed listless.

'Have you seen your friend *Señor* Finn recently?' she asked.

'Yes, I saw him today. He was eating something very like what we're eating.'

'Is he well?'

'Flourishing, by the looks of him. Becoming more talkative. In fact, he told me something rather disturbing, if it's true. I noticed his dog was tied up, which it never usually is, and asked why. He said they're rounding up the strays in the city and shooting them.'

'That's right, it was on the news.'

'Seems a bit extreme. There aren't that many.'

'Max says it'll be the people next.'

William rested his knife and fork on the plate. 'That's what *Señor* Finn said. "Today the dogs, *señor*," he said, "tomorrow the people." '

'Max says communist countries often do it when they're heading for a purge. It's one of the first signs of clampdown. He was in Peking when they did it there.'

'But this isn't a communist country.'

'It's becoming one, according to Max.'

William picked up his knife and fork. 'Maybe.'

They continued talking over coffee. He told her in greater detail about the events at Maria's and their aftermath, including his visit to Box and the embassy. He found he could mention Theresa without any spasm of guilt. This was partly because the whole thing – Theresa, Box, Carlos, the embassy, Maria's – sounded so unreal when he talked about it. It was as if bits of his life didn't connect with each other. Also, a recitation of events without an account of his own feelings contained nothing to feel guilty about. Sally seemed amused but not particularly curious.

Afterwards she mentioned the friend to whom she was writing – Jackie, who had remarried and had a baby. William had met Jackie - after several promptings he vaguely recalled a girl with curly brown hair who giggled – and the story of her first marriage was alternately funny and violent. It ended with her leaving her husband stuck in his car in a snowdrift. She married the brother of the man who gave her a lift home. Sally told the story, which William assumed had been sent to her in a novel-length letter, with a relish for detail he had not seen in her for some time. Her account of the baby made him wonder whether she now wanted one herself, though she always said she didn't. He realised that Jackie was not the girl he was remembering but it was too late to say so.

She continued talking over the washing-up. It pleased him to hear her talk, no matter what about. Interest in something – anything – was better than the polite disinterest which had characterised their relations for some time now. When she talked she became animated and was more attractive. It reminded him of when he had first known her, a lively, confident girl whom he could not at first believe could ever be interested in him. But he had made her laugh and that had helped.

Before going to bed that night he made brief notes of what he wanted to tell Box. He wrote them as a series of one-word reminders on a piece of paper on which he had already made notes about the next paper-run forecast. He was very tired now, but content. Sally was in bed already and he thought that, despite his tiredness, they might make love that night; it would be the first time for many months. But she was already asleep.

7

The envelope was brought to William in his office by one of the girls from the shop. It was plain white, with his name written in a rather flowery script. The girl said it must have been pushed through the letterbox in the night because it was amongst the other mail but there was no stamp. Afterwards he heard her giggling downstairs and wondered again why it was that encounters with him always provoked such giggles. Perhaps they giggled about the orange-seller. He was in his usual position. Could Ricardo be right about the man's infatuation? Possibly, but it wasn't incompatible with spying. William wondered which of the two girls might have captivated the man. He was never certain of being able to tell them apart.

He put aside the letter of intent from the Ministry of Information – it was a large order for certification of censorship forms – and opened the white envelope. It was dated the day before, with no address, and read:

Dear William, I should be grateful if you would deliver the goods you promised tomorrow night at eight-thirty. Please come by car. Do not use the front entrance nor either of the sides but come to the back where the garages and stables are. When they stop you at the gate, say that you are the interpreters who have come to interview the prisoners and ask for directions to the exercise yard. I will meet you there. C.

William had to quell his jealousy. He concentrated on an undramatic determination simply to do his duty by Britain and by Box. That at least should provide satisfaction, an opportunity to be loyal, useful, disinterested. It was necessary to see Box urgently.

He would have to use the telephone procedure Box had described at the hotel. After looking carefully at his watch and re-checking twice, he rang and asked for Mr Kronstadt. The extension was answered by a harsh, '*Ja*?' William introduced himself in Spanish and said he could not after all see Mr Kronstadt at one o'clock that day. Could they arrange another time? Box replied in rapid German. William said he was sorry, he did not speak German. There was a pause and then Box replied in convincingly fractured Spanish, with a heavy Teutonic accent, that he did not understand – could William repeat his message? William did so and there was another pause.

'You speak English?' Box asked, with a foreign accent.

William repeated his message in English. Box replied in his best German-accented English that it was okay, they would arrange another time when William was not so busy.

One o'clock in the message meant twelve o'clock. Saying they could not meet that day meant they must. The meeting-place was a newsagent that sold foreign papers within walking distance of William's office. It was on a busy junction near the main post office and opposite the national bank, a venerable and grave institution, magnificent in decay. There were a few tables on the pavement at which people sat reading papers and drinking coffee.

There was no sign of anyone serving when William arrived. There was no sign of Box. William searched for a while and found a *Daily Telegraph* more recent than the last he had received. The front-page news of the unfavourable balance of trade, a health service financial scandal and a survey of geographical ignorance was at once familiar and distant. He could guess how much it all seemed to matter in England, at least for the day. Here, people sat, read, drank coffee and talked in the sun. Economies, politics, even so-called communist takeovers were relegated to their proper places. He turned to the sports pages and read about the outstanding New Zealand touring team.

It was not like Box to be late. Men with clipped moustaches and polished shoes tended to be punctual. William glanced across at the massive studded wooden doors of the bank. They looked about eighteen feet high. He remembered again that he had once seen Theresa slip out through the similarly high doors of the treasury. Perhaps they had been the bank doors, after all. What could she have been doing in either? He felt another spasm of anger and jealousy, then thought of her set expression in the car and the flat tone in which she had asked if he disliked her. Whatever she was doing, she didn't like it and didn't do it for herself. He felt warmly towards her, a feeling as dominant as the spasm of a moment before.

The great doors began to close. It was approaching lunchtime and closing when most people would wish it open was one of the ways in which the national bank maintained its dignity. Just before the doors met with grim finality Box slipped through them and crossed the road.

He stood next to William, looking through the magazines on the rack. William was not to acknowledge him first; Box would speak when he judged it safe to do so. William continued reading about the cricket.

Box picked up a copy of *Der Speigel*. 'Anything important?' he asked out of the corner of his mouth.

'Quite important.'

'Can you tell me here or do we need to discuss?'

'We should discuss.'

'Right. I've recce'd a place. Let me go first and you follow about twenty yards behind.'

'*Señor*?'

The new voice startled them both. The proprietor held out his hands towards Box. 'I hope you will not forget to pay, *señor*,' he said in Spanish.

'Pardon?'

The proprietor turned to William. 'You are with him, *señor*?'

'No, no, he's a foreigner.'

'You too.'

'Yes, but he's German – I think, judging by the paper.'

'But you speak to him. I see you.'

'He speak – spoke to me. He asked me something.'

'*Señor.*' The proprietor was an old man with a sour expression. He leaned across his counter. 'Listen, *señor*. I don't care what you are, I don't care what you do with each other. It is your business. But I tell you this: in this country there are many people who do not like people like you, who do not like men like you. They beat you up. Sometimes they kill you. If you are wise you will prefer women. Now you must pay for the magazine. If someone has a paper for more than one minute, he pays. It is a rule.'

Box was still pretending to read *Der Spiegel*. 'He wants you to pay for it,' William said in English.

'Why? I'm not buying it.'

'You've been reading it for more than one minute. It's the rule here, he says.'

'I'm not sure the company will wear this. Foreign papers are four times their proper price.'

'I bought mine.'

'That's all right. I can claim yours for you. Not sure about mine, that's all.' Box paid. 'Not that I'm mean.'

'No.'

'Twenty yards, remember.'

Box left the shop with the magazine under his arm. William followed, watched by the proprietor. They walked towards the dock area and then after about ten minutes back again to the same street. With a glance behind to check that William was still following, Box entered a small restaurant next to a ladies' dress shop. As William reached the restaurant door it opened and Box stepped smartly out. The door shut behind him.

'Closed for lunch,' he whispered.

'It is a restaurant, isn't it?'

'Course it is. I recce'd it the other evening. Now they say they're always closed for lunch. It's not possible.'

'It must be one that opens only for dinner. Some do. Yes, look there's a notice in the window.'

'I'll swear it wasn't there before.'

'Where now, then?'

'Let me think.' They stood staring at the underwear in the window of the dress shop. They were still within sight of the newsagent. 'I don't think we should do this for very long,' said William.

'D'you know any other places?'

'One or two.'

'All right. You lead. I'll follow.'

'Mightn't we just as well walk together now?'

'Rather we didn't. Might look odd. You never know what people are thinking.'

Maria's seemed a sensible choice. It was not far, it was unlikely to be crowded during the day, it was particularly unlikely that the president and his entourage would be there again, there were rooms enough for quiet conversation and there was a good chance that he would bump into Theresa, whom he had to contact anyway. His being seen with Box shouldn't matter since he could always explain him as a client.

The house was open but quiet. A few people were drinking in the bar, a couple of girls sat on the big sofa in the hall, there were smells of food and the murmur of voices. Someone tinkled intermittently on a piano.

Box stopped at the coat-stand in the hall. 'What is this place?'

'It's Maria's, the tango club – the one I told you about.' William waited for protests on security grounds, but none came.

Box looked about him. 'Quite nice. Where do they tango?'

'In a room farther in. I don't think they're doing it now but we can have a look later. Should we get a drink and sit down? There are some armchairs through here.'

The figure sliding into vision from his left was, he realised too late, El Lizard. There was the usual horizontal projection of the neck and, on the end of it, the usual expression of concentrated gloom.

'*Buenas días, Señor* Wooding. I am delighted to see you

back so soon. I must apologise for the incident the other night. I hope you were not too inconvenienced?'

'Not at all. I should apologise for my part.' William wondered how the man knew who he was.

'Some people do not know how to behave.'

'That's true.'

'*Señor* Wooding . . .' El Lizard's voice reached greater depths and his neck veered to the left and downwards like a lop-sided crane jib. 'I knew your predecessor, *Señor* Wicks.'

'Ah yes, I think I knew that.'

'We used to have an arrangement regarding certain materials.'

'I'm afraid they're not in stock any more.'

'So I understand. But if you were short of – originals' – there was the slightest widening of El Lizard's lips – 'I could possibly help you out from my staff. Some of them would pose quite well. It would also provide them with business during the slack periods.'

'That's very good of you but the company policy has changed, I'm afraid.' William used to wish he could stop apologising whenever he refused anyone anything but now, having accepted it as an ineradicable habit, he made the most of it. 'Very, very sorry about that.'

El Lizard held up one long hand. '*Por favor, por favor, Señor* Wooding, you are very kind. I can help you to a drink?'

William asked Box what he would like, but before Box could reply El Lizard said in good English that he had everything available. He had never been caught out on drink.

'A Guinness, please,' said Box.

'Certainly, *señor*. Draught or bottled?'

'Draught, if you have it.' Box's eyes flickered about the hall. 'And a private room, if you have one.'

Comprehension did not so much spread across El Lizard's face as settle like a stone into the bottom of a pond. He nodded gravely. 'Of course, *señores*, my apologies for keeping you waiting.'

He turned to the two girls on the sofa. 'These two are ready now, but we can quickly get others if you prefer.'

'I think my friend meant lunch,' said William in Spanish.

The dining room was near the room where the band had played. It was shabby and comfortable with an open fire and a white fluffy cat curled up on one of the tables. From the dance room the piano still tinkled amidst talk.

'I like this place,' said Box.

'Yes, it's cosy.'

'I say,' Box rested his folded arms on the table and leaned forward. 'Those two girls on the sofa – were they on offer?'

'Yes.'

Tears filled Box's colourless eyes. 'Not a bad little aperitif, eh?' He compressed his thin lips and closed his eyes as laughter shook him. He took off his glasses and dabbed at the tears with his large white handkerchief. 'In fact, if I weren't a married man . . .' He was shaken again by suppressed laughter.

'You are married, are you?'

'Very. There's a Mrs Box in Bletchley.'

'Children?'

'Sadly not. Doesn't seem to have been possible. You any?'

'No.'

'Early days, I suppose?'

'I suppose.'

An elderly waiter poured unasked from a bottle of red wine and left them a bowl of bread. Four men came in and sat at one of the other tables.

'They could be surveillance,' Box said quietly. 'Sensible if we look away from them when we're talking.' He turned sideways in his chair towards the wall. 'You shouldn't have addressed me in English in the hall there.'

'I didn't. It was the owner. You replied in English. You ordered a Guinness.'

'You're right. And it hasn't come. My punishment for not replying in German. Wall, please.' Box waited until

William was facing the wall. 'Grateful if you'd pick me up on any little slips I make. I'll do the same for you.'

William told him about the visit to the factory, about Ricardo's identification of him and all his predecessors as British spies and about the president's command to bring Theresa that night. Box sat without expression for some time after William had finished. He clenched and unclenched his hands, then half turned to the wall.

'You've been blown, no doubt about that. People often get the right answer for the wrong reason. On the other hand, it sounds as if it's almost an open secret. No one minds. At least, not yet. The factory business sounds nasty, though. Party representative and all that. The beast is beginning to show itself. Wait till London hears. Make these embassy people look pretty silly. Now this chappie of yours – Ricardo – is he all right?'

'His heart's probably in the right place.'

'Bit of an unguided missile, eh? Works well under supervision, that sort of chap? Knew a lot of them in the army. But tonight's the urgent thing. The president wants his way with your lady friend. Obviously, you must be there, to talk to him.'

'Would he want that?'

'No. But our planning should be guided by what we want, not by what he wants. Question is, whether I should be there too. Would that make too big a party, do you think?'

'It might be rather a surprise for him.'

The elderly waiter reappeared with full bowls of soup in his trembling hands. He left some on the tablecloth and some on William's trousers.

'Did we order this?' asked Box.

'I don't think there's a menu.'

'What is it?'

'Meat soup.'

'Is that common here?'

'Universal.'

It was hot and thick. Box dipped his bread in it. William dipped bread in his wine, remembering the incident in the covered market. He hoped it might mean he would see her.

The waiter shuffled over again and muttered, '*Disculpen la molestia, señores.*' He took away the soups and gave them to two of the men at the other table. William and Box were left holding their spoons.

'What was that for?' asked Box.

'I've never known it happen before.'

The waiter reappeared with two more soups which he put before them and shuffled away again.

'If we keep these to the end we'll have had more than our share,' whispered Box. 'I'd had about a quarter of that other chap's.'

The soup was followed by steak, chips, tomatoes and mushrooms, with a little offal. Box's eyes widened.

'You didn't order this specially, did you?'

'No.'

'Not bad, is it?'

Another bottle of the nameless red wine appeared. 'How much do you think this stuff costs?' Box asked.

'About the same as the *Telegraph* in England.'

'Not bad.'

Between mouthfuls of steak Box said that the 'blowing' of William added urgency to everything. Fortunately, he had found a 'SH' – Safe Hole – in which to hide the EEC kit. The danger was that, since it seemed to be an open secret that William was a British spy – through no fault of William's or the company's – a watch on William might lead to him, Box, hence to the EEC kit. It was more than his life was worth to have that compromised to the enemy. A further urgency was that the country appeared to be slipping ever deeper into the morass of Marxism–Leninism and, if the president had even half a mind to stop it, he should be helped to do so now. They should find a way to talk frankly to him that night.

'I don't imagine he'd welcome that,' said William. 'After all, he's – you know – '

'Not during, no. Before or afterwards. Not sure which would be better. He might be inclined to agree to all sorts of things in the heat of anticipation but he might on the other hand be irritated and impatient. Afterwards he might be relaxed and persuadable or, having got what he wanted, indifferent and dismissive. All animals are sad after coition, Aristotle said. He might even have us arrested if he's very sad. Touch and go, you see.'

William did not want to think about it. He looked down at his *Telegraph*, where his interest was caught by a front-page announcment of an inside feature on South American economic problems and their political ramifications. He stopped eating and opened the paper.

'What I'm really looking forward to,' said Box, this time not waiting until he had finished his mouthful, 'is the reaction in London when we convince them that this place really is going to the dogs.'

'They don't need convincing. It's all in the paper here. That's just what it says. Look.' The feature predicted economic stagnation under a rigid socialist framework.

Box shook his head when he had finished reading. 'Unfortunate, yes, but not too serious. Real-world stuff, you see. Journalism. No interest in Whitehall. Unless there's a scandal.'

'But they must be worried, mustn't they? Otherwise they wouldn't have sent you. So they'll take this seriously.'

'But the government didn't send me, the company did. This is the good side of privatisation – awareness of market forces. Cobalt, remember? The government is a little uneasy but that's all. It's up to us to convince them that they've got every reason to be, and more. The opposition is this embassy and the Foreign Office. They don't want the government ever to be uneasy. They want them always to think everything's all right because they think that keeping things all right is their responsibility.' Box speared his last chip. 'They're wrong, of course, and they are the second most important reason for British decline in international standing since 1919.'

'What's the first?'

'Economic performance. Companies like yours – don't you think?'

'I've never thought.'

'Time you did.'

Coffees and brandies arrived with most of the coffee still in the cups. The brandy bottle was left on the table. Box drank several glasses quite quickly. He crossed one leg over the other and pulled out a couple of cigars from his breast pocket. 'You don't, do you?'

'No, thanks.'

'Nice place, this. Comfy.' Box struck the match on the heel of his shoe. When his cigar was lit he tapped the heel with his forefinger. 'Got my shoe.'

William looked. It seemed an ordinary black shoe, probably better quality than most, perhaps even what was called an Oxford. 'Yes, very nice.'

'Special.'

'Yes. Good quality.'

Box glanced round to see that the four men were not looking, then leaned forward. 'Just in case. Never know what you might find.' He gripped the heel with his hand and twisted. The heel, hinged at the back, opened to reveal a hollow space. 'For microfilm.'

William was impressed. 'Ideal.'

'Or messages.'

'Or' – William tried to think of other things spies might carry – 'money or bullets.'

Box snapped the heel shut. 'Not if they rattle.' He poured more brandy.

For some minutes there had been a change in the sounds from the next room. The voices had stopped and the piano continued, but differently. The same note was being repeated, softly, slowly, without variation. It sounded as if it were building up to something.

Box seemed not to have noticed. 'This SH I've found for the EEC is damn good. Bet you can't guess.'

'I can't.'

'Try.'

William wanted to listen to the piano. 'I don't know. In the hotel kitchens?'

'No. Try again.'

'In the sea?'

'No. Not a bad idea, though. Plenty of room. But it has one big disadvantage. What do you think that is?'

'It's wet.'

Box shook his head. 'Tides. Chaps have been caught out no end of times. Drop something in on the end of a rope in the dead of night and next morning there it is on the beach for all to see. Or you go and bury something in the sand one day and come back to find it covered by full fathom five the next. Difficult. Come on, one more guess. You've got to have three.'

The same soft note continued inexorably. It was surely leading to something. If it went on like that everyone would be driven mad.

'Come on,' said Box.

'You've buried it.'

Box exhaled a plume of smoke at the ceiling. 'Very close. Buried, yes, but not quite in the normal way. Buried in a wall. Have you been in the big cemetery near the cathedral?'

William knew where it was. A high wall, perhaps forty feet high, surrounded it. 'No.'

'Go this afternoon. Look for grave number 1066: name of Bustillo. I haven't actually moved the kit in yet and I shall want your help when I do. There should be room for both of us.'

He topped up their glasses. He was drinking much faster than William and his colourless eyes had acquired a dull shine. 'In emergencies,' he added.

'What?'

'In emergencies. Room for us too in emergencies. If we wanted. Guinness never came.'

William was barely listening. Slowly at first, then with increasing confidence, the theme had grown. Despite its familiarity it was still a while before he recognised it as 'Lili Marlene.' It was played very tentatively, as if the pianist were feeling his way. It was exquisitely nostalgic.

William stood. 'Im going to see what's going on.'

'Something going on?' Box looked about him. 'Is it the Guinness?'

'Won't be a minute.'

Seven or eight people were grouped around the piano in the dancing room. It stood on the floor to one side of the stage. Two of the people were army officers in uniform, one was a waiter and the rest were girls, Ines among them. She smiled and waved both arms at William, beckoning him over.

Theresa was playing the piano. It was clear that she had to concentrate and that the effort was absorbing. The normally vivid beauty of her features was softened as she gave herself to the music. She seemed unselfconscious, unaware, beyond herself. William felt at that moment that he loved her so dearly that for the rest of his life nothing he could say or do would express it.

She did not so much finish the tune as blend it back into the sequence from which it had grown. The others listened in silence as it declined into the softly repeated single note. The repetitions became slower and softer and finally stopped. Everyone clapped and cheered, the applause bursting as if long pent-up. The gentleness and absorption left her face and she smiled. William stood by the door, seeking to retain in his own stillness the impression of hers, until Ines called to him. As he walked over Theresa looked up and stopped smiling. Her dark eyes were concentrated and intense.

When he was closer she relaxed and smiled. 'William, I didn't see it was you. You were against the light. Have you come to sing for us?'

'I've been having lunch.'

Ines kissed him on the cheek and took his arm. 'Well, now you must sing. An English song.'

'I don't think I could. No one knows any any more.'

Ines's perfume was strong, by which he concluded it must be cheap since that was what people said about strong perfumes. He liked it, as he had Theresa's. 'That was beautiful,' he said to Theresa.

'*Gracias*.'

'The English do not sing?' asked Ines, nudging him with her shoulder.

'Not now. They used to but not now. No one sings in England now.'

'Only at football matches,' said one of the officers.

Ines shrugged. 'They are not songs.'

The officers were young and pleasant. The whole company smiled as if they had all had quite a lot but not too much to drink. One of the girls started humming 'Lili Marlene' again. There was an air of expectation and of reluctance to depart but no one seemed to have any idea what to do next. William was still looking at Theresa who, head down, moved her fingers over the keys in silent rehearsal. She wore a dark skirt and a white shirt, the sleeves buttoned at the wrists. It looked like a man's shirt and, though clean and pressed, it was frayed at the cuffs and collar. He wondered if she would let him buy her a new one.

Ines tugged again at his arm. Her big eyes had always the same degree of brightness, the slightly manic brightness of a nervous hostess. 'William, you must sing for us. You can dance. We have seen you. If you can dance, you can sing. Síng us an English love song.'

'In English,' said one of the girls. 'Theresa will accompany you.' She giggled.

The door banged. They looked up to see Box standing stiffly.

'Who is that? Is it another *Inglés*?' Ines asked.

'A client of mine,' said William. 'I was having lunch with him.'

'What does he want?'

William detached himself from Ines's grasp. 'I think perhaps he wants to go home.'

Box's stare was fixed and unrecognising. William tried a hopeful smile. While he was still some feet away Box raised one arm. A curious noise came out of him, like the first complaining notes of an old organ long disused. After a few notes it became recognisable as 'Lili Marlene', sung in German. Ines and the others clapped. Theresa began a honky-tonk rendering in time with Box's singing.

Box walked as he sang. He walked steadily and slowly, describing a curve to the left which brought him back not far from the point where he had begun. He started again, this time in a larger curve. He seemed to be making for the piano but veered continually to the left. Eventually he adopted an angle of start that gave him a far wider curve and brought him to the point where the stage and piano met. He was still singing. The others smilingly made way for him and he came to a halt with one hand resting on top of the piano and the other on the stage beside it. When the song had finished he began again. Theresa began again. Everyone laughed. Without pausing in his singing, Box tensed himself and made to vault on to the stage. One leg was up and the other in the air when his hand slipped. For a moment he seemed caught as if in a newspaper photograph in which readers are asked to guess whether the body was going up or down, though in his case there was no question. He fell with a crash, pushing the piano a foot or two away. There was a gasp and everyone moved to help.

William did not rush. He worried more about how to explain Box than about what had happened. It was hard to believe that anything that happened to Box could be serious.

They got him to his feet and propped him against the stage. He looked dazed. 'Are you all right? Are you broken?' Ines was asking. One of the girls went for water.

'It's all right, he's with me,' said William. Box's eyes stared without focus. 'He's a client. We were having lunch. I'll get a car to take him to his hotel.'

The waiter went to get a taxi while the two officers looked on in disdainful amusement. Theresa stayed at the piano.

Box could walk but he was unsteady. He remained passive and silent, his eyes blank. William felt he should go back with him to the hotel but he had also to speak to

Theresa about the president. Anyway, Box would doubtless be all right.

'Are you okay?' he asked in English.

Box returned a blank unfocused gaze. 'Perfectly.'

Ines put her arm around him, nearly concealing him. 'You will have a headache but we liked your song.'

'What did she say?' asked Box.

William told him.

'What song?'

William told him.

'Never heard of her.'

The taxi was prompt. William gave directions to the driver while Box, still a little shaky, was eased into the back by Ines. He clutched William's arm.

'One thing. 1066.'

'Okay.' The taxi drove off with Box sitting very upright in the centre of the rear seat.

'Is he also a spy?' asked Ines as they walked back in.

'A spy? Who?'

'That man, your client.' She looked serious. 'He cannot be a very good one. Spies are not supposed to be drunk.' Her face brightened. 'Unless he is pretending.'

William was spared further response by being presented with the bill for the meal. Ines intervened forcefully, causing the old waiter to totter back.

'*Estupido – bobo*,' she said sharply. '*Señor* Wooding is a friend of the president.'

The waiter mumbled his apologies and turned away. Ines stayed to talk to someone else and William went back to the dance room.

Theresa was sitting alone at the piano. 'You have a message for me?'

William hadn't wanted it to be as businesslike as this, although it was, he had to admit, business. 'I thought we might go for a walk. Walk and talk.'

She got up and smoothed her skirt. Ines and the two officers came back into the room.

'I have to go,' she told Ines.

'What, now?'

'Yes.'

'*Suerte*, Theresa. Good luck.'

'No, it's not yet. We won't be long.'

Ines smiled a farewell to William and put her arms through those of the officers. 'I will sing and we will all play.'

Theresa dressed as if it were seriously cold. She wore a black fur hat and coat which looked expensive, though many women in the city seemed able to afford furs of some sort. She looked askance at William's jacket and tie. 'You have no coat?'

'No. It's all right for me, this weather.'

'Ah, you English.' She smiled.

'Do you mind if we go to the cemetery?' he asked. 'I want to see it.'

'You have never been? It's very beautiful.'

The cemetery was behind the cathedral, a nineteenth-century gothic building dominating one of the two main hills on which the city was built. The cemetery was on the side of the hill that sloped towards the sea. Because of its very high walls William had thought for a long time that it was in fact a prison. Even now he was not sure where the gates were.

They went through streets of small shops and stalls, some of the latter set up right under the cathedral walls. Many of them sold cheap good leather goods. Even in that city, where beautiful women abounded, maté drinkers turned to watch Theresa, clutching their gourds and tubes like the brass section of an orchestra.

'What did the president say?' she asked.

William took Carlos's note from his pocket and gave it to her. Box would no doubt have disapproved of his not having destroyed it, but Box's standpoint was not so strong now.

She handed back the note. 'Where should we meet?'

'I thought we'd better discuss that.'

The breeze pressed some of the black fur of her hat against her cheek. He disciplined himself to be practical.

'Should I wait for you after I've dropped you at the palace, do you think?'

'Not unless the president says so.' She looked at him, her eyes screwed up slightly against the wind. 'You are kind.'

'No,' he said. 'It's not that.'

There was one entrance in the massive cemetery wall, a pair of wrought-iron gates. The arch was about twenty feet thick and at the far end was a smaller pair of gates. The cemetery was like a town in which the architectural fashion was ecclesiastical. It was filled with prodigiously ornate mausolea, some not much smaller than the buildings that housed families where Theresa lived. Well-kept cobbled streets ran between the tombs. People sauntered among them. There were many cats.

It was the high walls that were most striking. Each was lined with small doors on four levels, evenly spaced. A gap in the far wall led into another square in which there was another town surrounded by walls with doors. It seemed to William like the physical embodiment of an imaginary scene someone had once described to him, his reactions to which were supposedly revealing of character.

'Isn't it beautiful?' she said.

'Beautiful?'

She stared at the clean black and white tombs. 'It is my big ambition. If I can get enough money I will have all my family and myself buried here. But it is very expensive.'

William tried to view it more sympathetically. The place was well kept, which was all he could bring himself to say for it. 'Is it?'

'Yes, it is only for the rich people.'

The elaboration and the expense, the attempt to make permanent what had gone for ever, were to William grotesque and depressing. 'I expect there are flowers here in the summer.'

'Many, many flowers, all so beautiful. I come here and walk with Ines. It is the best part of the city. Where would you like to be buried?'

'I've never thought about it.'
She laughed. 'Die here.'
'My predecessors have.'
'Then you can have a box in the wall, if your company will pay.'
He looked up at the doors. 'What are they?'
'They're graves. Most of them take whole families. That is why the walls are big.'
'And they have numbers?'
'Yes. There are thousands. Nearly everyone has to go in the wall now because the ground is full.'
The cobbles and bricks of the little streets had been worn smooth by generations of mourners. Her heels clicked on them. William's rubber shoes made him move without sound.
'It's very quiet in here,' he said. 'You can't hear any traffic.'
'All the dead people are enjoying themselves in heaven.'
'*All* of them?'
She smiled. 'Nearly all. Nearly all are Catholic, you see. You are Protestant?'
'No.'
'What are you?'
'I'm not really anything.'
'William, you must be something.'
It was tempting to pretend that he was agonised by the issue. At one time he had felt vaguely that he might be something but it seemed more honest not to be anything.
'Look – English,' she said. 'They must have been something.'
In one corner was a row of six Imperial War Graves Commission headstones, plain and unadorned, the grass around them neat and trim. Four commemorated Scottish sailors killed in action on a cruiser off the coast during the Second World War, the other two Welsh soldiers from the Great War. 'Not quite English,' he said, 'but yes, probably they were something.'
From the next square of the cemetery he could see

another beyond that. The graves in the wall were now in the 1,000 series. He hoped number 1066 wasn't one of the high ones.

'I like your furs,' he said.

'They were given me but I had to sell them.'

'But you've still got them.'

'They were given me again.'

'By someone else?'

'No, by the same person. He bought them back. He was always giving me things.'

'He doesn't now, then?'

She nodded at the next square. 'He is through there.'

'He must have been very rich.'

'He was the governor of the national bank.'

He remembered the great doors of the treasury and the bank. 'Did you visit him at work?'

'Sometimes.'

'Did he die long ago?'

'Not long.'

Number 1066 was one of the bottom doors and was obviously old, made of black wood and studded with heavy metal. As Box had said, it was the grave of the family Bustillo. The door was about four feet high and three wide. Through a small iron grille William could just make out the corner of a coffin. The chill damp of the tomb seemed to reach into the sunlight. Anything to do with death horrified him.

He turned to Theresa. 'I am a British spy and I love you very much.'

'They have made a new cemetery near the river but it is not as nice as this.'

She had continued walking. He hurried after her. 'Theresa, did you hear what I said?'

'Of course.' She looked down at the points of her shoes.

'I know you can't love me but I wanted you to know.' He didn't know what to do with his hands. They had never been a problem before. She had hers in the pockets of the banker's fur coat. He clasped his behind his back and walked in step beside her, head lowered like hers. He thought they probably looked like a couple who had been visiting a dear departed – the banker, for instance - and were now subject to intimations of mortality. 'I could lose some weight,' he offered.

She smiled without looking up. 'No, no. You are William. That's enough.'

'We could run away. We could go to England. I could work there and support you and then you wouldn't have to be – to go through with tonight. Or we could go somewhere else. Anywhere.'

'You are very romantic.'

'I am very important – I mean, serious.' His Spanish was breaking down under pressure. 'You're laughing at me.'

She looked at him. 'It's funny, don't you think? We are here, in the cemetery, you are a British spy and tonight you are going to help the woman you love to be the mistress of the president. It is too ridiculous to be serious. It must be funny.'

'But you do not love me.'

'I didn't say so.'

'If you did, how could you do this with the president?'

'I could say, how could you take me to him if you loved me? But you will, won't you? And it won't mean you do not love me.'

'I suppose not.'

'It's quite funny, isn't it, this love?'

'I suppose it is.'

She nudged him with her elbow, as Ines had. 'William, please do not be so important.'

The next square was like the others but the walls were thinner, the doors smaller and apparently made of tin.

'They look like left-luggage lockers,' he said. 'They even have locks like them.'

'That's what they are. Waiting for collection on Judgement Day.'

'Only they're smaller.'

'They take ashes now. You can get many generations of a family in one.'

'More if you mix them all together.'

She led off to the left, walking faster. They met a portly woman in furs whom Theresa greeted politely.

'That was the banker's widow,' she said.

'Is he near here?'

'Number 4010 – up there.'

William looked at the name. 'I thought he was still the governor of the bank.'

'That is his son.'

'Does – did she, the widow, know – ?'

'Oh, yes. My mother used to work for her. She cleaned the house. That was why.'

'I see.'

He didn't, but didn't want to go on asking. 'We should arrange where to meet tonight, where I should pick you up. Will you being going home to change?'

'No. Meet me at the club at eight o'clock.'

'Won't that be a bit obvious?'

'People who don't know will think I'm going with you. That's all right.'

It felt to William as if they were both talking about what they would do after they were dead. 'Were you surprised when I said I was a British spy?'

'No.'

'Does everyone know?'

'Of course. It's your job, isn't it? With the company?'

'Not with the company, no. It's separate. But no one seems to mind. It doesn't seem to matter that I'm a spy. No one does anything about it.'

'Why should they? Spying doesn't do any harm.'

'What do they say about my client – the chap I was with?'

'They don't say anything. No one has seen him before. Does he work for you?'

'Not really, no, but he is involved. He wants to find out what the president wants.'

'I can tell you and you can tell him.'

'That's what he suggested.'

She nudged him again. 'William, I told you, a funny thing, this love.'

'But that isn't why I'm seeing you, why I want to go on seeing you.'

She smiled. 'Is it not?'

He smiled despite himself. 'No, really, it isn't. Of course it was part of it at first, it gave me an excuse. But I'd drop everything now, as I said. If you want to go, I'll take you. Anywhere.' He stared at her with an expression intended to reinforce his seriousness. 'You have only to say so. I'd rather take you anywhere than to Carlos. I never liked him much, even at school.'

She laughed and put her hand on his arm. 'William, you are a perfect English gentleman. But I could not let you take me away. You could never marry someone like me.'

'Why not?' He remembered Sally as he spoke. It was very odd that he should simply have forgotten her. 'Why not?'

'You don't know me.'

'You mean, because of what you do and where you come from? That would all change.' He felt certain that whatever now happened to him in life would be different as a result of this conversation, for good or ill. 'I would marry you, Theresa.'

'You cannot speak like this. You do not know me. I do not know you.'

'That's no problem. We'll have plenty of time to get to know each other. That's what it's all about, isn't it? Or supposed to be.'

'You should not be flippant about this.'

He stopped walking, making her do the same. 'Look, Theresa, I'll do anything to marry you, live anywhere, do any job, go on a diet, *anything*.'

She smiled again. 'That would not be necessary.'

'You mean you don't mind my being fat?'

'You're not fat or thin for me. You're William.'

This was the best news he had ever had. He wanted to

hug and kiss her but she kept the distance between them, not so much physically as by thinking it. He could feel her insisting. Frankness depended on it.

'If I could do it this afternoon, I would,' he continued. 'I'd have to get a divorce, of course, but I think it would be unopposed so it shouldn't take long.'

'You are married?'

'I thought you knew.'

'You never said.'

'I didn't think. I thought you knew.' He felt as if he had been caught out in some shabby deceit. 'Really, I didn't realise.'

'You propose to one woman when you are married to another?'

Her dark eyes were impregnable. He would have much preferred her to be hot and angry. 'It wasn't like that, Theresa, it isn't like that. I didn't mean to deceive you. I am not going to deceive Sally. I just thought you knew. I'm sorry.'

'Sally. Her name is Sally?'

'Yes. She's a teacher. She works at the American School of English.' He felt that the detail somehow ameliorated it.

'I had thought you were an English gentleman.'

She walked back up the cobbled path between the graves. William wanted to follow but it was she who dictated distance. He could still feel her insistence. When she had turned the corner he looked up at left-luggage locker number 4010. He hated the graves, the lockers, the people for being dead, for having been alive, the banker for having made Theresa his mistress, the president for being about to do the same, Theresa for always being someone's mistress but never his, not ever, not now. How could she, the whore, accuse him of not being an English gentleman? What right had she to expect that of him, even supposing that either of them knew what it meant? He had not sought to deceive, he had simply not thought.

William could not hate or be angry for more than about thirty seconds. He had disappointed, that was the point.

He had led her on – not intentionally – but that was what he had done. It mattered not that she was a prostitute nor that they had agreed no definition of a gentleman. The ideal did not need defining for one to know that one had fallen short, nor was it necessary for one to have tried to be a gentleman in order to have failed; being aware of the ideal was sufficient. Gentlemen who wished to marry prostitutes did not forget their wives.

It was markedly colder on his walk home that evening, cold enough to do up his dufflecoat and put his hands in the pockets. If it got much colder he would take his gloves down from the wardrobe shelf. They were sheepskin mittens and he hadn't worn them for a long time. He liked dressing against the cold.

The wind flattened the grass of the golf course and the stunted trees quivered. *Señor* Finn sat hunched over his fire. The sea was brown and choppy.

William had to go close because the noise drowned out conversation from his normal respectful distance. The old man had wrapped a grey blanket around his bulky clothes and the dog was still tied up nearby. The upturned boat looked as if it had been in the water. The dog barked once.

'All right?' William called.

'Bad weather coming.'

'Feels like it.'

The old man put his hands to his cheeks and rubbed his white bristles, at the same time sticking out one thumb almost at right-angles. 'They bring it with them.'

'Who?' William had to shout above the waves.

'They do. Them.'

Señor Finn indicated with his thumb and rolled his eyes to the right. When William looked he saw a black Mercedes parked some way down the road. There were some men in it but he could see only the backs of their heads.

'Who are they?'

Señor Finn's reply was smothered by a large wave. The

cold spray reached as far as William, stinging his cheeks and spattering his glasses.

'They want you,' *Señor* Finn called again.

'Me?'

'They ask about the foreigner. You are *Inglés*?'

'Yes.'

'I was in England. I was a sailor. Nice place.'

'What did they ask?'

'I was in Liverpool. Big city.'

'What did they say about me?'

'They asked if you ask questions. I say you ask only for money.'

'For money?'

'You are beggar. You beg from me.' *Señor* Finn sat back, clutching his blanket, his red cheeks wobbling with laughter. 'You beg from me,' he shouted.

'What did they say then?'

'They don't say anything. They don't like me. Also, they don't like you.' *Señor* Finn wiped tears from his eyes with his knuckles. 'They are waiting for you, I think. They will talk to you.'

'I'll tell them you had no money.' *Señor* Finn nodded, still laughing. A thought struck William. 'Would you like some?'

'Money?'

'Yes. Do you want any?'

Señor Finn stopped laughing. 'You have some?'

William took out all the loose change from his pocket, plus a couple of banknotes. Eyed by the terrier, he walked forward and held out his hand over the fire. *Señor* Finn's palm was broad and hard.

'*Gracias, señor.*'

It had never before occurred to William that *Señor* Finn might be in need of money. He could have given him a little every day. He would from now on.

'I'll see you again soon.'

'*Gracias, señor.*'

William approached the black Mercedes with a kind of lighthearted fatalism. He would see Theresa again that night, not all was lost, everything else was peripheral. A soldier wearing the olive-greens of the security police got out of the car and opened the rear door. Manuel Herrera got out. He too wore olive-greens but with a holster and pistol. His boots were polished and he looked spruce and pleased with himself. When he smiled, his big even teeth reminded William of the six Imperial War Graves.

'Perhaps your English masochism has a point, *Señor* Wooding. It is bracing to walk in such weather in such a place.'

'Soldiers' weather,' said William.

The thought seemed to please Manuel. They shook hands and Manuel held out his other arm. 'Let us walk on the beach for a while. I'm not detaining you?'

'Of course not.'

'It is your coat that should be detained, for carrying hammers. Tell me, *Señor* Wooding, why do you have such an old coat and such a strange one, so unfashionable? Surely you or your company could afford a new one? Your company particularly.'

'I like it. I've had it a long time.'

'You are a traditonalist?'

'Perhaps.'

'An interesting position in time of revolution.'

'At least people know where I stand.'

'That would he helpful if it were true.'

William did not respond. His instinct was to leave it to Manuel to say what he wanted. He did not want to be difficult nor to betray himself by being nervously helpful. They crunched along the shingle, heading away from *Señor* Finn's hut. The wind and spray whipped in from the sea. It wasn't easy to walk on the slippery shingle and they plodded for a while with heads down.

'*Señor* Wooding,' Manuel began again, now in the politely formal tone he had used when they first met in the covered market. '*Señor* Wooding, I have something to say, something informal – off the record, as journalists say. I like you and you are an asset to our country. We need people like you, foreigners who are sympathetic and understanding to help us build a prosperous and peaceful society. We do not want to drive foreign investment away, we want the opposite so that we can all work together, all be equal, no one poor, everyone happy and internationally peaceful and non-aligned. Do you understand me?'

The phrases were familiar to William from his readings of the local press. 'I think so.'

'Non-aligned.' Manuel repeated deliberately. 'And fair and prosperous. And we wish to help you so that you can help us. We can help in all sorts of ways. For instance, an order has been placed with your company by the Ministry of Information, has it not? Very good. I imagine your company welcomes business' – he paused just long enough to glance at William with a slight smile – 'and no doubt more government business could be arranged. Also, I understand you have a problem with strikes at present. Indeed you went to see for yourself, did you not?'

'Yes.'

'Yes. It does not look capable of resolution but I'm sure it could be if the right words were spoken. The problem is, how to get them spoken?'

There was a vindictive gust of wind and another shower of fine spray hit the sides of their faces. William saw with satisfaction that Manuel was discomforted; he stepped with un-soldierlike hesitation on the treacherous shingle and once or twice he shivered. He was waiting for a response. William, who enjoyed the weather and felt the cold less than most people, let him wait.

'Shall we turn round?' suggested Manuel.

'I'm sorry, I didn't realise you were in a hurry.'

'I am not, but I do not wish to keep them waiting.'

Manuel spoke almost crossly and there was another pause. He glanced at the sea, to which he was now closer than William. It was a thick menacing brown, a sign of more rain in the hills, and the waves fell upon the beach with sullen repeated spite.

'What is important is that you should not interfere,' Manuel continued, in a tone that was more crisp and curt. 'Do your job, by all means – we don't mind that – but don't interfere with what is happening here. If you do, I cannot answer for the consequences.'

'I don't want to interfere.'

'Good. Then we can agree.'

'But I'm not sure what you mean.'

'I think you know, *Señor* Wooding. You were at school with the president. That is fine. Naturally, you wish – perhaps for old times' sake or perhaps to help your business interests – to be friendly with him. That also is fine. But let it stop there. Our president is a young man who is still feeling his way. Do not plot with him, *Señor* Wooding. The masses – the people of our country – would be very unhappy if he were to lose his way and it would be very inconvenient for many people, including yourself. It would not help the cause of social justice. You enjoy special protection because of your friendship. Please do not abuse it. Do you understand what I say?'

Manuel ignored the spray now, watching for William's reply. William felt the nervousness he had so far kept at bay. His stomach tightened but he remained determined. 'I hear what you say.'

'You see, our country has had bad government for many years, for generations. Now we have a chance to bring good government. We will do anything – anything – to succeed. We will take any help we can from whoever will give it. We will pay any price to make sure that our country has the right sort of government for ever.'

'What if the people don't want it?'

'The people will not sabotage what is in their best interests. Neither will anyone else, *Señor* Wooding.'

Back at the car Manuel's manner was cheerful and offhand. He said farewell like one who had just played and won his weekly game of squash. William was pleased to see how wet he was down one side.

'Thank you for the walk,' he said. Manuel showed his big teeth again, and shut the door.

William continued on his way. He expected to be overtaken by the car but wasn't. When he reached the point where the road turned inland he looked back. The black

Mercedes had reversed until it was now opposite *Señor* Finn's hut. William smiled to think how little change they might be getting out of him.

8

'Are you all right?'

William started. 'Yes, I was looking out of the window.'

'You haven't done anything else since you got in.'

'Lot to think about. This big order from the Ministry of Information as well as all this . . . you know . . . funny business.'

'Oh yes, the funny business. How's it going?'

The entryphone rang. Sally answered it before William could move. He hadn't, in fact, been thinking about work or about Box's business. He'd been trying to decide what he should tell Sally about Theresa. The more he thought about it the less it seemed there was to tell. It amounted to: I am in love with the prostitute I told you about and have proposed marriage to her. She has not said that she's in love with me and I don't think she wants to marry. In fact, I'm not sure she's speaking to me at present. I thought you should know.

It wouldn't do; yet it was lodged like a great lump in the middle of his forehead and any other thoughts had somehow to find their way round it. Moreover, the idea of leaving Sally lost all credibility in her presence. In the abstract it was something he could contemplate but when he was with her it was impossible. She was Sally, as familiar to him now as he was to himself, a part of his life, not a separate section that could be hived off - privatised, as it were – but integral. It would feel like an amputation of half his nervous system.

She came back from the hall. 'It's Max, my boss. He's dropping some books off. I ought to give him a drink, do you mind? We can eat later.'

'Of course not. In fact, I've got to go out. More funny business.'

'More? Getting a bit much, isn't it? You'll be working for them full-time soon.'

She sounded as if she didn't mind and so he described very quickly what he had to do that night. She was neither resentful nor jealous, which made him feel more guilty.

'So you've just got to drop this woman off at the palace?'

'Yes.'

'Well, if you're not back by the time I eat I'll put your dinner in the oven.'

'Okay.'

Max Hueffer was a tall academic-looking man with black hair, chiselled features and large heavy-rimmed spectacles that seemed to do all the self-assertion necessary. His voice was quiet and his manner assured. William felt he might well have been shaking hands with a successful international lawyer or a distinguished specialist in nervous diseases. Max said he was very pleased to meet William, he'd heard a lot about him.

William asked Max where he came from.

'Wyoming.'

'Wyoming.' William rolled the word round his mouth. 'I've never met anyone from Wyoming.'

Max smiled. 'Not many people have. Not many there and not many leave it.'

'It's a romantic name. It feels good to say it. I'd like to go there.'

'William, don't be silly.' Sally was by the cupboard and she looked round with an excited smile. 'You're never romantic about places.'

'I am about places I've never been to.'

'He's right,' said Max. 'Don't chew him up. It is a romantic name and it is a romantic place. Big and beautiful. You should go there some day.'

Max had a whisky. William was in no hurry and so he had one, too. Sally had a gin and tonic, something she rarely did. For a while she and Max talked about the books Max had brought and about the school, where one of the courses was proving troublesome. Max turned courteously to William.

'At least in your business it's not so much people you're dealing with as things,' he said. 'People are trouble. You're better off with things.'

'Except that the people who are supposed to be working for me are all on strike at the moment.'

'Is that so?'

'Well, they don't work directly for me, that's part of the trouble. Because of all these new laws I've got no control.'

'Bad position to be in. What happened?'

William told him. Max was a sympathetic and informed listener. He asked intelligent questions and made sensible pronouncements. William described his visit to the factory and the apparent element of political control. It struck him that Max might be a useful source of more information which he could report to Box.

'Things are coming to a head,' said Max.

'In what way?'

'I reckon the Sovs and Cubans might move in seriously pretty soon if nobody does anything. And where they move, they stay. It's not a question of opposition. Once they're here there ain't any. Unless someone does something to stop them pretty damn quick.'

'Who could do that – the president?'

Max shrugged. 'Not sure he's got the freedom to manoeuvre. He's the joker in the pack, that's the trouble. No one knows how strong his position is, nor what he really wants. Including him, I guess.'

William would have liked to have told him what Manuel had said that evening, but he could not do that without revealing how he knew Manuel and why Manuel had spoken as he did. Box would not have approved of bringing the Americans in on the affair. 'What does your embassy think? Ours doesn't seem to have much of a clue.'

Max grinned and touched his heavy glasses. 'You know what embassy people are like – so scared of being wrong you have to practically beat them up in a corner before they commit themselves to anything more than another drink.' Sally laughed. 'But I did get one of the political section guys to tell me the other day that they wouldn't be surprised if half of them were expelled soon. There's been a lot of anti-US propaganda and it's increasing. It all fits a pattern.'

William finished his whisky and said he had to see a client. Max stood and said he supposed he'd better be getting along, too. William urged him to stay, to have one more whisky, like the embassy people. Max laughed and agreed.

'Won't be long,' William said to Sally, 'but don't wait.'

She smiled. 'I'll put it in the oven.'

It was another wet night, still blustery, with very little traffic and hardly any people. The tree-tops swayed and sheets of old newspaper were blown about the streets. At the corner by the city's only vegetarian restaurant, recently gone out of business, a broken billboard swung to and fro like the sail of an abandoned yacht. A black cat crouched to avoid it before disappearing into the grass behind. Flower baskets suspended from the lampposts jerked and twisted precariously. It was as if the city had abandoned itself.

There were cars parked outside the club, though, including Theresa's Dodge which had not moved since William's attempts to start it. Not much light showed through the curtains but the house gave its usual impression of shabby comfort and warmth. William noticed for the first time the size and proportion of the Georgian-style windows. Someone had said that El Lizard lived in the roof. That seemed appropriate.

She was standing in the hall talking to a group of people. When she saw him she broke off, picked up her handbag and fur coat from a chair and hurried towards him. She wore a black dress that seemed both tight and loose, simultaneously suggesting and accentuating the contours of her body. It was held in at the waist by a thin gold belt.

'All right?' he asked.

She nodded. They hurried to his Datsun, their heads bent against the squalls. Her presence in his car made him confident again. Once more everything became possible. 'I can't believe what I'm doing,' he said. 'I can only do it because it doesn't feel real.'

At first it seemed she was more interested in her fingernails. 'That is how to do it. Keep it from being real.'

'But it is real, isn't it? What we do matters.'

'It's only what we do. It's only a part. God sees the rest.'

She had to direct him to the palace. It was on the hill beyond the cathedral not far from the parliament building and the gaol. There was plenty of time and he drove slowly through the wet deserted streets.

They stopped at some traffic lights. 'I'm sorry about this afternoon,' he said.

She smiled. 'You are so English.'

'For apologising?'

'For stopping.'

'Oh, yes. Sorry.' The lights were still red. He drove through them. He kept forgetting – rather, had never properly acquired – the local custom of treating traffic lights as optional.

'I stopped at a pedestrian crossing once,' he said, 'and a policeman told me off. I also tried to cross on one and got told off again for nearly being run over.' The rain drummed on the roof of the car. 'But I am sorry, I really am. I never meant to deceive you.'

'Don't talk about it now.' She stared straight ahead. 'Tell me about England. Does it really rain all the time like this?'

'Not all the time, not even most of it. But in parts of the west it rains a lot. They have a saying – when you can see the hills you know it's going to rain, when you can't, you know it is.'

'Your prime minister is very strong.'

'Yes.'

'What would you like me to ask the president – for your spy work?'

'You don't need to bother, really. I'm only an amateur spy. It doesn't matter.'

'It makes it better for me if you tell me something you want to know.'

'Ask him, then, whether the Russians and Cubans are really taking over and whether that is what he wants. Is the People's Party really a communist party? But be careful. Manuel Herrera warned me this afternoon.' He described his visit to *Sẽnor* Finn. 'Ask him what Manuel Herrera does.'

'Herrera is dangerous,' she said. 'Even the army is frightened of him. People who do not agree disappear. He controls the president's guard and has many informers. The army don't like it but the officers can do nothing because it is Herrera and the Chief of the Police, Paulotti, and another general, Quinto, who control everything. Ines was told this by the officers she was with. Also Paulotti and Quinto come to the club sometimes.

'What for?'

'For us.'

The palace was not a very impressive building. It was partly barracks and much of it was anyway invisible behind the walls. Carlos's letter had said they were to enter at the back by the garages and stables. The streets around were broad and empty, laid out during the few years when the city aspired to international status. It took some time to drive all the way round the walls.

At the back a pair of large wooden gates led into a cobbled courtyard. Some soldiers were leaning on their rifles with unaffected nonchalance. When William pulled up one of them strolled over, catching his rifle butt on the cobbles.

'We are the interpreters who have come to interview the prisoners,' William said.

The soldier had a boy's face and an expression of premature indifference '*Qué?*'

William said it again but still the soldier didn't understand. He replied in a thick, incomprehensible accent. Theresa leaned across and spoke rapidly and harshly.

'*Sí*,' said the boy. 'Wait.' He ambled back to his comrades.

'These are peasants from the north,' she said. 'You have to speak to them hard, otherwise they don't understand. They know no politeness and if you speak politely it is like a foreign language for them. They have not heard the words said like that before.'

'Peasants, are they?' William wasn't sure he had seen a real peasant before, unless the street-traders counted.

'Animals.'

'You don't like them?'

'I know them.'

The soldier left his comrades and ambled to the guard room inside the gate. Presently a big square sergeant came purposefully towards them. He wore a sub-machine gun like a necklace and trod indifferently through the puddles. When he reached the car he bent down with one hand on the roof, letting the muzzle of his gun knock twice against the door frame. He pointed with his other arm.

'Straight through and turn right to the exercise yard. Someone is there for you.'

'*Gracias*,' said William.

The sergeant left them without a word.

'They don't understand "*gracias*",' Theresa said.

The only light in the exercise yard came from an open door-way. William drove towards it. He heard a series of small, perhaps nervous, movements at his side and glanced across. Theresa was looking at herself in the vanity mirror.

She turned to face him. 'Do I look all right?'

'You look very beautiful.'

She remained facing him. 'Do I make you unhappy?'

'Sometimes.'

'You must not be. All this has nothing to do with me. It is not me. You must remember.'

'You make me more happy than unhappy.'

'I cannot promise anything. You must undersand that. Will you wait here for me?'

'If he lets me.'

They stopped outside the lighted door. Inside, well

back from the rain, was the slim figure of Carlos. He leant against the green-painted wall, his arms folded. He wore a white jersey and blue jeans which made him look very youthful. His slack mouth seemed less out of place with casual clothes and his expression was alert and humorous. William thought, resentfully, that he looked pretty all right, too.

'This is an unusual way for the president to receive his guests,' Carlos said, 'hiding from his own guards in his own palace.' He smiled briefly at William but his eyes were on Theresa. 'They all think I've gone to bed early. I had to cross two courtyards without being seen by my own sentries. It was not easy but never mind. We are here.' His speech sounded prepared. He stood back for Theresa and touched her lightly on the elbow, indicating that she should walk on. As she passed he smiled directly into her face.

William remained by the door. Carlos made to follow Theresa and then hesitated.

'Wooding, you can wait, can you?'

'Yes.'

'Thank you. Leave your car where it is and come with us. I will show you where.'

It was a long corridor, freshly painted and harshly lit with white neon lights. Theresa's heels rang out on the stone. William felt each reverberation in his breastbone. There were carpeted wooden stairs and a door, then a room with a table, a number of wooden chairs, two armchairs and a sofa. On the table were magazines and newspapers. Two doors led off the room. Carlos opened one to reveal a small hall and two further doors.

He turned to William. 'If you wait here. We're going in' – he hesitated, slightly awkward – 'the other door through here is a lavatory if you need it.' He opened the nearer one for Theresa and she entered without looking back. 'No one should bother you. If they do, say you're waiting for your turn with the prisoner. This is the waiting-room of the officers' medical centre. It's all you need to know.' He glanced to confirm that Theresa was out of sight and then, holding the door to with one hand, put the other on William's shoulder. 'Thank you, my friend, for this service. I shall find a way to reward you. We shall not be long. Normally, of course, I should want all night' – he smiled – 'but this evening has been difficult to arrange. You will find newspapers on the table.'

William stood for a minute or so after the outer door had closed. Fortunately, he could hear nothing. What surprised him was that at first he also felt nothing – no indignation, no jealousy, no rejection, no shame. It was as if a part of him had been abruptly and painlessly cauterised. He considered how long he could remain before Sally became anxious. He had said he wouldn't be late. However, there was a telephone on the table, so he could ring her if it looked like being a long wait. But perhaps it would be only ten minutes or so.

He picked up some of the papers and sat down. They were a month or two old but it was noticeable how much the country had changed even since then. There was a dated innocence about them, about their continued rejoicing in the demise of the old regime, about their prescriptions for economic recovery, about their speculation as to the political future. Now all that was known; the future was the People's Party.

William rested the papers on his lap. It was of course absurd to be sitting reading while the woman he loved prostituted herself to the president in the next room. He had been accustomed to think of himself as a stable sort of man, not one to be blown hither and thither, yet here he was hourly determining to divorce his wife, deciding it was impossible, then that it was inevitable. But the events had about them a sort of logic. After all, she was a prostitute – if it had to be put like that – and he had fallen in love with her, knowing that. He had encouraged her relationship with the president for his own ends, despite an attempt to persuade her not to go through with it. The sort of logic it was, therefore, was the logic of his own choices, given which it all seemed inevitable – except that he need not have chosen.

He got up. Box was to blame, of course. It was at Arthur Box's behest that he had done it all. The reason he was there now was to do Box's bidding. Thank God he could hear nothing from next door. He reached for the phone.

An operator asked for the number with disconcerting promptness. The hotel answered after the usual delay and he asked for *Herr* Kronstadt. The ringing tone was abruptly terminated by a harsh voice.

'*Ja?*'

'*Herr* Kronstadt? This is William Wooding – we were–' William stumbled over his words. The charade made him self-conscious even though the likelihood of the palace telephones being bugged was remote. 'I was ringing to see if you are all right.'

'Yes, I am all right.'

'The lunch did not upset you?'

'No, the lunch did not upset me.'

Box's Germanic persona was not a helpful one. 'I was wondering if you would like to continue our discussion. I may have some business for you now. Would you be able to come over?'

'*Jawohl.*' Box rang off.

William rang back. 'I didn't tell you where I am. I'm at Carlos's place. Can you come here?'

'*Ja.*'

'Use the back entrance and when challenged say you have come to help in interpreting for the prisoners.'

'The prisoners, *ja.*'

'Head for the exercise yard and wait outside the lighted door. You will see my car.'

'*Ja.*'

Box's replies were so prompt that William wondered whether his message was really getting through. It was possible that Box was still concussed. 'Have you understood everything?'

'*Ja, ja.* And now something for you to understand. I am bringing my goods.'

'Your goods?'

'*Ja*, my goods. What I have showed you.'

'Oh, *ja* – yes – your goods, right.' William replaced the receiver and listened. No sound reached him. He hated to listen, but couldn't help it. He wasn't sure how long they'd been in there. Long enough in one sense, if not in any other. Too long, of course, as far as he was concerned. He had to do something. He picked up the phone and asked for his own number. Sally took a while to answer.

'Just thought I'd better let you know I've been a bit delayed. Might be late after all.'

'All right.'

'It'll keep in the oven, will it?' Thinking of food made him hungry.

'Yes, I'll switch it off. You can heat it up when you get in.'

'Fine. Everything all right?'

'Yes, fine.'

''Bye.'

''Bye.'

Next he wanted to urinate. He had meant to go before leaving home and it was now becoming urgent. Carlos had pointed to the door beyond theirs as being a lavatory. He supposed that the room they were in was the surgery. The two were very close and he would no doubt be able to hear them, and they him. There must be other lavatories. The second door opening off the waiting room was locked. He went to the green-painted corridor and looked for other doors. There was none open and he was soon outside, where his car was parked. There seemed to be no one about. He went to one side of the lighted doorway, but the wind was too blustery. He hurried round the corner. There he found a row of single-storey brick huts linked by open paths with corrugated roofs. They looked like the kind of post-war hospital accommodation in Britain that had become permanent. The entrances were lit, so he made for a dark patch at the far end of the nearest hut.

The rain came in spiteful gusts. He was about to pass the lighted entrance where the roofed path joined the hut when he heard voices. He ran across the grass and ducked into the darkened doorway of the next hut. His need was now desperate.

Two soldiers came out of the hut. Their rifles were slung over their shoulders and they dragged a man between them. They had him by the arms with his back towards the ground, his bare heels dragging along the cinder path. His body looked young though his head was shielded from view by the soldiers' thighs. William was close enough to see a large wet patch in the man's jeans where he had wet himself. The shock made him forget his own desire for a moment. As the soldiers passed William glimpsed the man's face. The whole of one side was crinkled and red where the hair had been torn out. Blood glistened in the neon light. His head lolled back as if he were unconscious.

The sight shocked and frightened William. He wanted to get back to the waiting room as quickly as possible, but felt he would burst. He hurried through the wet grass to the next corner. His eyes, particularly weak in the dark, gave him no warning of the sitting figure and he fell heavily. The figure toppled over with a muffled grunt. There were four of them, blindfolded and handcuffed, sitting in the grass with no shoes or socks. They were grouped around a short flight of concrete steps leading into the end of the hut. Squatting on the top step, the door closed behind him, was a soldier in a cape, his rifle with fixed bayonet resting across his legs.

William was back on his feet before he consciously thought. He had a vivid impression of the soldier's startled young face and of the blind immobility of the wet hunched figures. As he turned he saw similar figures grouped around the steps of the adjoining huts. He ran back the way he had come, aware of shouting only after he had passed the roofed path. Twice he slipped on the grass, once his glasses nearly came off.

He ran across the exercise yard to the doorway by his car and panting, closed the door behind him. It locked with bars that pushed down and could not be opened from without. He flicked the brass switch on the green wall and the strip-lights went out. He leaned against the door, panting and listening. There were footsteps and shouts and he caught the word '*coche*' – car – after which the voices faded. His chest still heaved, his heart thumped and his thigh muscles quivered. It crossed his mind that that was probably the farthest he had run since leaving school. It wouldn't do; he would begin exercising when he returned to normal life.

He felt his way up the corridor, helped by some light from the waiting-room at the top. His breathing was still not normal when he got there. The far door opened and Carlos came out, composed and smiling.

'Ah, Wooding. You see, I have not been long. Did anyone disturb you?'

'No one disturbed me. I disturbed someone else. I'll tell you about it. Is it all right if I go to the lavatory first?'

'Of course. You may find Theresa in there.'

She was not. Relief was beyond words, at first even a little painful, but he knew the bliss to come. The cistern was as noisy as he had feared but there was no minding that now. On his way out he could not help looking into the open door. It was, as he had thought, the doctor's surgery. There was a narrow untidy bed with a metal frame. Beside the bed stood Theresa, wearing white knickers and a white bra. She was adjusting the left shoulder-strap, her hair spread across both shoulders and over her breasts. Her face was turned towards the strap but she saw him out of the corner of her eye. She met his gaze calmly, unsmiling. Neither spoke. The strap adjusted, she bent to pick up her suspender belt. William went back to Carlos.

'Something nasty is happening in your palace.'

Carlos was stretching like Ricardo, staring at his fingertips. Like Ricardo, he stopped in mid-stretch. 'Something nasty?'

William told what he had seen.

'Oh, the prisoners.' Carlos abandoned his stretch. 'Yes, they're always here now.'

'But they're being tortured.'

'That's Manuel and the security police.'

'Can't you stop it?'

'Me?'

'You're the president, aren't you?'

Carlos looked surprised and irritated. 'Of course I'm the president, but I can't *do* any thing. I can *do* nothing, nothing at all. Why do you think I have to come secretly to the medical centre for my pleasure? I am a fugitive in my own palace. I can do nothing without the agreement of the triumvirate - Herrera, Paulotti and Quinto. These prisoners are political prisoners, *their* prisoners. Everything political is theirs. I am political and I am theirs. Otherwise, do you think I would tolerate having my women for twenty minutes on a doctor's couch?'

'Are you really powerless?'

'How does it look to you?' Carlos stretched again, then his loose lips widened into a smile. 'Mind you, that twenty minutes was worth the candle, as we used to say in England. I am very grateful to you.'

A klaxon sounded deafeningly in the corridor. Carlos hurried to a cupboard and the noise stopped. The remaining corridor lights went out.

'Fuses,' he said, 'the only way.' Other klaxons were sounding outside. 'It's the general alarm. There must be an intruder. Now they'll surround my quarters and I shan't be able to get back in. They don't know I'm out. *Dios mío*, what it is to be president. Who would believe me?' He looked angry and frightened.

'It's probably me they're looking for.'

'You must stay here. You can't leave until they give up.'

'But they'll find my car.'

'Well, they'll just tow it away or blow it up.'

Theresa appeared, dressed now and with her coat over one arm. Carlos smiled extravagantly.

'Please accept my apologies for this small disturbance. It will mean some delay in your leaving. Perhaps we should have coffee.' He took out some keys and unlocked the other door. 'There's a kettle and some things in there.' He sat in one of the armchairs, indicating to William to do likewise.

Theresa put down her coat and handbag and went into the other room where she could be heard moving cups. Carlos turned to William. 'Not bad at all,' he said in English. 'Very good, considering the circumstances. I shall see her again, but we must try to make better arrangements. We should find someone for you, too. I felt a little guilty' – he laughed – 'well, no, a little concerned, about your hanging around without anything to do.'

'You don't need to worry about me.'

'Of course not, but you know what I mean. I should like to reward you in some way.' He leaned across and, looking very serious, held out his hand. 'William, now I think we can be even better friends than we were at school.'

William tried to think only of doing his duty by Box. 'I'm pleased to be asked to help.'

'You are the only man I can trust.'

'Why?'

'Because you are a spy.'

'Does that make me trustworthy?'

'Yes, you are in my power. You are the only man in the country who is. I could have you shot. Manuel Herrera would organise it – he has said so – but I asked him not to because you are a friend of mine and because, being a British spy, you do no harm. Not like the Americans. So I asked Manuel to leave you alone and he said, okay, so long as you don't do anything such as seeking unauthorised contact with me – like this.' Carlos beamed. 'If you are caught you are shot. So you are in my power. So we are friends and we can trust each other.'

'What about you? Might they not shoot you as well?'

'Not while I am popular with the people. But one does not know how long that will last. The people are fickle. If things go wrong, Manuel and the others will blame me; then they will shoot me.'

'Does that worry you?'

'Of course it does. I want to live a long and peaceful and selfish life. I don't want to harm anyone or even do anythihg. But they want me to do things, and things go wrong when you start doing them. At least, that is my experience.'

Theresa came in with two coffees on a tray. William was as aware of her moving near him as he would have been of a source of heat. Now on his neck, now the side of his face, now the back of his hand. It was difficult to concentrate.

'But what can you do about it?' he asked.

Carlos shrugged. 'I don't know. At first I liked being president. It was better than being a colonel. But now it is hard and there is no fun. I wish I could be president without being in the government.'

Theresa was leaving them. William turned. 'Aren't you having any?'

Carlos looked as if he had just remembered her. He waved his arm. 'Yes, have your coffee with us. Bring it in.'

There were sounds of vehicles and shouting outside. The klaxons continued.

'Won't they realise you're missing?' asked William.

'Not yet. This is the outside guard and I left orders not to be disturbed. We should be all right in here. But I have to get back soon. I look to you for that. The British Secret Service is famous for that sort of thing, is it not?' He smiled at Theresa.

'I have sent for assistance.'

Carlos looked gratifyingly surprised. 'You have? But how will they get in here?'

'They – he – will find a way.'

'He? Is there only one?'

'Yes, but he's very good and the more people you have the more likely they are to be seen.' William was pleased with his answer.

Carlos looked doubtful. 'All this noise outside – it might mean they've caught him.'

'He's probably creating a diversion.'

'He can do that sort of thing?'

'Oh yes.' Once launched, it was easy to sail on confidently. The fact that each claim might be taking him farther from reality did not make it more difficult; it became easier. 'He's a master of disguise and infiltration.'

'Is he armed?'

'He doesn't need to be.'

'What's his name?'

'That's up to him. I never know in advance.'

Carlos was impressed. 'Could you and he get a message to the Americans for me?'

'Of course.'

'Ask them to intervene and get rid of this government, and then set up a new government with me as president again.'

'Okay.'

'And give us lots of money.'

'Right.'

'It seems absurdly simple but when you think about it, that's really all it needs. Will he be able to fix that, this man?'

'Bound to.'

'William, again I thank you.'

They stood to shake hands. William felt fraudulent in front of Theresa.

There was renewed shouting outside but Carlos was unworried. 'Good. I am pleased that is settled. This has been a good evening.' He looked at Theresa. 'Now, we shall go and see what they are doing out there. Perhaps we shall see your friend evade them, William. There is a window that overlooks this part of the palace. Follow me.'

He led them into the darkened corridor and up several flights of stone steps. Arc-lights had been switched on outside and there were enough windows to let some light in. They came to a small square room littered with broken chairs, old mattresses and planks of wood. There were windows in each wall through which they could see the palace lit like a football stadium. The area swarmed with troops and vehicles. William looked for the huts where he had seen the prisoners. The nearest was blocked out by the roof of the medical centre but those beyond were bathed in light. Two soldiers guarded each door, one facing outwards, the other inwards. The windows, he now saw, were boarded up.

'There's your car,' said Carlos.

It was being towed round the corner of some sheds by a lorry, the boot and bonnet open. The lorry took the corner too sharply and the side of the car was dragged along the wall.

'They'll probably take it to pieces now,' said Carlos.

Theresa was at another window. 'Something is happening here.'

On the far side of the exercise yard was a hearse and coffin surrounded by soldiers. A short man stood on the bonnet, gesticulating, while soldiers pointed their rifles at him. A tall man, apparently an officer, appeared and the short man got off the bonnet. They stood apart, talking.

'Have they killed someone?' asked Carlos.

'Perhaps they are going to,' Theresa said.

'That is our rescue,' said William. After a while, the officer saluted, turned away from Box and shouted at the soldiers. They quickly formed up on either side of the hearse, and, with Box driving, began to escort it at slow march pace across the yard.

'Your friend knows what he's doing,' said Carlos, admiringly.

'He won't be able to get in,' said William. 'I locked the door and told him to look for the lights, like you told me.'

They went quickly downstairs and Carlos reconnected the fuse. The klaxons had stopped but the main corridor lights came on. They decided William should be at the door to receive Box. The chances of his being recognised as the man who had blundered amongst the prisoners were not great, whereas Carlos was certain to be recognised. Exposing Theresa was also out of the question. The soldiers might just be controllable in the presence of the officer but the officer himself could not be trusted, Carlos said.

'I know my officers,' he continued. 'He would be in here in thirty seconds – less, if he is a colonel.'

'Why if he is a colonel?'

'Colonels have more honour.'

'Then couldn't he be more trusted?'

Carlos smiled. 'You have an English conception of honour, Wooding. For us it is dishonour not to seduce a beautiful woman. When I was a young officer a colonel of my regiment shot himself because it became known he had failed with the wife of the adjutant. The adjutant shot his wife for bringing dishonour upon him and then himself for bringing dishonour upon the regiment. You see, women are a serious matter for us. Not like with you English.'

'I think something is happening outside,' said Theresa.

Carlos took her hand. 'Wooding will see to it. He will bring his friend to us. We will go back to the surgery and wait.' He turned to William. 'You need not hurry.'

William watched in the corridor. He could hear feet marking time, then shouted commands. He knocked up the bar that locked the door.

The hearse was drawn up outside flanked by soldiers at attention. Box gave William a nonchalant wave as he got out.

'Ah, there you are,' he said in English.

'What is all this?'

'EEC kit. I want to bury it. It's all right, no one here speaks English. I told them I'd come to collect a dead admiral. They weren't going to let me in otherwise – well, they didn't anyway, I just drove in and kept going until they stopped me. All hell on the loose when I got here. They after someone?'

'Yes, me, actually.'

'Good. You've been active. Well done.'

The officer was looking on, his sword drawn. 'What are they doing now?' William asked.

'Guard of honour. I told them the admiral died under interrogation and the president wanted him buried in secret. Pretty difficult with my Spanish.'

'Difficult with any Spanish. There aren't any admirals. There isn't a navy.'

'That must have been what the officer chappie was on about. Couldn't make it out. "*Imposible, imposible,*" he kept saying. I slipped him 500 US and then it became "*Por su puesto, señor*, at once, *señor*." Best thing that's ever come out of old uncle Sam, the old greenback. Works the world over.'

For the sake of verisimilitude the coffin had to be taken in. Síx soldiers were detailed as bearers. They were the peasants Theresa had described, square strong men with broad shoulders and no necks, but even they staggered for a moment beneath the supposedly empty coffin. William told them it was lead-lined. They carried it into the waiting-room and laid it on the creaking table. The officer dismissed them and, seeing the coffee cups, took off his cap.

'Don't want him, do we?' asked Box.

'No.'

'*Colonel.*' Box went to the officer. There was an exchange of words and their hands touched briefly. The officer put on his cap, saluted and left.

'Hard to believe this place could really be communist if everyone's as corrupt as that,' said William.

'They'd be ten times worse, only more systematic.' Box put his wallet back in his pocket. 'Right, fill me in.'

William did so. When he had finished Box stood motionless, arms still folded. 'You have done well. As I see it, it's both good and bad. Good in that the president wants help, bad in that he wants American help. Would he accept British?'

'Possibly, but what could we do? We couldn't invade.'

'Probably not.'

'And even if we could, we couldn't offer to prop up the country afterwards, could we?'

'No.'

'Better do as he asks, then.'

Box shook his head. 'I don't like giving away secrets. All very well in the old days but they matter more now.

It's business. London wouldn't like it. We should try to do something ourselves and pass it on to the Americans only if it doesn't work.' He recommenced his pacing around the coffin. 'One thing puzzles me – nothing for you to worry about, not your fault at all, nothing to do with you – but it's London. Heard nothing from them, which is very unusual. This is a high priority operation and they haven't even acknowledged the intelligence I've sent so far. Nor has the embassy, of course, though that's not surprising. But for us nowadays intelligence is money. It's how we survive. You'd think they'd want more.'

There was a sound from the surgery, like furniture being moved. Box stopped. 'What was that?'

'It's the president. He's next door.'

'What's he doing?'

'The same as before.'

'With the prostitute?'

'With the woman I love'. It made William feel better to say it.

'Bit soon, isn't it?'

'I suppose he's very ardent.'

'You'll have to marry her. It's the only thing to do if you fall for a prostitute.'

'I am married.'

'Point.' Box took out a hip-flask from his inside pocket. 'Have a pull at this.'

William took a swig of whisky. He had a vision of the lolling head of the prisoner, normal on one side, red and hairless on the other. 'It ought to be possible to do something,' he said, handing back the flask. 'Carlos will agree to whatever gets him out of his mess.'

Box took a swig and replaced the flask. 'Of course it's possible. It's a question of finding the way through.' He sat on a chair opposite William. 'We must think.'

'May I ask a question?' William enquired after a while. Box nodded, without expression. 'What you said about marriage being the only way with prostitutes – you know about that sort of thing, do you?'

Box nodded again. 'Not that Mrs Box –'

'No, of course, I didn't mean –'

'British, you see. Wouldn't do in Britain. Prostitutes are sordid there. Here they're much more acceptable, almost respectable. Only ever marry foreign prostitutes. Anyway, things seem different when you're abroad. Every man is a bachelor east of Gibraltar, Nelson said.'

'But we're west and my wife is with me.'

'Would you feel guilty if you divorced your wife and married Theresa?'

'Yes.'

'Don't do it, then.'

Carlos reappeared, pulling on his white jersey over his head. William introduced him to Box. Carlos was distracted by the coffin. Box explained. Carlos didn't like it.

'Please understand,' he said, 'I am grateful to Special Information Services plc for coming to help me, but I do not like coffins. They remind me of death. Can it not be taken away?'

'Not until we go,' said Box.

'Then we must pretend it is not here. That is what we do all the time, anyway.' Carlos flopped on to the sofa and turned to William. 'Again, I am grateful to you. It was very good. Even better. She will make coffee when she is dressed, if you would like some.'

Box took out a notebook and began writing. For a while no one spoke.

When Theresa returned Carlos indicated that she should sit by him on the sofa. At first she sat a little way away but with his long fingers he tapped irritably on the cushion and she moved closer. He put his hand on her thigh. Box, meanwhile, had got to his feet and put his notepad back in his pocket. He stood facing them with his arms behind his back, rocking on the balls of his feet.

'Now, our aim is the overthrow of the government while retaining the president as president – as it were, knocking away the ladder on which you are standing and replacing it with another, more sympathetic ladder before you fall.' Box looked at William. 'Will you interpret?'

'Carlos speaks English.'

'But Theresa does not.'

'She needs to know?' asked Carlos.

'Of course.' Box's tone was formal and serious.

William had difficulty with the 'sympathetic ladder'. Carlos helped. Theresa nodded.

'Problem,' continued Box. 'The removal would have to be effected before Soviet or Cuban allies had a chance to interfere. But we should remember that it is necessary only to remove leading elements of the government.'

'Three people,' said Carlos.

'Precisely. The question is how. This is where we come to method.' Box glanced at William. 'Translate, please.'

William translated. Carlos repeated and embellished what he had said.

'We'll decide method later,' Box continued. 'We have a more immediate task: Aim – to get the president back into his quarters undetected and to get ourselves out; Problem – the palace guard; Method – the coffin.' He tapped it. 'The president can be carried out in it and unloaded in his chambers. The guard will provide bearers and escort. We, the two interpreters and the undertaker, then leave with the coffin.'

Carlos shook his head. 'I will not go in that.'

'There's plenty of room. It has a raised lid, you see. There's some equipment in the bottom half but there is space for a man to lie on top. I've tried it. It was specially made with airholes.'

'You've been in it?' Disgust distorted Carlos's features. 'I don't care. I am not travelling in a coffin.' Carlos got up suddenly, ignoring Theresa. He looked excited and angry. 'I am the president, the head of the government, in my own palace. I am not going to hide in a coffin.'

Box was unmoved. 'It will take only ten minutes.'

'Is this how the great British Secret Service treats presidents and heads of government?'

'Special Information Services plc treats people well. It is policy. The live body exfiltration method has a long and distinguished history. Presidents and prime ministers, kings, queens, party leaders and nannies have all availed themselves of it.'

'Nannies?'

'Very useful people to talk to: they know what goes on in a house, who comes and goes, what is said, what is not said. Some of our best agents have been nannies. Now, let me show you.' Box stepped forward and undid the coffin lid. With William's help, he lifted it off to reveal a purple lining and a white mattress about half-way down. There was, as he had said, plenty of room in the high lid.

Carlos peered in. 'What's underneath?'

'Equipment. I told you. It's quite safe.'

The door at the end of the corridor banged open. William looked through the waiting-room door. The tall colonel was striding towards them.

'Pay him to go away,' said Carlos quickly.

'I've paid him twice,' said Box.

'How much?'

Box told him.

'Not enough. He's a colonel; his honour is more expensive.'

'Right leave him to me.' Box put his hand on Carlos's arm. 'Now, you jump in in case he sees you.'

Carlos glanced at the surgery, then at the door. The colonel sounded about half-way down the corridor.

'Come on, come on,' urged Box.

Carlos grabbed Theresa and pulled her to her feet. He kissed her passionately on the lips and climbed into the coffin.

'You two put the lid on,' Box said and went out into the corridor.

There were six butterfly screws, easily fastened by finger and thumb. The expression on Carlos's face as they lowered the lid changed from affected nonchalance to uninhibited horror. William caught Theresa's eye as they fastened the screws. He started to laugh. Her dark eyes moistened and became warmer. Within seconds they were both convulsed with silent, near-helpless laughter. He rested his forehead on the lid and she turned away, her hands over her mouth, her hair shaking.

Box reappeared, closing the door firmly behind him. 'Honour is not cheap here.' He stared at them.

'Sorry,' said William.

'Not to worry. Nerves take people like that sometimes, especially in this business. Now.' Box pushed back his shoulders, a gesture that William recognised as habitual when decisions were to be anounced. 'The bearer party is on its way. We'd better compose ourselves.'

The soldiers carried the coffin with difficulty back down the green corridor. One of them slipped and banged it against the wall. The officer shouted. He had drawn his sword and for the seventh time, to William's count, looked long and hard at Theresa.

They all three climbed in the hearse. The colonel formed up the guard on either side.

'I must have paid him too well,' said Box. 'They want to escort us off the premises.'

They set off in time with the slow-marching troops.

'Where are we going?' William asked. 'We don't know where Carlos's quarters are. We can't very well ask him now.'

'Point. You'll have to ask the colonel.'

William waved to the colonel to come alongside. He told him that the president wished to inspect the body and it was therefore necessary for the cortège to call first at the president's private quarters. The colonel was disposed to discuss the matter, his eyes all the time on Theresa. It was very strange for the president to wish to see the body of a prisoner, he said. But this had been a very important prisoner, William told him, a friend of the president's who had proven treacherous. There had been several such, the colonel said, and the People's Party Investigation Committee was uncovering more daily. Perhaps the president wished to see the body with his own eyes in order to ensure that his treacherous friend was dead? The colonel's eyes flickered up and down Theresa's body until, with a last lingering attempt to catch her glance, he went back to the escort.

The president's private quarters were in a wing of the palace. The alarm was now over and the lights were out, so it was difficult to see much. They knocked on a door that was manned by a guard in the uniform of the security police. These troops were responsible for the inside of the palace while the army guarded the outside. A security police officer was summoned. He appeared yawning and scratching, his jacket undone. He and the colonel lost their tempers on sight and shouted at each other across the threshold. After intercession from William, it was agreed that the coffin could be brought in while the officer summoned the president, but that the colonel could not remain in the building.

'Tell them to bring it in quickly,' William said.

The soldiers stumbled and the coffin was saved only by the door jamb. William wanted to laugh again. He did not dare look at Theresa, beside whom the colonel marched with oppressive attentiveness, his sword erect and quivering. Box walked solemnly ahead, very upright, his hands behind his back.

The coffin was placed on a table in the guards' mess room. The colonel was again disposed to hang around but Box dismissed him. When they removed the coffin lid Carlos sat up immediately, his face was red and angry. 'Who was throwing me about?'

'The bearers slipped,' said Box.

'And what is under this mattress? It was digging into me.'

'Equipment, I told you.' Box's manner was brisk and authoritative. 'Get out and get into your quarters. The officer of the guard has gone to summon you to see if it's true that you want to view the body. You must go and be summoned and then come back and do it.'

Carlos climbed out. Irritability and sulkiness made him look younger, almost adolescent. 'I tell you something,

Mr Special Information Services plc, I'm not going in another coffin again, ever, for you or anyone.'

'Put that in your will.'

Carlos was too taken aback to be offended. He hesitated by the door. 'Go on,' urged Box. 'There's no one in the corridor.'

Carlos held out his arm towards Theresa. 'Come with me.'

'No,' said Box.

'But she's an excuse,' said Carlos. 'If I'm seen, she's what I've been doing.'

'*No.*'

Carlos left the room. 'Next thing is to get this in the tomb I told you about,' said Box. 'We must do that tonight. If I have to leave the hotel and go to ground, I shall go in the tomb with it. That's where you'll find me.'

'Okay.'

'You can use it, too, if you need. Now, point four.'

'Point four?'

'Of my notes.' Box tapped his pocket. 'I learned them. Write, read, remember, never refer. The four Rs. Trick of the trade. Impresses people like Carlos, demonstrates mastery of the situation and gets them to obey. Very important. Appearances count in this business even more than in others.' He crossed the room to look at the pictures of past presidents hanging on the wall. They were mostly fat, glossy men with enormous moustaches and layers of medals, though the country had never been to war.

'But what is point four?'

Box turned round. 'Point four. Yes. Point four is contact arrangements between us and the president. We must agree them when he returns. There is also point five, our plan of action. We'll have to agree that, too.'

'What is it?'

'I don't know yet.'

William translated for Theresa. He could see her smiling while she conducted a minute examination of the hem of her fur coat.

There were footsteps and voices in the corridor and the

door was opened by the officer of the guard, now fully buttoned and assiduously respectful. Carlos entered, looking haughty, behind him the tall colonel. He and the officer of the guard engaged in a silent tussle to follow Carlos into the room.

Carlos frowned at them. 'Close the door and wait outside.' He waited until the door was closed, then turned and smiled. 'I hadn't reached my quarters when the oficer found me, so I pretended I had been disturbed by the noise and wanted to know what it was all about. I was angry with him. It is easy when you're president.' He sat in the chair by Theresa.

'Contact arrangements,' Box announced. He went through them. They involved as little telephoning as possible, sensible use of the tango club and, in emergency, calls on the palace in the guise of interpreters for the prisoners.

Carlos nodded. 'Okay but what do we do?'

'That's point five. It's what we have to decide.'

'But we only have a minute. I can't stay longer, or they'll think I'm necrophiliac as well.' Carlos was pleased with his remark and translated for Theresa.

'Any ideas, William?' asked Box.

'No.'

'Me neither,' said Carlos.

'Nor me,' said Box. 'Theresa?'

'She won't know,' said Carlos. 'She doesn't know anything about this sort of thing.'

'Ask her anyway.' Box's tone was light but insistent. Carlos stared at him. Box stared back. Carlos offhandedly asked Theresa if she had any ideas.

She stood up and moved away from Carlos. She seemed to have followed what had been said. '*Se llama, no*?' she said cautiously, looking at William. 'Is that what it's called?'

'Yes, it is.' William translated for Box. 'Honey-trap.'

Box looked pleased. 'Honey-trap, yes, it is called that. Go on, Theresa.'

'Bring Herrera and Paulotti and Quinto to Maria's. Ines

and the girls will look after them – compromise them, do you say? – and then you can arrest them. They are the leaders and that is the only place where they will all be together without their guards. If you lock them up, no one else will know what to do and everyone will obey the president.'

Carlos's irritation was replaced by pride. He held up both arms for her to come to him, smiling hugely. When she was near enough, he pulled her on to his lap and kissed her.

William translated for Box.

'Brilliant.' Box stared at the back of Theresa's head. 'Like all great ideas, very simple. I knew it would be worth asking her.'

'It may not be easy to arrange.'

Box waved one arm. 'Details to follow. We'll work it out.'

It was not until they were back in the hearse, flanked by the soldiers and heading for the gate, that William noticed the time.

'All right?' asked Box, seeing him stare.

'I didn't realise it was so late.'

'Missus expecting you?'

'Yes.'

'Queen and country. She'll understand.'

They passed an arc-lit area in which a vehicle was being dismantled by soldiers in overalls.

'That's my car,' said William. 'They're searching it for bombs.'

Box stared. 'Not any more, they're not. You don't need to break it into that many pieces. Cannibalising, that's what they're doing. Your car's going to be distributed amongst a dozen others by breakfast. Don't worry, the company will be pleased to get you another if we pull this job off. Also, given the fact that they've pinched it, they're hardly likely to get the police to trace the owner and make enquiries. All things considered, therefore, probably just as well.'

William watched a door being carried away. 'What if we don't pull it off?'

Box barked his brief discordant laugh. 'Then your not having a car will be the least of our problems.'

At the gate they had to stop because of an army lorry coming in. The guards were paying it a good deal of attention, two of them talking to the driver and several standing staring at the back. They were embarrassed by the arrival of the hearse, though, and waved the lorry on almost before the tall colonel had begun to shout. As the lorry pulled past the gate, they could see two rows of huddled blindfolded figures in the back.

The colonel put his face in the open window by William, smiling past him at Theresa. 'More live ones come in, *señora*. You will come again to take them away when they are finished with?'

Theresa uttered a short expletive unknown to William. The colonel looked surprised, his features stiffened and he disappeared.

'What did you say?' William asked.

'A bad word.' It seemed she wouldn't continue but then she smiled at her hands folded in her lap. 'He would be used to hearing it only from his peasant soldiers, not from – not from . . .'

'From a lady.'

She nodded, looking down at her hands.

9

The cemetery gates were closed. Box was incredulous. 'Locked. How can they be?'

'It's night,' said William.

'What's the point of locking them at night? People might want to come here.'

'Surely not.'

'I bet they do.' Box kept the headlights on them, focused like his own insistent stare. 'It would be the one time I haven't got my lock-picking kit.'

William asked Theresa about the gates. 'They're shut because too many people wish to go here at night,' she said. 'Homeless people and vagrants. They sleep in the tombs.'

'I've never seen any homeless people in the city,' said William. 'Well, one, but he's not really homeless. He has a home of his own on the beach.'

'There used to be many but not now, not since the new government.'

'It's done something good, then.'

'They disappear.'

'We can't sit here like this until the gates open,' said Box.

'Try them,' said Theresa.

Wiliam got out and pushed at the gates. They opened.

'Extraordinary,' Box said as he and William closed them behind the hearse. 'She must have some sort of sixth sense.'

'She has a friend buried here. She knows it quite well.'

At night the cemetery was even more like a small town than during the day. The slowly traversing headlights picked out dozens of pairs of furtive green eyes.

'You're sure there are no guards?' asked William.

'Yes, I checked. There's nowhere for them unless they

live in the tombs. And now we're in, we can't be seen from outside. The high walls prevent that. But if we are caught we have to pretend to be tomb robbers. Lesson there.' He looked across at William. 'If you're ever caught with your trousers down and there's no hope of innocent justification, always try to hide the greater crime behind the lesser, like adultery or something. Once they find one unsavoury explanation people tend to be so pleased they don't look any farther.'

'But is tomb-robbing a lesser crime?'

'I should think so. Ask.'

Theresa shook her head. 'It's much more serious. No one minds about spying, especially if it's the British.'

'I find that hard to believe,' said Box.

They found the right stretch of wall and then door number 1066. Its black wood was dull in the light of Box's torch. The beams seemed unable to penetrate the gloom behind the small iron grille.

'Is it unlocked?' asked William.

'Yes, yes. I checked.' Box bent and opened the door. It creaked but not very much. His torch illuminated six coffins of the family Bustillo, piled four and two. The fourth and highest was on a level with the door. 'If we move that on to the others, they'll be even and we can just slide ours on top.'

'Move it?'

'Yes.'

Box climbed in, stepping carefully on the lower coffin. 'Plenty of room in here.' His voice echoed. 'If you get in and take it from your end, I'll manage this.'

William glanced at Theresa, who had stayed in the hearse. 'You're sure we'll be able to move your coffin? It took all those soldiers and they found it heavy.'

'No problem. We'll unload some of it. Come on.'

'What . . . what if the surviving family Bustillo come to visit the grave and find a new coffin? I mean, are you sure this is a good idea?'

'The door hasn't been opened for years. And the most

recent coffin in here is 1937. Come on, we haven't got all night.'

William eased his way through the door, feeling with his feet for the lower coffin. He thought the lid bent beneath his weight and said so.

'Nonsense,' said Box.

'They might be cheap ones. Feels like plywood.'

'Stop worrying about it.' Box had to put his torch in his pocket in order to grapple with the coffin. 'If we each take a handle and edge it towards us, then get an arm underneath and step back on to the ground as we lower it, we should be okay.'

William thought of Box's short legs. 'It's a big step down, two coffins' height.'

'Manageable. On the count of three?'

It was very heavy and at first difficult even to slide. The lowering was more a barely-controlled fall. William's feet found the floor much closer than he thought.

'Perfectly manageable,' Box said, panting. 'Must have been a chap about your build, though, this Bustillo. Big uncle Bustillo.'

There was a sudden splintering and William experienced an abrupt descent.

'What was that?' asked Box.

'The floor's given way beneath me.'

'Can't have. You all right?'

'Think so.' The descent had jarred William, but he remained in otherwise exactly the same position. His legs felt normal and whatever was now beneath his feet felt solid.

'Can't have given way.' Box pulled his torch from his pocket and shone it down. They had both been standing on an older and lower coffin, but William was now standing in it. The coffin rested on the grave floor and its top, except the broken part around William's legs, was as dirty as the floor. 'Good lord.' said Box.

William was standing in the broad end, roughly where the chest and throat would be. His calves tingled in anticipation of the touch of unmentionable slime. He waited for the stench but there was only a cold damp smell.

'Extraordinary,' said Box. 'I thought it was the floor. Maybe you were right about the plywood, just goes to show. You never know in this business.'

They climbed out of the tomb. William did not like to look at his feet in case something was clinging to them. Box set about unpacking their coffin but first insisted William get into the back of the hearse with him so that he could see once more how the kit worked. It was stowed neatly below the mattress and it was even possible, Box demonstrated, to lie in the coffin and operate both transmitter and receiver.

'All this up to the pelvis is the batteries. Trunk is transmitter and receiver, head and neck the controls, as you can see. They're just as they were in the hotel room when I showed you before, only closer. Power switch here, look, and that gives you enough light to see by even when the lid's down.'

'Who designed it?'

'I did. Made good use of coffins in my time. Very adaptable articles. I've never known that before, though, someone going through the top. They must be cheap ones here. In West Africa they're even cheaper – just cardboard painted as cars and aeroplanes and things. Also, bodies go off so quickly there that no one hangs around for very long. We got one mixed up once. Awful muddle. Thousands of pounds worth of sensitive kit buried in a Cadillac coffin in Kumasi and a decomposing mother of ten landed in a Mercedes coffin at RAF Brize Norton. Frightful legal complications, coroner and all that. Press nearly got on to it. I was sent to training department for a while as a sort of punishment posting.' His thin lips parted. 'Spent my time there designing new coffins. That's where this one comes from.'

The batteries were the heaviest part. They unloaded them separately and reloaded them once the coffin was in the tomb. Box demonstrated how the aerial should be attached to the grille and in which direction it should point.

'Reception here shouldn't be too difficult, depending on climatic conditions. Now – the next problem is her.'

William didn't like to hear Theresa referred to as 'her'. She had remained in the hearse throughout, the collar of her fur coat turned up, her hands in her pockets, her long hair pushed forward by the collar. She stared straight ahead at the opposite wall. Perhaps she was thinking of the banker. William felt more jealous of the dead banker than of Carlos.

'What problem?' he asked.

Security. She knows what we're up to with Carlos and she knows our hideout, but can we trust her?'

'Of course we can. She's in it as much as we are. Anyway, she's that sort of person.'

'All the same, I'd rather pay her something.'

'Why?'

'To buy her loyalty.'

'Can you buy loyalty?'

'Yes, temporarily.'

'You couldn't buy hers.'

'She needs money, doesn't she? She must have taken it from Carlos. That's what she was there for. I wonder how much.'

There were moments when William disliked Box. 'She doesn't take it from just anyone.'

'Depends how much she needs it. Family, that sort of thing. They don't live well, these people.' Box shrugged. 'You know her better, of course, but there's plenty of it if she wants it.

William didn't want Theresa to be further degraded, as he saw it, by the offer of money. On the other hand, he didn't want to deny it her. Also, if Box paid her well she might not need to go to Carlos again.

'I'll sound her out,' he said.

They drove away from the cemetery as a glimmer of light spread far out to sea. William's watch had stopped at twenty past three. 'It can't be that late,' he said. 'How *can* it be that late?'

The other two looked at their watches. The dull thin gleam spread along the horizon. 'Eleven minutes past five,' said Box. 'Never mind, a shave and a shower will see you right. Good night's work. London will be delighted: a real coup. All we have to do is work out the detail.' He regretted that daylight made it impossible for him to take them to their respective homes. He didn't want them seen in the hearse.

'Just drop us both near the beach,' said William. Theresa was going back to Maria's rather than home and he was so late that another hour or so would make no difference. He didn't want to leave her yet.

'Shall we walk by the sea?' he asked.

She nodded.

Box dropped them by the golf course. The sun was still not visible but its rays reddened the undersides of the clouds. The sea was leaden and a damp wind scythed off it. William led the way to the beach, thinking there was enough light to see where to tread, but he slipped on a bit of driftwood. His glasses didn't help in poor light. Theresa put her arm in his and they walked by the sullen waves, staring at the brightening horizon. Her face was wet with what he at first thought was spray. When the sun rose, partially concealed by cloud, it reddened the sea. The colour was reflected faintly in her features. She kept her eyes on the horizon.

'Are you all right?' he asked.

'Yes.'

'Do you want to go back?'

'No. Keep walking. It's beautiful.'

It became light enough for him to see properly. The sand and shingle beach was littered with driftwood, tins and bits of plastic. A long line of breaking surf curved around the bend by *Señor* Finn's hut. Her hand on his arm made him feel that all his nerves were concentrated on that point. He kept noticing, then forgetting, then again noticing the beauty of her face.

They walked in silence. She wept continuously, without sound, without grimacing, the tears dripping unhindered from her chin. The fur of her collar was wet where the wind flapped it against her face.

'You know I would marry you,' he said. 'I meant it.'

She nodded.

'Even after Carlos and everything. It makes no difference. It's you.'

'You cannot marry me. You are married.'

'I can get divorced.'

'You cannot.'

'Why not? I'm not a Catholic. Neither is Sally.'

'It is wrong to leave your wife.'

'I'll do it nonetheless.' He spoke more confidently than he felt.

'I could not like you if you did.'

The outline of *Señor* Finn's hut looked unfamiliar. William supposed it was because he was approaching from an unusual angle but as they got closer he saw that the corrugated roof was hanging down and that one whole side, which had been made of a door and assorted drift-wood, was missing. The sagging roof creaked in the wind and the surrounding grass and rushes had been trampled. For a few moments he nearly convinced himself that there had been gales in the night but he recalled Manuel Herrera's black Mercedes reversing towards the hut, and the doors opening. He recalled also *Señor* Finn's red-faced chuckles at having told Manuel that William was a beggar. He remembered giving *Señor* Finn money.

'Where are we going?'

'This is where my friend lives.'

She stared at the litter of trampled grass and scattered wood. 'Your friend?'

There was a hole in the upturned boat, the pots and pans lay amidst the ashes of the fire, the earth was churned, the table was on its side and the chair on its back. Inside the hut a mattress and blankets were strewn in confusion. The wind had fastened a sheet of newspaper against the splintered prow of the boat.

'You have a friend who lives here?'

'Lived.'

What looked at first like a crumpled rag turned out to be the terrier. It had a dark hole in the side of its head and its lips were drawn back over its teeth.

She put her hand through his arm again. 'Who was he?'

'I didn't know his name. He just lived here, that's all.'

'He was a vagrant?'

'I suppose so.'

'It is against the new law. They will have taken him to a home.'

'This was his home.'

He began to feel as if he were no longer the centre of his own world. All his concerns, his future, his marriage, his desires, were peripheral not the main thing. There was something else. It was like realising that throughout his life there had been another person in the house, for years unnoticed but now, once seen, forever present, in every room, at every meal. Unawareness was no longer possible. Henceforward, he would be living for something or against it, no longer floating but swimming. A gust of wind tore the newspaper from the boat and sent it fluttering out of sight.

She tugged at his arm. 'There is nothing you can do.'

'It was partly my fault. It was because I spoke to him. I gave him money so they probably thought he was spying for me, or something. It was Manuel Herrera who did it.'

'You can do nothing now.'

'We must get rid of them, Herrera and the others.'

'That's what we are doing.'

'But now it's serious.'

'It wasn't before?'

'It didn't feel serious. Did it for you?'

She shrugged. They walked back towards the golf course. 'Are you cold?' he asked.

'A bit.'

'Are you a fatalist?'

She smiled. 'God is a fatalist.'

'If we go to the covered market, will God permit breakfast?'

'He might.'

'Arthur Box says you can be paid for the work you are doing – the spying work.'

She raised her eyebrows. 'He will pay me for it?'

'Yes, if you want it for your family or whatever – if you like.'

'I would like it very much. It's better than the other work.'

He smiled. 'That's good.'

10

'Can you come now?'

Nightingale's tone was peremptory. William held the telephone away from his ear. 'As I said, it's a bit awkward. I've only just got into the office. I'm late myself and there's no one else here. I ought to stay until there is.'

'It is urgent. We've got to get something off.'

'I'm pretty tired and there's a lot here I should be getting on with. I've been up all night.'

'I know you have. It's about that.'

'All right. It may take me some time to reach the embassy, though. I've lost my car.'

'We'll send you one.'

Nightingale met him beneath the chandelier. He seemed hurried and distracted. His spotted bow-tie was loose and lopsided.

'Awfully nice of you to come. The car will take you back again. It's about this business of your friend – your secret friend, you know, the little funny – and what he wants us to send to London for him. He left a message and then disappeared and now we can't find him. We're not very happy about his message and Peter suggested we seek confirmation from you. Feather thinks we should just tear it up and forget it.' Nightingale relaxed enough to smile as they went upstairs. 'But that was first thing this morning and Feather's early-morning reactions are sometimes a little – well, briskly decisive. I'm a hopeless prevaricator and Peter's a natural compromiser, so we thought we'd call you to make up our minds for us.'

Nightingale's coffee was a help. The ambassador was as good-naturedly miserable as on the other occasions when William had met him. It seemed that the wrinkles would be smoothed and the furrows lifted from the man's face if only someone would tell him he need no longer be ambassador.

'Sorry to drag you in' he said. 'Can't find your friend anywhere. We had various names to ring at the hotel but no one answered any of them. Then we discovered they'd all checked out first thing. Who were they, anyway – agents of his?'

'They were all him, I think.'

'Well, he or they have gone to earth good and proper now, leaving us with a tidy problem.' The ambassador handed William several sheets of dense black handwriting. 'I say it's a bit of a problem, Nightingale says it's a crisis, Feather says it's a disaster.' He laughed uneasily. 'You seem to have had an eventful night of it, anyhow.'

'More coffee?' asked Nightingale.

'Please.' William sat down to read Box's notes.

'Where's Feather?' the ambassador asked Nightingale.

'In his bath, the brute. He's got his brandy so he won't be long. Then we'll see a new man.'

Box's crabbed, precise handwriting summarised the night's events as he knew them. The major part dealt with the scheme to entrap the president's advisors. Paragraphs were headed: 'The Sítuation', 'The Proposal' and 'The Way Ahead'. The final one was entitled 'Back Up'. It comprised a request for immediate diplomatic recognition of the new government whenever it was declared, a statement of support for the president from the City, an announcement of substantial low interest development aid to be provided by merchant banks and a request for a pair of frigates as a 'demonstration of intent'. The message ended on a personal note: 'Why no answer to my last? Please send soon. Wooding doing well but needs encouragement. Self ditto. Allowances just adequate. EEC transmissions fine. Weather cool.'

'All a bit far-fetched, I thought,' ventured the ambassador. William said nothing. The ambassador hurried on 'perhaps it's not, though, perhaps you're right and it's all rather . . . you know, serious . . .' He trailed off, looking at Nightingale.

'Out of the question,' said Nightingale. 'We can't set about undermining our host government. After all, we're here to get on with them, not to get rid of them.'

'And things aren't that bad.' The ambassador stressed the two last words. 'Are they? Perhaps they are, I don't know.' He scratched his head.

William remembered his conversation with Max, Sally's boss. 'The American embassy seems to think they are. They're expecting to be expelled.'

'Oh, the *Americans*,' said Nightingale.

The ambassador smiled. 'Very alarmist, I always thought.'

William persisted. 'People have started disappearing.'

'Really? Who?' Nightingale asked.

'Well, I don't know them all, of course, except one. A chap who used to live in a hut on the beach.'

'Ah.'

'And they announced on the radio this morning that they've suppressed the newspapers – they've all got to re-apply for licences except the government one.'

The door opened as William was speaking. 'Which makes this the same as half the other countries in the world,' said Feather. 'No change except a little for the worse.' He went straight to the coffee. He was a big man and gave the impression of moving slowly while covering a lot of ground. His haggard, handsome face looked unhealthy when scrubbed. 'Everything and everyone ends in disaster,' he continued. 'No reason why this place should be different. Your attempt to alter history's decline into barbarism can only hasten the undesired end. This is no place for improvers.' He gulped his coffee, poured another and in two long strides reached and reclined full-length on the ambassador's sofa.

The ambassador smiled at William. 'That doesn't mean you haven't done jolly well.'

Feather insisted from his recumbent position that it was no good, it wouldn't do, they couldn't send nonsense like that to London. London would think they were barmy. Nightingale regretted that the office no longer had any influence over the funnies now that the funnies were privatised, though the office still had to act as a channel of communication for them. Was it permissible to refuse to transmit material they didn't agree with? No one knew. Feather thought the main thing was to prevent that lunatic Box from doing or saying anything more.

'Box is not a lunatic. At least he's trying to do something. You may not agree with it but at least he – he –' William sought to avoid the caring cliche – 'he is concerned about things.' He felt like someone who had mistimed his leap over a puddle.

Feather lit a cigar.

'Perhaps the answer,' the ambassador said tentatively, 'is to send the thing as it is and for us to send a – a – you know –'

'A dissenting telegram,' said Nightingale, as if he had been waiting a long time. 'What a brilliant idea, Peter.'

The ambassador beamed at William. 'Yes, perhaps that's the answer.'

'What did you need me for?' William asked.

'Oh, well, we needed you to – to . . .'

'To put you in the picture,' said Nightingale.

'Exactly, exactly so,' the ambassador stood. 'Thank you so much for coming, Mr Wooding. A most useful mind-clearing exercise.' He looked at the others.

Feather raised himself and turned towards William. 'The real point', he said slowly, 'is the futility of ever doing anything. Things happen, but we don't *do* them. Whenever we try, they go wrong. The temptation to action must always be resisted.' He lay back and put his cigar in his mouth. 'It is the one temptation I have always been able to resist.'

Nightingale giggled and the ambassador smiled unhappily as William closed the door.

The two girls were at the shop by the time the embassy car dropped William. As he suspected, they had been delayed by the bus strike but that was now over, they said. The government had ordered the strikers back to work and had issued a proclamation: strikes were not illegal but because the government governed for the people any strike against it – which this one had been – was an act against the people, and acts against the people were treason. There had been some arrests.

The girls competed almost breathlessly with each other as if to show how well they had learnt the message. They seemed pleased and excited. William wondered why they weren't worried. He gazed at the orange-seller, hunched beside his stall. There was less breeze now and the sun was warmer but the man still dressed as if against a chill wind. So far as William knew, Box remained the only customer. Presumably the oranges were changed sometimes.

'Possibly our strike will be finished,' he said to the girls.

They were round-eyed and serious. 'Our strike? We do not make a strike, *señor*.'

'At the factory, I mean. Our strike at the factory.'

'The factory, yes, yes.' The girls nodded.

The factory was nothing to do with them; he wasn't sure that they had ever understood its connection with the shop. 'But maybe that is not a strike against the government,' he added with a smile. 'Not treason.'

'No, *señor*, not treason.'

As he went upstairs, he heard them whispering and laughing.

There was a telex from London that morning, the first since he had sent his lengthy report on the strike. It asked what progress he had made in resolving it. His description of the political situation and his points about his own impotence to intervene under the new laws and about the government attitude towards foreign-owned companies had all been ignored. He could imagine the remarks being made in London about failure to get a grip, about things going downhill and about the need for radical surgery. This meant a senior visitor from head office with a kill-or-cure brief. There would also be staff restaurant gossip about his going native like his predecessors. There would be rumours of a bar girl, quite without foundation and only coincidentally true.

Sally had not been at home when he had got back that morning. She must have gone to work early. His dinner was still in the oven, which had been turned off, and she had left no note. Angelica, the maid, was already there, back from her holiday. She had started on the washing. Diminutive and smiling, she behaved as if there were nothing unusual in his tired and unshaven appearance. No, *Señora* had left no message, only instructions about the washing, that was all. *Señora* had gone to work at her usual time.

William showered and tried to ring her but she was teaching. He did not feel guilty at having been away all night, only a little at having had breakfast in the covered market when he could have got back. But it had been a very good breakfast. He and Theresa had laughed about Box and the coffin, she had talked of her brothers and sisters and had asked him about the Queen and Mrs Thatcher who, along with Churchill, were the Britons most admired or known about. They had eaten a vast breakfast, drunk many cups of coffee and had finished with two or three glasses of whisky. She laughed helplessly when he described Box's tactics for street meetings, coughing over her coffee as she clutched his arm for fear she would fall off her stool. He felt a twinge of disloyalty in holding Box up for ridicule, but twinges were bearable. After all, they were getting on with their task, no matter what the embassy people thought. When they parted she kissed him on the lips.

He tried ringing Sally from the office, but again she was teaching. Presumably she wasn't too worried or she would have rung him.

There was sudden laughter from downstairs and a few seconds later Ricardo bounced up. He entered grinning and reached for William's hand, taking it in both his.

'William, I congratulate you. Now at last you are a man.'

'I am?'

'You have a mistress.'

'A mistress?'

Ricardo threw himself into his chair and put his feet on the desk. 'No man is really a man until he has a mistress. Of course, any man can have a wife, that is easy, but to have a mistress – and such a mistress – is very good. You were seen at breakfast in the covered market. By lunch you will be famous. And to have the president's mistress, that is really something.'

'Things aren't always what they appear.'

'That is English modesty. It suits you but it is not true. She looked tired and happy. You must have been making love all night.'

'No, we weren't.'

Ricardo held up his hand. 'It was breakfast. You both ate a lot and you were happy. She was laughing. When you parted, she kissed you. A woman who does that has always been making love.'

'Who saw us?'

'Manuel Herrera's men. He told me this morning. I had to see him to make my report. I was very nervous because it was him, but he was all right. I had nothing to report' – he grinned – 'of course, but he did not mind. He said you are a sensible man. He will come to see you this morning but he said I must not be here so I will go for coffee.'

'He's coming here?'

Ricardo stood. 'Please – don't tell him I told you. He must believe I am spying on you. What do you want me to do?'

'You could go to the factory and find out what's happening. I haven't been able to get through to them this morning.'

Ricardo grimaced. 'Not that kind of work. Spying. What spy work do you want me to do?'

William thought. 'You can find me another car. My old one was stolen.'

Ricardo's face lit up. 'Another car? Any sort, any price?'

William remembered Box's promise as to who would pay. 'Any sort, any price.'

'I will find you a beautiful car. *Chau*, William.' He paused at the door. 'We work together well, eh?'

William smiled. 'We do.'

'*Chau*, William.'

'*Chau*.'

Manuel made no secret of his visit. His black Mercedes drew up by the orange-seller's stall. He got out with two other men and spoke to the orange-seller. His step was light on the stairs, his olive-greens were clean and pressed and he wore tight black leather gloves, which he removed delicately.

He could not stay long, he explained. It was a social call, one of what he liked to call his 'pleasure visits'. Things were going well and he was pleased that William had heeded their little talk on the beach the day before. He had done the right thing.

William smiled. 'You are well informed.'

Manuel held up his hand, as Ricardo had done. 'There is very little that escapes attention in this city, especially where women are concerned. Your companion for the night was an excellent choice in every sense. Better that you spend your time with her than with the president. He will not want her as his mistress when he knows she is sleeping with you . . . as he shall, in good time.' His eyes rested steadily, almost warmly on William's. 'Also, I was never sure about that girl. Her attitude is suspect. Girls in general are not to be trusted. They are confused and unpredictable. But it is better that she is with you than with the president.'

'You know them well, these girls?'

'Well enough to know that there are better choices a man can make.' He continued to gaze warmly and assessingly at William. 'Also, I have good news for you. The strike at your factory will be finished. The workers will return this afternoon. It was a simple matter to resolve. We are keen to have more foreign investment, therefore strikes against foreign companies whose attitude is favourable to us could be construed as sabotage. What is more, your Ministry of Information tender will be accepted. That should mean much business for you.'

William inclined his head. 'This is all very unexpected.'

'Of course, you may see the president whenever you or he wish. We would like you to see a little of him. It is important that he should feel he has friends who can reassure him, perhaps even guide him. And it is equally important that you should feel free to discuss with me any worries that the president may confide in you.'

Manuel's manner was soft but precise. His eyes never left William's. William always felt uneasy in his presence, sometimes frightened. He had to remind himself that the man was not invincible, that he didn't like getting wet. But it was best to appear to go along with him.

'I understand you.'

'Good. There is one small question I have to ask: why should the British Embassy wish to see you this morning and send a car to pick you up and bring you back?'

The orange-seller, thought William. Box was right. 'They asked me if I'd seen the president. They wanted to know what was happening.'

'It is not usual for them to be so curious. The Americans, yes, they wish to know everything. But the British are not usually so interested. They have been trying to contact all sorts of strange people.'

'They are confused.'

'Like the girls, yes. We men understand each other better, don't you think?' Manuel smiled. 'We shall meet soon. It is important that we keep in touch, especially now we are getting on so well.'

His apparent success made William more confident. 'I have a question in return. The man on the beach I used to speak to, the tramp – what has happened to him?'

'Ah yes, the nice old man. He has been re-housed.'

'Where?'

'In suitable accommodation provided by the government. It used to be the responsibility of the Church but, happily, the secular authorities now acknowledge their duties.' Manuel smiled again and stood. 'I should not worry about it if I were you, *Señor* Wooding. That hut of his was really very cold and damp and rather insanitary.'

'But he didn't want to leave it.'

'I'm sure he is happier where he is. He appreciates his new place; he has company there.'

'He's in prison?'

Mañuel appeared to give all his attention to pulling on his gloves. 'I wouldn't call it that.'

'Who shot his dog?'

Mañuel stopped. He had one glove on and held the hand before him, fingers outstretched. 'I did. What is it to you? It was only a dog.'

'Today the dogs,' said William, recalling *Señor* Finn's words.

'What do you mean?'

'Tomorrow the people . . . But he was only a tramp, I suppose.'

'Exactly. *Buenas días, Señor* Wooding.'

William stared through one of the clean panes of glass as the black Mercedes drove away. He had not started on a new pane since this business with Box, nor had he done any work to speak of. It seemed to make little difference whether or not he tried; success or failure depended, as Manuel had just illustrated, on extraneous factors. Anyway, the company, the factory, London were hard to take seriously any more. Perhaps he never had taken them seriously, not really, and only now was he realising it. His job was no longer the point, if it ever had been.

The fate of *Señor* Finn was something he couldn't imagine. But although there was no positive image there was something there all the time, passively present, something that would be sickening to know if he knew it. He kept recalling the lolling, glistening head of the prisoner.

He went downstairs, startling the two girls. Outside, the orange-seller stood with his hands in his pockets. He had not moved during his conversation with the men from the Mercedes and now continued his unstinting stare at the shop door. William was pleased to see that his approach caused consternation.

'*Buenos días, señor*,' he said. The man grunted. 'You have many oranges?'

'*Sí.*'

'But you do not sell many?'

'Enough.'

'I will help you. I will buy all your oranges.'

The man stared.

'Yes, all. We have sacks in the shop to carry them in. I will pay now.' He pulled out his wallet. 'How much?'

'No, *señor, imposible.*'

'Why not?'

'It is bad for trade.'

'I will get the girls to fill the sacks.'

The girls enjoyed the job. It was something to do. They filled the sacks and William carried them in while the orange-seller watched in melancholy silence. When they had cleared his stall he took William's money as if it were a dismissal notice.

Afterwards William sat at his desk and stared again through the cleared panes. The orange-seller remained disconsolately by his empty stall. He had not moved but his posture indicated despondency and confusion. Eventually he looked at his stall, then cautiously back at the shop and then very furtively up at William's window. Finally, like one joining a funeral procession, he took up the handle of the stall and left.

William was home early that evening. It seemed tactful. Besides, he was very tired and he thought that after an explanation to Sally and a meal he would go to bed. He had still not managed to contact her.

She was not there. The flat was tidy, smelt of polish – Angelica's work – and was filled with the warmth and light of the late afternoon sun. The wind had dropped and the clouds had broken up, transforming the day. The sea was a flat pale grey, silvered by the sun and reflecting on the ceilings a clear shifting light. He pottered about for some minutes feeling pleasantly unreal, knowing that if he sat he would sleep.

When Sally returned, she greeted him with a smile and a kiss. 'I was getting worried. I thought you'd either been kidnapped by dancing girls or made president.' She wore cream and black, always a sign with her of confidence and good humour.

'I rang several times but you were teaching.'

'Yes, one of my full days today.' She flung her handbag on to a chair and headed for the kitchen. 'I'm very thirsty. Do you want a drink?'

'Tea, please. Sorry, I should have been making it.'

'I'll do it.'

He sat with his eyes closed and let the sun warm his face, listening to the sounds of water, kettle and 'fridge. He could also hear birds and traffic and, distantly, the sea. It was pleasant to do nothing.

'Angelica was back today,' she called.

'I know, I saw her this morning.'

'She's done the ironing. She must have spent hours on these shirts – she's still not as good as you, though.'

He dozed. Images of Theresa, the sea, the prisoners and coffins galloped in kaleidoscopic succession across his forehead.

'What's your secret?' Sally asked when she came in with the tea.

'What?' He opened his eyes.

'With the ironing. You must give her another lesson, show her what she's doing wrong.'

'I can't. It's temperament.'

'But she must have the patience for it. She's not like me.'

'It needs passion'

'*Passion?*' She laughed.

'Passion for exactitude. You have to like being exact.'

'I'd never thought of it like that.'

He described what had happened the night before. Relief that she wasn't angry and pleasure in talking about it revived him. He even mentioned that he had had breakfast with Theresa. She laughed at what he said about the orange-seller, at first refusing to believe him.

'But that poor dog,' she said when he had finished.

'I know.'

'Max was right. First they shoot the dogs.'

'So was *Señor* Finn.'

'But it really must be getting serious. Max said that there was a convoy of Russian lorries going into the palace this morning and one of the military airfields is now entirely Russian. He said the Americans are evacuating some of their embassy staff.'

The telephone rang. She got up before he could. 'It's Ricardo,' she said.

Ricardo's tone was excited and conspiratorial. 'William?'

'Yes?'

'It's me.'

'Yes.'

'I have a message for you.'

'Yes.'

'Are you listening?'

'Yes.'

'The message is from your friend of the night. I have seen her. She says the important visitors are coming tomorrow night. That is all.'

'Thank you. If you see her tell her I'll be in touch as soon as possible.'

'She has gone home. She is not at work. She will come back tomorrow.'

'Never mind, I'll see her tomorrow.'

'It was all right to telephone you?'

'Yes, you have done well. Thank you.'

'I have not said who she is. I have not used her name.'

'No.'

'Today I spoke to the workers at the factory, and now they have gone back to work.'

William hesitated. 'I heard they had. That was very good. You did very well.'

Ricardo laughed. 'You are pleased with your assistant, eh, William?'

'Very pleased. I could not manage without him.'

'Tonight I will find a new girl-friend.'

'Good hunting.'

'Good hunting for her, too.' Ricardo laughed again. 'I will come into the office soon. Maybe I will find you a car.'

'Good.'

'*Chau*, William.'

'*Chau*.' He told Sally he would have to go out again to warn Box.

'So this honey-trap is on for tomorrow night?'

'Looks like it.'

'But you're so tired. You don't have to tell Box now, do you? Especially as we haven't got a car.'

'I don't have to but I'd rather. There won't be much time tomorrow.' The news had revived him. 'Also, I've got to find him. I'm only assuming he's in the grave because the embassy couldn't get hold of him.'

'Max says that some of the American embassy people have already secretly been told to leave by the government. It hasn't been announced. He says they think they're kicking out the CIA ones, but apparently they're not. They've got it all wrong.'

'I won't be very long. I'll get a taxi.'

She came to the door. 'So it's definitely all on for tomorrow? You'll be exhausted.'

'It'll have to be on if that's when the junta is going. I won't be long, I really won't.'

She kissed him again. 'Make sure you find the right grave. See you later.'

It was still light when he reached the cemetery. The gates were open and people were strolling about. Some were courting couples, others carried flowers. Outside the gates was a stall-holder with a poor and expensive floral selection. William supposed winter was the excuse, then remembered that florists in the city never closed, day or night. It was the custom to present flowers to corpses as soon after death as possible. When the cemetery was shut, the man probably pushed his stall round to the hospital. William bought some stale carnations to make it look more like a graveside visit. He would tell Box the cost so that it could be added to the car; Box would approve of that.

The wooden door of number 1066 looked as they had left it. It was impossible to see in through the grille and it would have seemed odd to peer. Other, presumably genuine, mourners were lingering by the 1030s. There was an old broken flower-pot by the side of the door. William knelt and began scooping earth to fill it.

'Are you in there?' he called softly. There was no answer. He glanced round, knocked and called again. 'Arthur.' There was scrabbling. 'Arthur.'

'What?'

'It's me. William.'

'I know that. What do you want?'

'I've got something to report.'

'Hang on.'

There was more scuffling. William suspected that Box had been sleeping. Presently he saw a pale patch in the gloom behind the grille.

'Can you come in?' asked Box.

'No.'

'There's plenty of room.'

'There are people watching. I'll talk while I'm planting the flowers.'

'What flowers?'

'The flowers I brought for visiting the grave.'

'You'd better take them with you when you go. It might look odd, flowers for the family Bustillo suddenly appearing after all these years.'

'It'll look odder still if I bring them in, put them in a pot and take them away again.'

'Point.'

Box was excited when William told him what had happened. There was more scuffling. He would draft a message for London, he said, and take it to the embassy first thing in the morning. William told him about the embassy's reaction to the last message. Box was furious. They had no right, it was sabotage, he would use the EEC and tell London that night. He was worried, though, about Mañuel's visit. It was good that Mañuel thought he had secured William's cooperation, but the man was dangerous and had to be watched. That was partly why he, Box, had gone to ground – too many people were getting to know, there was activity now and activity attracted attention. It was inevitable in the run-up phase to an operation. With luck, though, Mañuel would be safely nailed with a floosie the following night. But who was to carry out the arrests? It all needed discussion. The four of them – they two plus Theresa and the president – would have to meet tomorrow. Meanwhile he would get on to London. It was very odd not to have had a reply, essential that they got one by H-hour. The whole thing was pointless without follow-up from London.

'Stop now. People are coming,' said William, fiddling with the flower-pot while a family of happy mourners wandered past. The children stared as he tried vainly to make the carnations stand upright. 'How long can you stay in there?' he asked when they had gone.

'Water and rations for three days.'

'Isn't it cold?'

'Sleeping-bag. The coffin's lined.'

'You get in?'

'Of course.'

'What about . . .'

'Polythene bags for emergencies.'

'Anything I can bring you?' He hoped he wouldn't be asked to dispose of the bags.

'You can get me a top-up.' Box's fingers gripped the grille and the door opened sufficiently for his other hand to appear, proffering his silver hip-flask. 'Teachers if you can find any. Otherwise anything as long as it's Scotch.'

'Okay. I may be some time.'

'Just so long as I know it's coming.'

There was a bar not far away. The barman wouldn't sell a bottle of whisky but ill-naturedly agreed to fill the flask with several measures. It was almost dark by then and a man in uniform was about to close the gates.

'We are closing, *señor.*'

William held up the flask. 'For the flowers. One minute. *Gracias.*'

He knelt at the grave again. There was hardly any danger of being seen now. Box's hand reached out from impenetrable darkness.

'Teachers?'

'Bells.'

'I've discovered why no answer from London. Bank Holiday.'

'Sounds more like my head office.'

'Yes, odd. You'd think they would be working, especially since privatisation. Mind you, they all get BMWs now. Have to go away in them, I suppose.'

William paused before getting to his feet. 'Did they give you one?'

'Refused it. I prefer Shanks's pony. Otherwise taxis. More secure because less traceable provided you change at least once in a journey. Mrs B. has a Metro. See you tomorrow.'

The attendant eyed William suspiciously as he passed through the gates. William raised his empty hands. '*Los espiritos tienen sed* – the spirits are thirsty.'

'*Sí, señor.*' The big gates closed behind him.

11

The streets, never very busy even in the rush hour, were unusually empty when William walked to work the next morning. It was sunny and the parrots in the trees below the flat flapped and squawked.

He liked walking along the wide deserted avenues. Perhaps there had been a revolution. If so, it was odd that only he and Sally hadn't known about it. He had woken late and couldn't remember her having the radio on before going to work. An old Dodge approached the traffic lights. For a moment he thought it was Theresa's and, quite ridiculously, his knees began trembling against his trouser-legs. The Dodge cruised through on red.

The shop was shut when he arrived, but that was normal. The orange-seller was not there. This was a small triumph, though William didn't like to think of having put the man out of business. Perhaps there had been an overnight plague or perhaps there was a curfew – but then there would have been troops and tanks patrolling the streets. Presumably that was how one would know there was a curfew. He couldn't remember having seen much newsreel coverage of curfews, no doubt because they were not easily filmed. As with the trembling knees, he was suddenly surprised by an intense spasm of home-sickness. He yearned for England, its greenness, its friendliness, its ordinariness, even its shabbiness. Sprawling, dirty London seemed like a comfortable old dressing-gown which he longed to put on again. Things were normal there; it didn't matter what you did, much, and not at all what you said. He imagined himself showing it all to Theresa.

There was no answer from the factory. He tried a couple of other calls and was thinking that it was past the time for the girls to arrive when his eye fell on the calendar. It was Síerra Blanca Day, a national holiday named after the country's only mountain in honour of a war supposedly fought over its possession. In fact, no war had been fought. Soldiers had been despatched but the enemy had failed to find the mountain in the cloudy region inland. It was acclaimed a great victory.

He worked on some papers for a while. It was increasingly difficult to feel that they had anything to do with him. He would have to feel otherwise pretty soon or else find something different. Meanwhile, there was not much he could usefully do – a good day, therefore, for bringing down governments.

He locked the shop and headed for Maria's. There were a few people about now. He remembered reading that Síerra Blanca Day was celebrated by enormous family meals beginning at lunchtime and lasting well into the evening. There were no processions or parades and the entire population became comatose. The incidence of strokes and heart attacks increased sharply during the days following. This was viewed not with horror but as an appropriate end for people whose appreciation of life was primarily gastronomic.

Theresa's Dodge was in the same place. To William it was now a lopsided and lovable creature, not, like most mechanical things, an enemy. There were no stalls under the trees in the square. The house looked asleep but as he approached he saw that the door was open. Perhaps, like the florists, Maria's served a need that had no end.

Inside there was a smell of furniture polish. Sunbeams slanted through the windows on to the floorboards and the battered, comfortable furniture. William felt suddenly and intensely happy, a physical sensation that caused him to remain standing just inside the door, unmoving. It reminded him of something from childhood, but he could not remember what.

'Ah, *Señor* Wooding, a welcome surprise.' El Lizard spoke from the shadow by the bar where he was doing something to the till.

'A beautiful morning.'

'It is Síerra Blanca Day. It is always beautiful, but everyone is inside preparing for the feast.'

'Are you having a feast?'

'We cater for after the feast. You want Theresa?'

'Yes, please.'

'It is very early still. I don't know if she is available.'

'No, I mean just to talk, you know?'

'Ah, to talk.' El Lizard nodded ponderously. 'I will send for her. Please go through. I will send brandy.'

'This time I must pay you.'

El Lizard smiled. 'No, *señor*. You bring business and honour to our house. We are proud of our connection.'

William walked through to the dance room and sat at one of the tables. Presently the clinking of crockery announced the trembling waiter with coffees and brandies. The cups and glasses shivered as if on board ship.

It struck him that there was no reason why his assumption that she would be at the club should have been right. It was surely more natural for her to be at home in the shanties at this time of the morning. The club was unlikely to do business early in the day, though perhaps there were girls on call for twenty-four hours. Perhaps there was even a duty roster. It was curious how indifferently he could think of this. He wondered how much Carlos had paid her, which reminded him that she had said she would take money from Box. Quite rightly. Box would approve. William approved, now.

She came quickly across the dance floor through alternating bars of sun and shadow. She was smiling and when he stood she kissed him.

'I knew you would come,' she said.

'I wasn't sure you would be here this early.'

'I wanted to bath. It's easier here than at home.' She laughed. 'Ricardo telephoned you?'

'Yes. With relish.'

'I couldn't think how else to get hold of you. I didn't want to ring you at home and the only other way was to go to the cemetery to see if Arthur was there.'

'He is now. He's living there.'

'Is he happy?'
'I think so. I took him some whisky.'
'He has some interesting ghosts for company.'
'Have you ever seen a ghost?'
'Yes, many. Have you?'
'No.'
'You see ghosts of the living as well as the dead. They are quite common. I saw you before you came here this morning.'
William's hands remained on the coffee pot.
'You were standing just inside the front door when I got here,' she continued. 'You were standing in the sun, staring. At first I thought it really was you, but then I realised it wasn't.'
'How?'
'I don't know, it's just different. It's more an impression of someone than a vision, though you do see them as well. Anyway' – she smiled – 'that was how I knew you would come.'
'I did stand there, just as you described, just now.'
'Of course, but I saw you first.' She laughed. 'You see, I know what you do before you do it.' She took the coffee from him. 'It is very strange for a man to serve me.'
'A nice change.'
'I think so, I'm not sure.'
'You know, I really am in love with you. Absolutely. Hopelessly. Without limit.' He could not help smiling.
'That is also a nice change.'
'What do you mean? Hundreds of men must have fallen in love with you.'
'Yes, but usually they are in love with me only because they want to sleep with me.'
'Well, I want to sleep with you, too.'
'Yes, but you are different.'
'How?'
'You are William.' She put her hand on his knee. 'Many women must have fallen in love with you.'
'I don't know. I don't think so.' It was a novel thought. She took her hand away before he could cover it with his.

'What about your banker? He must have been in love with you.'

'Yes.'

'And you with him?'

'I only really loved him when he was dead.' She sipped and smiled. 'Now you are looking serious and sad.'

'I am serious.'

'It is not necessary to look it, it never helps. I know when you are serious. Is that not enough?'

'Have some brandy.'

'It is very early.'

'It is.' He handed her a glass. 'To our new government.'

'Our revolution.'

'Are you serious about that?'

She raised her eyebrows. 'Of course.'

She told him that Carlos had sent a message to the club saying that he and the junta would come in late afternoon or early evening. There was a feast in the palace for their families, after which the menfolk would repair to the club to continue drinking and to have some girls. This was a tradition inherited from the previous government. The message had also said that the president expected a special effort to be made. She thought this must be a coded reference to themselves but El Lizard, not knowing of the plot, was worried about it. He thought something extra was required but didn't know what – whether more girls, different girls, unusual clothes or some sort of live act. He was keen to find out but frightened to go to the palace himself. He had never been there and, besides, did not know the new leaders as well as the old. He did not know their tastes.

'So you could offer to go for him and talk to Carlos. Then you can plan,' she said.

William thought. 'We need to know who's coming, we need to know who's going to make the arrests and where. And whether soldiers or police and which ones can be trusted.'

'Soldiers can be trusted if the president tells them. He is popular with the army.'

'What about the security police?'

'I don't know about them.'

'And where will it happen and what will they do? I mean – physically – where?'

'Easy. I will show you.' She led him to the front of the house and up the main staircase, a grand construction with polished banisters and a faded red carpet. On the first floor were rooms where she said people played cards or were 'private together'. The two floors above were bedrooms and massage rooms.

A small staircase at the back led to the top floor and gave on to two corridors, each with doors opening off at regular intervals. She explained that they had been the maids' bedrooms many years before the house was a club, before anyone living could remember. Then, a year or so ago, they had been converted into massage rooms.

'That must have been expensive.'

'It cost nothing. The Minister of the Interior wanted it. Government workmen came.'

In alcoves by the windows there were armchairs and small tables. These, she said, were where people sat and drank while waiting to go in. She took him into the first of the rooms. It was on two levels, with varnished floorboards and clean white walls. On the first level, to the right of the door, was a bath set low in the floor. Leaning against the wall beside it was an inflated lilo. On the second level were two armchairs and a large round bed with, above it, a circular ceiling mirror. Wall mirrors formed the corner behind the bed. High on one wall was an air-conditioner, and on the other a large clock which looked like old school furniture. There was no window.

'We have twelve of these.'

'Do you like them?'

'*Sí*, they are much better than the other rooms. Much cleaner.' It was stuffy. She switched on the air-conditioner, which started with a clatter and quickly settled into a monotonous rushing sound.

'Why the clock?' he asked.

'So the girl knows the time. A massage is an hour. If

the man wants more, he must pay for it – except that the government men pay nothing, of course.'

'Do they usually want massages, the government men?'

'Always. And not only hand massage, they want full body massage.'

'What is that?'

'It's when you take off your clothes and rub their body with yours. It is more expensive.'

'Does it stop there?'

'They can have sex if they want it and if the girl wants. Normally they have to pay her extra, not the club. They pay the club for the massage. But the government people do not pay.' She refolded a towel on a rail by the bath. 'You never had massage in England?'

'No. They have them in England but they're not . . . well, I don't know what they're like. I don't know what happens.'

'Have you been with girls like – from places like this?'

'No.'

She smiled. 'You are not like other men, William.'

'Is that good or bad?'

She took his arm. 'Good, of course. Now, please switch off the air-conditioner. We must go downstairs.'

She thought the massage rooms would be the best place for the arrests to take place. The generals would be naked then and naked men were always more vulnerable. They would be ashamed and would not resist. They would not have their guards with them. They could be photographed and the photographs published if they misbehaved whenever they were let out of prison. And the girls would like it because they would be famous.

'You sound as if you've done it before,' he said.

She laughed. 'No, but when you start to imagine many things become possible and why not do them? What else is the future? The government will get worse, I will get old, the president will tire of me and I will live at home with my family and we will all be poor even if I make money now.'

'There is an alternative. I offered—'

'You are married to a nice girl. You cannot marry me and be cruel to her.'

'It might not be cruel. It's very common in England.'

'It would be cruel to make her unhappy. It would hurt her, wouldn't it?'

'I expect so.' He thought. 'But I don't really know any more.'

He wanted to go on talking but she walked quickly downstairs. El Lizard was at the bottom. Theresa told him that William had been inspecting the massage rooms in advance of the visits that afternoon and that he would now, if El Lizard wished, talk to his friend the president in order to find out if there were any special requirements. It needed only that El Lizard should ring the palace, refer to the message he had received, and say that someone was coming to discuss it.

Her tone was direct and business-like. El Lizard was obsequious and grateful to William.

'I am delighted you had time to inspect our suite of massage rooms,' he said,with the faintest glint of humour in his lidded eye. 'I hope everything was satisfactory.'

'*Sí, gracias.*'

'Theresa is an expert masseuse.'

'She is a remarkable lady.'

El Lizard's head dropped. '*Gracias, señor.* We try to do our best.'

He went off to the telephone. William looked at Theresa but she was doing something to her hair. When he did catch her eye she smiled from beneath her raised arm. 'You will come also this evening?'

'Yes, with Arthur. We must see that it works and that you are all right.'

'I shall have to be with Carlos.'

'Of course.'

In the palace reception rooms military personnel and uniformed functionaries guarded, aided, prevented, bullied, cringed and lounged. A group of civilians wearing suits talked in low voices amidst the thick cloud of cigarette and cigar smoke. They were, William learned, members of the chamber of deputies, the body that had replaced the elected parliament – summoned even on Síerra Blanca Day to approve an urgent measure connected with the press. Approval would be automatic and they had been told they would be home in time for the feast.

William was directed to the side door that led to the president's living quarters. As he followed the soldier who accompanied him he recognised the passage where they had smuggled in Carlos. He was shown into a white-panelled room overlooking a small courtyard of rose bushes and lawn. French windows gave on to the courtyard where Carlos sat eating breakfast at a white table. He wore a white silk dressing-gown and waved William to a chair with the same gesture that dismissed the soldier.

He held up a silver pot. 'I hoped it would be you. Tea, or have you had breakfast?'

'Yes and yes.'

Carlos smiled and poured untidily, splashing tea on to the tablecloth. He had a copy of the *New Yorker* on his lap.

'A lot of people here today,' William said. 'I was surprised.'

'Yes. I've got to sign something later. So I'm told.' Carlos smiled. 'I think they've all been informed that the junta has been in all-night session and that we're still wrestling with our consciences over this new measure. In fact, we're going to meet later and make an announcement. I don't suppose the others are up yet apart from Herrera, of course. He's around. He always is.'

'Will he come here?'

'No. He knows I don't like to talk business so early in the day. Or later, really.' He smiled again. 'He's such a bore, Manuel. Always so serious, though he can be quite charming. I can't imagine how he will take it when we lock him up. Have you come from Theresa?'

'Yes.'

'I assumed you'd get the message. How is she?'

'Very well.'

Carlos looked thoughtful. He pushed out his long lower lip with his finger. 'She's not the most beautiful woman I've ever had. That was an English girl from Wolverhampton, strangely enough. But Theresa is probably the best all round. Probably. It's too early to say, of course. My wife is also beautiful.'

'I didn't know you were married.'

'Naturally, I am married. An unmarried president is inconceivable. That's why I tell Mañuel he could never be president even if there were no other reason. Even an unmarried officer is unusual. That is also why I have three children. But I keep my family in another part of the palace, for security reasons. Also, one needs one's privacy.'

William looked around the courtyard. 'It's very pleasant here.'

'Yes, I am quite fond of it. It's quiet, which is important to me. If only one didn't have to work. Mind you, it's not really work. It's just talking to people. That's all you do when you're president. Talk, talk, talk and sign things. That's how I became president, just by talking. But my ranch is even more pleasant than this. You must come there when we have everything sorted out here.' He leaned back and stretched, exposing the tanned skin of his chest and stomach. 'What will you do with my generals?'

'That was what I was going to ask you.'

'I thought Special Information Services plc would have a plan.'

'I'm sure they will – have – but I haven't talked to Arthur yet. I wanted to find out from you what was happening first.'

'Arthur, yes. He is an excellent fellow. I like him. He will have a plan. But no more coffins, please.' Carlos laughed. 'Tell him we are all having a big feast with our wives and families here and afterwards we will come to the club. There will not be any guards because it is a holiday and a celebration and no one knows. The arrests will have to be made by my old regiment. They are the only ones I can trust. They are very loyal to me. The security police troops are not controlled by me and even other parts of the army I am no longer so sure about. Tell Arthur he will need to plan how this is to be done.'

'And what then?'

'When my colleagues are in prison I shall be very pleased.'

'But what after that?'

'What do you mean?'

'What we do when you've locked them up. What next?'

Carlos looked irritated. 'I head the new government, as I head this one, but with new poeple.'

'Which new people? How? I mean, how does it actually happen?'

'I will make a broadcast. I will speak to the people.'

'But you might need help. I mean, if the security police or the Russians or Cubans—'

Carlos held up a hand. 'Thank you, William. You have no experience of politics. Things can be done. Also, you do not know how my people love me. They will support me. And in order to get help from your country, I will write to your Queen. Your secret service can give her the message.' He picked up a small hand-bell and rang it. 'They are used to passing her messages, I suppose?'

'I don't know.'

'Please do not look so worried. Believe me, I know how to manage these things. I will write a letter and tomorrow your government can send warships and soldiers and lots of money.'

'I was just wondering whether the Queen is the right person.'

'The prime minister, do you think?'

'Possibly.'

'But I am both a political figure and a head of state. So I am like both of them in one.'

'Either, then.'

'I will send it: "To Whom It May Concern". That is the formula, I believe?' He chuckled. A servant appeared and he ordered pen and paper to be brought. 'Normally, of course, I dictate, but this time perhaps writing would be more discreet. I am enjoying this. Are you?'

'Yes.'

'Especially as I shall make love with Theresa while the arrests are being made. Last night I made love with my wife. She surprises me sometimes. But the secret is not to do it very often with one's wife. One needs variety otherwise one loses interest and becomes impotent. The feast should be good.'

Paper and pen were brought on a tray. Carlos's flippancy was affecting William; he could feel himself becoming nonchalant when in fact he wanted to be filled with enthusiasm. It seemed to him that he had not done much in his life and now at last he was – or hoped he was – he wanted it to be big, dramatic and serious, not silly. He began to see Box's dog-like dedication in a better light.

'There.' Carlos passed his letter across the table. His hand was elaborate and childlike, with many loops. The letter read: 'To Whom It May Concern: I, Carlos Calvaros, President and General, request all such assistance in maintaining my country as I may require. Sígned, Carlos Calvaros.'

'It is quite concise, don't you think?'

'Very.'

'Did you know I had trained to be a barrister in London?'

'No.'

'That is where I learned to write legal letters. But I didn't train for very long. It was not necessary. You will give it to the Queen or the prime minister?'

'Okay.'

Carlos rested one hand on his bare chest and gazed at the roses. William could not decide what, if anything, went on behind the happy loose smile. Perhaps it was better to be inconsequential and invincibly vain. Carlos looked like a man without a worry on his mind.

'I'll go and find Arthur,' William said.

'You will send him to me?'

'Yes.'

'He will have to sort out all the details. I can't be bothered with them. They obscure my vision.'

'Arthur is keen on detail.'

'Tell him to come as you came. No one will realise today. Things are very slack. *Buenas días*.'

The taxi dropped William by the flower-seller outside the cemetery and he bought another bunch. A larger number of people were strolling there that morning and children ran in and out of the avenues and mausolea. As he walked he noticed there were no women amongst the strollers, then that nearly all the children were boys. Presumably the women and girls were at home preparing the feast. Next he realised that no one was mourning. Talk and laughter, the squeals of children, cigarette and cigar smoke filled the air. They had all come, as Theresa had said she used to, because it was a nice place.

'Looking for me?'

Box stood proprietorially in the entrance to a large gothic sepulchre, smoking a cigar. He had one hand in his pocket and looked like a man taking his Sunday constitutional in an English suburb, at a time when constitutionals were regularly and properly taken. William stepped off the cobbled path.

'Came out for my morning exercise,' Box said. 'Got caught out. Place suddenly filled with people. Can't get back in without causing a scandal or religious sighting.'

'Just as well you saw me. I'd have been shouting into the grave otherwise.'

'Come in here. We won't be overlooked.'

The sepulchre was an architectural copy in miniature of a medieval European cathedral, complete with gargoyles. They had to stoop to get in the door, William particularly. Inside were two stone seats running the length of the nave, each with room for five or six people. There was also a number of old coca-cola tins and bits of newspaper. It was damp and dark but not as bad as the grave.

'Still no news from London,' said Box. 'I don't understand it.'

'The embassy must have put its spoke in.'

"No doubt. But they can't stop the message being sent. Not allowed. London can contact me independently. They know the EEC is live now. But nothing. Not a dickie. I don't get it.'

Box sounded seriously worried. From nearby came the squeals of children. William pulled out Carlos's letter.

'I've got news, anyway.'

Box leaned against the wall of the sepulchre with his cigar in one hand and the letter in the other. William wondered if he ever tired of his job. Presumably he had done this sort of thing often enough. Was it exciting? Did it pall? Was it worth it? How was he regarded by his colleagues? Were they all like him? Was he senior or junior? What did he do with his time off? Did he have any? It was hard to imagine that he did. Arthur never seemed to be anything other than what he was doing, and that completely.

'One problem about going to the palace,' Box said. 'I am in need of a wash. You may have noticed.'

'No, no.'

'Shaving was all right – I could do that off the batteries – but not washing. Clothes are all right, too. I've kept these uncrumpled. Can we go down to the beach, do you think?'

'Come back to my flat. Sally went off to work as usual this morning, so her school must be open today. She knows about you, anyway.'

'You told her?'

'Yes. Was that wrong?'

'Not necessarily.'

'Angelica, the maid, might be there.'

'She doesn't—'

'No.'

'Good. Never know with domestics.'

A scream filled the sepulchre and William's stomach contracted as if he had been punched. Box ducked and dropped his cigar. The child in the doorway ran crying back to his father.

Box picked up his cigar. 'Never done that before. Must

be getting old. Time we weren't here. Don't forget your flowers.'

As they left the sepulchre the child was still audible from somewhere behind the other tombs. He was being comforted by his father, who was asking to be shown the two spirits.

'You must have done a lot of operations like this,' said William.

'Like and not like. The same but different.'

'Do you ever get bored?'

'Not bored. Weary sometimes. You have to make yourself keep going. Remind yourself of why you're doing it. Like a war, it's not all battle, it's mainly just keeping going and waiting. Only this war never ends.'

William didn't like to think of Box being made weary. To be properly himself, he should be enthusiastic. 'Why do you do it?' he asked.

'Think of everything good.'

'Everything?'

'Everything you can think of in life that's good. In the end it all depends on one thing: having the freedom to choose it. That means there must also be the freedom to choose what's bad. But it's what we stand for. And it's what all creeds are against. All. They fear people choosing for themselves.'

'You sound as if you've been through this once or twice before.'

'Only in my head. On planes, in hotels. Lot of time for navel-gazing. Different for the chaps back in London, of course. They're too busy with paperwork to think about why they're doing it.' Box stubbed his cigar into the ground, grinding it thoroughly with his foot. 'But this silence from London worries me. I shouldn't admit that I'm worried, of course, so this is very much *entre nous*.' He emphasised the two words. 'I have a growing feeling of operating alone, with no one behind me. Never had it before. It's my first operation since privatisation. Perhaps it's the new style – more autonomy and all that – but it's odd. Maybe I'm getting out of touch, getting past it, but you'd think they'd be keen. At least, if they didn't want us to do it you'd think they'd jolly well say so. Puts us in an awkward position with Carlos, not knowing what support will be forthcoming.'

'Perhaps they're organising all that now.'

'Perhaps.'

'Mind you, I haven't heard from my head office, either. Perhaps the revolution is in London.'

'Twenty yards.'

'What?'

'Twenty yards. Gap between us from now on. I'll follow.'

They had reached the cemetery gates. Box was already dropping back.

Angelica was not in the flat but Box walked from room to room opening cupboards and looking behind doors.

'Checking that we're alone,' he explained. 'Always a wise precaution. Don't want to find gorillas in the kitchen.' He inspected the 'fridge. 'Nice flat, good views, not overlooked. Vulnerable to bugging, though.'

'Is it?'

'Flats above and below. They can drill through. Mind if I turn the radio on?'

'No, it's in the bedroom.'

'I know.'

Box fetched the radio and placed it on the dining-room table. He fiddled with it until he found classical music, then listened for a while. 'Mahler's Resurrection Symphony. Possibly the most . . .' his voice trailed off. He stood looking out of the window, his pale face rapt, his gaze somewhere between the parrot-favoured trees and the blue and white sea. When the symphony finished he remained as he was.

'A good view,' said William after a while.

Box nodded. 'One can live on a view. Almost.'

Mahler had given way to the radio news, read by a woman whose voice was famed throughout the country. She read slowly, caressing the Spanish vowels. It was a list of favourable trade statistics. Since government control of the media had been tightened, all internal news was good. Foreign news was good if it featured what were called fraternal allies, bad if it featured the United States. The woman's voice curled above, around, below and between the statistics like an endless tongue. She had made it the country's most popular station.

'One can live for a voice,' Box added with a smile.

'I think one could.'

'Almost.'

Box took his shower. He was still in it when William heard the key in the front door and Sally entered. He was as surprised as she and even started guiltily. Behind her stood the tall figure of Max Hueffer.

William and Sally each said, 'Hello,' to each other, rather stiffly.

'I didn't realise it was a public holiday,' he said. 'I was at work but no one else was.'

'Same here. We had no students. Max came in and told me. He's come to pick up a book.'

Max shook hands. 'Nice to meet you again, William. Sorry to walk in on your holiday. I knew it was one but so many of our students said they were coming in that I thought we should stay open. Then they didn't show, not one of them. Typical. I should have known.' His eyes, enlarged by spectacles, were kindly and warm.

'What are these?' Sally pointed at the flowers William had bought to place outside Box's grave.

'Ah. They're mine – yours.'

'Mine?'

'Yes, I bought them this morning.'

She looked at him. 'Thank you.' She picked them up and went into the kitchen.

William didn't want to mention Box in front of Max. 'Warmer now,' he said.

'You ain't seen nothing yet. You can boil lobsters in your sweat in the summer here.'

'Drown them in mine.'

'Can lobsters drown?'

'Well, I daresay they can have too much of a good thing.'

Max smiled.

'Which book?' asked William.

'Have you left the shower running?' called Sally from the kitchen.

'Yes, yes, I have.' He hurried into the kitchen and explained.

'So the flowers aren't mine?' she whispered.

'No – well – yes, they are now. They weren't originally – but you can have them.'

She smiled as she cut the stems under the tap. 'I might have known.'

'I'll buy some especially for you tomorrow.'

'What are you going to do this afternoon?'

'Arrest the government.'

She stopped cutting. 'You're really going ahead with it?'

'Yes.'

'Isn't it dangerous?

'Maybe. A bit. But the difficult part will be getting help afterwards. The president is sending an appeal via us.' He showed her Carlos's note. She dried her hands to take it. The water in the shower stopped. 'I'd better warn Arthur,' he added quietly. He went along the corridor and knocked softly on the shower door, which opened at once to reveal Box's small face. Pink as a lobster now, William thought. He whispered what had happened.

'I can't move while he's here,' said Box. 'He's CIA. He'll smell a rat. Then they'll try and barge in and do it themselves.'

'CIA? How do you know?'

'Professional instinct.'

William could hear Sally talking to Max. 'He may stay some time.'

'Is there another way out?'

'Only out on to the balcony. There's nowhere to go from there.'

'Try to get him on to the balcony so that I can slip out. Knock twice.' The door closed.

William went back along the corridor. Sally was in the kitchen again and Max was using the telephone.

'Okay, about five minutes,' he said as William entered, and put down the receiver.

'It's better out on the balcony,' said William, unlocking the sliding windows. 'Come and have a look.'

'I'd rather use your bathroom first, if I may.'

'Of course, yes, I'll show you.'

He led Max past the shower room to the lavatory. When the door was safely closed he touched the shower door twice. Box opened it and William pointed to the lavatory door. Box nodded, retreated and reappeared wearing a pair of Y-fronts and carrying his shoes and clothes. His wet hair was plastered thinly against his scalp. He tiptoed along the corridor and into the kitchen. There was a small gasp from Sally. He backed out, still holding up his shoes and clothes and half bowing in apology. William showed him to the front door. 'Good luck at the palace,' he whispered.

'What?' There were drops of water on Box's pink face.

'Good luck at the palace.'

'Meet me at Maria's at six unless I ring you.'

'Right.' As he closed the door William could hear Max talking to Sally in the kitchen. The telephone rang. An American asked for Max. 'It's for you, Max,' he called.

Max took the receiver. 'Hello. Yes. Fine.' He put it down. 'I have to go.'

'Already?'

He held out his hand. 'Nice to see you again, William. I hope we get the chance for a longer talk next time.' He took a couple of paces towards the kitchen. ''Bye, Sally. I have to go.'

'What? Already?' Sally came out of the kitchen.

William opened the door. Box, still clutching his clothes, was waiting by the lift.

'Something's cropped up,' Max was saying. 'I'll see you tomorrow.'

William's sign language was vigorous but unnecessary. Box scuttled down the stairs. As he turned the first corner one of his shoes fell and bounced noisily ahead of him. The lift came. 'See you, William,' said Max, getting into it.

'Yes, goodbye.' He wondered whether Box would have the sense to pause on the way down or whether they would meet at the bottom. He shut the door and went back to the kitchen. 'That was close.'

'I nearly dropped the vase when he came in with his Y-fronts. He's rather sweet, isn't he?'

'He thinks Max must be CIA.'

'What on earth for?'

'Instinct, he says.' He noticed his copy of *First Among Equals* lying by the sink.

'Oh, Max has forgotten his book,' said Sally. 'Your book. You don't mind, do you? I said you wouldn't.'

'What does he want it for?'

'To read. I told him we had it.'

'Wouldn't have thought it was his sort of thing.'

'Really? Why not?'

William shrugged, picked up the book and put it down, while Sally took the vase of flowers through to the dining room and put them on the table. 'There. I wish you'd go to the cemetery every day.' She smiled. 'Now, tell me all. I only understood half of what you were saying.'

12

William was at the club at six. There were a few more people on the streets but for many the big feast was still not finished. It was a clear evening and the city had an air of repletion and calm. An aeroplane climbed in a widening curve from the airport inland – probably the twice-weekly flight to Rio, he thought. From all that he had heard, he was happy not to be in Rio. It sounded too big and noisy and violent; too much happened there.

Theresa and Ines and about half a dozen other girls were in the dance room. The piano was open but no one sat at it. They all sat in a group on and by the stage, drinking from cups.

Ines called out as soon as she saw him. 'What do you do here? Do you come with the president and the generals? I hope so.' She stood and held up her big face to be kissed. He did so three times on the cheeks, as seemed to be the custom. 'I would rather massage you than a horrible old general,' she said.

The girls laughed. Theresa had smiled at his approach but was not looking at him now. He smiled back at them. they were all attractive. Indeed, the effect of the group was to enhance the attractiveness of each. He felt like a clumsy interloper amidst flowers, afraid to move a foot.

'Would you like some tea?' asked Ines.

'That's really tea?' His surprise was so genuine that they all laughed again. 'I'd love some, thank you.'

One of the girls hurried into the kitchen.

'Have you had your feast?' asked Ines.

'No – well, not a big feast. Only a snack.' He had had sandwiches with Sally after Max and Arthur had gone.

There was a chorus of concern. 'But you should have a big feast today. It is traditional,' Ines said.

'Unless like us he is working,' said one of the other girls.

'I was.'

'No, it is holiday for you.'

William explained how he had turned up to work. They were curious about the shop and the business. Did he own it, was it a big business, could you travel if you worked for his business, did he have a telephone of his own? The girl returned with his tea and he sat on the edge of the stage. The tea was almost undrinkably strong and the milk was off. Theresa remained quiet and withdrawn. She had tied up her hair and her cheeks had a sculptured look, their bones more prominent. Her eyes were languorous and veiled and as always he had to keep himself from staring.

El Lizard appeared, grinning, nodding and rubbing his hands. '*Señor* Wooding, you are very welcome.' The girls made way and he seated himself next to William. 'Are the generals nearly ready?' he asked confidentially.

'Nearly, when I left,' said William. 'One or two wanted to come then, the others wanted to wait a while.'

'You come to see that everything is okay?'

'Yes.'

'I think you will find everything is okay.'

'I think so.'

'The girls are very beautiful.'

'They are.'

El Lizard's lips parted. 'Expert at massage. You will sample for yourself, I hope?'

'If I have time.'

The girls were whispering. Ines nodded and looked at William.

'Please,' said Ines to El Lizard, 'we have tea, we have you, we have piano – can we have tea dance before we start work?'

'Tea dance?'

They all looked hopeful. El Lizard glanced at William. 'I think so,' said William. 'It will warm them up.'

El Lizard's head dropped and rose solemnly. 'Yes, yes, they are better warm.'

They all got up, laughing and talking. El Lizard approached the piano. He gazed at the keyboard as at a friend dressed for burial, then sat and began abruptly with a cheerful waltz. Ines and another girl started dancing together. The others joined them and soon only Theresa was left. William raised his eyebrows at her. She smiled and nodded.

He fumbled the first few steps. As he put his arm around her and took her hand he could again feel his knees trembling against his trouser legs. It was ridiculous. He knew her well enough by now. The effect should have worn off with time instead of getting worse. The other girls danced around them, their dresses swishing. Perhaps loose dresses made it easier to massage, he thought. Theresa wore a dark pleated skirt and cream blouse that emphasised her breasts. With her hair up, she looked like somebody's dauntingly efficient and glamorous PA. He felt the pressure of her hand on his shoulder and of her stomach against his as she pressed and manoeuvred him through his hesitant steps.

'Sorry,' he said. 'I *can* waltz but today I can't.'

'You are nervous. You're crushing my hand.'

'Sorry.'

'Arthur is here.'

'What?'

'He's hiding upstairs in one of the massage rooms, the last on the left. He's been to the palace and it's all going ahead. He wants to speak to you.'

'Do you know what time they're coming?'

'They'll come when they get rid of their wives and children, which should be soon. They'll be full of food and drink and talk and cigars. Pleased with themselves. The soldiers from Carlos's regiment will arrive afterwards; Arthur has organised it. We will have to give a signal when they are all being massaged so that they can be arrested naked and at the same time.'

'It sounds unreal.'

'Arthur is very determined about it.'

'I'm sure he is.'

'We must be serious. None of the girls knows, it will be a big surprise.'

The other girls continued to swish around, laughing whenever they made mistakes. Ines called out that Theresa should not have all the men all the time. The decrepit waiter stood in the door with a tray under his arm. The last of the afternoon sun shone through a window in an adjoining room, reflecting off the polished floorboards on to the girls' twinkling legs.

Ricardo appeared behind the waiter in the doorway. He grinned and waved at William. El Lizard motioned to him to go away but when he saw him wave to William he made a brief apologetic gesture.

'I wonder what he wants here today,' said William.

'He wants a woman.'

'You think so?'

'He's very arrogant. He thinks that because his father is in the army, his family is very good. They are not really so good and they owe much money.'

'You know them?'

'My banker knew his grandfather.'

'Well, he'll be disappointed today. The girls will be busy.'

'Not too disappointed. There'll be something left over for him. There will be more girls than customers.'

William smiled. 'You don't like him, do you?'

'He made Ines pregnant and it cost her much money. But still she goes with him.'

William didn't want to know more. He pulled her closer and she pressed herself willingly against him. 'Pelvis to pelvis,' she said with a smile. 'This is correct dancing – also easier. You can feel where the other person is gone.'

When El Lizard had stopped playing Ricardo walked over, smiling from girl to girl.

'Hi, William.'

'Hello, Ricardo.'

'You have no feast today?'

'No, I went to work. I didn't know about the holiday.'

Ricardo laughed. 'You should have asked me. I would have told you. My family is still eating but I wanted different food. Can I talk to you?'

The girls had clustered around El Lizard at the piano and Theresa began to go towards them but Ricardo motioned her to stay. 'Is it true that the president and the generals are coming?' he whispered.

William hesitated. 'Yes.'

'I will stay and help you.'

'But Mañuel Herrera will be here. You don't want him to see, do you?'

'I will tell him I have come to see what you do on your holiday. He will like that.'

El Lizard began playing a quickstep. Ricardo made off towards the girls.

'Does he really report to Manuel?' asked Theresa.

'Yes, but he tells me about it. He wants to help us.'

'You trust him?'

'I think so. Do you?'

'I don't like him.'

'He doesn't know what we're doing, anyway.'

'You ought to go to Arthur. They will be here soon.'

The intimacy of the dance had gone. 'I'll see you later,' he said.

'Yes.'

He put his hand on her arm. A minute before he had been happy but now he felt sick with apprehension. 'Don't worry,' he told her, as if it were she that felt sick.

'I am not worried. I am tired. It's the thought of pretending again. It's very tiring having to pretend you like something.'

'It'll soon be over. You won't have to do it anymore.'

'Perhaps.' For a moment her features became heavier and she seemed to sag. Then she squeezed his hand and smiled.

'It doesn't matter. We will make it happen. It will happen.'

The door of the last massage room on the left was

locked. William knocked and said who he was and Box, spruce and dapper, let him in. The room was identical with the one Theresa had shown him except that on the round bed was Box's open briefcase and a number of papers.

'You got away then?' William asked.

'Got away?'

'From the flat. Max Hueffer didn't see you?'

'No, thank God. They'd be in like a shot if they knew what we were up to.'

'Are you sure he's CIA?'

'Positive.' Box nodded. His moustache looked freshly clipped. His clothes, his bearing, his briefcase and papers all suggested a visiting accountant. 'People like Hueffer don't run language schools in places like this. What else would he be doing here?'

'I don't know. But you've never set eyes on him, have you?'

'Yes, I have. Outside your flat, more than once. He's interested in your wife.'

'Sally?'

'That is what you call her, isn't it? Yes, well, she works for him, we know that much. But I reckon he reckons you're up to something, and he's trying to find out through her what it is. He'll know you know the president and he'll know you work for British Intelligence.'

'How?'

'Because of your company. It's what everyone else thinks, isn't it?'

'Yes, but they're wrong.'

'Are they?'

'Well, not now, no, but they were. They've got no good reason for being right. It's unfair.'

Box patted William's arm. 'There's a lot that's unfair in this man's world. Have a seat.'

'I'd rather walk.'

He paced the room while Box sat on the bed sorting through his papers.

'With you in a moment,' Box said. 'Just putting my affairs in order.'

'What do you mean?'

'Will, expenses, that sort of thing.'

'Is that necessary?'

'It may be.'

'Shouldn't you have done that in England?'

'The will, yes, but I was sent out in a rush. Don't want Mrs B. to be inconvenienced if I'm killed, so I'll do it now. I'll ask you to be a witness if you'll be so good. Have you done one?'

'No.'

'It's not too late, you know. Expenses, too. You must let me know of any more you've incurred. Estimated cost of replacing your car, for instance. Any hiring you may have to do meanwhile. If anything happens to me I'd like you to see that these get back to the embassy. They'll send them on. You'll get what's owing to you in due course. Also a bonus for Theresa.'

'Is this the first time you've tried to bring down a government?'

'Outside Africa, yes.'

'What other preparations are you making? I mean, guns—'

'Never carry them. More a liability than an asset. Got my shoes, though.' He tapped them. 'Special shoes, remember?'

'Ah, yes.' William resumed his pacing. 'What's going to happen?'

Box spoke without looking up. 'Fairly straightforward. The girls will bring them all up here to be massaged. You stay in this room until you get the signal from Theresa that they're all in an appropriate state of undress and helplessness. You then come downstairs to me and I give the signal to the officer from Carlos's regiment who will be waiting with his men in nearby streets. They will come in and make the arrests. The officer is the chap we met the other night with the hearse. The prisoners will then be taken to the palace and Carlos will make an announcement on state radio and television. He will say that there was an attempted coup involving a foreign power, that the conspirators are all under arrest and that he is assuming full powers until a new government is appointed. Meanwhile, the army will have been instructed to disarm the security police, and the Russians, Cubans and anyone else we think of are to be given notice to quit. Carlos will then make a personal appeal to the Western democracies for aid and will summon the British ambassador to ensure our message gets through to the appropriate quarters in London.'

Box had spoken while totting up a list of figures. He continued counting when he had finished.

'Have you always been able to do that?' asked William.

'What?'

'Count and speak simultaneously.'

'Yes, Can't everybody?'

'No.'

'I'm sure they can if they try.'

'The plan sounds very – well – simple.'

'Coups always are. There's no subtle way of mounting one. They're either simple and successful or simple and catastrophic. Just hope the embassy and London do what they should. Sad to say, I don't trust either.'

'What did Carlos say?'

'Agreed with everything. Very easy chap to work with. I even wrote his broadcast for him. Mind you, I think his mind was more on getting his way with Theresa again. All he had to do was sort out his old regiment.'

'Can they be trusted?'

'I think so. We have no choice. Mind you, they haven't been told exactly what's going on. They'll find out at the last minute. But they should be loyal. They hate Herrera and the security police even more than the rest of the army and they're very protective of Carlos.'

'What remains to be done?'

'Nothing except for me to get myself downstairs and into hiding. Theresa will tell you where to find me. She's down there now, isn't she?'

'Yes.'

There were sounds of voices and laughter. A man shouted a verse of song, another something dismissive. There was more laughter.

'Too late,' said Box. 'Damn.'

William opened the door a crack. From the far end by the stairs a group of people advanced towards the massage rooms. He glimpsed uniforms, cigar smoke, bottles and girls. He locked the door.

'That was silly,' said Box.

'They didn't see me.'

'But they could have. You knew what was happening. You didn't need to look. Unnecessary risk.'

'Sorry.'

'They're very early. They must have come straight up the moment they got here. Hot with lust, no doubt. Keen to be at it like a lot of bulls.'

The noise diminished as the generals were herded into the massage rooms with their girls. There was still laughter and some calling out, but doors closed and water gurgled through the pipes.

'Were they all there?' asked Box.

'I couldn't see. How many should there be?'

'Four – Carlos, Herrera, Quinto and Paulottio. We'll give them a few minutes, then I'll go downstairs. Trouble is, you won't know where I'm hiding.'

'Do you have to hide? Why not wait in the bar?'

'I can't do that.'

'Why not? People do hang around in bars.'

'I know.' Box frowned. 'Nonetheless, secret signals should be secret.'

'But if no one knows you're making signals it's still secret, isn't it?'

'Point.' Box's frown cleared and he began collecting his papers. 'All right, I'll wait in the bar. You're learning, you know.'

William examined the bath. It looked clean. 'What goes on in these massage sessions?'

'Oh, nothing you wouldn't expect.' Box closed his briefcase. 'Most of my experiences were in the Far East, Bangkok mainly – all in the line of duty, of course – but I imagine it's much the same here as anywhere else. The number of things you can do with the human body is really quite limited. It's all masturbatory, anyway, despite people trying to pretend otherwise. That's what the girls assume they're here for.'

William thought of the graceful dancing girls and the fat generals – fatter than himself, full of wine and food. Manuel was not fat, of course, and Ines was supposed to be with him. She was big and generous and would make a great fuss of him. He hoped so, anyway. They did not want Manuel anything other than engrossed. He didn't let himself think of Theresa and Carlos.

'Extras are extra,' Box continued. 'You come to a private arrangement with the girl. Not that I've indulged – unfair on Mrs B. – but I won't say I wasn't tempted.' His teeth showed briefly. 'I used to have the same girl each time when I had to go regularly. B29 – they have numbers out there. Lovely girl. Called Mina, when I got to know her better. Earned the same as a major in the Thai army – better than factory work, which was the alternative for her. Who's to say she wasn't right?'

'You *had* to go?'

'Yes, on a job. I was trying to get alongside a chap.'

'A chap?'

'A customer of the establishment, not an employee. Used to have two at a time, I remember.'

'Can't have been very easy to get alongside him.'

'Not too difficult. You just find someone who can.'

'B29?'

Box winked lugubriously. 'State secret. Need to know.'

William opened the door and peered out. 'All clear.'

Box breathed deeply a few times. 'Good luck.'

'And you.' They shook hands. Box walked quickly along the corridor, briefcase in hand, jacket buttoned. William closed the door and sat in one of the armchairs. The air-conditioner was not switched on but he could hear that the others were. The wall clock ticked, one of the bath taps gurgled a few drops of water. He looked at the round bed with its red cover reflected in the ceiling mirror. The towels were red, the shower fitting was red and the inflated lilo that stood against the wall was red. He wondered what people had done on that bed. Did they get more out of it for being able to see themselves in the mirror? He rather thought he wouldn't. He would prefer to look at the girl, but presumably she would have to look at him. Not a very fair exchange. But then it was her job. She would be getting paid for it and must be used to it, like nurses. He thought again of the graceful girls ministering to obese generals.

He got up stretched and began pacing the perimeter of the room, his hands behind his back. He recalled seeing an interview with a woman who had spent seven years in solitary confinement in Russia. She said that in such circumstances people either became introverted and withdrew from everything or they clung to self-imposed routines and tasks. She was the latter sort and she had measured the width of her tiny cell, then paced it so many times a day until eventually she had walked the distance between her prison and Paris. She walked to Paris three times during her sentence.

He had seen the interview on television in England. It was curious how little he and Sally missed television. They had not bothered to get one while in South America and noticed the lack not at all. He could not imagine how they would find time to watch it, anyway. People must do nothing else in England. The capacity for adapting to what was new and strange was disconcertingly strong. Things so quickly became normal that there was a danger of losing all perspective. One could easily cease to judge or, rather, one's criteria for judging shifted with the ice-floe one happened to be stuck on.

The door opened and closed behind him. Theresa was brisk and business like. 'You should keep it locked. Where is Arthur?'

'Downstairs in the bar, waiting for me to give him the signal. Shall I tell him?'

'No, it will be some time yet. We have to wait until they are at their most helpless. Probably about an hour.'

'Is that how long a massage takes?'

She looked at him for some moments before replying. Her manner changed. She became less busy, more sympathetic. 'I will show you. I will give you one.'

'Me?'

She laughed. 'Why not? You will like it. You have to wait, anyway.'

'What about Carlos?'

'I have left him in his room. We haven't started. We are waiting to see if everything is all right. I told him Arthur said I had to keep coming out to check. He is very keen to have his massage before the arrests but I think he is a small bit frightened of Arthur.' She went to the bath, turned on the taps and sprinkled something in the water. 'Take off your clothes,' she called over her shoulder.

William was wearing his usual corduroys, tweed jacket, veldtskoen, which he polished daily, shirt and tie. The corduroys, jacket and shoes were old and he was therefore fond of them. Undressing was to him more than a matter of taking off his clothes; it was divesting himself of an important part of himself. He did not feel more essential when naked – rather the opposite. He was also ashamed of his body.

'All my clothes?'

She was kneeling by the bath and looked round, laughing. 'Yes, all. Even your tie.'

He took off his jacket and folded it on the chair, then began taking off his tie. 'I'm rather fat, you know.'

'Not so very fat. Anyway, fat can be nice. It is better to cuddle fat people than thin ones. They are more comfortable in bed. Could you switch on the air-conditioning, please?'

William did so. The machine made a lot of noise and at first was icy cold. He took off his shoes and socks, pushing the socks into the shoes and shoving them under the chair in case they smelt.

She dried her hands on the red towel. 'I must go back

to Carlos and start with him. When the bath is ready, you can get in and wait. But you must lock the door and you'll have to get out to let me in.' She put her right arm through his and smiled. 'William, don't be so serious. It is not a terrible thing, a massage. It is quite nice – really.'

'I was thinking about our plan,' he lied. 'Are you sure they're all being massaged?'

'Now I am, yes. At first Manuel and Ines were left behind. I don't know why. She was to go with him, he must have known that, and I thought it wasn't going to work, you know, because he wouldn't come with the others, but when I came out from Carlos I heard Ines laughing in the room next to mine so it is all right. She laughs very loudly. I don't know what he was doing to her.'

'You are fond of Ines, aren't you?'

'She is my friend.'

He glanced along the corridor when he let her out. All the doors were closed. The only sounds were the hum of the air-conditioners and the noise of water running through the pipes. She signalled to him to go back and walked quickly towards the room at the end.

He finished undressing. The water was very hot beneath the bubble bath and he ran some cold. It was the first time for years that he had been in a bath without reading. He lay back. The water soothed and comforted him. He moved his hands gently through it, shaping mountain ranges of foam. The pleasant sensation added to his growing sense of unreality. Even the small thought that perhaps it was he who was being set up and not the generals, that perhaps the security police were going to burst in upon him and drag him dripping and slipping from the building, did no more than ripple his composure. If it would happen, it would happen; probably it wouldn't. If it did it would be because Theresa had betrayed him. And if she betrayed him – well, then anyone was capable of anything and there was no longer any hope. One may as well give up.

The tap on the door, just audible above the air-conditioner, was unlikely to be the security police. He wrapped the towel around himself, keeping it as high as possible so as to cover more of his stomach. He also scooped up foam and put it on his chest, hoping it would distract attention. She was now in a thin white dressing gown of silk or some imitation, with black underwear beneath it. Her hair was still up.

'I've started him off,' she said. 'He's in the bath. It is extraordinary. What is going on, you would think it would put him off, but not at all. He is not interested, he wants only one thing. It is very irresponsible.' She rubbed her arms and looked at the air-conditioner. 'That thing is so cold but we have to have it on because of the condensation. Can we put something over it?'

'I'm sure we can.' He looked around for something.

'Your towel. Why are you wearing it, anyway? Were you expecting someone else?' She smiled.

He gave her the towel. She moved one of the chairs and stood on it to fasten the towel over the air-conditioner. She was unable to manage both corners of the towel simultaneously so he got up on the chair beside her.

'Can't the air-conditioner be adjusted?' he asked.

'No, they are cheap ones.'

Twice they thought they had fastened it and it blew back over their heads. They laughed and once, when the chair nearly tipped, she clung to him. Eventually the towel stayed in place and they climbed down.

'Get in the bath,' she said. 'We must be quick. I cannot leave him long.' She took off her dressing-gown and stood in her underwear, stockings and suspenders. 'He insists on this,' she said apologetically. 'He likes me to do it with him in all this. I would rather be naked.'

William got into the bath. She seemed not to notice his body. Probably she had seen so many. She took off her underclothes and joined him sitting between his legs and facing him. With a quick expert movement she slid her legs behind his back, then pulled his head forward and wet his hair with a sponge. She put soap on the sponge and began gently washing his arms, shoulders and chest.

He closed his eyes while she squeezed more warm water over his head. 'I haven't been bathed since childhood.'

'It's a nice thing to do for someone.'

'Nice to have it done.'

'Better with people you like. Lie back.' She washed the rest of him.

'How many of these do you have to do in a week?' he asked.

'It depends. Not so many recently and now, since Carlos, none. I can keep myself for him. But when I first started, I had to do it for whoever wanted, like the new girls now. It's quite hard work if you have several in an evening.'

'It must be.'

'It's better when you can choose. Sít up.' She climbed behind and knelt against him, her thighs supporting his back.

'Close your eyes.' She washed his hair, her fingers splaying across his scalp.

'I wish I could do something as pleasant as this for you,' he said.

'I like to do it. Women get pleasure from pleasing men. Provided they like them.'

'Some women wouldn't like to hear that.'

'They are *bobos, estupido*. Prudes. They have no pleasure in being women.' She kneaded his shoulders with her thumbs and knuckles, pressing hard into the loosening muscle. 'Stand up. I must be quick.'

She unhooked the shower attachment, tested the temperature and held it above his head. Water and shampoo streamed down his face.

'Wait,' she said. 'Can you hold me?' She put one hand on his shoulder and got upon the sides of the bath, a foot on either edge. He held her by the hips. She swayed against him a little, laughing. Once she nearly slipped and he had to grip her wet hips tightly. When she had finished she got nimbly down. 'I must go to Carlos. Can you prepare for the next part? Empty the bath and put the lilo on the floor here, where I am, and cover it in hot water and soap so it it is all slippery.' She began drying herself.

'Right.' He wanted to be businesslike. 'Both sides or one?'

'You can only lie on one.'

'And me?'

'You?'

'What should I do about myself?'

'Don't do anything. Stay as you are.' She put on her underclothes. 'But lock the door.'

'Why are you so worried about the door if they're all doing this? They won't want to come out.'

'Sometimes they want more than one girl or they want to see what the others are doing. They are generals, remember. But it is unlikely today. They are very full and lazy. They will just lie there and the girls will have to work very hard.' She opened the door carefully and looked round it before slipping away.

Being alone and naked in a windowless room was even more like how he imagined prison to be. He wondered how long the generals would be imprisoned, what Carlos would have done with them. Presumably nothing too unpleasant. There was no need for firing-squads or anything like that, though he could imagine that Carlos might have a vicious streak. He cleaned the bath thoroughly and got to work on the lilo. Twice he slipped on the wet tiled floor when the lilo moved as he scrubbed it. He wasn't sure whether he was supposed simply to cover it with hot soapy water so that it would be welcoming, or whether there was also a cleansing function. He opted for the latter, not knowing who might have been there before.

Afterwards, wanting the towel back on, he balanced on the chair and tried to unfasten it from the air-conditioner. He had got one end off when he heard Theresa's knock. Trying to get down quickly, he slipped and fell to the floor, hurting his elbow and hip.

She was solicitous, predicting bruises. They righted the chair and both stood on it again to reposition the towel.

Her skin was wet and where the dressing-gown touched her body it clung. When she took it off he could see that her underclothes and stockings were soaked.

'What have you been doing?'

'The same as with you but Carlos likes me to keep these on. I told you. I don't like it and it's uncomfortable when they're wet.' She took them off. 'Can you make the lilo wet again? It's drying.'

He held the lilo still with his knees, kneeling modestly so as not to present his buttocks to her. It must, he felt, be the least appealing of all his unappealing aspects.

'Lie on your stomach,' she said.

He lay with his chin on his hands. The dips and swellings of the lilo beneath him were teasing. She filled a red plastic bowl with more soapy water and knelt beside him, rubbing him gently from neck to heel with her wet hands.

'This is more than pleasant,' he said, feeling he should say something.

'I'm sorry I have to be quicker than I like.'

'Carlos is impatient for more?'

'Yes. Also, I listened at some of the other doors. They are getting on quite fast. We don't have much time.'

'You'll tell me when I have to signal Arthur? I'll need to get dressed, you see.'

'I think you will.' She laughed and tipped some water over his back. It trickled swiftly down his sides and formed a stream down his spinal column. The remainder she tipped down her own back, her head bent forward and one hand protecting her hair. Then she lay on him, her back against his, and began moving slowly up and down. She pressed quite hard with her shoulders and slid her buttocks backwards and forwards over his, aided by the soapy water. Her hands gripped the sides of the lilo and her knees were raised so that she could push with her feet. Twice she slid right down the backs of his legs and up again.

She rolled off him and picked up the bowl. 'Turn over.'

It was an effort to move. He was very comfortable and bits of him had been pressed into the declivities of the lilo. He heaved himself inelegantly round while she put more hot water in the bowl. He surveyed the unwelcome spread of his belly, now – thanks to the lilo – adorned by red weals. Her stomach had dips and hollows where his bulged. She smiled as she covered his front with water and then did the same to her own, dipping both hands in the bowl and running them over and under her breasts and down her belly.

She lay on him, her hands against the sides of his face. Her elbows rested on the lilo and she pushed herself up and down while he rested his hands lightly on her shoulders.

'This is body massage?'

'Yes.'

'Do most people have this?'

'Usually, unless they are poor. But not many poor people come here.'

'And do they – you know – is it just massage usually?' He winced. One section of the lilo had deflated and his coccyx was being ground against the tiled floor as she moved.

'It depends on the man and on the girl. Sometimes the man doesn't want to, or can't, and sometimes he is horrible and the girl has enough money for the week and so she will not. But if she likes him – well, you know, even if he has not much money.' She slithered the length of his body, down and up. 'Or perhaps the girl is tired. It is quite hard work if you do it properly. There is not really time for more than three in an evening because she has to get dressed again and put on her make-up and everything.'

She rotated her pelvis into his. He held his breath as his coccyx was rotated in turn on a crack in the tile. He didn't want her to stop but his mind was focused almost entirely on the pain.

'Most of the men who come here are married?' he asked.

'Nearly all. And they tell their wives they are going for massage and that it is only massage, it is not sex.'

She turned over again and slid up and down on her

back. Then, with the adroitness which he felt rather than saw, she turned about, slid her legs between his and lay back so that they were like open scissors meeting, crotch to crotch.

The relief of pressure on his coccyx was blissful. She rotated tantalisingly. He stared at the ceiling. 'Their wives must know,' he said.

'Of course. The men always lie to their wives and the wives lie to themselves.'

'Do the wives really mind, do you think?' It was pleasing to talk dispassionately, as if nothing else were happening.

'Yes, they mind. How can they not? But you cannot change men. The only wives who do not mind have no longer any interest in their men, but even they would have minded once.' She sat up. 'I must go, I have been too long. What is the matter?'

'It's all right – it's just – you see, the thing went down and when you pressed there – '

'But you should have said.' She got up, laughing. When he stood she examined his coccyx. 'Yes, there is a mark. It will bruise. Now you will have three, with your elbow and hip.' She sqeezed his hand. 'You are silly, William. You must be more careful when you take your clothes off.'

'I shall. Now, what next?'

'Put away the lilo and the bowl. Next we move to the bed.' She began putting on her underclothes.

'You're going to do the same with Carlos now?'

'Yes. It hurts me, you know, the bra hurts my breasts when I press on them.' She fiddled with the strap. 'It's funny, isn't it, for him to want me in my underclothes? Perhaps he will start wearing them. Some men are like that. He will be very impatient now. He cannot bear to be kept waiting.'

William tidied up when she had gone, making everything neat and exact. He straightened the red cover on the bed but did not get on it. He wished again there were no mirror above. Perhaps they could get under the cover

to do whatever was done next. There didn't seem very much left to do, short of doing it. Perhaps that was it. She was now doing with Carlos what she had been doing with him. Could she be intending to make love with them both? Or was she prepared to do all this with him because she felt sure she wouldn't be forced to go on and do more? He realised with some surprise that he no longer minded very much one way or the other. He wanted to make love with her, of course, but it no longer upset him to think that he wouldn't, or even that she might be doing it with Carlos. Yet he believed he loved her. He longed to help, to surprise, to please, to feel her dependent, to care for her. But the sex, the simple sheer sex, didn't seem important in the way it had.

He was still musing when she knocked. She slipped in and put her hands on his arms. 'You are unhappy. What is the matter?'

'Nothing. I was thinking.'

'You have bad thoughts?'

'No, no. I always look like this when I'm thinking. My face relaxes.'

She gripped him. 'No more thought. We must act.'

She explained that when she had left him she had found that Carlos had been out of his room, looking for her. Fortunately, he had not gone far, because he had become intrigued to know what Manuel and the two generals were doing. He had listened at one or two of the doors – luckily not theirs – and had heard that things were well under way. One door had been unlocked so he had opened it and peeped in unobserved. What he had seen had so amused him that he had had to retreat to his room, doubled up. Only there could he laugh. He was still laughing when she got back. He was on the lilo now. She had left him because she had said she must give the signal but he had made her promise she would be back in tim to finish him off. If he was not finished, he would b angry and then he was quite capable of upsetting th whole thing. But the others were now at their most vulne

able stage; they would be helpless and humiliated. William must tell Arthur.

She was still gripping his arms as he pulled her to him and kissed her on the lips. She neither resisted nor responded. When he stopped she moved her head back.

'You must hurry.' She went to the door. 'You must be quick. Don't forget your clothes.'

'No. I'm sorry I kissed you.'

'It's all right.' She hesitated as if to speak again, but turned and went.

William dressed quickly. When he put his foot on the chair to tie his shoelace he felt the whole of his leg shake, though in himself he felt calm and fatalistic. It was everything else that seemed to be getting out of control.

Box was alone in the smaller bar, a dark room with racing prints on the walls, and an open fire. He was concealed behind a German newspaper but was obvious by his polished shoes – his special shoes, William remembered. There was a glass of whisky on the table.

'All right,' said William. 'They're ready.'

The newspaper remained still. William shut the bar door. 'We're okay, it's me.'

Box lowered his paper. 'Open the door.'

'Isn't it better closed?'

'Looks odd.'

William opened it. Someone was playing the piano again. 'Right. They're all ready but we've got to move fast.'

'Important to stick to operational procedures even when they seem unnecessary. Perhaps especially then, so that the habit sticks. You should have waited for me to speak.'

'Okay, but we'd better get moving.'

Box folded his paper. 'Never show haste. Important to reassure the troops. If you panic, they'll panic. The essentials of a good officer are a cool manner, a reliable wristwatch, a steady blow on the whistle and an exemplary death on the parapet. It's all a matter of setting the tone. The men will do the rest themselves.'

William could see only one glass on the table. There was no sign of a bottle. 'Are you all right?'

'Perfectly.' Box downed the whisky. 'Are you?'

'Yes. I just think we'd better get a move on, that's all.'

'Don't worry, it's only nerves. They make good servants but bad masters. You'll get better of them as you become more experienced.' He stood and stretched.

'I just think we should hurry, that's all.'

'That's how it takes you. Try not to think about it. Pretend we're doing something quite different. But keep your eye on the ball.' He put the newspaper under his arm. 'Keep close to me. We may need your Spanish.'

On the way out Box waved his newspaper imperiously at El Lizard, who nodded and smiled. William felt a spasm of guilt. The man was shortly to have his club invaded by soldiers and his most prestigious clients arrested. He was to be unwitting host to a coup or a revolution or counter-revolution or whatever it would be called. On the other hand, there should be no violence and it should be good publicity for the club. Carlos would no doubt continue to patronise it and the new generals and ministers would doubtless continue where their predecessors had left off. William smiled back.

It was dusk outside and the birds were twittering noisily in the plane trees. Four black Mercedes were parked in the square. The drivers were all sitting in the first one, filling it with smoke. Cathedral bells were ringing. Box seemed no more disposed to hurry than the dawdling couples.

'Where are the soldiers?' William asked.

'Twenty yards.'

'What's the point? We came out of the building together.'

'Security is a state of mind. Always seek what is most secure at the time, even if you haven't been doing so.' Box tucked his paper under his arm and clasped his hands behind his back. He had spoken without looking at William. William dropped back a few yards.

They turned the corner at the end of the square, crossed

the road and turned another. The waiting soldiers were not in sight. After a while they passed William's shop. He half expected to see the orange-seller back with new stock but there was no one in the street, just the two of them, walking slowly. He caught up with Box.

'Where are they supposed to be?'

'Twenty yards.'

'You're not lost are you?'

'Anti-surveillance. Making sure we're not followed.'

The stiffness of Box's manner and bearing indicated strong disapproval. William dropped back again.

The minutes passed. Street gave way to street. At one time they were heading towards the cemetery, at another towards the docks. Once they almost turned back into the square but veered away. William's exasperation and impatience increased. When they passed his shop the second time, he hurried forward again.

'Look, this is daft. Time's running out in there. They'll all be gone by the time we get back. You are lost, aren't you?'

Box's pale cheeks were tense. 'I'm not lost. They are.'

'Where did they say they'd be?'

'Round the corner.'

'Which corner?'

'The second one out of the square.'

'Very unlike you to accept anything so imprecise.'

Box went a shade paler. This was clearly a professional humiliation.

'Let's go back and start again from there,' William added in a more conciliatory tone. 'I'm more familiar with the ground.'

This time they walked side by side. 'Never trust other people,' was all Box said, slowly and through clenched teeth.

At the second corner from the square there were a few closed shops, some sleepy-looking houses, a courting couple and a black dog.

'This was definitely it?'

'Definitely.'

The black dog cocked its leg against a drainpipe and then wandered along the pavement, pausing at an open doorway in one of the houses. It started to go in but recoiled before a boot, then continued on its way as if kicking were routine. William, however, had seen the boot. It was long, brown and polished.

'Let's have a look down there.'

In the doorway a tall uniformed officer was negotiating with an ample middle-aged woman with very blond hair. She was shaking her head and smiling as he stroked her plump arm.

'That must be him,' said William.

'Not sure. They all look alike in uniform.'

'It's the one from the palace, the tall chap, the colonel who accompanied the coffin. The one you bribed.'

'That's it, that's the one. The colonel in Carlos's old regiment.'

They went over. The tall colonel was about to be affronted by the interruption but, realising who they were, changed his manner.

'*No ahora, señora*, you must wait. I have important business. I shall return.' He closed the door on the woman.

'We are friends of Carlos,' said Box in careful Spanish.

'Of course, we have met. The undertaker and the interpreter. *Saludos, señores*. You have no body this evening?'

The colonel laughed. They all shook hands.

'We bring orders from the president,' continued Box.

'*Donde – ?*' He turned to William. 'You'd better ask. Not sure my Spanish is up to it.'

'Where are your men?'

The colonel held up his hands. 'They are no longer here, *señor*.' His accent was a northern one; he spoke as if translating from his own dialect.

'Where are they?'

'They were tired of waiting and they have gone.'

'Where?'

The colonel slapped the gloves he was holding against

his thigh. '*Señores*, I am told to come and wait here. I do not know for how long or for what. I am told a man from the president will come to tell me what to do but I do not know which man until now. It is the holiday. Everyone has holiday, even the president, but not us. I am told I cannot tell my soldiers what we are here for. They want to know why they must work on the holiday. I cannot tell them. And so they wish to have a drink. Naturally, I do not stop them.' He stared as if boasting of an achievement.

'Tell him,' said Box.

'The president wishes us to arrest members of his government. He wishes to be saved from them. But it has to be done quickly and secretly before the security police find out.'

The colonel's eyes widened. 'This is the counter-revolution?'

'Yes.'

The colonel straightened himself. '*Señores*, I am honoured to take part. My children and my grandchildren will honour me. I lay down my life for the president.' They all shook hands again.

'Where are your soldiers?'

'It is not a problem, *señores*. It is near here. There is a tango club. It is the only place that is open. I will show you.'

Two army lorries were now parked near the club, behind the four Mercedes. Inside, the larger of the bars was packed by soldiers, their weapons slung over their shoulders, glasses and cigarettes in their hands. Of the few other customers who had earlier crept in there was now no sign.

El Lizard came out of the bar. '*Señor* Wooding, it is not possible. These soldiers, they want women. I tell them the girls are busy but they are not satisfied. They wish to interrupt. I tell them they must wait their turn, but they will not wait. I cannot tell them who is with the girls, so I have to give them drinks and promise there will be girls, otherwise they break the furniture. They have guns. *Señor*, you can control them, please?'

'We will see to it. The colonel here will see to it.'

El Lizard looked at the colonel. 'Normally we have more girls, but today with the holiday' – his forehead wrinkled, his face grew longer and he raised his hands, palms upward – 'I have sent for some but it takes a little time. The soldiers are impatient.'

'The girls are coming here?' asked the colonel.

'In time, *señor,* in time. Please be calm.'

'If they come here, my soldiers will not leave.'

William translated for Box, who nodded. 'Tell the troops you will be sending the new girls to the palace where the prisoners are to be taken.'

The colonel agreed. El Lizard was relieved but puzzled. 'The palace? They will not be the best girls, these who are coming. Normally for the palace I would want the best girls, the ones upstairs. But the best ones are wasted on soldiers, so perhaps it is good.'

William told him the colonel would provide a lorry for the girls. Meanwhile, the colonel had brought the soldiers here for a purpose: he had been ordered to make some arrests. El Lizard was appalled – the club would be ruined, his staff and his girls were dear to him, his reputation would be destroyed. The president himself would be embarrassed.

William said that the colonel and his men were acting on the orders of the president. The club would be famous and for ever patronised by the best people for the best reasons. No members of staff would be involved.

El Lizard took one of William's hands in both of his. He was almost tearful. '*Gracias, muchas gracias*. I will bring you a special drink.'

The colonel was confident that his men would leave the bar provided they were told they would have the girls at the palace afterwards. It wouldn't matter that they were not the same girls - the soldiers wouldn't notice by then – or that the soldiers recognised the men they were arresting. They were democratic, they didn't care who they arrested. In any case, their loyalty was to the president, not to these jumped-up generals and traitors who made alliances with communists, while all the time feathering their own nests and promoting only their relatives and friends and ingratiating themselves with Herrera and his Russians and Cubans.

Box held up his hand. 'The president blesses you. He will thank you, your relatives and your friends many times.'

The colonel saluted. 'To battle, *señores*.'

Box took the salute. 'To battle.'

They mounted the wide wooden staircase, William and Box side by side and in step.

'I'm finding it difficult to take this seriously,' said William.

Box nodded like a doctor who was hearing what he knew only too well. 'Same with everything when you think about it. All your normal daily business. Look at any bit of it closely enough and it soon becomes unreal and impossible to take seriously. The difference with our work is that it confronts you with the fact instead of covering it with habit so you never notice.'

'Do you often think like this?'

'Not often, there's no point.' They had reached the second set of stairs. 'Up you go. I'll look after the colonel and his merry men and make sure they come up quietly.'

The upstairs corridor was quiet. There was water running, but not as much as before. William listened at two of the doors and heard nothing apart from the air-conditioners. He opened his own door cautiously, and stared at the part of the floor where he had been with Theresa on the lilo. Those few minutes now seemed as unreal as everything else. He walked back to the top of the stairs and gave the signal.

There was murmuring and muffled heavy footsteps. Box came first and then the colonel, bristling and eager. The soldiers, their broad shoulders encumbered by weapons and webbing, barely fitted the narrow staircase. They smelt of alcohol.

The party assembled at the end of the corridor. The floorboards creaked. There were three soldiers to a prisoner, Box whispered, and a camera to each group. Two men would escort the prisoner, the third would photograph him and then carry his belongings. William was to point out which rooms they were to enter and the colonel would see to the rest. The president was to stay in his room throughout.

William showed them the rooms. He felt almost as if he were opening a country house one day a year for the villagers.

'Are the rooms locked?'

'One isn't, the others may be.'

'Do you know who's in which?'

'No.'

'Right. Ask the colonel to get the men to fall in outside each door.'

The soldiers were detailed off, their weapons unslung and at the ready. One or two eased off the safety catches.

'Tell them there should be no need to do any shooting,' William said to the colonel. The colonel told them. They fixed bayonets. 'It should be enough just to show the bayonets,' added William. 'They won't have to use them.'

The colonel smiled proudly. 'Our soldiers are very fond of the bayonet. For them it is a symbol.'

Box turned to William. 'I'll give the signal when you're ready.'

'Well, okay, I'm ready.'

Box nodded to the colonel. 'Right.'

The colonel stood to attention, drew his sword and held it aloft. All the men looked at it. He held his pose for some seconds, the point quivering.

'Tell him to get on with it,' Box whispered.

The colonel brought down his sword as if starting a race.

Two of the doors opened at the first attempt, the third was locked but yielded to a hefty shoulder. William, Box and the colonel were left in the corridor. The colonel held his sword as if to stab at escapees. Nothing happened. There were no shouts and no sounds of struggle.

'May as well have a butchers,' said Box.

William followed him. A fat naked man with white hair was lying on his back, his arms outstretched. He had a white moustache and his face was red and staring. The mirror above him made him look like a beached whale. Sitting on the bed beside him and also naked was the slim girl who had been one of the dancers. Two of the soldiers were pointing their guns at the couple while the third took photographs. No one spoke.

'Tell them to get a move on,' said Box.

William's Spanish was not up to military commands, so he simply told them to proceed. One of the soldiers made a move towards the bed. William looked at the fat man whom he thought he recognised as Paulotti, chief of the Police. 'You must go with the soldiers,' he said to him. 'You have been arrested.'

Paulotti sat up with difficulty. 'Who is arresting me? Who has ordered this? I cannot be arrested.'

'The president has ordered it. You are arrested.'

William's Spanish was more stilted than usual. He turned to the soldiers. 'Go. Continue. Arrest him.'

Paulotti became angry. He got clumsily to his feet, his thighs and buttocks wobbling. William hated to watch because he thought that was how he himself might appear. Paulotti turned to the soldiers. 'You are arresting me? You have no power. I will have you shot. Who ordered this? Who are these foreigners? Get out of my room!'

The soldiers hesitated, looking at William and Box. William stepped back to the door to call the colonel but couldn't see him. He tried to think of some confident-sounding reply but his Spanish had gone to pieces. When he looked back he saw Box step purposefully forward. The girl rolled out of the way. Paulotti stared like an affronted walrus. Box stepped on to the bed beside him amd with one swift movement hit him on the buttock with his rolled newspaper.

'Out!' he shouted, pointing with his other hand at the door. 'Under arrest! Move, move, move! Run, run, run!'

With each word he struck at Paulotti's buttocks. Paulotti jumped and nearly fell, uttering small affronted squeals. He tried to grab the newspaper but missed and Box brought it down with a final resounding slap. '*Out!*'

One of the soldiers grabbed Paulotti by the arm, another moved to push him off the bed. Once they felt struggling flesh, they regained their momentum. By the time Paulotti had been hustled to the door he was cowed and looked shocked again. The third soldier began to follow.

'Tell him to bring the clothes,' said Box.

The soldier gathered them, taking his time to look at the girl who was wrapping herself in a towel.

'*Rapido!* Quick!' Box shouted at him. The soldier gathered up the remainder of the clothing and left.

The corridor was filled with soldiers again. Quinto, the other general, was there with one naked girl and one wearing a towel. There was a dangerous air of hesitancy and aimlessness. The colonel was not to be seen. Something seemed to be happening in the third room which William assumed to be occupied by Ines and Manuel.

'Tell them to get moving,' said Box. 'Take the prisoners downstairs to the lorries and wait for the colonel. Make sure they leave the girls alone. Where's number three?' He went towards Manuel's room.

William's Spanish was returning. Raising his voice gave him confidence. The soldiers and prisoners eddied around the stairs. William went to the group still in the doorway of Manuel's room. Inside he saw Ines, naked and expostulating, her pendulous breasts shaking. She was arguing with the colonel, who stood with his sword pointing at Ricardo's naked stomach. Ricardo was also arguing. Box stood to one side of them, looking puzzled.

He was the first to see William. 'You'd better come and sort this out. Seems to be a bit of confusion.'

The contrast between Ines's enveloping proportions and Ricardo's slim litheness was transfixing. William tried not to dwell upon either and eventually focused on the colonel's sword.

They greeted him as a saviour and competed in rapid explanations. He had to ask them to slow down.

'He is trying to arrest us,' said Ines, pointing at the

colonel. 'He says we are communists and that Manuel Herrera is here. Where, where? I ask him. In the lilo? Down the plug-hole? There is no one here. He says he will castrate Ricardo.'

Ricardo stared in wide-eyed appeal. 'He talks like a madman. Take his sword away. If he touches me I will kill his family.'

William held up his hand to the colonel. 'He doesn't want you,' he told Ricardo. 'He thought Manuel Herrera was in here, that's all. That's what we all thought.'

'Is this the counter-revolution?'

'I suppose it is, yes.'

Ricardo opened his arms. 'Why didn't you tell me? I could have helped you. I could have told you that you would never catch Herrera here with Ines. Never in his life. He would not touch her.'

Everyone looked at Ines, who stood with her legs apart and her hands on her hips. She nodded. 'Herrera is homosexual. He doesn't want women. I discovered today, this afternoon. I thought he didn't like me but it was not that. Ricardo told me.'

The colonel lowered his sword. 'The army will hate him even more for this.'

'Where is he now?' William asked Ricardo.

'He is with his driver. I saw them go together. His driver is his boyfriend. Once when I was going to meet Manuel – you know, when he wanted to talk to me – I was early and I saw them doing it.'

'Why didn't you tell me?'

'You never asked. Why didn't you tell me you were going to do this? Then I would have told you.'

'What were they doing?' asked the colonel.

'They were kissing each other in the car.'

The colonel stepped back as if Ricardo were infectious.

'What's going on?' Box asked.

William explained. Box said they'd better get after Manuel. He was easily the most dangerous one to have at large. The security police were his people and would be loyal to him so long as he was free. It would be ideal to catch him with his driver, even better than with a prostitute. Where would they be?

'I don't know,' answered Ricardo. 'At his house, I suppose. Wherever he lives, I don't know.'

'Where does he live?' asked Box. No one knew. 'Carlos will know.'

The soldiers at the door were told that there was no one to arrest and that they should join the others. The colonel went with them to see that the prisoners were taken back to the palace. He tried not to go because he wanted to see the president but Box insisted. 'Tell him he must be ready at the palace with more men to arrest Manuel and that Carlos will see him afterwards and give him a medal.'

William stayed with Ines and Ricardo. 'I'm sorry about all this.'

'What is happening? What are you going to do with the president?' Ines came close to him, unselfconscious, her big face angry.

He put his hand on her shoulder. 'Nothing, they are doing nothing to the president. He supports this, he wants it, it is on his orders. He wants a new government. He's next door with Theresa.'

'He will not be put in prison?'

'Of course not. He will be head of a better government.'

'Which government? Who will be in it? Will they free my father?'

'I don't know. That's not my side of it. The president will choose people.' He was about to add that Britain would be helping the new government but remembered that London had not replied. Perhaps London would disapprove of what they had done. It was presumably regarded as a serious thing, bringing down governments though to look at the two fat old men being shuffled off downstairs, it didn't seem serious.

Ricardo went over to his clothes. 'You should have told me. I helped you, I told you things. Now you leave me out.'

'It wasn't like that, it wasn't deliberate. You were very

useful and the president is very pleased with you. And you can still help. There's more to do.'

'You did not trust me.'

'No, it wasn't that,' William recalled as he spoke how little he had trusted Ricardo. 'It wasn't that at all. It wasn't in my hands, you see. I played quite a small part.' It was unpleasant how rapidly power involved one in deceit. He tried smiling at them both. 'I am sorry you were interrupted.'

Ricardo pulled on his underpants. 'We were finished.'

Carlos and Theresa were with Box in the corridor, dressed and surrounded by the other girls. The colonel had reappeared and was asking what should be done with the Mercedes outside. Carlos, who had been pleased at first, was now frowning and looking worried.

'We must find him,' he was saying to Box. 'We must find him quickly. He is the most dangerous.'

'But we don't know where he lives.' Box sounded as if he were repeating himself. 'Or where the driver lives.'

'He lives in several places. I remember the places but not the addresses.'

'Can you describe them to the colonel? Then we'll take soldiers to each.'

Carlos stood like a sulky child. 'I won't feel safe until he is caught.'

'Therefore we will go and catch him. If you can tell us where.'

Theresa was whispering to the girls. Her eyes briefly met William's but there was no message. The girls would not know she had been party to the plot all along, and she might not want them to.

Box urged Carlos to return to the palace and make television and radio broadcasts. He had to ensure that the security police were either disarmed or accepted his authority. He must show himself. He must ensure that the television and radio stations were guarded by his own men. He must warn the newspaper editors.

Carlos listened abstractedly. When he noticed William, he spoke across Box. 'Herrera has escaped.'

'We must find him.'

'If I had known he was homosexual I could have got rid of him easily. They are not liked here. But now it is too late.'

'Not too late,' said Box. He went on talking earnestly. Carlos continued to look distracted.

William already disliked the whole business. It had seemed like fun at first or, if not quite that, somehow not exactly serious, either. It didn't even seem fully serious now, certainly not momentous, but it wasn't fun. People were not happy. Ines looked worried. Ricardo was obviously resentful. Lies were already necessary. Carlos's troubled face was reflected in the colonel's. Only Box seemed fully engaged, to have any idea what to do or any desire to do it. They all began drifting downstairs.

At the bottom they met El Lizard. His head now projected even farther forward and downwards from his shoulders. He rubbed his hands like Uriah Heep.

'*Señores . . .*'

Carlos, perhaps feeling himself on display, held up his hand with regal decisiveness. '*Gracias, señor.* You will be rewarded.'

El Lizard bowed but as the party passed he looked anxiously among them. 'My girls, *Señor* Wooding,' he whispered. 'They are all right?'

'They are all right. Everything is okay.'

'Only I did not know what was happening. I run an orderly house –'

'*Sí, sí*, and so you shall. It's all right. The president is grateful.'

'*Gracias, señor.*'

There was talk of getting back to the palace as quickly as possible. The Mercedes, minus Manuel's car, was still outside. The remaining three drivers stared at their recent masters now wrapped in blankets and sitting glumly in the back of the army lorry. William caught Theresa's eye again. They were all in the front hall of the club. Box and the president were talking, two soldiers had come in to listen, the colonel was saying something to one of the girls.

'You are going to the palace?' William asked Theresa, trying to sound matter-of-fact.

'I think so.' Her hair was still up and the edges behind her ears were still wet. 'No one else left upstairs?' he asked, pointlessly.

'No.'

The others began moving through the door. 'I'll see you later then,' he said.

'Yes.'

Carlos turned to her and she followed obediently, bowing her head as they walked. There seemed no trace of the confident energetic woman who had massaged him. Either she was a superb actress, he thought, or she was remorseful. He wanted to take her hand and say something comforting but dared not in front of the others. Yet what if he had, he asked himself the moment after she had moved away. No one would have done anything, not even Carlos. Nothing would have happened. It would have been quickly forgotten amidst all that was going on. But it was too late.

'Got a moment?' Box was at his shoulder. They went out and walked a few yards along the road. It was dark but a dozen or so people were in the square, staring at the army lorries and the Mercedes. 'What do you think?' Box asked.

'I think you were right in what you said to Carlos just now.'

Box looked thoughtful. 'I'll get off to the palace with him. He needs his hand held. I don't trust his resolution. He'll bend with the wind. As soon as the news has broken – ideally before – I'd like you to tell the embassy so that they can tell London. If they can't or won't, use the EEC. You remember how it works?'

'What, get in the grave with it?'

'Of course.' Box pushed his chin into his chest. 'Now, if anything happens to me I'd like you to tell London the full story so that they will know what to tell Mrs B. She doesn't know where I am or what I'm doing, you see. And I'd like her to know if anything happens.'

'Where does she think you are?'

'Brussels. She thinks I work for the Department of Trade, negotiating tractor agreements, that sort of thing.'

'Why did you tell her that?'

'Cover.'

'But why? Can't you trust her?'

'No, no, trust her absolutely. It's just that she'd sit at home worrying. You know what they're like.'

They turned back towards the club. 'But it's not as if anything's going to – likely to – happen, is it?' asked William. 'I mean, it's almost over with. So long as Carlos insists it will work it will, even if Herrera isn't found straight away. I mean, there can't be a Russian counter-coup overnight.'

'If there's one thing you know in this business, it's that you never know.' Box looked at the group of figures waiting for them and stopped walking. 'If anything does happen to me, I'd like you to know that I've been grateful for your help and companionship and that I nominate you my successor. You are in charge.' His pale face was serious. 'I daresay it seems rather a lot to take on but I'm certain you're up to it.'

'That's very kind but I'm not sure I know—'

'Don't worry, just keep going. Remember, we're on the right side, the side of all the good things. That's why we have to do it. No one else will if we don't.'

'No, but I still don't see—'

'You will find a list of your expenses with the EEC. Make sure it gets to London. They'll pay in full in any currency you like. Don't forget to add anything you might incur as a result of tonight. We won't shake hands in front of the others. Looks rather too final, bad for their confidence. So I'll say cheerio.'

'Cheerio.'

Box rejoined the others, addressing them briskly and decisively. They all got into the vehicles and drove off. William remained. It would be terrible if he were never to see Theresa or Box again – or even Carlos, in an odd sort of way. But there was no reason to think he wouldn't. Indeed, there was every reason to feel pleased. If it went on like this it would all work.

El Lizard crept out of the club, still rubbing his hands. 'I keep an orderly house, *señor*. Always, I have kept an orderly house.'

'Yes, you do. You keep an orderly house.'

El Lizard stared after the vehicles. 'It is still an orderly house.'

'It is.' Through the open door William could see Ines, dressed now and talking to Ricardo and the other girls. She stood with one arm folded and gesticulated widely with the other. The girls nodded. Ricardo spoke, bunching the fingers of one hand together and pointing at himself with the other.

'You like a drink, *Señor* Wooding?'

'No, thank you. I'm afraid I have work to do.'

'Good luck, *señor*.'

13

Sally was in the bedroom when he got back, folding clothes. She wore a green jersey she had recently bought. He had the impression she had not been in long.

'Do you mind if we have the radio on?' he called. 'I want to hear the news.'

'Of course not, no.' She came through, holding a white blouse by the shoulders as she folded it. 'How's the revolution?'

'It's started.'

'Really?'

'Yes. We – the army – have arrested the generals. We missed Manuel Herrera but they're trying to find him now.'

'At the bordello?'

'Yes. Naked, in the massage rooms.'

'I kept wondering if you were really going to do it. It didn't seem serious.'

'It still doesn't.'

'Do you want a drink?'

'No, but I'd love a cup of tea. I'll make it. Do you want one?'

'No, thanks.' She had folded the arms of the blouse flat against the back and stood now with it hanging over her arms.

There was music on the radio. He turned it down so that it was just audible. She said something he didn't hear because he was filling the kettle.

'I said this is yours, you ought to have it.' She pointed at a piece of paper on top of the fridge. 'It's the president's appeal for help. You showed it to me earlier, remember?'

'Oh yes, I'd forgotten you'd got it. The message was sent, though, or should have been. I suppose it's of historical interest now.' He picked it up. 'That's odd. It's a photocopy.'

'Is it?'

'Yes.' He looked at her. She stood just outside the kitchen, resting her back against the wall of the passage. The blouse still hung over her folded arms. Her eyes seemed slightly wider than usual.

'I gave the original to Max,' she said. 'He must have returned the photocopy by mistake. I said you'd want it back, you see.'

'You gave it to Max?'

'Yes. He's in the CIA.'

William looked at her.

'I gave it to him when he was here,' she continued, speaking more quickly than usual, 'when he turned up just after you'd shown it to me. That was why he left in a hurry. He wanted to take it to the embassy.'

'You mean, when he called here to pick up that book?'

'Yes, except that wasn't really what he came for.'

'Wasn't it?'

'No. I'm going off with him.'

William stared.

'He thinks he might have to leave the country in a hurry if your plan goes off at half-cock – which he thinks it will – and he's asked me to go with him.'

'To leave – you mean, with him?' He felt heavy and stupid. 'You mean, you want to leave me for him?'

'Yes. Also, he says it would be dangerous for me to stay here with you if it all goes wrong. But that's not really why I'm going with him. I've fallen in love with him and he has with me. We've fallen in love with each other.'

'Have you?'

'Yes. Are you surprised?'

'Not at the moment.' He felt nothing at all, a complete absence. The kettle boiled. 'You're sure you don't want a cup?'

'No, thanks – I mean, yes, I'm sure.'

'When – how long has this been going on?' There was no avoiding the cliché.

'Oh, not long but long enough for us both to know.'

She remained staring, her back pressed against the wall, her eyes slightly widened, her arms still folded. She looked pale, though that might have been because of the harsh kitchen light. He waited for the tea to brew. It was odd how everything else carried on as normal. No doubt it was the same when you died: the alarm would ring at the time you set, the paper you had ordered would thump on the mat, the letters you had written would be answered, your voice on the answer machine would promise to ring back.

'You don't seem to mind very much,' she said.

'I don't know what I think.'

She went on nervously, as if he had said something quite different. 'Yes, because it's not as if you haven't had your bordello girl to play with.'

'What do you mean?'

'You've been having an affair with her, haven't you?' She laughed a short laugh.

'Not an affair, no.'

'More fool you.' She laughed again. 'I assumed you had.'

'Is this why you've decided to go off with Max?'

'No, it's nothing to do with that. In fact, it began . . . well, I don't want to go through it all but we became aware that we couldn't live without each other. Neither of us intended to get involved at the start. It just happened. It was inevitable.'

William wasn't sure that love affairs were inevitable. People chose them. He would have chosen if he'd been allowed – had chosen, in fact, but had been prevented. He was tempted to unrighteous anger at her having taken advantage where he couldn't, but he said nothing.

'It can't have come as a great surprise,' she said. 'It was obvious we haven't been getting on for some time.'

'Haven't we?'

'Well, no, not having rows or anything but just not . . .

well . . . going anywhere. Our relationship wasn't progressing.'

William wasn't sure about the linear view of relationships, either. 'I'm sorry about that.'

'Not that it was ever much anyway.'

'Wasn't it?'

'I don't think so, do you? We just got along with each other, that was all. It was a habit. We were a habit for each other.'

'Which is now broken.'

'Yes.'

They stared. There was an edge of defiance to her tone as if she were prepared for, perhaps even wanted, argument. He felt no jealousy of Max, none whatever. It seemed to have nothing to do with Max. If it hadn't been him it would have been another. The essential fact was anterior to all that.

'You love him?'

'Oh yes. It's like nothing I've ever known.'

It felt as if he were talking to a born-again Christian. Even the thought of her making love with Max did not move him. It seemed to involve someone wholly other than the Sally he had last made love with, quite a time ago. Anyway, he had no right to jealousy. He poured the tea. 'Are you sure you don't want any?'

'Yes. I'd better get on with my packing.'

She went back into the bedroom, refolding the blouse. There was a change in the muted tones of the radio. He took his tea into the sitting room and turned up the sound. It was martial music. When it stopped an announcer slowly read the repeat of an earlier statement. There had been an attempt to overthrow the government but it had failed. The president was safe and the two generals who had been temporarily imprisoned were free. The conspirators had been arrested by the security police. Investigations were continuing but foreign elements were believed to have been involved. The president, who would shortly appear on television to make an announcement to the nation, had already issued a statement deploring the attempt, promising a full investigation and retribution according to the law, and thanking Colonel Herrera for his prompt and loyal action. The music resumed.

Sally stood in the doorway. 'It hasn't worked, then?'

William said nothing.

'Max said it wouldn't. He said something much bigger would be needed. What's happened to your friends?'

'They've been arrested.'

'Will they come and arrest you?'

'I suppose they will.'

She came closer to him. 'I don't like to leave you if you're going to be arrested.'

'There's not much to be done.'

'No, but I do care about you. I love Max but I care for you.'

'Perhaps I should go into hiding.'

'I hope you'll go on caring for me.'

'Oh yes.'

'There's no reason why we shouldn't be friends.'

'No, there isn't.'

'You do mean that, don't you?'

'Yes.'

He watched her go back into the bedroom. It was probably as well she was running away with Max; he would be able to protect her or get her out. She came back with a suitcase and her raincoat, looking smart and lively, just as whenever they had set off anywhere new together.

'I booked a taxi,' she said. 'It should be down there by now.' She put the suitcase by the door and turned to face him. The raincoat was folded like the blouse over her clasped hands. 'I'm glad you came back in time for me to tell you. Otherwise I was going to have to leave a note and that would have seemed so unfriendly.'

'Yes, it would.' He felt as if he were floating.

'Thank you for being so sweet about it.'

'That's all right.'

'You will look after yourself, won't you? Try not to get arrested.'

'Okay.'

'And we will stay friends, won't we?'

'Of course.'

She picked up the suitcase and smiled. 'Don't look so sad. You make me feel awful.'

'I'm all right.'

'Poor William. It's not been a very good day for you, has it?'

'Don't worry, it's all right.'

'Take care.'

It was an expression she had adopted since working at the American school. He nodded. 'And you.'

''Bye.'

'Cheerio.'

He did not know how long he stood there after the door had closed. The music on the radio continued until the announcer made an identical announcement. William noticed that his teacup was empty. The more that happened, the less he felt. There was a growing blankness which stilled mental and emotional responses. The longer he stood the more likely it seemed that the blankness would envelope his physical responses as well. That would be an interesting phenomenon: for how long could one remain simply standing? Days and nights, presumably. Weeks in some cases, the sort that got into the Guinness Book of Records.

When he did move it was in a determined stupor. He thought of one thing at a time and, when that was done, moved on to the next. He poured more tea, ate six pieces of toast with cheese and Marmite, changed his shirt, pocketed his passport, cheque-book and cards, collected all the money he could find, polished his shoes. Finally, he turned off the lights and the radio and stood for a while on the balcony. The trees, moved by the breeze, were now rustling masses of denser dark. Beyond them the sea was a faint uneven line of foam. Beyond that was nothing but dark. He stared at the spot where *Señor* Finn's fire used to burn. That was why they had been right to try. It would have worked if Manuel hadn't liked his driver.

He didn't let himself imagine what might have happened – be happening – to Theresa and Box.

He left the building on foot. A few people were strolling, muffled against the warm night breeze, but most were no doubt comatose after the feast. Many of the street lights were not working and voices, cigar smoke and relaxed rolling laughter floated through the darkness. William walked quickly towards the British Embassy. The leather soles of his polished veldtskoen sounded reassuringly purposeful. The people he passed did not seem excited. Perhaps they had not seen the news, or perhaps they had become used to this sort of thing. Twice he saw police cars travelling at speed and once an army lorry lurched round the corner, almost keeling over like a ship. There were distant sirens.

It was difficult to wake the Embassy guard. William pressed the big brass bell at the gate for some time, feeling increasingly conspicuous. The guard when he came was querulous and smelt of alcohol. He told William that the visa office was not open until ten in the morning. William said again that he wished to speak to Mr Nightingale, Mr Feather or the ambassador. The guard repeated that no visas could be issued until ten. William showed him his passport to prove that he was British and did not require a visa. The guard said he knew someone in the visa office who, for a consideration, could speed up the process. William demanded to see Mr Nightingale. The guard said it was not possible at night; not even his friend in the visa office could fix that. William became angry and shouted that he was British.

The guard shrugged and held open the gate. 'You come with me, *señor*.'

In the reception hall the guard pointed to a telephone and a list of numbers, then shuffled into an office and shut the door.

Of course, the ambassador did not live at the embassy. Nor did Nightingale or Feather. He should have thought of it, but his idea had been to avoid using the telephone. Now he would have to use it anyway. Nightingale and

Feather shared the same home number. Nightingale answered. Yes, he had seen the news. He knew no details but it could have worse. At least there was no mention of British involvement though the reference to foreign elements was worrying. They would seek a meeting with the Ministry of Foreign Affairs first thing in the morning in order to stress that, whatever appeared to be the case, there was no official British connection with the rebels. They could say that with their hands on their hearts. It was the one positive thing about the privatisation policy. They would also send congratulations to the president. With luck embarrassment might be averted.

'What about my friend?' asked William.

'Your friend? Oh, the little man, yes.' He could sense Nightingale's smile. 'You think he was arrested, don't you? Well, that's all right, then. Nothing we can do.'

'But shouldn't we try to get him out?'

'Why?' Nightingale let the word fall like a drop of water.

'Because he's British. And there are others, not British but they—'

'They got themselves into it. They tried to overthrow the government, they broke the law and they got caught. That's what happened, isn't it?'

'Yes, but—'

'It's not our job to pull people out of the fire after they've jumped into it. We thought it was a bad idea from the start, as you know.'

William was trying not to argue. 'I'd like you to send a message to London on Arthur's behalf. I want them to know what's happened.'

'It'll wait until tomorrow, won't it? Nothing's going to affect anything now.'

'But it's urgent. They ought to know.'

'They haven't asked, have they? Not exactly falling over themselves with enthusiasm.' There was a pause. 'Have you written it yet?'

'No.'

'Well, then. Bring it in in the morning and we'll have a look.'

William was too angry to continue and, anyway, would have said all the wrong things. Nightingale was right, in a sense. He could see that. But was it enough to be right in that way? Whatever he had argued, it would have done nothing for Box and Theresa. He would have to use the EEC.

The wind had got up. It buffeted about the sky, and the polished stars sped between ragged strips of cloud. The roses near the gate – in summer a good show, William remembered – were tossed wildly against the railings. He thought of the embassy parrot that raised its claw in greeting. What happened to parrots on nights like this?

He had closed the wrought-iron gates behind him and was already across the road in a smaller street when he heard the sirens. The street lamps were still out and he stood by a dark wall as two police cars came up the road he had left. They stopped outside the embassy. Several policemen got out and stood looking through the gates until a gust of wind sent their caps spinning along the road. They chased after them, then huddled together as they sorted out which was whose. After that they got back in their cars and watched.

William moved on up the street, keeping close to the wall and, so far as his eyes would permit in the dark, spying out gates or gaps ahead. His heart beat faster and his legs felt weak but at least they weren't trembling, as when he had danced with Theresa that afternoon. Was it really only a few hours before? It seemed another life now. It was surely not coincidence that the police had arrived when they had. His call to Nightingale must have been monitored. Just as well he was prepared not to go back to the flat.

He did not make straight for the cemetery. That would be too much like running to a hole and hiding in it. He felt he should at least find out what was going on so that he would have more to report. He walked quickly towards the city centre. The wind sent paper, cardboard boxes, bottles and cans spinning and bouncing through the streets. A sheet of newspaper rose suddenly before him as high as the roof-tops, hovered, slid back down to the eaves, then shot out of sight like a thing possessed.

He walked more steadily as he neared his shop. He would check that, then the club – not for anything in particular, but just to see. It would be too dangerous to go near the palace and anyway he would have no hope of getting in. It might be possible, though, to ring Carlos, so long as he kept away from the embassy telephones or his own. There were still sirens and whenever he heard a vehicle he hid. Once, at a junction, seven or eight army lorries crossed on the red light, their canvas backs flapping in the wind. There were no sounds of gunfire and no people now. Perhaps a curfew had been announced.

He stopped well down the street from the shop. Three police cars and an army lorry were outside, their red tail-lights making a glow. The shop lights and his own office lights were also on. Figures moved to and fro. He stood in a doorway, knowing it was foolish to stay. Other police cars could come up the road and see him at any time. He was frightened and fascinated. Door by door, he edged up the road.

He stopped when he was near enough to hear their voices. The lorry's engine was ticking over, its diesel throb shaking the vehicle. A policeman was reporting on one of the car radios. Several soldiers came out of the shop with boxes which they stacked in the lorry. Another soldier shouted to know how much there was, then gathered an armful of empty cardboard boxes and took them inside. Someone else shouted something indistinct.

William could see that what they were taking was all his office files and paper-work. It was strange to see familiar objects which he had come to regard as his own being handled as if – well, as if they were someone else's. Perhaps the same was happening at the flat to his books, records, cutlery, clothes. It showed how independent things were. We did not own them. We had them on loan, like spouses. He was relieved not to be able to think very much about that. Watching his life being dismantled was a kind of freedom.

A group of policemen came out of the shop and walked slowly towards the car nearest him. He realised that he was too close. Two of the policemen put their hands to their caps as the wind gusted. They seemed concerned with someone in the centre of the group. When a driver opened the car door the interior lights came on and William recognised Ricardo. He was handcuffed to one of the policemen who held a truncheon in his other hand and every so often jabbed it into Ricardo's stomach. He didn't appear to jab hard but it was enough to make Ricardo double up each time, only to be jerked upright. Instead of putting him in the car they took him round to the front and forced him to his knees so that his face was inches from the headlights. The driver switched them on. They held him so that he had to kneel upright, his arms twisted behind him and his head pulled back by his hair. One of the policemen slapped his face and another, with a slow casual movement as if he were tossing a log on to a fire, laid his truncheon across the lower part of Ricardo's back. Ricardo cried out. Behind them the soldiers carried boxes to and fro.

They were asking questions. William caught odd words and phrases. Two or three were repeated, interspersed by slaps and blows. Ricardo was half crying, half choking. They were asking where William was and where the secret signals were sent from. Ricardo kept saying he didn't know, then was hit again. The blows to the body seemed to cause the most pain – the kidneys, William supposed, in that part of his mind that went on thinking whatever happened.

A gust of wind sent one of the policemen's caps tumbling down the road. It stopped three or four yards from William. The others laughed. As the hatless one walked down the road, William flattened himself in the doorway. The man approached slowly, calling over his shoulder to the others. William pressed himself harder against the door, wishing he hadn't seen what he had seen, wishing fervently that he had not come that far forward, that he was at home in England, going to work every day on the train, cocooned in routine. Another gust rolled the cap a couple of feet nearer. He felt like crying out, kicking the hat, running. He could hear the policeman's boots on the cobbles. The policeman picked up his cap, laughed and shouted to the others. William caught the smell of the man's breath. He had not been so frightened since childhood. The policeman's steps receded. William stayed as he was, upright and unseeing. As he became less fearful he felt more ashamed, as if he had abandoned and betrayed Ricardo. He knew he had not but that did not lessen the feeling. The selfishness of his fear made him wretched and bitter.

He heard a car start and pull away and when he looked again there were only two police cars and the lorry. He slipped out of the doorway and walked back down the street – wanting to run the moment he turned the corner but not letting himself. He felt guilty about Ricardo. He thought of Ricardo's daily evasions, his laziness, his complacency, his arrogance, his pride, but it did not make it any easier. If Ricardo had been kept informed the scheme probably would have worked. Instead, no one had thought of him and now he was going through all that.

He headed for the club. A few heavy drops of rain fell, the wind lessened, the streets were still deserted. As soon as he reached the square he looked carefully round for patrolling soldiers or policemen, but there seemed to be no one. The windows of the club were lit, the curtains drawn back, the front door open, though the other buildings in the square were either unlit or tightly shuttered. The few cars were parked where they had been. No sounds came from the club.

William approached. It was unnecessary and stupid, he knew. Probably he was walking into a trap but he felt he had to know, almost as if in atonement for his own freedom. He stood outside the main door and looked in. If they were waiting for him they could grab him now, he thought as he stepped forward. Inside were overturned chairs, a couple of broken bottles, an up-ended table. The sofas and armchairs were still in place but both the bars were in disarray. Spirit bottles had been wrenched from their holders, shelves ransacked. His footsteps sounded loudly on the big bare floorboards. In the dancing room a towel of the sort used in the massage rooms lay across the piano. On it was a woman's black shoe. Coffee cups and saucers were on a couple of the tables and lying on the stage was a broken violin, its halves still joined by the strings. He stopped walking and listened: the only sounds were the rattling of the sash windows.

He went upstairs, not bothering to tread quietly. If there were anyone waiting, he wanted them to know he was coming. After climbing the main staircase he went along the corridor and up the narrow one that led to the massage rooms. He could hear before he reached the top that some of the air-conditioning units were still on. Most of the room doors were open. Two towels were on the floor and a man's sock lay on the top stair.

He looked in each room. Two still had water in the baths, in one the shower was running. He turned it off. The school clocks said nine-forty. There was something touching about the way the time still faithfully announced itself after everything else had stopped.

He went to the room where he had been with Theresa and sat on the edge of the bed. He wanted more than anything to talk to her. He always had, but there had been so little time. He felt that the room should somehow suggest to others the significance it held for him. It should have a special feel, an atmosphere, but it was like all the others. The noise of the air-conditioners reminded him of Box's EEC. He hoped he would remember how to work it. He would go while it was dark because he couldn't risk entering the grave in daylight. He no longer minded about getting into the grave; it was the living he hid from now.

He didn't hear the footsteps until they were close. They were slow, as his own must have been. He sat without moving. If this was it, then it was it. There was nothing to do but wait. The steps came closer. He looked down and didn't look up until they stopped at the door.

When he did he felt his face change. 'You're all right?'

'Yes.'

'I was so worried, I thought you'd been arrested.'

'Not yet.'

She stood in the doorway looking exactly as when he had seen her last. She was obviously, wonderfully, all right. Her manner, though, was listless and her expression remote.

'What happened?' he asked.

'Manuel Herrera was in the palace with his driver. He heard about it before anyone got to him. He alerted the security police and there was a fight and they freed the generals. Everything is finished.' She spoke as if without interest. 'There is a state of emergency and they have told all the people to stay indoors. Everyone is being arrested except Carlos. They don't know how involved he was but even when they find out I think they will not arrest him yet because he is popular with the people. They will keep him president and prisoner.'

'How did you get away?'

'I was with Carlos and so I was not arrested. I walked out the way we came in with your car. The soldiers on the gate recognised me and let me through. I left Carlos. They will find out I was involved and then he will not want me again, so I left him first.'

'What is he doing – Carlos?'

'Whatever Herrera tells him. He is scared now, he is with his wife and children.'

'Have they arrested many?'

'Everyone who was here. That is why it is empty. They think it was planned here: Ines, the girls, Ricardo, El Lizard, everyone.'

'I saw Ricardo. They had taken him to my shop, looking for me.'

'They will torture them all.'

He got up. 'We must hide.'

'I will go to my family and warn them. They can hide.

It's better that I am found. Then they might leave my family alone. But you are British. You can leave, your embassy will protect you.'

'They won't.'

'They shot your friend.'

'Arthur?'

'With machine guns. He had taken the colonel's sword to protect Ines and the girls when the soldiers wanted to rape them. He would not put down the sword and so they shot him.'

'Dead?'

'Afterwards they took Ines and the girls away.'

'Poor Arthur.'

'If he is dead he cannot be tortured.'

'Come with me and we'll run away. Then we can marry. Sally has left me.'

'She has left you?'

'With an American called Max. He's in the CIA and she's run off with him. I think they're leaving the country, too. We could do the same.'

She came forward and put one hand on his arm. 'Poor William.'

'It's all right, I don't mind. It's all right.'

'You do mind – it is in your face.'

'No, I'm sad for Arthur and Ricardo and all the others.'

'You must not ignore yourself.'

He took her hand. 'But what about you? We must do something.'

'Perhaps the CIA will rescue us and the Americans come. That is our only hope.'

'They seem to be going rather than coming.'

She let go of his hand but continued to stand close. 'Shall we undress?' She smiled slowly at his surprise. 'Always you say you want to talk to me. You cannot really talk with a woman unless you make love with her. Your conversation is unfinished.'

'Make love now?'

'If you want to talk.'

He undressed, this time without self consciousness.

When they were naked she knelt by him and unpinned her hair.

'When I first saw you in the covered market that day,' she said, 'I thought you were a priest. You looked so serious. But you had a kind smile.'

'I was frightened of you.'

'Why?'

'You were too beautiful.'

'Does it worry you that I have been a prostitute?'

'Yes.'

'But you still like me?'

'I love you.'

'I will not be a prostitute any more.'

'Come away with me. I will look after you.'

She smiled. 'First you must talk to me.'

Later she sat up suddenly. 'Why do you love me? Is it because I'm beautiful?'

He propped himself on one elbow. 'That and something else. I want to go on talking to you, on and on.'

'I have never really loved any man.'

'Why not?'

'Perhaps my banker, a little. He was kind.' She stretched out her arms and looked at them; the upper parts were slightly plump. 'Did you like making love with me?'

'Yes.' He was worried by the question. 'Yes, I did. Very much.'

'*Really* like?'

'Yes, really.'

'I don't think you did, not really. I think you were too worried. Is it long since you made love with your wife?'

'Many months. I'm sorry it was over so quickly.'

She looked along her outstretched arms, rotating them slowly. 'You should not worry about such things. It takes time to know someone. Men are always in such a hurry. Also, perhaps I am like a fantasy for you.'

He sat up. 'No, it's not that, it never has been. It's you

I like, yourself, ever since you spoke to me. It was speaking that did it.'

She smiled and took his hands in hers. 'You look like a priest again. We can be friends and then maybe I will love you. To be friends is the big thing. All my life I have thought if I can find a man to be my friend, I will stay with him. But normally I cannot be friends with men. They do not want it. They want the sex, they want me for their mistress and that is all.'

'We will be friends. I will take you away, anywhere. We will send money to your family. You must come with me.'

'I have never been anywhere. You will get fed up with me and then you will send me back.'

'I won't. I won't ever get fed up, I will always look after you. I like to have someone to look after.'

'You will miss your wife and she will come back.'

'She won't, not now. Our marriage was dead for a long time. Anyway, she never wanted me to look after her. She never wanted me to do anything for her. I think she never wanted me at all.' He felt as if his marriage had ended years ago. Theresa listened with downcast eyes. Her dark eyebrows arched strongly and evenly. He pulled her forward and kissed them. 'We will hide and then we will go away together.'

She shook her head. 'It is not possible.'

'Why not?'

She looked up. Her eyes were impregnable, as in the cemetery when he had told her he was married. 'Things do not work for me.'

He argued, pleaded, insisted. More in her tone than her words, he had felt the brush of the wing of despair – the outer feathers merely, but it was as if they had darkened the corners of his vision. He felt he was arguing with her to stay alive and his words became more impassioned as he became more fearful. She remained calmly negative. There was no hope for her, she said. She had always known that. Her life might be short, but he would grow old. She was not a magician but some things she knew and was nearly always right about. This was one. She was not sad – it was God's way. It made no difference what she did but at least she had done something for her family. She hoped she would be with God and the Blessed Virgin.

'You want this,' he said. 'You're talking yourself into it.'

She stroked his face. 'Poor William, I am making you miserable. But you are really my friend?'

'Yes, I keep telling you. *Yes.*'

She kissed him. 'We will be friends for all our lives.'

It was some time later that the soldiers came. She heard them first and broke away from him, her eyes hard and glittering. 'It is now. It is happening.'

'What?'

'They are coming. It is what I knew – it is starting.' She grabbed his hand. 'You will always be my friend?'

'Yes, yes.' He sat up.

'We will be friends in heaven.'

'Yes, don't worry, don't worry.' He was still trying to reassure her when the door opened.

The soldiers paused but only for a moment. They had none of the embarrassment which had afflicted those who arrested the generals. There were five or six of them, clumsy but purposeful. They pulled Theresa and William away from each other, the one in charge excitedly repeating, 'Search them, search their clothes, search them.'

William at first felt paralysingly vulnerable, but when he looked at Theresa the feeling left him. She stood simply, passively, unembarrassed. She already had a dignity that made the soldiers at her side uneasy about holding her. Their hands rested lightly on her arms and the one who was going through her clothes looked awkward.

William's clothes they went through vigorously and carelessly. A soldier threw his trousers and underpants across to him and the one in charge ordered him to put them on. When he had done so he looked again at Theresa. They had done nothing with her. He was held apart from her as if they were two people who had been caught fighting. When he tried to catch her eye the soldiers pulled him back by the arms and pushed him towards the door. He turned and this time caught her eye. She gazed at him without expression or recognition, as if she were not fully recovered from an anaesthetic. Four of the soldiers stayed with her, the other two pulled William roughly by the arms. The door closed on her.

When they left the building a blanket was thrown over his head and he was made to walk stooping, his arms pushed up behind his back. All he could see was his bare feet on the wet cobbles. It was raining heavily. His head felt the drops through the blanket and the wind flapped its edges against his legs.

He was pushed into a vehicle and made to sit with his head between his knees. It was uncomfortable and whenever he tried to raise his head a hand pushed it down again. No one spoke. The vehicle lurched frequently and the gearbox whined. He listened to every change in noise, tried to judge from each change in direction where they were going – he assumed the palace but couldn't tell. He wasn't at all frightened. What was happening to him seemed of little account; it was only him. His thoughts remained with Theresa, with her muted, submerged look, and the four soldiers.

The car stopped twice in quick succession, then moved slowly over rough ground and stopped again. There were voices and the sound of rain on the roof. A hand was pressed on the back of his head, keeping it down. After some time he was made to get out. His feet were on rough ground and, just beyond the edge of the blanket, he could see rain spattering into a puddle. Someone took his arm and he was pushed forward. The ground hurt his feet, he banged his toes on stones and slipped in mud. The soldiers took no account of his difficulties, treading confidently in their boots. Only when they reached a small flight of brick steps did they make allowances, waiting for him to feel with his feet from one step to the next.

They were in a building, brightly lit and with cold green lino. Mud trickled from his wet feet. Doors opened and closed and there were voices giving orders; then he was pushed forward again, this time with someone holding the blanket so that he could not see even the floor any more. Once, and then again a few yards further on, they used his head to open swing doors. The lino ended and they went down steps of brick or stone, then along another corridor with more lino. A telephone rang. They approached and then passed it before stopping abruptly and turning in through a door.

This was a room with different lino. No one was touching him and he stood as he had been left, bowed in the blanket. There was some coming and going, then the blanket was pulled off and he was told to stand up. It was a green-painted functional room with a radiator, a filing cabinet, a desk and chair and a blanked out metal window. On one wall was a photograph of Carlos, beneath it photographs of the generals.

For a moment he thought he was alone but when he tried to turn round his shoulder was pushed roughly forward. An officer came into view and sat at the desk. He was younger than William and looked like Ricardo.

'Undress,' he said.

William took off his trousers and underpants. He saw then that two soldiers stood behind him. They were very young and looking precociously solemn. He had the feeling that both the officer and the soldiers were embarrassed by him. He felt vulnerable but not frightened. His vulnerability was complete, he was defenceless, there was no room for pretence. He felt this gave him a strength which his captors, who had everything to protect, lacked.

'Face the wall and bend over,' said the officer. 'Right down.'

Before his glasses fell off William could see between his legs that the man was still stitting at his desk. One of the soldiers took the glasses away. There was then a face between his legs and a pair of thumbs pulled his buttocks apart and examined his anus with a torch. He had to force himself not to clench his buttocks. The torch was switched off and the face disappeared.

'Stand up,' said the officer.

William stood and went to turn round but was pushed back to face the wall. He could hear movements behind him. The blanket was thrown over his head and he was made to stoop again. A hand took him by the arm and pulled him towards the door.

There was more lino, more descending stairs, then a cold damp concrete floor and finally a cell. He was pushed in, the blanket was pulled off and the door closed in one movement. The cell was bare and the walls again were green, the paintwork marked and smeared reddish-brown in places. A single bright light was flush with the ceiling behind wire mesh. Panels of dark glass were set in at the top of two of the walls, behind which it was just possible to make out camera lenses. The only furniture was a three-legged stool.

The cell was cold and smelt damp. William was more conscious of his nakedness now than when he had been in the office with the soldiers. He walked the perimeter, trying to see whether the camera lenses followed him, but his eyes were not good enough. His feet were very cold. He sat on the stool, testing it first, and put his feet on the bottom rung. He became colder. Next he squatted on his feet on the stool, which had by then been warmed. It was uncomfortable and he was about to get off when the door opened and the two soldiers rushed in. He stepped clumsily backwards off the stool. They snatched it away and went out, slamming the bolts home. He resisted the urge to look up at the cameras and continued pacing the room. After some time he sat on the floor with his back against the wall; it was very hard and very cold. He pulled his knees up to his chest and put his arms around them but soon started to shiver, so he got up and began pacing again. It was four paces one way and three and a half the other. He thought again of the woman who had walked from Russia to Paris in her cell.

He had no idea how much time passed. It didn't *feel* long, but there was nothing by which to judge – no sounds, no change in light. It might have been very little time, since he was neither hungry nor thirsty nor conscious of his bladder. He would worry about that when it happened. He began to feel that despite the cold, the confinement and the bleakness of his future, he had a kind of freedom. All that might have worried and concerned him had fallen away, leaving what was essential. He still wasn't sure what that was but felt he was beginning to find it out. Perhaps he was to suffer greatly. There was nothing he could do about that. It would happen when it would. Even thoughts of what might be happening to Theresa, what was happening to Ricardo, what had happened to Box were more bearable now that he was locked up and helpless. He wished they could know he was there and how he felt about them. He would have liked Box to know, too; he couldn't really believe he would not.

He sat against the wall again, tired but not sleepy. The cold put sleep out of the question, anyway. Time passed. It was odd to have no measure of it. He could recall no occasion in his adult life when he had not any idea of the passing of time – no possibility, ever, of dusk or dawn. He realised how his day was hourly parcelled out, how he lived life like someone on a boat, so busy taking bearings he had no time for sea or sky.

His bladder recalled him and with nothing else to hold his attention, the desire grew stronger. It was not yet as bad as when he had been in the medical centre and he was determined not to let it get that far. Perhaps he was meant to go on the floor. He got up and knocked on the door.

It was opened abruptly. They must be watching his every movement. 'I want to go to the toilet,' he said unthinkingly in English.

The two soldiers stared. He repeated it in Spanish. They threw the blanket over his head, pulled his arms behind his back and pushed him out along the corridor. They came to a junction where he had to step up but before he could do so they stopped him.

'Lie down,' ordered one.

'I want to go to the toilet.'

His arms were twisted and yanked upwards, forcing him to his knees. He lay down on the stone floor, his top half still covered by the blanket. He wanted to urinate more urgently now, and not only that. Perhaps they were going to make him do it there. Perhaps they were going to torture him or pull his legs apart and kick him. The thought made his buttocks quiver, though he did not feel fear. He felt detached from himself. His chin rested painfully on the concrete and his eyes focused on the tiny ridges an inch or two away. He felt he was more vividly aware of detail than he had ever been.

A door banged. There was some grunting, a few muttered words and the sound of something being dragged along the corridor in front of him. As it came closer he heard boots on concrete and heavy breathing with, amidst it, whimpering. The sounds passed, another door banged and there was silence.

'Get up,' said one of the soldiers.

The toilet had neither door nor seat but it was clean and there was paper. The two soldiers stood and watched.

Back in the cell there was only cold and silence. No doubt if they made him cold enough, tired enough and hungry enough for long enough he would give in, whatever that involved, but he felt that by then it wouldn't really be him who was surrendering: it would be what was left. Everything good and strong would have been used up.

Yet it was the past that interested him more than the future, particularly now that all his past should have come down to this. Until now he had simply drifted with the current. Job, marriage and South America had followed each other as one thing after another. Símilarly, involvement with Theresa, Box and Carlos. He had initiated nothing, had just let it happen. It was the same with Sally. He had been considerate of her but not really attentive to her. Now, quite suddenly, he was washed up on a rock. Other currents swept onwards, but his had stopped. What was left were memories and the impressions of personality, particularly of those who had given of themselves. They left more behind. For him it had all just been easy or fun or desirable. It had become serious with *Señor* Finn. That was when he was first faced with consequence.

The cell now seemed the result of his whole life, not only of the past few days. Layers of habit and illusion, years of accretion, had fallen away with his clothes. He felt that at last he might know where to begin again, if he were permitted.

14

'*Estupido*. You are stupid, *Señor* Wooding, and you are dangerous. Stupid people are more dangerous than clever people. They do things so stupid that no one would think of them, and sometimes they nearly work.'

Manuel Herrera sat behind the desk with his hands resting on his chest and his fingertips just touching. He looked tired. It was the office in which William had been searched. William stood before him, still naked, but flanked by two different soldiers. It was much later but he did not know how much; he assumed it was day. He felt hungry, weak, cold and tired.

Manuel looked at William's body. 'Why do you let yourself get so fat?'

William did not answer. It was another rhetorical question. He was there to be lectured, perhaps condemned, but not interrogated. So far it seemed they knew all he knew.

'And because of your stupidity and the stupidity of those who sent you, other gullible stupid people get themselves into trouble. All your people in the tango club, little turncoat Ricardo, the president's whore – they will all suffer because of you. Treason is a capital offence here, like espionage. It is not necessary to involve the courts since it is the prerogative of the People's Party to decide punishment. All these others will suffer because you did the bidding of your British spy master. Even the British Embassy acknowledges the stupidity of the affair. They have told us it was nothing to do with them and clearly they do not approve.'

That meant it must be day, thought William. Getting some idea of the time was a small triumph. 'The people at the club were nothing to do with it, they didn't know.'

'That is not possible. It was arranged with them.'

'It wasn't.'

'Who knew, then?'

'Box and me.'

'Plus at least two. One is too important to be punished and is saying he now regrets his foolishness. The other has got what she deserves.' Manuel smiled. He added that Ricardo would also get what he deserved and that El Lizard was being foolishly intractable, trying to deny everything. So were some of the girls. He hoped William would be more cooperative than his colleagues and would feel able to recall, without too much persuasion, the whereabouts of Box's secret transmitter.

Manuel's tone as he said that Theresa had got what she deserved, his playful little smile, distilled all William's feelings into one. It was a feeling as definite and intoxicating as desire, an illicit release from the sense, if not the fact, of responsibility. He would do something at last, something all his own. Before he died, he would kill Manuel Herrera. He was as certain of that as Theresa had been that things would not work out. He wanted to tell Manuel, to watch his expression change, but instead he said, 'I don't know where he hid his transmitter. I know he had one, but he was very security-conscious. He only told me what he thought I needed to know.'

Manuel nodded. 'Maybe. He did seem to go to great lengths – unnecessary and futile lengths. A strange man. Why did they send him, do you think?'

'I don't know.'

'It's hard to believe they were serious. Did they tell you he was coming when they sent you?'

'They didn't send me; he recruited me.'

Manuel smiled again. 'I find that very hard to believe.' He nodded to the soldiers, who took William by the arms. 'One thing.' The soldiers stopped. 'We haven't yet decided whether to shoot you or to keep you for a while. You may be useful later. If you are sensible, you will be. Meanwhile, I think you will find the regime here will help with your weight problem. *Chau.*'

They took him back to a different cell. The paint and layout were the same but there were fewer reddish-brown smears on the walls. It unsettled him for the first hour or so. He had not realised he had become accustomed to the old cell. Though weak and tired, he paced the four wals while trying to recall Manuel's every word and nuance of tone. This was what they counted on, he assumed, provided they weren't actually torturing you. You thought about nothing but your predicament, obsessively, despairingly, with no end in sight, and your only contact with the world was your interrogator. All he had to do was to make you tired and keep you waiting and in the end you would want to talk to him. Even with Manuel, there had been moments when he had felt like explaining everything – it would have been so good to have rest – but that was before Manuel had said what he had about Theresa.

The door opened and a soldier came in holding a metal tray with a mug of water, a bowl of brown soup and a chunk of bread. He put it down and went out. William lay on the cold floor, propped on his elbow, and ate and drank quickly. He did not mind that the cameras would see how hungry he was. When he had finished he felt hungrier than before and got up feeling slightly warmed but shivering again. The door opened, the soldier took the tray, the door closed, the bolts rammed home and there was silence.

Once he thought he heard a fly. He had read that in some Chinese prisons the prisoners lived off them. They also ate the corn found in horse-dung. Solitary confinement didn't so far seem so bad. It was an opportunity to look back on a half-life of partial decisions and easy options. It was better, too, than the overcrowding of British gaols. If only he could get warm and the light would go off and there were more food. Sometimes it was as if time wasn't passing at all.

The door opened. This time it was another soldier carrying a plastic bag. He held it upside down, emptied it of William's possessions, and went out.

William stared. His clothes were familiar yet strange;

he was slightly reluctant to put them on despite the offered warmth. He felt he would be resuming his old life, that the change he felt he had undergone would be nullified. When he started to dress, though, he did so quickly. It was surprising what a difference shoes and socks made. His money was there but not his credit cards, cheque book or passport.

The door opened. 'Come on,' the soldier said.

This time there was no blanket, no arms behind his back. They were in another green corridor with bright lights, steps going up at one end and double doors opened by push-bars at the other. They walked towards the doors. Perhaps he was to be shot. Would they dress him for that? Quite likely. Even his glasses were in his trouser pockets. He put them on but they showed no more than that the green paint was in worse condition than he had thought.

'Where are we going?' he asked.

'You are being freed.'

'Why?'

They did not answer. Their footsteps echoed in the corridor. Perhaps this was what they always said to prevent panic. One of the soldiers knocked open the push-bar doors. It was dark outside. William stopped. Surely it could not be the same night as his arrest? No, he knew it wasn't. It must be the one after, perhaps even the one after that. His eyes being so bad at night, they took some time to make what adjustments they could. He realised he was in one of the palace huts where he had previously seen the prisoners crouching on the steps. The steps led down to the grass. To either side he could see other huts, linked by the covered walkways along which he had seen them drag the bloodied prisoner.

He went gingerly down the steps. The soldiers seemed to realise it was difficult for him and took his arm.

'Where are we going?' he asked again.

'To the guard-room. They are letting you go. You can walk out. Free.'

As they crossed the grass there were sounds of distant gunfire – small-arms fire with occasional louder crumps.

Both soldiers stiffened and one said something about the airport. Alarm bells rang. The soldier who had spoken ran off, while the other indicated to William to keep walking. There were shouts and running figures in the darkness, vehicles were started and revved a klaxon sounded, drowning the alarms. The remaining soldier looked worried and confused. 'This is full alert,' he said. 'I must be at my position.'

He was a boy, really. William nodded. 'I know my way.'

'You know your way out?'

'I have been here before.' The soldier left him. The darkness seethed with movement, much of it invisible to William. The klaxon made an unbearable noise. There was no sound of nearer gunfire. Perhaps this was an exercise or maybe just panic. Anyway, who would be attacking the palace? He wasn't far from the entrance he had used before. Maybe they would let him out now, maybe he would be shot as an intruder. Why should he have been allowed to go, anyway? It was suspicious.

He stood still long enough to get his bearings and to make his decision. Twice groups of soldiers ran past without noticing him. When most of the immediate activity had died down, he headed for Carlos's quarters. The door through which they had carried the coffin was locked but one of the side-room windows was ajar. He climbed in, which was more difficult than he had thought, and closed the window behind him. He headed for the white-panelled room that led to Carlos's private quarters, walking as confidently as he could since there was no hope of hiding in the passage and his only chance on meeting someone would be to brazen it out.

By the time he reached the panelled room the klaxon and bells had stopped. There were sounds of troops outside but the building itself was eerily quiet. Carlos's private garden was deserted and there were no lights in his quarters. Perhaps he was with his family or imprisoned at his ranch. Deciding he would wait a while, William sat in an armchair behind the door.

He must have slept because when he heard voices and footsteps they sounded on top of him. They were just outside the door and one voice was definitely that of Carlos. The handle turned, the door opened a few inches and stopped. William did not move. He could not, anyway; his limbs were leaden with sleep and would not obey him. He heard Carlos saying, '*Sí, sí*. I'm sure you're right to try. Neither of them ever mentioned it to me, but I don't know.' He sounded as if he were trying to get away. The other speaker said something indistinct. 'Good,' continued Carlos. 'He got away before the alarm? Just as well. That will leave you free to attend to the airport business.'

Carlos came in and closed the door. He was wearing his general's uniform and looked tense. He would have gone through without noticing if William had not spoken. At first he was startled, then angry and fearful.

'They'll kill me if they find you here. They'll think I got you in. How did you get here?'

William told him. He did not get up.

'What do you want?' Carlos asked. 'I can get you money if that's what you need but you can't stay here. They'll think we're colluding.'

'I want to know what happened.'

'Nothing happened, that's the trouble. It all went wrong, just fizzled out. Isn't it obvious?' He paused as if hoping that might satisfy William. 'When they got back here with Quinto and Paulotti no one knew what to do with them. People lost their nerves and hung around. Someone told the security police troops and one of their officers contacted Manuel who was in the apartment he uses here. He'd been down at the club with us, you see, and had then come back. By the time I got here, they'd shot some of my soldiers and freed Quinto and Paulotti and then they attacked our party. They thought I might be a prisoner, too. They still think that – even Quinto and Paulotti – except that Manuel knows it's not true. He worked it out straight away when he saw I was with Theresa – only he hasn't told anyone, I think, so I'm even more in his power. I don't know what he's planning but he'll get rid of me, I know he will.' Carlos looked petulant and seemed close to tears. 'If he finds you here, he'll kill us both.'

'What happened to Arthur Box?'

'I don't know. It was dark. They took the colonel prisoner and they were going to take the girls back to their barracks but Arthur wouldn't let them. He said it was ungentlemanly or something stupid. He got hold of the colonel's sword and shouted to Theresa and me to run away while he held them off from the girls. They still hadn't realised I was there, you see. I ran away with Theresa and they shot Arthur. Why didn't he have a gun? Are your people never armed?'

'What happened to the colonel?'

'Being interrogated, I suppose.' Carlos's petulance faded and he sat wearily in one of the armchairs. 'Same as all the others.'

'Which others?'

'El Lizard and your assistant and some of the girls.'

'What's happened to Theresa? They caught her with me.'

'I don't know. She came back here with me. Then she escaped.'

'Has Herrera said anything about her?'

'He said, "You will be pleased to hear that your treacherous mistress has met the fate she deserved at the hands of a number of soldiers." I remember it exactly because it sounded as if he had been saving it for me.'

Every utterance was an effort for William, a raising for a few seconds of the great blanket of weariness. 'Why did Herrera let me go?'

'He thinks Arthur must have had other accomplices and that you might lead him to them. He thinks someone must be keeping a secret radio transmitter for Arthur and that you might know them even if you don't know they're involved. They were going to keep you under surveillance from the time you left the guard-room. Then they'll arrest you again.'

There was more distant gunfire.

'I was sorry about Arthur,' Carlos added. 'I liked him. I suppose I might have done something, but it was difficult. I kept quiet and just ran when he said.'

'Is that gunfire coming from the airport?'

'Yes, they think it may be some rebel soldiers from another part of the army. You see, even I call them rebels now.' Carlos grinned humourlessly. 'The control tower said the airport was under attack but we haven't been able to get anything more out of them. Manuel says I mustn't make my television appearance until we've found out what's happened.'

'What are you going to say?'

'It's being written for me.' Carlos stared at his shoes, then looked up. 'Did you send my message to your Queen and prime minister?'

'Yes. Also the Americans know about it. My wife's lover turned out to be a CIA man and she showed it him.'

Carlos cheered up. 'That is good, very good. Maybe the Americans will do something – they are more likely to do something than the British, aren't they?'

'I suppose they are.'

'It was kind of your wife to show it to her lover. Please thank her from me.'

'She's gone off with him now.'

'Well, when you next write.'

William got to his feet. 'I'd better go.'

'It won't very very easy for them to follow you with this alert going on.'

'That's good, too.'

'I'm sorry it has not worked, William. I hope you escape. If they catch you, please don't tell them you have seen me.'

'All right.'

'It is not for myself, it is for my family. I am worried for them.'

'Yes.'

'You do not look well.'

William looked at himself in the wall mirror. He was

unshaven and bleary and he thought he looked disgusting. 'I've been in the cells.'

'Of course, I was forgetting.'

'Do you have any food?'

Carlos's irritation and anxiety returned. 'Food? I can't feed you. Someone would realise.'

'Anything will do.'

Carlos went to another room and came back with two bars of chocolate. William ate one and put the other in his pocket. Then he held out his hand. 'Good luck.'

'And you.' Carlos was much happier now. 'It was a shame it didn't work, but if you can persuade your embassy to get you out of the country you should be safe. Herrera and the others have enough to do here. Perhaps we will meet again. If I can stay president, I will visit London one day. It's a pity about Theresa, too. She was one of the best I've had – possibly *the* best.'

William opened the door and stepped out into the corridor.

15

Whoever had searched the flat had indulged a malicious pleasure in destruction. The wardrobe hung open, clothes were trodden on the floor, the mattresses lay half off the beds, the carpets were pulled up, the crockery broken. The fridge lay on its side in the middle of the kitchen, the washing machine was pulled away from its plumbing points. William's stamp collection was scattered over the floor of the spare bedroom. The windows had been left open but the door was locked, the lock unforced. Presumably they had got keys from the owners.

William was too tired to do more than close the windows and pull the mattress back onto the main bed. He couldn't move without treading on things. Whatever they'd wanted to find, they'd failed, and that was something. If they had been following him from the palace they'd been further disappointed because he'd simply gone home – and that was also something. And if they were waiting outside now they'd have to wait all night. He drank a lot of water, ate the other bar of chocolate, set the alarm and stretched out on the mattress.

When the alarm woke him he couldn't move. His heart wouldn't seem to pump enough to get him going. He was like a sheep on its back, unable even to roll onto his side. He had never felt so heavy. Eventually he rolled onto the floor on all fours, then got up and went to the bathroom where he washed and shaved without turning on the light; he felt his eyes wouldn't stand it, and there was just enough daylight for him to see where things were. The shave was wonderful; it was like food, drink and sleep all in one. Afterwards he drank more water, ate all the cheese that had been in the fridge and put two apples in his pocket.

He could see through the window that there was a thick

sea-mist, which was perfect. The tree-tops showed above it but below all was white and impenetrable. Confident that no one would be able to see him from below, he stood on the balcony and breathed in the morning air. The balcony rails were wet and cold, the air clear, the day absolutely silent. The mist muffled everything, even the sound of the sea.

He used the stairs rather than the lift but there was no doorman anyway. He slipped out and crossed the road. As soon as he had gone far enough for the building to be invisible, he paused beneath a tree and listened. There was no sound of hurrying footsteps. They would need to keep close if they wanted to follow him in that mist. Box would have approved, he thought.

He cut across towards the golf course. The remains of *Señor* Finn's hut still stood among the pampas grass. Beyond he could hear the small lapping waves. The sea must be calm.

The mist was lifting by the time he reached the cemetery but there was no one about, not even the flower-seller, and the gate opened. The mist made the sepulchres and tombs even more grotesque than usual. As he reached the second square, he became aware that his footsteps on the path were being echoed by the walls. It was the only sound and it was far too loud. He stopped and listened. The sound continued. There were footsteps ahead of him, distant but receding. The mist was shifting and he could see twenty yards, sometimes thirty, sometimes ten. He walked carefully through the arch and turned off towards number 1066.

The grave was just as when Box had left it. William removed the coffin lid, carefully avoiding the one he had fallen through. The equipment looked formidable at first and he had to use the torch. He remembered more than he had thought of Box's instructions; also – evidently not trusting him – Box had added labels to some of the switches. Written in Box's meticulous hand, they brought his voice to William's ear: 'Start – switch to Start when you wish to start;' 'Off – do not switch to Off until you have finished.' William switched on, the green light glowed and the machine hummed. He lay full-length in the coffin, the controls before him. It was necessary to wait thirty seconds before slotting in the cartridge; one cartridge per message.

He didn't mind about coffins now, he minded only about Manuel Herrera. For thirty seconds he pondered the novelty of this vengeful urge. He had never been vengeful; his disposition was to ignore, to forget, to walk away, but with Manuel it had always been different. Manuel had awoken in him a different capacity. It had started when they met, before there was anything to be revenged: something visceral, irreconcilable, the sense – which he had not recognised – of an absolute emnity. It was intoxicating.

After thirty seconds the other light came on and he began typing his message on the small keyboard. He had worked out what he would say during his walk: FOLLOWING PRESIDENT'S REQUEST FOR HELP, BOX AND PRESIDENT ORGANISED COUP WHICH FAILED BECAUSE HERRERA ESCAPED. BOX AND OTHERS KILLED. PRESIDENT STILL THERE BUT POWERLESS, RULED BY HERRERA. FIGHTING GOING ON AT AIRPORT. EMBASSY UNHELPFUL. AMERICANS KNOW ABOUT PRESIDENT'S REQUEST AND COUP BECAUSE MY WIFE'S LOVER IS CIA MAN HUEFFER. PLEASE SEND INSTRUCTIONS RE BOX'S EFFECTS AND MESSAGES FOR WIDOW. AM STILL AT LARGE BUT MAY NOT BE FOR MUCH LONGER. WOODING.

Box had said that replies could usually be expected at twelve-hourly intervals except in cases of urgency, but even then it would take an hour or two. William switched the machine to Receive.

The clicking of the incoming message woke him and he watched the letters come up on the screen. The message read: PARA ONE. THIS PROJECT HAS BEEN SOLD TO CIA. FUTURE DEVELOPMENT IN THEIR HANDS. WE ARE SENDING DETAILS TO EMBASSY. PARA TWO. BAD LUCK CASUALTIES. WE WILL CONTACT WIDOW AND REVERT RE EFFECTS. DO YOU HAVE BODY? PARA THREE. PLEASE SEND EXPENSE CLAIM WITHIN 24 HOURS. EXPENSE CLAIMS RE DEAD OPERATIONS

NOT ACCEPTABLE AFTER THAT PERIOD. PLEASE ALSO SEND DATE OF BIRTH, MAIDEN NAME OF WIFE AND FULL UK ADDRESS. THANKS FOR HELP. CONTACT US IF EVER IN LONDON. MESSAGE ENDS.

William tapped in the one word, 'NOBODY', and shut down.

The mist still lingered in the streets but it was more a haze now and the sun was beginning to break through. There were a few early cars, coughing and misfiring, and the usual battered buses. Street-traders trundled their trolleys over the cobbles, shouting to each other. Wheezing old pick-up trucks rumbled in from the country filled with produce and peasants. Whatever had happened to the government, life seemed to go on. William saw no police cars but there were military vehicles. Surprisingly, people stopped to watch them pass and some waved. It was odd that they should be so popular. Vehicles and troops looked both familiar and different; the soldiers wore the usual olive-greens, but there was something else about them. William did not stare because he did not want to attract attention.

His office had been dealt with more kindly than the flat. Files and papers had been removed but the furniture had not been overturned. It was too early for the two girls – he would have to see them later and explain. He would also have to say something to London. He switched on the telex machine and found a message waiting. It was brief: the Board had met and in view of the recent industrial and political troubles had decided to cut the company's losses and close down the operation. He was to return to London pending reassignment.

He knew that this last was sometimes a euphemism for the sack. He replied: REVOLUTION IN PROGRESS. ARREST IMMINENT. WILL REVERT WHEN POSSIBLE. That should give them something to think about. They would enjoy telling each other that nothing had ever gone right there and if he never returned it would take them months to sort everything out. He left a note for the girls, telling them to come back the next day and meanwhile to help themselves to the petty cash.

The smell as well as the thought of food drew him towards the covered market. He salivated at the image of sizzling steaks, mushrooms, tomatoes, sausages and offal thrown together by the loud, happy, fat men. He was not put off by having last breakfasted there with Theresa; it was a reason for going, something she would have urged. Still he did not let himself think directly about her.

The market was as crowded as if it were already lunchtime. The clock as always said ten-past four, the smoke from the fires curled around it, everyone ate, drank and talked simultaneously. The nearby streets were so busy with people hurrying into the market that he checked his watch to make sure that it wasn't somehow already lunchtime. He sat down at the bar where he had first met Theresa and Ines.

The sweating *padrón* asked him what he wanted.

'Everything.'

'And coffee, *señor*?'

'And coffee.'

'And whisky?'

It was unforgivably early. The stool felt even smaller than he remembered. He ought to say 'No' to something.

'Is free, *señor*. To celebrate our new government.'

'Ah, yes. The new government.'

The *padrón*'s grin seemed as wide as his arms. 'Everyone comes here to talk today, no one is serious for work. It is carnival. We are pleased the Americans come to save our president. Now he is safe and we can have good government: no more Cubans, no more Russian officers. You will have whisky?'

William remembered the military vehicles, their familiarity and their strangeness. It took him some time to reply. 'Yes, I will have whisky.'

'You American?'

'No, *Inglés*.'

'Do not worry, is similar.'

When his food came he ate and drank hugely. The talk

around him was of how the president had been saved from a coup mounted by the spy Herrera and the treacherous generals. They had arrested the president and his beautiful mistress in the tango club but the president had escaped and, relying on local troops of the army, had held out against the security police. Then, faced with the threat of Russian and Cuban intervention, he had called for American help and the American marines and soldiers had landed at the airport, and now America was going to help the economy and there would be more money for everyone. But some people had been killed; there had been fighting, especially at the airport. The spy Herrera was being sought but had gone into hiding. One thing was certain: if the people found him he would be killed. It had been discovered that he was homosexual. That was only to be expected. He would be lynched and castrated. Anyone who attempted to overthrow the president deserved at least that.

William listened and said nothing. He hoped Manuel was still alive.

There was talk of a broadcast and a small black and white television was rigged up on the clock tower. The picture was fuzzy and the sound irregular. William stood at the back of the crowd but he could see quite clearly that it was Carlos on the screen. He was in uniform and looked vigorous and cheerful. He described how he had sent a message to heads of government of the international community asking for help in his and the army's fight against the rebels who had tried to overthrow him, how the American president had responded, how he himself had fought the rebels with a sword taken from the body of a loyal assistant, how a beautiful woman had suffered in order that he and the country might be free.

There was cheering when the broadcast finished, then the television fell from the clock tower to more cheering and laughter. A band began playing outside one of the tobacconists' kiosks, each player with a cigar between grinning lips. A few girls began dancing. Some men joined in, others clapped. The bodies swayed like ripples on water, suggestive of deeper motions. The man beside William nudged him and grinned.

Nightingale stood at the foot of the embassy stairs, barring the way.

'There just is not time,' he said. 'We're all terribly busy. This kind of intervention in a host country's affairs is highly irregular, to say the least. We're asking London for instructions.'

'You've had no message for Box or for me?'

Nightingale tossed his head. 'I didn't say that, I never said that. I said I hadn't *read* anything. There is a message, I believe, but there has not been time to decode it. Ralph's much too busy with our traffic to worry about yours.'

The embassy guard was listening with apparent indifference. He gave no impression of having recognised William from the night of the telephone call.

'I need to know what it says,' said William.

'Why the hurry? I should have thought it was somewhat overtaken by events.' Nightingale smiled.

William was learning that making one resolution in one area of life led to a more general stiffening of resolve. The fact that his resolution was still secret added to its potency. 'I'll stay here until I know.'

'You can't do that.'

'I can.'

'I'll have you thrown out.'

'Go on, then.' William looked complacently about him. He wasn't going to fight but it would take several good men to carry him. The guard was barely up to moving himself. 'No use calling the police; they're terribly busy, too.' He sensed victory. The important thing now was to make surrender easy for the about-to-be-defeated. 'See what you can do. I'll go for a walk in the garden.'

The grass was still wet with dew but the sun was warmer than for some time. Summer was on its way. The man tending the rhododendrons turned out to be the ambassador.

'Quite a to-do,' he said. 'All this business.'

'Sorry if it's upset you,' said William.
'Upset me?'
'Well, upset Feather.'
'Feather's been drunk for days. I've never known him so bad. I'm wondering whether I should tell London.'
'You don't mind, then?'
'Mind what?'
'About our coup attempt and the Americans taking over.'
The ambassador shook his head. 'Well, that's all out of our hands, isn't it? Thank goodness. Yes. So long as London don't blame us. I wish my leave had started a week earlier. Do you think the flights will be all right?'
'Probably.'
'Pity about your friend Box. He seemed a decent sort of chap.'
'Yes.'
Nightingale hurried over the lawn. 'Sorry to keep you, William. Ralph's frantic. He couldn't do the whole thing properly but he gave me the gist. Nothing to worry about, Peter.' He smiled at the ambassador and turned to William. 'Apparently your lot in London – Box's lot, I should say, the Funnies plc – have done a deal with the Americans and sold them what they call the "development rights" to this project, recognising CIA's position as market leaders in South America. They were already in discussion with the Americans when the Americans received information from their own sources here about the imminent coup attempt. Somehow the Americans got hold of a written request for help from the president; it was then decided to sell out lock, stock and barrel to the CIA in return for part-share in the cobalt concessions that are in the president's gift and a similar trade-off with something in Africa. So there you are, you see. The president doesn't need you any more. All's well that ends well.' He grinned.
'Except for those who were killed,' said William.
'Yes, bad luck for them.'
There was a commotion near the embassy. Several

limousines drew up, headed by a vast gold Mercedes. A number of people were milling about. Even at that distance, William recognised the uniformed figure of Carlos.

'Good lord, it's the president,' said Nightingale.

The ambassador's mouth opened. 'He hasn't come to see us, has he?'

'Perhaps he's come to ask for help.' Nightingale ran across the lawn.

'Oh dear,' said the ambassador. His frowns seemed to run right round his face. 'I suppose I ought to go and see him.'

'No need' said William. 'He won't know you're here.'

The ambassador looked grateful. 'I suppose he won't. He probably doesn't want to talk to me anyway. He never has. I could wait here by the rhododendrons and you could call me if I'm needed.'

The people with Carlos were both civilian and military. He was resplendent in braid and tassels and carried a swagger-stick with which he frequently gesticulated. It was hard to tell whether he was shouting or laughing. For a moment he was eclipsed by his entourage, then by Nightingale and the lumbering, dishevelled Feather. He wielded the stick and they parted suddenly. He strolled across the lawn towards William, arms outstretched.

'William, William! Comrade-in-arms!' He embraced William. He beamed and his eyes shone. 'I am cruising round the city, showing myself to the people – look, my beautiful new car.' He pointed his stick at the gold Mercedes. 'A present from the president of the United States. "From one great president to another," he said.' He laughed. 'And then a small cloud comes upon me when I am cruising. What has happened to my friend, Wooding, I ask, the friend of my childhood? Then I think I will call on the British Embassy and see if they know and, look, you are here!' He embraced William again. 'These embassy people, they cannot understand I want to see you, not them. What do I want with them? What did they do when I needed help? I have new friends now, I have a CIA escort as well as my own. Come, we will walk arm in arm towards them and show them who is my favourite British representative.' His expression became momentarily sorrowful. 'I'm sorry not to have Arthur Box on the other arm.'

'So am I.'

'I don't think these embassy people liked Arthur. When I mentioned him they started to apologise. I don't like these people. Now that I am properly president, I don't think I shall have them here. I shall ask for them to be withdrawn. We don't need so many, anyway. A consulate will do. But there is still another cloud on my mind: Herrera.'

'He's still at large?'

'They are looking for him. All the CIA agents in the city and soon all the people will be asked to look for him. Also, I regret Theresa. She is dead to me and to every man now. It is a pity.'

When they reached the gold Mercedes, Carlos held up William's arm like a boxer's. William was his friend and comrade-in-arms, he announced. They had fought together along with another British comrade who had died gallantly. William and his colleague had been symbols of British support and they would be appropriately honoured. The new government would restore honour and the economy. There would be no more security police and plenty of money for everyone, especially the poor. The fishing agreements with the Soviet Union would be revoked, cobalt production put on a proper footing, international aid directed to wherever it was most needed.

William's arm ached. It was difficult to know where to look. Carlos spoke as if to a large public meeting. The three journalists present took photographs and notes. The rest of the audience was either Carlos's own guard, embassy people or sober-suited civilians who were presumably the CIA bodyguard. Nightingale and Feather were at the front, Nightingale looked uncomfortable, Feather crumpled and gloomy.

The tall man at the back of the group nodded and

smiled. William recognised him as Max Hueffer only after he had smiled back, a reflex action. Carlos finished and there was dutiful applause which he took with grinning satisfaction.

Max walked over to William. 'Hi.'

'Hello.'

They shook hands. Max's grip was as firm as his gaze, his features remorselessly pleasant. 'I've been thinking we should have a talk. Couldn't find you anywhere. I've been worrying about you. So has Sally.'

'I've been busy.'

They walked down the lawn. The ambassador, seeing them coming, moved further into the rhododendrons.

'Hope you don't mind us cashing in like this on the good work done by you and Arthur Box,' said Max. 'It was now or never so far as intervention was concerned, and your people back in London seemed to have gone cool on the project. I guess they didn't want to invest much in terms of aid and the future, so we worked out a deal. It's a real tragedy our intervention force didn't take the airport twenty-four hours or so earlier. Might have saved Arthur Box.'

'Do you know where his body is?'

'In the city morgue, I guess. All the fatalities are there, including the ones we inflicted. It's just a pity Herrera isn't with them.'

'Any idea where he is?'

'Not yet. Could be taking refuge in the Russian Embassy. But they're all going to be hoofed out pretty soon, though they don't know it yet. Herrera may run but he can't hide. We'll find him.'

Max offered cigarettes. William didn't smoke but accepted. They both assumed a matter-of-fact businesslike attitude. At least, he assumed Max was assuming it. Perhaps this was what Max was really like. Perhaps that was what Sally liked about him.

'Arthur Box was an operator of genius, in my opinion,' Max continued. 'We didn't even know he was here and we thought we knew pretty well every sparrow in this city. Except what to do about it. We could see what was happening but we couldn't figure out how to stop it. On the other hand, your Arthur knew nothing about the place but he just came in and went straight for it, straight to the jugular. And the weird thing is, your people in London don't seem to rate him at all: prehistoric and freakish, they reckon. I wonder how serious they ever really were about this project.'

'I don't know. They're not really my people, you see. I've never met them.'

'That's what Sally told me but I couldn't believe it at first. I mean, you've done so well, so professional – getting past Herrera to the president, getting him a girlfriend, getting Arthur alongside him, getting him to cooperate. We had fifty-plus operatives here and we couldn't get anywhere near him.'

William had to remind himself that this man was his wife's lover; it didn't seem to make the difference it should. 'Is it true that Herrera comes from an old city family?'

'One of the oldest. But it's no use looking for him with them. They died out. We did some research. He's got some cousins somewhere up the coast but all his immediate family are in the cemetery and he doesn't exactly look set to prolong the line.'

The cigarette was good only for the first few puffs, like all that William had ever tried. He watched the rest of it burn in his fingers.

'I – guess I should say something about me and Sally,' Max continued.

'There's no need.'

'I feel under obligation to say something.'

'You needn't.'

'She's a very fine lady.' Max's tone was unctuous. 'I just wanted to say, no hard feelings.'

'No.' William wished he would stop.

'We both wanted you to know how very much we appreciate your attitude.'

'Don't mention it.'

Max's features burgeoned with sincerity 'We both want to humbly thank you.'

'Don't.'

Max transferred his cigarette and held out his hand. 'William, thank you.'

Not to have shaken would have been misinterpreted, so William transferred his own cigarette. 'No need ever to mention it again.'

Max held on to his hand. 'William, I count myself a big man, but I reckon you're bigger.'

The parrot was in the trees again. William raised his other hand. The parrot waved back. Max looked round.

'Just saying goodbye to the parrot,' said William.

The street markets were busy that day, the traders boisterous even by their own standards. Colour photographs of Carlos adorned most of the barrows. William stopped at the first one which had guns. A flintlock, a shot-gun and two rifles were strung up, while on the table revolvers and pistols were scattered amongst gardening tools, old shoes and elaborate riding-crops with silver handles. A couple of biscuit tins contained assorted ammunition. The stall-holder was a short moustachioed man who looked like the orange-seller, except that he smiled.

William said he wanted a hand-gun. The man nodded. '*Sí, señor*, a little or big one?'

'Nothing too large. Just – well – comfortable.'

He held two or three. The man commented favourably upon each but even more favourably on a fourth which he found beneath the shoes.

'It is more expensive,' he said. 'But better. You want a holster?'

'Yes, please.'

'For the shoulder?'

'Er – yes.'

He was offered a smooth black leather holster but the fourth pistol wouldn't fit. A smaller silver revolver, yet more expensive, was found.

'Revolvers are simpler, easier, more reliable,' said the

man, divining William's inexperience. 'And it fits the holster with clips – let me show – there – or there.' He clipped the holster and revolver to William's belt, then to the left breast pocket of his shirt. It was heavy and made the shirt sag, but it fitted snugly beneath the jacket.

'And some bullets, please,' said William.

They sorted through the biscuit tins for some that would fit. The revolver held only four. 'That should be enough,' said William.

'Is for animals, *señor*?'

'No.'

'For business?'

William thought. 'Business involving my wife.'

The man was immediately sympathetic. 'You take more.'

William ended up with a dozen more bullets which he had to put in his pockets. He had never held a gun before and tried to spin the chamber as he had seen in films. 'It seems a bit stiff. Doesn't seem to move.'

The man shrugged. 'Is not important. You can oil. Anyway, is necessary only for one movement at a time when you fire.'

William walked away feeling self-conscious and awkward rather than lethal. He kept his jacket buttoned though it was now very warm. People were already sitting and drinking maté in the shade of the plane trees. Perhaps they drank it throughout the summer, too. He was free to try it now.

The cemetery flower-seller was busy. Inside, flowers had appeared on many of the graves and were even placed in small holders by the doors of the lockers high in the walls. Tall aluminium step-ladders were provided and people waited patiently to use them, laughing and talking. The white walls were clean in the sun, the atmosphere festive – not, William thought, a suitable day for a killing. There were plenty of bodies there already, of course, but a fresh one might seem indecent. Also, there were children around, so there had to be no stray bullets. It seemed that once you decided on something there were immediately other things to be taken into account.

There was a small door in the wall by the main gate where Theresa had told him they kept books relating grave numbers to family names. The books were large, strong ones like those he had seen in war cemeteries in Europe. There were two families Herrera but one, because of the dates of recent internments, he could discount. The other, by its number, could not be far from Theresa's banker. The footsteps in the mist that morning had seemed so clear, so elusive and so threatening that he was unreasonably confident of finding what he sought.

Walking past 1066, William wondered whether he should buy it for Theresa. Carlos had said she was dead to him and all men now. As with Box, he couldn't really bring himself to believe in her death, but had to accept it. She had said she wanted to be buried there. Box would more appropriately be buried in England, perhaps with military honours.

The Herrera grave was high in the wall. Manuel would have needed a ladder to get into it and, having got in, he couldn't have moved the ladder away. Nor were there signs on the ground of a ladder having been there. All this was clear, but William nevertheless stood and stared for some time at the small high door, unwilling to accept the failure of his theory.

He turned away and stared instead at the city of obelisks, turrets and sepulchres before walking slowly back towards 1066. Some children were playing around the mini-cathedral in which he and Box had talked. They laughed and shouted. Two ran into the cathedral but came out subdued, they spoke to the others and all walked away.

William approached. His inclination was to hesitate outside and try to see in, but that was stupid. It would take too long for his eyes to adjust. Nor did he feel he could draw his gun. That was unnecessarily dramatic and, anyway, might seriously frighten innocent people. He approached from the side, then ducked through the door and stepped into the gloom.

Manuel was seated at the end of one of the stone seats, leaning against the wall. He was wearing the robes of a priest. William remained crouched in the doorway. The revolver weighed heavily upon his heart. He did not attempt to draw it. He had imagined doing so many times but now it seemed unthinkable, an almost ludicrous breach of manners. But it was what he was there for.

Manuel smiled in the gloom. 'Why have you come here?'

'To find you.'

'Why here?'

'I guessed. You came in this morning, didn't you, in the mist?'

'Yes.' Manuel's tone, like his smile, was perceptive and disconcerting. 'Why did you want to find me?'

'I came to kill you.'

Manuel looked politely surprised, as if he had received a proposition from an unexpected quarter. 'Why is that?'

'In revenge for Arthur Box and Theresa and all the others.'

'That seems a little harsh, if you don't mind my saying so. I'm not responsible for everything.'

'Nevertheless.' William's hatred had evaporated. He kept going only because he had started.

'Are you really going to shoot me?'

There were voices outside and a breath of breeze. An insect hummed.

'That's what I came for.'

'I never thought of you as a man of action, *Señor* Wooding. After all, things don't always turn out as you plan them, as we both know now.' He laughed. 'So, you are going to shoot me, an unarmed man, in cold blood. Well, you may as well do so.'

Even thinking of Theresa and Box didn't help now. They wouldn't have done this. He knew he wouldn't. Some people could justify it, and there were no doubt others who would say it was his duty, but it wasn't. It wasn't quite right enough. A pity because it was the only big thing he had ever set out to do.

'Are you going to do it here?' asked Manuel. 'Or outside? Standing or sitting? Am I allowed to pray first?'

'I'm thinking.'

William was aware of Manuel's movement but not of any threat. He seemed to fold his arms and change position as if to see William without having to turn his head so much. William's last sight was of the small dark 'O' of the gun barrel. It was so brief a glimpse that he had no time even to be alarmed. There was an explosion in his ears and chest and a pain beyond anything. It lasted an instant yet seemed for ever expanding. Next there was a feeling of being free, of floating, that again seemed both instantaneous and timeless. Then a sudden decline, an abrupt and bottomless fall.

16

'The Cross of Honour, second class. It should be first, but I'll compromise.'

'No.'

'I can't go lower than that. Third class is for diplomats and I don't want you lumped in with them.'

'I don't want a medal. I wasn't being brave.'

'Of course you were. Anyway, it's useful that you should be recognised for what you did. It lends dignity to the lynching, at least in international eyes.'

Carlos's own eyes were drawn again to the window, through which he could see nurses sunbathing on the military hospital lawn. William's private room was sunny and filled with flowers. They had brought him the remains of his stamp collection that morning. He could walk and talk and eat now, and though there was a dull pain all the time it was excruciating only when he sneezed or coughed. His chest was still discoloured and swollen; the doctors said there was nothing to be done with fractured sternum and ribs except to let them heal. On his bedside table was the silver revolver in its holster, the leather torn and the chamber flattened on one side where Manuel's bullet had hit it. The shock had actually stopped his heart, they told him. He had seven stitches in his head where he had cut it when thrown back against the tomb. The concussion was wearing off now and the headaches came only if he moved suddenly.

Manuel had been caught fleeing the cemetery. He had been surrounded by a mob, tied to a trader's stall and dragged to the covered market where, after castration, he had been hanged from the clock tower. His testicles were rumoured to have been thrown in with other offal and cooked. The incident had threatened to cause public relations problems for the new government but with

American help United Nations criticisms had been headed off. There were to be no executions.

Carlos was wearing another new uniform with many medals. He had been inaugurated as president for life the day before. The reconstituted parliament had voted unanimously and an estimated million people had thronged the streets. His uncle, the prime minister, would actually run the government. There had been dancing all night and that evening Maria's was to be officially reopened by Carlos. El Lizard would continue to run it but it was to be given the status of a government hostel and run by a board of trustees, chaired by Carlos's cousin. This was to ensure that it remained, as El Lizard desired, an orderly house.

William had refused the chairmanship, but had agreed to sit on the board. He was to have special responsibility for the welfare of staff.

'That nurse who was in here when I came?' Carlos asked.

'Camilla. She's on in the mornings.'

'I thought she was reasonably beautiful. She reminded me of Theresa. I shall send for her.'

'I'm seeing Theresa this afternoon.'

'How is she? Have they moved her now?'

'The same but yes, thank you, she's on the floor below.'

Carlos stood. 'I shall have tea with my wife and children and then, I think, a short sleep before going to Maria's tonight.' He straightened his uniform. 'You know, idleness is so agreeable to me. I've never liked doing things. I only get bored when I'm busy.'

'You look very well on it.'

'I feel well on it. Are we agreed – second class?'

'I'll think about it.'

'It should really be first, but it is conditional on your accepting my other offer.'

'The British Foreign Office won't like that.'

'We all have to accept things we don't like sometimes. At least, some people do.' Carlos smiled. 'If they want a representative here and they want cobalt, they'll agree.

Otherwise neither. Anyway, Special Information Services plc owes it to you to use their influence. *Chau*, William.'

William waited a while after Carlos had gone, then got carefully out of bed and put on his dressing-gown. It tired him to be up for very long so he built his days around visits to Theresa. Now that, through Carlos, he had got her moved out of the appalling and hopeless mental wing into a room below his, visits were much easier.

The worst period had been the two days of fluctuating consciousness and persistent pain when, propped up in bed, he had seen the mental patients walking behind the wire on the grass outside their wing. He had thought at first that his sightings of her were cruel tricks of his poor eyesight, then that he was suffering hallucinations. That was why he had said nothing as she wandered, withdrawn and apparently unseeing, amidst the sad aimless people. They looked as if they were all either under heavy sedation or beyond it. She wore the same dull green overalls as the others and her hair had been ruthlessly cut. William had become obsessed. It was the way she held herself and the way she moved. Even her smallest gesture suggested something beyond itself. By the end of the second day he was convinced.

It had not been difficult to find out. As national hero and friend of the president, he was given everything he requested. Yes, they said, she had been the president's mistress and she had been raped by Herrera's security police. They had treated her badly and after the coup she had been found wandering the streets. She had not spoken a word since; her mind was gone. It was sad, such a beautiful girl, and as mistress of the president she would never have been poor. Now, of course, it was impossible for the president to touch her, now she had been raped. Nor would any other man accept her. She was dead to all men now.

As soon as he could walk far enough William had gone to see her. She had not known him. He talked to her but she did not reply. Her dark eyes rested on him without recognition. She was utterly passive. She would walk beside him and would respond to simple statements about change of direction or standing or sitting, but anything beyond that it was impossible to know whether she even heard. After the first visit he had gone back to bed and resolved to die if she died, otherwise never to leave her.

Since then he had got used to talking to her. He would put her arm through his and every day they would walk in the grounds. He would tell her everything, hoping that one day something would get through. She was no longer in overalls but in clothes he had ordered for her. The private room where she now slept was bright and quiet. It was imposible to tell whether she noticed her surroundings but she showed no sign of unhappiness. The doctors had described her as 'deeply withdrawn'.

Ines had been to see her twice in the early days but had been distressed by the experience. It was not in her nature to be anything other than cheerful and she could not be cheerful when faced by no response at all. After the second visit she had cried, saying she could not bear to do it again. William had promised to call her if Theresa's powers of recognition ever returned and meanwhile secured for her a permanent position at the club as El Lizard's secretary, responsible for bookings. She was petitioning the new government to release her father from prison.

William decided he would sit with Theresa that day rather than walk. He was still prone to headaches on exertion which, they told him, should wear off after a year or so. He was particularly tired because Carlos's visit had not been the first that day. In the morning Sally had come with Max Hueffer and flowers and chocolates. Sally described how she had cleaned up the flat and removed her things. She wanted to talk about divorce arrangements. William said he would go along with anything. Max formally asked for his blessing on their union while Sally, who used to be so dismissive of displays of emotion or sentiment, looked on with the exaggerated meekness of the born-again. William had had another headache.

Theresa sat in one of the cane chairs by the open window of her room. It was not as quiet as it should have been because one of the nurses on the lawn had her radio on. Theresa might have been looking out or she might have been looking at the window-frame. William took the chair next to hers, held her hand and began talking. Her eyes moved to him briefly, then back to the window. He told her that the mystery of Box's body was almost resolved. It had begun when he had asked for Box's special shoes as a memento and had been sent the wrong pair. Further requests failed to elicit the right ones. He had then asked for other items of Box's clothes, but the only article forthcoming was the colonel's sword with which Box had tried to defend Ines and the girls. It had been cleaned and polished. Box's body was by then said to be en route for London in the EE(C) coffin, which was no doubt as Box would have wished. Special Information Services plc had behaved decently. They had chartered an aeroplane for the coffin and had sent William a particularly favourable offer on the new share issue. They had also said that if he stayed on they would appoint him their permanent salaried representative. His own company had meanwhile changed their decision about pulling out; they wanted him to stay and were prepared to drop the new name, Britbooks, and revert to the English Bookshop. They had also offered a pay rise but he still hadn't replied. He was considering putting Ricardo, who was now out of hospital, in charge. They would accept whatever he said now that he was so well established in the country and he felt he still owed Ricardo something, even though Ricardo was already boasting everywhere about his wounds received in the civil war and the patronage of his new friend, the president; and even though his father, formerly a colonel in an obscure regiment, was now the general in charge of the palace guard.

Next there had been an urgent message from Special Information Services sent via the embassy and unfortunately indecipherable because it used the code known only to the departed coffin. London reluctantly agreed to send it again in an accessible but restricted format, but the cipher operator succumbed to professional stress and had to be flown home to be dried out. At the same time Feather went missing on a diplomatic bag run to Rio, where he was thought to have submerged himself in one of his periodic debaucheries; Nightingale was apparently on leave; and the plane bringing the replacement cipher operator from Rio had diverted to La Paz, where a national holiday had just started. London's message had eventually been delivered to William by Max Hueffer.

'I guess your guys prefer to trust it to our guys than to their guys in the embassy,' he said. 'I can see why. It would be embarrassing for your headquarters if it got out.'

The signal said that the body in the coffin was not Box's but that of an unknown man with a beard and one eye. This had become apparent only when Mrs Box had viewed the remains. Legal complications arising from the importation and possession of an unknown corpse meant that there could be no question of a rapid re-export. The police had got to hear about it, customs had impounded the EE(C), and the company had had to engage and fully brief one of the City's top law firms. There was also serious concern as to whether or not the equipment had been compromised before the despatch. Security Section (abbreviated to SS) was prepared to concede that the unknown corpse might pose no threat but was most anxious that William should identify it and discover the circumstances of death and substitution. Tests were being carried out to establish date and cause of death. Had the coffin been handled and filled by security-vetted personnel, as requested? William was to locate and despatch the correct body with all speed. He was not to worry about expenses.

All that had been over a week ago. He had done what he could, he told Theresa, but even if he'd been more mobile he'd have been unlikely to have any more success. None of the corpses known to the city authorities was Box's. The most likely explanation was that he had been buried instead of the bearded one-eyed man and was now inhabiting the cemetery that had sheltered the last days of his life, though the local custom of displaying corpses before burial made it most unlikely that the differences would have gone unnoticed. Nevertheless – all William's enquiries were channeled through the presidential office – the authorities were anxious to exhume every body buried since the coup and arrange them for inspection. William thought not; he also thought he should not tell London that the offer had been made. He remembered Box telling him about a dead African lady who had been despatched to London under similar circumstances. Box would have revelled in this one, he thought; and the more he thought it the more he felt that one day Box would do so indeed.

Then there had been the rumour from the hospital about the foreigner with gunshot wounds who had discharged himself, or at least disappeared, before the hospital records had caught up with the influx of casualties at the time of the coup. There had been many with gunshot wounds, and patients who could nearly always left with something like alacrity since the hospital was widely known as a place where people came out with more diseases than they brought in with them. The foreigner had been operated on and treated afterwards, but no one could remember precisely what for or by whom; he had simply disappeared and dropped out of mind, one problem fewer.

This was when William had become convinced. He did not dare say so, partly out of superstition and partly because he did not want to provoke a torrent of unanswerable questions from London. He was finding that all bureaucracies were alike, that his own firm and Special Information Services plc had more in common with each other than either would like to believe. But for him it was the very lack of detail that made it all but certain; that was Box's style. It was one of the two best bits of news he could have had, and in the privacy of his room he had done a little jig for joy, which had brought on an immediate headache.

And now there was something else. Max had handed over a plain envelope at the end of his visit with Sally that morning. He had winked and grinned and said: 'One of your eat-before-reading messages. More problems for the folks back home.'

William took it from his pocket for the fourth time. He

would read it aloud before Theresa's quiet face. Security Section would presumably be horrified, though if she couldn't take it in, would it constitute infringement? He didn't mind, he was so happy. He took her hand and held the paper up before them both: 'Further complications. Widow's grant, first installment of widow's pension, deceased's terminal bonus and death-in-service lump sum all paid to Mrs B, but payments hazarded now by lack of proof of death. Legal position on re-claiming under examination. Payments possibly further invalidated by following plain speech unclassified telegram received yesterday from unknown source in La Paz: GONE TO GROUND STOP INJURIES IMPROVING STOP NO NEWS SUCCESS OR FAILURE PLANS DUE TO INCAPACITATION COMA FLIGHT AND PRESENT PRIMITIVE CIRCS STOP POSSIBLE DEAD PARTNER HAD EXPENSES CLAIM WHICH SHOULD BE PAID WIDOW UNLESS HE LIVES STOP TELL OWN WIFE BACK BEFORE XMAS STOP WILL SURFACE AGAIN THIS MEANS AFTER LOCAL HOLS STOP PLEASE REPLY POST OFFICE STOP REGARDS ALL END. Could this be the deceased? Grateful your urgent views in view of possible court action by Mrs B. Missing eye of bearded corpse found. Any luck your end? Suggest you consider advertising. Please report soonest.'

William put the message carefully on the table. 'Serious bureaucratic complications,' he said to Theresa, grinning broadly. 'Months of work for desk officers, huge legal fees, adverse publicity, Mrs Box indignant and the cause of it all due for a triumphant return. All very serious. I think I'll read it again.'

Afterwards he told her how that afternoon Carlos had asked him if he would accept a decoration and stay on as British Consul. Carlos was fed up with the embassy people and wanted them withdrawn; a consulate should be sufficient, provided the consul was William. The Foreign Office might not like it, but it was either that or no rights to cobalt or any other minerals that Britain was to be allowed to share with the Americans. Carlos wanted an answer soon. William wasn't sure. Being consul quite appealed, especially if he could combine it with overseeing his old job and representing Special Information Services. But he didn't want to do any of them unless Theresa stayed with him as his wife. Not yet, of course, but one day, when she was ready.

'If you feel you can,' he said.

He stared at the section of the window she was staring at, not expecting an answer. Then, for the first time, he felt a pressure from her hand. It was almost nothing, so slight that he wondered if he had imagined it. He looked again at her face. Her eyes were still vacant, but she was moving her head, very slightly, to the music from the nurse's radio. William clasped her hand more firmly. One day, he thought, if Box could return from the dead, one day Theresa and he would tango again. He took both her hands in his, watching the tiny movements of her head. Perhaps it would all turn out to have been worth it after all; and perhaps he would send in his expenses claim.